A Cunning Plan

Book One -
Sloane Harper series

Astrid Arditi

CROOKED
CAT

Discover us online:
www.crookedcatpublishing.com

Join us on facebook:
www.facebook.com/crookedcatpublishing

*Tweet a photo of yourself holding
this book to @crookedcatbooks
and something nice will happen.*

To Sasha and Alec,
Thank you both for making my life complete.

Acknowledgements

As *A Cunning Plan* takes its first baby steps into the world, I couldn't be more grateful. A childhood dream finally comes alive. A big thank you to Crooked Cat Publishing, the fairy godmother who's made this possible.

I wouldn't be anything without the love of my family.

Thanks to my father, the pillar who's supported me and nurtured my dreams with his unwavering love. Dad, in the words of Gustave Flaubert: "If you could read my heart, you would see the place I have given you there."

To my mom, my first reader always and literary cheerleader: thank you for believing in me and my stories. Sloane wouldn't exist if it weren't for you. You're a true inspiration and the mother I hope to be.

To my sister, favorite enemy and partner in crime; to my little brother who's been towering over me for some time now; thanks for always having my back.

To my cousin Olivia Wildenstein, brilliant author and force of nature: Thanks for your precious help on my manuscript and everything literary related.

Finally to my husband, Jeremy. You challenge me and make me believe anything is possible if I set my mind to it. Thank you for giving me the two most wonderful kids and for always keeping me on my toes. Life with you is an adventure, in Paris, London or New York soon, and I'm pretty sure it hasn't reached the end of its surprises yet. I'd follow you to the moon.

Last but not least, many thanks to you, readers, for picking up A Cunning Plan and following my beloved

Sloane on her tentative path to self-fulfillment. Hope you enjoy the ride.

Love xx
Astrid

The Author

Astrid Arditi was born from a French father and Swedish mother. She lived in Paris and Rome before moving to London with her husband and daughter in 2013.

After dabbling in journalism, interning at Glamour magazine, and teaching kindergarten, Astrid returned to her first love: writing.

She now splits her time between raising her kids (a brand new baby boy just joined the family) and making up stories.

A Cunning Plan is Astrid's first published work.

Follow Astrid at **www.astridarditi.com**

A Cunning Plan

Chapter One

So far, I have spent more than ten hours this week parked on the exact same street, in front of the exact same building, staking out my husband's mistress. To be exact, Tom was my ex-husband now, but I was pretty sure he was still my husband when Katherine Stappleton started screwing him.

A sideways glance confirmed Claudia's eyelids had finally closed, and I sighed in relief. If I had to listen to one more minute of heavy metal, I would hurl myself or my *housekeeper extraordinaire* out of the car window.

I shot my hand toward the Mini Austin's radio. But just as the angry voices faded in favor of a monotonous radio show, Claudia's hand lashed out and slapped my wrist away.

"Go back. I love that song."

"But I don't understand Polish," I said with a pout.

"It's music, you don't need to understand it," she countered, her eyes still closed.

My teeth hurt from the loud screeching she called music. I considered looking for Magic FM again, but Claudia read my mind first. She snapped open one fierce blue eye.

"Don't," she warned.

Heavy metal music wasn't nearly bad enough to risk incurring Claudia's wrath and chancing her leaving. Listening to any kind of music with her definitely beat sitting in the car alone.

I gave a last, longing stare at the radio then turned my attention to the dashboard's digital clock. It was 3:43 p.m. according to the flashing orange numbers. Sighing, I thought again of how much time I'd spent here.

The details of my husband's 'infidelity' mattered; they changed the way one perceived things. On one side, you had my ex's new girlfriend, and on the other, the tramp who stole my husband. Doesn't have the same ring to it, right?

The same way if you asked Katherine Stappleton, she might have described my endeavor as 'stalking' rather than 'staking out'. *If* she knew I was hiding in front of her work place, that is, and I was extremely careful not be noticed. Plus, I never left the car or followed her home – the definition of stalking. Legally speaking, I was in the clear. I'd checked on *Yahoo Answers*.

Claudia was now fully awake beside me, blowing bubble gum as pink as her chin-length bob. Disapproval oozed from her. I didn't care as long as she kept me company. The divorce had left me quite friendless. As a result, Claudia had graduated from housekeeper to life coach, and had become the Robin to my Batman when the Kate issue arose.

This mistress, so artfully hidden during the divorce, had come as quite the surprise. It had been a relief too. When my husband, Tom, left me six months ago, I had felt totally blindsided. Ten years together, two wonderful daughters, sex once a week and sometimes twice on holidays, a cozy home, and a fabulous group of friends – wasn't that the very definition of a happy marriage?

And then one day – *Bam!* – he filed for divorce. I didn't fight it. Why look like a hag when all I had to do was wait it out? I smiled and said I understood his *need* for change. I let his lawyer represent us both. I agreed to the terms of the divorce without any negotiations – I got to keep the house, and most importantly, custody of my girls so it wasn't such a bad deal anyway. Surely, Tom had felt very magnanimous.

I pretended I didn't know about the offshore accounts. I figured they would be ours once again when we remarried so there was no reason to bring them up and look petty.

But no matter how much I smiled and consoled Tom, no matter how well I swallowed my tears to look cheerful just like he loved me, my bed was still empty and my girls' home was broken.

"Movement by the door," Claudia pointed out sullenly.

As the revolving doors came to life, I ducked for cover under my seat, banging my forehead against the dashboard in the process. Tears sprang to my eyes, a mix of pain and burning humiliation. I fought them off, holding onto on my newfound hope. If Tom had left me for someone else, it didn't mean he'd stopped loving me. I could now attribute his wandering to lust.

From my pitiful hiding spot, I pictured Kate the goddess's long brown hair swaying gently in the London spring breeze as she exited the building, her impossibly long legs taking on Maddox Street in elegant strides, her hips sashaying in a pencil skirt.

"It's just some security guy," Claudia interrupted my masochistic reverie. "The coast is clear. No Kate in sight."

I scrambled back onto the driver's seat and peeled a chocolate chip cookie from my leg, courtesy of one of my daughters, no doubt. Claudia seethed silently next to me. Five more minutes and her patience wore off.

"*Kurva*! Can you tell me what we're doing here?" When Claudia got mad her accent became thicker and her vocabulary more colorful. Fortunately for me, her favorite curse words were in Polish. "Sitting here all day is sad. Every day for a week! You have no life, maybe, but I have better things to do."

Like cleaning my house. I was too chicken to say it aloud.

"If you're trying to scare her off, I know people. Or at least let her see you. You're scary enough."

I chose not to let her taunt get to me. "I don't know what I'm waiting for. I just want my husband—"

"Ex," Claudia said.

"Back," I continued. "I guess I'm waiting for a sign."

"Signs, mediums, past lives. You are worse than my grandnanna!"

"Thank you. I'm sure you grandmother is very wise," I said.

"You know he's not worth it," Claudia said.

"Kate wouldn't agree," I snorted.

"She doesn't know Tom yet."

5

"He's handsome, brilliant—" I ticked my thumb and index fingers.

"He's good looking for an old guy, and rich," she translated. "He's also conniving and full of himself."

"He's not old! He's only forty-three. And he's worked hard to succeed. Nothing was handed to him on a silver platter."

"Boohoo! Why do you keep on defending him? He's a selfish bastard."

I was tired of this argument. Tom might be all of these things, but he was my husband – well, ex for the time being – the only man I had ever truly loved, and a fantastic father. None of his countless flaws changed that.

"You're young. You can start a new life."

She was right. I was young. I simply couldn't make Claudia understand this was precisely why I needed Tom back.

I wasn't one to kid myself. If the man I had dedicated most of my adult life to, the one I had left my New York's life for and followed half-way across the world, had cast me aside without so much as a hint of regret, I couldn't expect any new relationship to be different. I was obviously lacking, underserving of a man's love.

Not to mention that thirty-two with two daughters equaled a decade older for a single woman. I pushed my fears away.

"I don't want to start over," I said.

"Fine." She rolled her eyes. "Anyway, I'm out of here. It's too stuffy."

"I can open the window if you want?"

Claudia pretended not to hear me.

"This is not good for you, Sloane," she said, as she grabbed her studded jean jacket and black messenger bag.

The Wiccan star on her right wrist showed as her sleeve hiked up her elbow.

"Don't stay out too long. You need to eat something."

I showed the crushed cookie in the cup holder. "I'm all

set."

She waved me off. "Real food. You eat too much junk. Not good for you."

Said the twenty-six-year-old who was so thin she could slip between two pages of a closed book.

"Don't worry," I replied calmly.

"The beds sheets need changing, there's a load of laundry in the dryer…" Claudia paused to scratch her head, trying to be as thorough as possible as she shoved her chores on me, "and you have to clean the witch's bathroom."

The witch – that would be my mother, Claudia's arch nemesis.

"Maybe you can go home and get a head start?" I suggested tactfully, not too hopeful since Claudia had mentioned my mother.

"Too far. I could be working, but you insisted I come with you. Now I'm claustrophobic. I need to go home and rest."

We'd only been in the car for an hour and a half. She opened the door and stomped a black Doc Martens with Hello Kitty laces outside of the car.

Claudia was a battery: tiny and full of energy. She bent back inside the car and winked warmly.

"See you tomorrow, okay?"

She slammed the door and hurried down the street toward the closest tube station.

I immediately seized control of the radio, experiencing the simple joy of having power over something for once. I sighed as I laced my fingers behind my head and listened to Joe Cocker promise me love would lift me up where I belonged.

After a week camping here as often as my schedule allowed, the only conclusions I had come up with were that Kate had no set working hours and that she rocked a power suit. Somehow, she managed to look very professional with a touch of naughty schoolteacher – maybe it was the pearls.

Kate was a personal art buyer who, at this time, was redecorating Varela Global's headquarters in London. They

7

were located on Maddox Street number thirty-two, in a modern glass and aluminium building currently under my surveillance. Apparently, she had done some work for Gabriel Varela, sole heir to Varela Global, and he had been so impressed by her many talents, he had offered her the artistic selection for the group worldwide.

I knew this, and so much more trivia about Katherine Stappleton through Tom, who had been more than happy to brag about his lover when I had broached the subject while picking up the girls last Sunday.

Apparently, once he'd decided it was safe to let their relationship out of the bag, the gloves were off and he would spare me no detail. I had only wanted to know where she worked but had received much more than I had bargained for. From her cup size to her sky high IQ, I could have written Kate's biography. She was an Oxford graduate, originating from London, where she had gone back after a few years in Asia working for some of the top galleries. She had never married and was insatiable sexually – well, the last part I had deduced from the satiated wolf smile he sported lately.

Though I had found some information useful, this need to flaunt his happiness in my face had felt cruel. This was the attitude one would expect from the dumpee, some pathetic attempt to salvage a semblance of dignity, but not from the dumper.

Maybe I deserved this. After all, I now realized I was to blame for our divorce. Or so my mother, who had moved in with us to offer assistance after the break up, loved to tell me. I should have taken better care of myself, I should have seduced him every day, should have paid closer attention to his needs. I had felt too confident, had grown negligent.

I couldn't help but find daunting the list of my many flaws and shortcomings. Countless times a day, I dreamt of packing my mother onto the first flight to New York. Unfortunately, she had a point. Her voice resounded in my ears as I slowly zoned out.

My own snoring woke me, along with a sharp pain in my hand from sleeping against it. I massaged my palm gingerly, moving my numb fingers to activate the blood flow. I'd dozed for half an hour according to my new best friend, the car's digital clock. Cher had replaced Joe Cocker on the radio. I silenced her by dialing to the next radio program. The voice of the speaker started to fade away, the telltale sign of a song to come.

My panties had turned into a thong while I'd slept. I wriggled in my seat to try to put them back in place. Yet another reason I needed Tom back. I could not wear thongs again and only single women would pretend a tanga was comfortable.

This technique wasn't working, so I propelled myself on one butt cheek, hitched a hand inside my pants, and pulled with relief on the rebellious panties. Then I fell back on the seat, an ecstatic grin on my face, still sitting on my hand. Which was when I noticed a man staring at me through my windshield.

Blood rushed to my cheeks as his handsome face broke into a grin. I held my breath and willed myself to stay immobile. The exact same way my four-year-old, Poppy, did when she hoped she would not get caught.

Seriously… The one time a good-looking man glanced at me!

Through the shame buzzing in my ears, my brain registered the new song playing. Of course it would be the most romantic song of all – Roxette's *It Must Have Been Love*, from *Pretty Woman*. Well, to quote the singer, it was definitely over now. With my left hand, the right one still stuck in my pants, I shut off the radio, happy to find an excuse to avoid looking at the man outside. He seemed familiar. I figured he probably worked on the street. When I raised my eyes again, he was gone – probably off to tell some friends about the classy lady in the Mini Austin.

I got both my hands back and buried my face in them.

"Stupid, stupid, stupid," I chanted over and over, till the words lost their meaning and I was finally ready to move again.

Catching my reflection in the rearview mirror, I sighed. What a mess. My white skin was dry and in dire need of care. My straight hair lay limp on my shoulders. Highlighted properly and cared for, it looked good, but my natural ash blonde color appeared quite forlorn. I was washed out, like the ghost of the pretty girl I could have been. I made a mental note to book an appointment with Gustav, my fabulous colorist whom I seldom saw these days.

My eyes that changed colors constantly, from green to blue to grey, were my only outstanding features. But even there, tiny lines had started to bloom. I was quite against plastic surgery but this was one of those days when I contemplated Botox. I put two fingers on each side of my eyes and pulled to see what it would look like.

Even from the bottom of my depressed state, I realized I looked quite ridiculous. I dropped my hands on the steering wheel and decided to call it a day. There was only so much my ego could take and I had just about reached it. Plus, Kate could have come and gone a thousand times while I'd napped. I might as well get back to my daughters. As usual, the thought of them made me feel lighter.

I fiddled with the radio, turned the key in the ignition, and bent down toward the handbag at my feet. My face plastered against my knee, I searched for my cell with the tip of my fingers. I hummed along with Freddy Mercury, who must've been turning over in his grave, as I took hold of the phone at last.

"Show must…" I belted triumphantly.

Before I could finish the chorus, a cool draft of wind on the nape of my neck paralyzed me. Someone had opened the passenger door. Fear ran down my spine, soon joined by shame as I realized it was windshield man who had invaded my car. I found myself hoping he had found the panties episode so hilarious, he had come for more.

He sat with his knees crammed against his chest as he tried to fit into Claudia's place. My panic was kept in check for a second longer than it should have when I noticed his eyes fixed on me. They were quite ordinary except for – surely, I was mistaken – a twinkle of amusement dancing in them.

The reality of the situation was slowly creeping up on me. A stranger was inside *my* car. I inched toward the door handle, knowing my best solution would be to escape. My only knowledge of martial arts came from watching *The Karate Kid*. I harbored a strong suspicion it wouldn't help much. I would probably hurt myself if I tried to pull off a crane move. Shoving all movie references away from my overwrought brain, I wondered what was wrong with me?

A burning sensation in my lungs reminded me to breathe. I gulped as much air as I could, getting ready to scream for help. All the while, I kept my eyes trained on him, trying to conjure a reassuring expression that wouldn't set him off. Would I make it out of the door if he lunged toward me? Doubtful. Although he lounged back in the seat casually, I could feel the tension in his lean body, a panther ready to pounce on his prey.

I focused on his face, hoping to decipher his intentions. Besides his brown eyes that had lost their humor, the intruder had light chestnut hair clipped short, a nose that must have been straight once, and a square jaw sporting a five o'clock shadow.

At last, my hand connected with the metal handle and I tensed, ready to spring the hell out of here. Let him have the car, I just wanted out.

His hand shot in my direction, but he stopped it right before it touched my arm. "Please. Just give me a minute."

I cringed, my nails biting into my palm from holding the handle so tight. Please don't kill me, I pleaded silently. At the thought of my body, flawed as it may be, dead, and my girls becoming orphans, I finally freaked out. It was a relief. At least it kicked me into action. I fumbled with the key, pulling it out of the ignition.

"Here…" I stuttered as I aimed for his lap. "Have the key."

It bounced off his grey shirt before landing with unstable equilibrium on his knee. His stare never wavered from me.

"Take the car. I mean here's the key to the car. I'll just go?"

He gazed at the key and back at me, eyebrow cocked. Maybe he wasn't after the car. I dove for my handbag, struggled to untangle my foot from its handle, and moaned in frustration. He made a gesture to help just as I managed to break free. I scooted as far away from him as I could while hugging the bag. His mouth twitched as if trying to suppress a smile. I almost thanked him before remembering who he was. Or rather, who he wasn't – aka someone I knew.

Rummaging through my Mary Poppins bag, I promised myself that from now on I would only carry clutches. I was too afraid to look away from him. In scary movies, the murderer always waited for the victim to be distracted to strike. Lip balm, pack of chips, a pen, my mostly empty calendar, keys to my house – possibly interesting to him but completely out of the question, so I fished them out discreetly and sat on them – and gum.

"Mrs.…" Windshield Man said.

Honking nearby made me jump in my seat. Jittery from nerves, I gave up and threw the whole bag at the man.

"Have it. Have it all."

Half of the bag emptied onto his lap and the ground. I was way past caring about the tampon that fell at his feet, which was a good thing because otherwise it would have been mortifying. "There's my wallet inside. 2789. Want to write it down? It's the pin to my credit card. I'm afraid there's not much money on it." I bit my lip as I tried to recall my last bank statement then subtracted my last expenses. "Four hundred and sixty pounds give or take ten or twenty. It's not much." How much was my life valued? "Sorry. It's debit only."

He shook his head. "Listen…"

Obviously, he wanted more money. I remembered the shared account with relief. "There's another card. With much more money." It was to be used only for my daughters' welfare but I figured keeping their mother alive qualified as such. I scratched my head, my scrambled brain having a hard time coming up with the code. "Aha!" I exclaimed finally. "9876. Easy!"

By now, Windshield Man looked puzzled. I ran my hands in my hair and scanned the car on the lookout for some other bargaining chip. Besides the 'I love you mommy' clay heart dangling from the rearview mirror, the crushed cookie in the cup holder was the most valuable thing left.

This was so frustrating!

Out of my wits, I picked up the cookie and threw it right into the man's face. I watched it tumble down his jaw and land on his lap, leaving a brown chocolate smudge on the edge of his nose. The level of stupidity characterizing this last impulse had the effect of an ice bucket over my hysteria. I caught my breath and waited for his reaction. I was way off the wagon. He couldn't possibly be interested in my cookie.

He touched his nose gingerly, as if I might have damaged it then broke into a grin.

"You threw a cookie at me," he said, his voice full of wonder.

My jaw went slack. "Huh?"

"Begging, bargaining, crying, punching," he recited.

"What?"

"Possible reactions to this scenario," he answered. "A cookie throw? It's a first."

When he started to laugh, it confirmed my thoughts. The guy was certifiably insane.

Yet his chuckle was warm, playful, suggesting he was probably younger than he looked, around my age, and for some reason that made him feel less threatening. Or maybe it was his American accent. As if a common citizenship would protect me. Somehow, his laughter eased my fears and made me postpone my escape plans.

The moment lasted only a few seconds before a more serious expression replaced his wide smile. His tone still teetered on the edge of humor when he asked, "Are you done assaulting me?"

I choked on indignation. *I assaulted him?* He didn't see my pre-heart attack redness or the smoke coming out of my nostrils because he was too busy repacking my handbag. His face was turned away from me and a fleeting thought of running away crossed my mind. But I was too curious to go. Who was this man? Not a thief, apparently, I concluded as he handed me back my handbag.

"Wait," he said, pulling back the bag. "First promise there's no glass of milk hidden in the car. I really like this shirt."

I stared daggers but kept my mouth shut. I kind of deserved that one. *Stupid, stupid, stupid me!*

"Mrs. Gennaio…"

"Sloane," I corrected automatically. Even after nine years, I still winced when I heard my married name. Out of all the gorgeous Italian last names available, how unlucky was I to have landed *Mrs. January*? "How do you know my name?"

Apparently, my question was irrelevant.

"Agent Ethan Cunning." He extended his hand for me to shake.

I stubbornly folded my arms and retreated against the window. He returned his hand on his lap, looking unfazed.

"I work for the US government. We need your help."

A hysterical giggle escaped my lips. I clasped a hand over my mouth to regain control. He waited patiently, shoulders squared and mouth thinned, for me to calm down. The guy was a good actor, I had to give him that.

"Hah hah! And I'm Sloane, the Martian," I said in a high-pitched voice. "Joking aside, who put you up to this?"

Fake Agent Cunning's mouth twitched. His brown eyes, mischievous just minutes ago, screamed murder now. I swallowed painfully; afraid I had taken the sarcasm too far. Perhaps it wasn't a joke after all.

"Seriously. How can you expect me to believe you?"

As if he'd been waiting for my question, Agent Cunning

14

drew his driving license before I could finish my sentence. Men could be thick sometimes.

It confirmed his name was Ethan Cunning, the picture clearly his – same wholesome American boy face, but clean-shaven and less intense. It was a good picture, as far as ID pictures went. Although it was a far cry from the handsome, focused man sitting close to me.

I diverted my stare away from his strong jaw covered with light stubble, fearing I might lose the few wits I had left if I kept admiring him. I had yet to see proof of his government affiliation. Before I could ask to see his credentials, Agent Cunning spoke again.

"We hope you can help us in a current investigation."

I bit back another caustic response, pretending instead that Ethan Cunning wasn't giving me a cartload of bullshit.

"How? How could *I* be of any help to the mighty government?"

"You have a strategic position to collect intelligence for us."

Sure. If what he needed was second-grade gossip, I was his man. Somehow, I doubted that's what he meant.

"We've chosen you because you are a highly capable woman—"

"Really?" I squealed.

Pink rushed to my cheeks, the unexpected praise making me sit up taller. Compliments were too hard to come by these days not to fully savor them.

Agent Cunning's nonplussed expression morphed into one I didn't quite identify as he moved onto his second argument.

"And you could get access to a high profile individual we are interested in." He stared intently, making me catch my breath.

His dark gaze was smoldering. I batted my lashes uncomfortably, unused to a man paying such close attention to me. I was reminded again of the small distance separating us but this time the dread was gone.

I meant to ask clever questions, like who was the high profile individual I had access to or who'd decided to play April's Fool on me one month late, but instead I found myself asking, "What would I need to do?"

"You would be my CI."

I knew that meant confidential informant. I was well versed in cop shows and their lingo.

Agent Cunning now spoke in hushed tones, low enough that he had to draw closer to me. I fixated on the dimple on his chin. So much that I worried I might drool. I shook myself and stared pointedly at his earlobe instead, a safe enough feature. Or so I thought till my mind wandered again. *Stop it!* In my defense, six months without a sliver of action was a very, very long time.

"Before I reveal classified information, I need to ask for your complete discretion. If you agree to help us, you won't be able to talk about our dealings to anyone."

In all honesty, that might turn out to be a problem. I was kind of a blabbermouth, especially now, when I pictured Tom or my mother's condescending expressions, my fingers itched to grab my phone and tell them everything. *Stick that in your pipe and smoke it!* Someone wanted me, thought I was worth noticing, the government no less!

Then I thought of my daughters and the secret part seemed insignificant.

"It's too dangerous. I can't."

Agent Cunning seemed taken aback by my reaction. Feeling guilty, I hurried to explain myself.

"I'm a mom. My daughters are my priority."

"I don't see how they are relevant here."

"I have responsibilities."

"And what about your duty?" he countered. "Don't you want to help your country? Be a hero?"

"I'm pretty sure my country doesn't need me. Aren't there other agents you can use?"

"I told you discretion is very important here." He shook his head. "Forget about it. I must have profiled you wrong."

What else was in this profile of mine?

"I thought you were brave," he said flatly.

This stung. He didn't know me so I shouldn't care but I wanted to be brave. I simply couldn't afford it. What would happen to my daughters if I accepted his offer?

"I'm sorry. I told you. I can't." My voice broke down from disappointment.

All my life I'd been waiting for a moment like this. A chance to prove myself, to be more than what people saw when they looked at me. I often fantasized about heroic scenarios like this. Even as a girl, I would wonder: if I saw a woman getting assaulted in the metro, would I help or walk away? If a building was burning, would I save the baby from the flames? I loved thinking I would rise to the challenge and be brave but you never knew how you would react till it actually really happened to you. Considering the disappointment in Agent Cunning's gaze, it seemed like I had finally gotten my answer.

"I'm just a mom," I said as a way of apology.

"You wouldn't be in danger," he said at last. "But I can't tell you more if you don't agree to help. The information I want to share with you is classified."

I tried to overlook the thrill these words evoked for me. Instead, I conjured up my daughters' innocent faces and kept a stubborn silence. We had some sort of staring contest for a while, Agent Cunning and me, which wasn't at all unpleasant while it lasted.

I saw his resolve dissolve as he drew away from me. He had finally given up. I felt a pang of regret.

"Here's what we're going to do," he said, his long fingers holding a manila folder. "I'm going to leave now and give you the night to think it through. You can give me your answer tomorrow."

Didn't he hear what I said?

I tried to tame the little monster inside me, thrilled at the thought of seeing him again. Before I could say a word, he swung the door open. I stopped him just in time, only one of his feet dangling outside the car. In his shirt, jeans, and sneakers, he didn't look very professional. Then again, maybe it was his undercover attire.

"Where? When? How?" I asked.

Again, I could have sworn the bemused glimmer shone in his eyes but it was gone just as fast as before. He jumped gracefully out of the Mini, unfurling his tall body as his feet hit the sidewalk. I thought he was gone, but then he bent back inside, scaring me out of my wits.

"I'll find you," he said, and then slammed the door and jogged down the street.

I watched his slender silhouette turn the corner of Maddox and Davies streets. The fear I had experienced wasn't completely gone from my system yet, and I finally succumbed to it. Every muscle in my body started jerking erratically all at once, so much so I had to sit on my hands to calm their tremor. I rested my sweat-beaded forehead on the steering wheel with a little too much forcefulness, resulting in a loud *bang*, and indulged in a good, nerve-relieving cry.

Chapter Two

The Mini Austin was stuck in one of the completely unexplainable London traffic jams. I kept replaying my conversation with Agent Cunning. What would happen when he showed tomorrow? Worse, what if he didn't show at all? And what was hidden in his folder? Was it intended for me? Knowing I would never get to see what was inside drove me insane.

In a futile attempt to change my mind, I tried to assess the level this day had reached on my personal *disastometer*. It was high up there, next to the day when Tom had announced he was leaving me between bites of his breakfast, and the day my mother moved in with us.

It wasn't 5 o'clock yet but I had banged my head twice, been humiliated countless times, and a government agent had hijacked my car. I kept returning to the folder in his hands, wondering what information it had contained.

The rest of the day also promised to be a bust. My house would be a mess, just like I'd left it today, and all because I had asked Claudia to tag along on my empty quest. And I had a looming migraine that would only get worse.

A gap in traffic finally appeared and I gunned my car through, eager to get home to my daughters but not to the household chores awaiting me there. Undoubtedly, my mother would manage to make a comment about the mess without lifting her pinkie to help straighten the house. Bizzy Harper did not partake in domestic tasks. I was pretty sure she thought laundry folded itself and a duster was some kind of kinky accessory. No need to try to enlighten her. That ship had sailed a long time ago.

I drove down Sloane Street with relief, knowing I had

almost made it home. As chance would will it, I had fallen in love with my namesake street my first time in London. It was located in the Chelsea neighborhood, a charming place where tiny townhouses sold for exorbitant prices and every inhabitant belonged to a Ralph Lauren ad – stylish, thin, and glowing. To discover what lay behind the dazzling smiles and expensive trench coats, you had to be one of them or at least be wealthy enough to let them think so. You had to be a member of the same clubs, posh places where tea tasted just the same as anywhere else but cost a zillion times more, send your kids to the same elitist prep schools, and attend the same parties. All the while being bored out of your mind and dreaming of a quiet night home with a good novel. Or maybe that was just me. Tom had seemed to enjoy this life very much.

The corners of my mouth lifted as I spotted my house nestled between many more almost identical ones. The entire street shone, the townhouses' white walls gleaming under the spring sun. As was tradition in London, my home was very narrow; three bedrooms spread over three floors, with six windows on the façade. Many people I knew complained about the way the rooms were laid out, two living rooms required to make one, but I thought it was cozy. I had grown up between Park and Madison in New York City, in a thirty-story building with doorman and full amenities. The reception room was wide enough to host a skate park but the windows were always sealed close. On my street, I could see the sky, and my house was human sized, perfect really.

No sooner had I set foot in my hallway, I kicked off my shoes and launched my raincoat toward the peg by the door. I was no Michael Jordan. It missed and fell in a heap on the floor. I considered not picking it up but then thought: *What if Tom stopped by?* So I bent to retrieve it. I dropped my keys on top of the console on my right. They sunk in the mess of unopened mail and trinkets brought home by the girls.

The living room was eerily quiet for this time of day.

This could mean my mother, Bizzy, had taken my daughters out for an afternoon snack or they were playing in the girls' bedroom. Enjoying the respite, I relaxed a little bit and stepped into the living room, the worn wooden floor cool under my bare feet.

"Where have you been?"

I flinched, my poor heart vaulting in my chest. Pivoting to my right, I glared at the silhouette under the window. All I could see at first was a straight silhouette sitting in a wide armchair, her hand holding a tall glass.

"You almost scared me to death! Why don't you turn on the light?"

My eyes adjusted to the feeble light filtering through the window. I saw Bizzy blink as she realized I was right.

"It was much lighter when I first sat here," she said, her manicured hand gripping her drink while the other one patted her pale hair in a neat French twist.

Judging by how little liquid remained in the glass, I believed her easily.

"Where are the girls?" I asked.

"In their room. Pretending to sleep."

I smiled and strode across the living room. Since Rose had watched *Sleeping Beauty,* I regularly caught the girls in bed, waiting to be kissed.

"Want me to fix you a drink?" Bizzy asked.

"It's a tad early for a martini, Mom," I replied. Although after the day I'd had, it should have been mandatory.

"Of course it is!" she scoffed. "You know I never drink a martini before six. It's not proper. I meant lemonade."

"Just lemonade?" I asked wearily, craning my neck in her direction.

"Why would I drink that?" she wondered.

"I'm okay, Mom. Thanks."

The girls' room was on the second floor. Pre-divorce they'd both had their bedrooms but when Bizzy had *kindly* moved in, they had been forced to bunk up together. Fortunately, they seemed to enjoy it – most days.

"Knock, knock, knock," I said, while rasping gently

21

against the door.

"Who's there?" Poppy's mellifluous voice asked.

Rose's voice was muffled, like she was talking from underneath her comforter. "Poppy! We're supposed to be sleeping!"

"Sorry." Poppy giggled.

"May I come in?" I asked. "I'm Prince Charming looking for my true love's kiss."

I lay my forehead against the door, my hand resting on the brass doorknob, while my daughters conferred in urgent whispers. I thought of Agent Cunning and renewed my decision not to help him. I simply couldn't gamble with my precious angels' welfare.

"You may come in," Rose said solemnly.

I commended myself on my resolution as I stepped into a princess's fantasy. This was the kingdom of Barbies and glitter, tiaras and ponies. Inside this head-spinning realm, two blonde fairies slept in identical beds. I suppressed a chuckle, a warm sense of calm spreading through me. On my right was Rose, her serious, heart-shaped face still as marble. The comforter was firmly tucked under her chin, her delicate lips puckered gracefully for a kiss. I moved toward her first but my youngest demanded I veer off track.

"Kiss me first, Mummy! Pretty, pretty please!"

I knew Rose would understand, her maturity way beyond that of a typical eight-year-old. Poppy's golden curls were spread over her pillow, as was the rest of her plump body, sprawled across the pale pink sheets. Her skirt was hiked all the way up to her stomach, displaying her favorite princess undies. Ever so impatient, Poppy tapped her foot and opened one eye to see what the holdup was. I kneeled before her bed and kissed the tip of her nose before tickling her.

"No, Mummy!" She giggled.

I kissed both her eyes and her round nose again then turned to poor Rose, still waiting to be awakened. I pushed a straight, darker blonde strand of hair from her forehead and deposited a kiss on her soft skin.

"A true love's kiss is on the lips," Rose said.

"A mother's kiss is always true," I told her, hugging her small shoulders tight against me.

I helped her up.

Meanwhile Poppy was circling the room like a fury, singing, "Twinkle, Twinkle Little Star" at full blast.

"So what news today, little mommy?"

Rose was the perfect little lady, all posh British accent and cool behavior. Oftentimes, she was too serious and I felt responsible for it. Those traits had been reinforced since the divorce. I tried to make her understand it was okay to be a child, just as she tried unburdening me by playing the adult. I wished she didn't feel like she had to be a second mother to Poppy but since I couldn't control it, I made light of the situation by teasing her kindly.

Rose thought for a moment then recounted her day. "And Poppy got a note from her teacher for you. She gave it to Bizzy because you were not here."

As always when I was reminded I'd missed something in my daughters' life, I experienced a deep pang of guilt. This was much more frequent since the divorce. I complained a lot about Bizzy moving in with us but she was great with the girls; she was there when I couldn't be. Even though my mother did her best to hide it, she was a doting grandmother.

Between Bizzy's constant presence – no way would she allow the girls to call her *Grandma* – and the fact that we had registered our daughters in every afternoon club available, they hadn't seemed to suffer from the divorce. We had also established an open door policy, allowing Tom to visit as often as he pleased. Of course, the policy didn't swing both ways and the door to his new flat was shut to me. I had a feeling Katherine Stappleton wouldn't have a key made for me anytime soon, especially if she learned of my recent afternoon activities.

Sometimes, the level of maturity I showed in all this impressed me. My daughters and I had handled the divorce beautifully. So long as this regrettable separation didn't last too long, we would come out of it unscathed. I simply couldn't consider what would happen if Tom didn't return to us. To quote one of his favorite sayings: *Failure was not an option.*

The following morning, I woke up with Rose's head on my stomach and Poppy's foot against my cheek. I remembered picking Poppy up before going back to sleep. Rose must have come of her own volition later in the night.

My back was damp from sleeping in the cashmere sweater I had shrugged on to roam the house the night before. Or maybe it was the two extra bodies in my bed. I nuzzled Poppy's foot, breathing in her warm baby smell, letting it soothe me.

My eyes stung from lack of sleep. Agent Cunning's mysterious mission had kept me awake most of the night, imagining heavily armed men invading my home. I pictured them lurking in the shadows, hiding in closets, or nestled inside the chimney conduit, holding on to their Katanas or Kalashnikovs, hoping to pry government secrets out of me.

The sound of the rain against my window made me yearn to fall back asleep but school would start soon and I needed to get the girls ready. Also, the heavenly smell of freshly brewed coffee wafting in from the kitchen had me drooling. Bizzy was an early riser and despite her contempt for electrical appliances, she knew how to work the coffee machine.

I untangled myself from my resting angels and went to the bathroom. After splashing water over my face, I went to make breakfast. The kitchen was deserted except for the coffee pot, my saving grace. The rusty pipes shook. Bizzy was in the shower.

Taking the eggs from the fridge, I relaxed in the ambient silence. A few minutes of solitude; the early bird's reward.

I hummed while I baked, doing my best to keep all thoughts relative to Agent Cunning at bay. I was helped in this task by Tom's face popping in the kitchen just as I finished making waffles, my surprise resulting in a waffle crashing pitifully against the beige tiles.

"Hi, babe!" Crow's feet bloomed around Tom's eyes as he smiled.

I beamed, thrilled that he still had a pet name for me and was still using his keys. It was a good sign he felt free to come and go as he pleased.

"It smells great in here! Fix me a plate, will you? I have a hell of a day coming up," he said as he hung his tailored jacket on the back of a bar stool, rolled up his immaculate white shirtsleeves and sat down.

"How are my flowers doing today?" he asked.

"Blooming," I replied, grateful for the simple ritual and the intimacy it implied. *Take that, Katherine Stappleton!*

As if on cue, the girls galloped in and fought to perch themselves on Tom's knees. I breathed easier, seeing my family as it should be, together and happy.

"Did you sleep over, Daddy?" Poppy asked as she rubbed her sleepy eyes.

"Of course he didn't!" Rose answered. "We slept with Mommy, remember?"

Tom's lips curled into a smug smile.

Yes, I slept with my daughters because I felt lonely. I missed him.

"Maybe Daddy slept in our bed," Poppy argued.

Rose rolled her eyes.

I ended the argument quickly. "Dad didn't sleep over. He's here to have breakfast with us."

"There is no breakfast at your new flat?" Poppy asked.

"Of course there is," Tom answered. "Only not as good as your mom's waffles." For my benefit, he added, "Kate isn't much of a cook. She's a free spirit, you know. Not the kind of woman who enjoys spending her time in front of the stove. And her schedule is way too busy to plan Waffle Thursdays."

It was clearly meant as a compliment to Kate and a criticism to me. Yet here he was, asking for my waffles. I wondered if I should forbid him the access to my stove but then worried he'd never come again.

Fifteen minutes later, in a whirlwind of energy, Bizzy stepped into the kitchen. She wore designer jeans and a peach silk blouse that shimmered as she walked. Her hair was tied in her signature French twist and she'd applied mascara on her lashes and a little rouge on her cheeks. She was a picture of elegance. My hair was a mess and I had yet to brush my teeth. In our case, the apple had fallen so far from the tree I might as well be a cantaloupe. As she spotted Tom, her smile got wider and she extended her arms in his direction.

"Tom, my dear! What a pleasant surprise!"

I sulked a little. I never got that type of greeting. And wasn't my mom supposed to take my side? Instead, she was nice to Tom, seemingly more so since the divorce.

He dropped the girls on the stools next to him and stood up. "Bizzy, always a pleasure."

"Flatterer! I see you've come for some family peace and quiet. Sorry to disturb the moment but I'm afraid the girls will be late for school. Shouldn't they be getting ready?"

I glanced at the oven's clock. *Crap!* Only thirty minutes before classes started. I breathed deeply to keep the panic at bay. I didn't do well under pressure. "Girls, are you done with breakfast?"

Rose nodded while Poppy somersaulted off her stool and began dancing wildly. I took it as a *yes*. Bizzy poured herself a cup of coffee and grabbed her Sudoku. Clearly, there was no point asking for her help now.

"Go put on your uniform; I'll come in a minute to fix your hair." I turned to Tom. "You need to help me. Please take them to school, I'll owe you one."

"Can't," he said as he unrolled his shirtsleeves and tried to make an escape. "I'm meeting Sir Ashton at the club."

I followed Tom outside the kitchen, hoping I could convince him to help.

"Pants, Sloane," my mom reminded me. "Don't forget to put on pants."

I looked down at my bare legs in surprise. She was right; I had forgotten this critical piece of clothing. I blamed

Agent Cunning for it. My feet were cozy inside UGG boots, the cashmere sweater kept my chest warm and – I held my breath in prayers and exhaled sadly when I saw they were not granted – my tushy was snuggled in granny panties. *Oh! Sexy me!*

Tom shrugged on his jacket. "Did I tell you about Sir Ashton? He's such a nice fellow." With a sly smile, he finally dropped the genteel British act, and added, "Fucking loaded."

I didn't give a damn about Sir Ashton.

As so often, I wondered why I loved Tom so much. He had so thoroughly erased the Tommaso I had fallen for. Gone was the faint Jersey accent, the childlike dreams of grandeur, and the free smiles. Now everything was calculated, every smile dispensed in the hope to serve his cold ambition, every action supposed to help him fit into London's posh society. Katherine Stappleton was the final touch to his transformation. The man was a real chameleon and I often wondered if the man I'd known was still somewhere to be found.

"Please, Tom, take the girls today. I'll never make it on time."

"Really, Sloane." His dark stare turned cold. "I don't want to be mean but it's the only thing you do all day, every day. Can't you at least do it right? I don't have time to fix your mistakes. I need to work to pay for your lifestyle, in case you've forgotten."

I stumbled backward from the blow his words inflicted.. *Jerk.* In order to keep calm, I pretended his head was a giant pincushion. With each imaginary needle I stuck in him, my anger receded, replaced by a beatific grin.

Tom grabbed his briefcase. His smug smile had returned as he checked his reflection in the gilt-framed mirror on the wall by the door. He carefully smoothed his dark brown hair streaked with silver.

"You should have this frame fixed," he said, pointing at a crack in the gold-covered wood. "It's a family heirloom, you know."

One more needle. Of course I knew it. It was *my* family heirloom. Just like most of the objects we had shared during the divorce. At this point, I was grateful when I saw him turn the doorknob. If he stayed one second longer, I would smother him.

Poppy rushed past me in a swirl of navy blue and blonde curls. Tom's eyes mirrored the love in hers as he dropped his briefcase and twirled her. He tickled her throat with butterfly kisses, making my youngest howl with glee. I was amazed at how fast my resentment dissolved when I saw Tom with our daughters. Despite his countless flaws, he was a fantastic father. I hurried to my room to fetch some sweatpants. We had no time to lose and Ms. Giles, the dean, frightened me to death.

By some miracle, I parked the Mini in front of Belgravia Prep School at seventeen past eight, only two minutes late. The pristine, three-story building was huddled between the embassy of Congo and the Royal Ballet Academy in a discreet side alley. I pulled on my sweater hood to fend off the rain and held a cheap plastic umbrella above the girls till we reached the front steps.

We struggled to make our way against the stream of perfectly put-together mothers exiting the school after dropping off their kids – on time. I was rarely as groomed, but I usually blended in, priding myself on punctuality.

Rose fidgeted, anxious to get to class. At the bottom of the massive staircase leading to the Dragons' classroom, Rose blew me a kiss and hurried up the stairs. I watched her straight little frame struggle against the weight of her school bag with a fondness that scared me. That kind of love was overwhelming at times.

Meanwhile, Poppy tugged on my arm with all her might. "Mummy, can we go? Please!"

"Sorry, baby," I said, while leading her to another set of stairs. The kindergarten classes were in the basement. All the rooms were large with wide windows opening onto a private garden, a rare luxury for a London school. The Ladybugs classroom was the second on the left. Poppy hugged my waist tight then ran inside. I smiled apologetically to Miss Adriana and Miss Lakshmi, her stunning teachers. Miss Adriana nodded back with a smile.

I waved one last time to my blonde fury, very busy climbing on her chair, before hurrying outside. I had been fortunate enough not to run into anyone I knew and hoped to make it out of there before I did. My hand was on the door when I was stopped in my tracks.

"Hello, Ms. Gennaio. May I assume your alarm clock broke down this morning?"

I turned to face my least favorite Cerberus, Miss Stevenson, the school's secretary and spy for Ms. Giles. Her red hair was tied in a strict ponytail, her grey eyes magnified by huge tortoiseshell glasses. She was thirty going on seventy-five and she hated Americans with a passion. Next to her stood my other nemesis, my former best friend, Nisha Kothari. I smiled feebly at her and was repaid by a look of complete disgust as she gave me the once-over. Clearly, my hoodie and sweatpants didn't compare to her sleek black dress and kitten heels. She shook her head ever so slightly, making her lush curtain of midnight-colored hair swish against her shoulders.

"Mrs. Kothari was helping me plan the International Awareness Gala," Miss Stevenson declared. Nisha nodded amiably in return.

I understood her glee. Nisha had this thing about her that made you feel so blessed when she gave you her attention. Like you were the luckiest and most important person around.

She had been a great friend to me when I'd landed in London eight years ago. She knew everyone in the city because her father had been the Indian ambassador here when she was a teenager. Her husband worked with Tom, which was how we had met. Now our daughters attended Belgravia together. Selma was in Rose's class. They'd remained best friends despite our fallout.

Why Nisha had chosen to side with Tom was an enigma to me. No matter which way I spun it, I was pretty sure I

29

hadn't done anything to deserve it. I was the victim in this separation. But it definitely made starting the day a fun experience – comparable to that dream where you realize you've turned invisible – considering I had to face her indifference every single morning. And her attitude now extended to most of the other moms at school. I was a pariah because I had joined the infamous ranks of the divorcees. It was a well-known fact: divorcees were soulless pirates that would collar every husband as soon as their wife dropped their guard.

"I'd love to help out for the gala," I told Miss Stevenson as I pried open the door.

She stared at Nisha before turning to face me. "Of course. I will keep you informed."

"Great. Thank you," I said.

Finally outside, I breathed in deeply and ran to the car without bothering to use my umbrella. I wouldn't be so lucky as to drown in a puddle. I turned on the heating system, the rain having settled deep inside my bones with a viselike grip. Or maybe the cold came from Nisha's obvious disdain. I shivered and bit my lip so as not to cry. Focusing on the day ahead, I tried to decide whether I should start with grocery shopping or go grab Rose's extra uniform at the shop. I also tried to figure out when it would be most strategic to go spy on Kate again.

A gust of wind invaded my car, accompanied by a frozen sheet of rain. Agent Cunning settled comfortably inside next to me. I leapt while doing my best not to yell at him. I was in enough trouble already without causing a scene in front of the school. I glanced outside to make sure no one had spotted him entering my car. I couldn't afford the bad press. The rain was so intense it served as a makeshift curtain, shielding us from the outside. I pressed my hands to my chest to quiet down my furious heartbeat.

"You've got to stop doing that!"

"What?" he asked. His hair looked darker because it was wet. It was messy, plastered against his forehead. A few drops of rain hung on to his eyelashes. His plaid shirt clung to his chest, showing yummy muscles. Despite my best efforts, I found myself grinning.

"Are you all right?" he asked me.

"Sure, why?"

"You look like you just had a stroke," he said.

I dropped the smile and sat up straighter. A dimple formed fleetingly on his chin as he looked at me.

"Didn't get much sleep, did you?" he asked.

"How did you guess?"

"Did you give our conversation some thought?"

"No. Well…yes…" I wanted to tell him my answer was still no, but then I thought seeing him was the better part of my day – well, of my day so far – so I paused for a second.

Tom's words resonated inside my ears: *waffle Thursdays, all you do all day, free spirit*. Obviously, Kate sounded more glamorous with her thrilling job and freedom to do whatever she wanted.

I sometimes too wished I could travel on a whim or even simply leave my house in the morning without reviewing my endless mental checklist. A mom's life was bound to be predictable and a tad boring. Could this be my last occasion for an adventure? A chance to prove Tom wrong about me?

I could be surprising and fun too.

"I'll do it," I said.

Agent Cunning stared dumbly for a second, like he had been prepared for battle, and the army before him had just forfeited. Not for more than a second though; he seemed like the kind of man who landed back on his feet quickly.

"And you understand what it means? You can't talk about it. To anyone."

"Yes, yes," I said, waving my hand.

I looked for the manila folder without success.

"So…what do you need me to do?"

My curiosity was becoming an avid monster. I also feared this might be a prank played on me by Tom or Nisha. They always made fun of how gullible I was.

"You need to keep an eye on someone for me," he finally answered.

So far, it seemed to fit into my range of capacities. "Who?"

"This man has embezzled money from the US government."

The air got caught in my throat and I wheezed painfully. I had to grip my seat not to fall over against the steering wheel. Tom's offshore accounts! Yesterday, Agent Cunning had said I had access to some individual. Did he seriously think I would help him imprison my own husband? There must be a law against it. A wife couldn't testify against her husband. Then I remembered: I wasn't his wife anymore. Not right now at least.

"I… I can't…"

"I told you. No danger. I promise."

I shook my head. I wasn't afraid for my life anymore. It was worse. I feared for my family.

"The suspect is very careful. He knows there's an outstanding warrant against him in the US. That's why we must arrest him here."

When was the last time we'd traveled to New York together? Not last Christmas, we had already divorced by then. The Christmas before that. Was Tom already aware the government was onto him? A flicker of hope danced in my chest. Was it the reason he'd left? To protect the girls and me?

"He's meant to arrive in London soon. According to my sources, he'll stay for one month. It might be our only window of opportunity to catch him."

"Arrive? You mean he's not here yet?"

"Yes. That's precisely what I mean." He frowned. "Are you okay?"

"Sure." I smiled. *Not Tom then.* I was as relieved as I was disappointed. Well, maybe a little more relieved than disappointed. I simply couldn't picture pancake Tuesdays in jail. I felt like I'd dodged a bullet. I needed to talk to Tom about closing the offshore accounts. The risk wasn't worth taking.

"But I know him?" It seemed only logical if I had access

to this person.

"No, but you spend a lot of time parked in front of this person's property."

"He's a *he,* right?" Not that I wouldn't welcome an opportunity to put Katherine Stappleton away for good.

Agent Cunning seemed to get to whom I was alluding. The dimple creased his chin again.

"He's *her* boss. Here," he said as he untucked his shirt.

I caught my breath, hoping to get a glimpse of abs. Instead he pulled something from behind his back – the manila folder. *Yes!* I noticed it was slightly wrinkled as he handed it to me. My hand trembled as I took it.

"Kept it dry," he said, nodding for me to open it. Behind the cover was a picture. "This is Gabriel Varela, heir to Varela Global. We've been waiting to catch him for a while."

"You and me both, brother," I replied absentmindedly as I considered making out with the picture – pale skin, Caribbean sea green eyes, black hair that curled at the neck.

Behind the picture were four or five pages of data and a couple of other pictures. Way less attractive than the first one so I barely gave them a glance. When I looked up, Agent Cunning's brow was raised. I realized I had spoken the last part aloud. I blushed all the way to my hairline.

"Are you okay?" he asked.

I nodded.

"We'll get back to the rest of the file later. Mister Varela is a suspicious man. This is why we can't use one of our own to survey him."

"*Your own*? Who are you? FBI? CIA?"

"IRS," he answered flatly.

Humiliation washed over me. I felt mortified! I had been worried sick, picturing dangerous spies coming after me when he was only an IRS agent.

"Why didn't you say so yesterday?" I demanded, my tone more peeved than I'd wished it to be.

"Would it have changed anything?"

"Of course! I thought you were the real deal!"

He made a sour face at that so I hurried to correct myself.

"I thought you had a dangerous job," I said.

I took a mental step backward to see what this implied for me. This new development quenched my hesitation for good. "At least, I don't need to be afraid anymore…"

"That's what I told you," Ethan Cunning grumbled.

"Yes, you did," I admitted as a way of apology. I may have insulted him back there. "Are you seriously worried Gabriel Varela might spot IRS agents?"

"Yes. At least we can't take the chance without jeopardizing the whole operation. You, on the other hand, will fly under his radar, so you can keep me informed of his comings and goings."

"How do you know…?" I asked, embarrassment forbidding me to finish my sentence.

"That you spy on Katherine Stappleton?"

I nodded again.

"You're not exactly inconspicuous."

"I'm not?"

"Your car. Baby blue? Really? Was pink not available?" he asked.

I didn't think he wanted to hurt my feelings. Not on purpose at least. But it did feel like payback for my ungenerous comment about his job.

"I've been observing you for a few days now."

I ran my hands through my hair, pushing back my hood as I did so. *This was so creepy.* Ethan Cunning chuckled. I looked up and caught my reflection in the rearview mirror. My hair stood up straight on top of my head. Apparently, Mohawks were making a comeback. I was too preoccupied to do anything about it, although I did resent Ethan for mocking me.

"If you've noticed me, don't you think he will too?" I asked, while pointing at the picture on my lap.

"He might. But he won't pay attention to you. You're just a desperate ex-wife following one of his employees."

He could've slapped me, it would have hurt less. Was this how he saw me? *Desperate?* Tears stung my eyes but I kept the dam firmly shut. I refused to humiliate myself any further.

"Out! Now!" I yelled, way past the point of caring that anyone could overhear us. I pointed at the passenger door.

At first, he looked taken aback by my reaction. Then he relaxed in his seat and pretended he hadn't heard me. My head was a kettle past the boiling point, smoke coming out of my ears and nostrils. If he thought I'd get over it, he would be sorely disappointed. I had enough nasty comments at home without strangers starting in on me.

"You ask for my help and then you throw insults. I want you out of here. Now!" I repeated.

"But—"

"Now." I maintained my finger trained on the door, my expression impenetrable. I kept channeling my best bad-cop-mom persona till he reluctantly opened the car door.

Deep inside, I was shocked and proud of my outburst. This was the kind of dialogue I usually made up in my mind after people had offended me and they were long gone. For once, I had stood up for myself. It felt like I was making up for Tom's belittling attitude, my mother's nagging comments, and everyone who had ever been rude to me. I nearly considered apologizing to Ethan Cunning because of how grateful I felt toward him for having brought this out of me.

Then he winked. "I'll find you," he promised.

I watched as he jumped out of the car and slammed the door shut. Somehow, he had managed to get the last word. I lowered the window.

"No, you won't." I stared at the manila folder on my lap, hesitated for a second, took out Gabriel Varela's picture, and threw the rest of the folder out the window. "And take this with you!"

I registered Ethan Cunning's staggered expression with delight, switched the windshield wipers on, and gunned the car out of my parking spot.

Chapter Three

It was an absolute miracle that I made it to the house alive. Between the torrential rain, the total lack of survival instinct shown by British drivers, and my own agitated state, I had my lucky stars to thank for my safe travel.

I was still trying to come to terms with the implication of what I'd done. Thousands of questions jostled in my mind. Had I miraculously turned into a kickass goddess? Or like in Cinderella's tale, was I about to turn back into a pumpkin? Obviously, I favored the first answer, but as I'd known myself for the past thirty-two years, I didn't keep my hopes up.

On a bigger scale, what would be the punishment for my outburst? The reason why I never stood up to anyone – correction, to an adult; my daughters thought I was tough as a dragon – was in part due to my constant fear of retaliation. I wasn't witty enough or mean enough to stand my ground in an argument. Even when I was right, I ended up losing because I lacked the weapons to defend myself. This morning, for once, I had forgotten my limitations and Ethan Cunning had been surprised enough to let me get away with it. But what had I unleashed for the future?

Now that I knew he was an IRS agent, I wasn't afraid for my life any longer. Yet surely, he had means to get back at me? I still lived in London with a visa. Could he possibly have it revoked? What would happen to us if he did? Would we have to move back to New York? Or could he have Tom investigated as revenge?

Oddly enough, not even all those worries could quite dampen my elated mood. I was Wonder Woman in sweatpants. My blood thrummed with adrenaline.

I stepped inside my house with a determined spring in my step. *I am the master of this kingdom.* I wanted to do something crazy like get naked and roam the house, but I could hear the familiar sound of my mother and Claudia's bickering coming from the kitchen. I doubted Claudia would even notice if I walked around stark naked, but Bizzy hadn't seen me *au naturel* since I was about ten, and I intended to keep it that way. WASPs were modest things, so long as they didn't drink Bizzy's spiked lemonade. I shuddered at the thought of Aunt Daisy's annual Hamptons' pool party.

I dropped my sweater on the floor, a large puddle forming instantly on the carpet. I took a couple cautious steps inside the living room. I was just close enough to the kitchen to hear snippets of the conversation. Bizzy and Claudia were busy taking digs at each other, my bold housekeeper inflaming the row by calling her an "old hag." I could picture Bizzy's face turning purple at that, which added to my good disposition.

But then as I prepared to join them, a strong pull led me back toward the front door. Bizzy and Claudia had the same argument every day. For the largest part, it was fun to observe, a well-oiled vaudeville performance. They were so different, the simple fact they came into contact was a wonder to behold – as rare an occurrence, and as awe-inspiring, as a comet falling from the sky. You could see the sparks as the two strong-headed women quarreled.

But then I knew where the squabbling would go from here. Bizzy would bring Tom up and Claudia would say how sleazy he was and I was better off without him. Then Bizzy would argue that had I made a little more effort he'd still be here. None of these were things I wanted to hear.

Nothing would ruin my serenity today. I grabbed my raincoat, fetched the keys from the jumble on the console, and headed out. I deserved to savor my win over Ethan Cunning a while longer.

As soon as my feet hit the pavement, the weight on my chest lifted. But I also almost drowned instantly. In a second, I was drenched from head to toes. *Raincoat, my –*

What was the use if it didn't keep you dry?

I was determined not to go back. Pestering against that god-awful rain, I started down the street, half-walking, half-skating my way toward a nearby, busier street.

By the time I reached it, my teeth were chattering and I cursed my stubbornness. *Who is dumb enough to take a walk in this weather?*

All the shops were still closed because it was so early. In a flash of genius, my frozen brain conjured up an image of a cup of hot cocoa. The thought of my favorite teahouse – once our usual place with Nisha – just down the street filled me with a warm, simple joy. I didn't know if Nisha still went there; thought it strange to picture her at our table sitting with some other woman desperate for her affection. But I was too cold to care if I ran into her. That hot cocoa was so good it could melt the icicles her cat-shaped eyes threw at me.

The feeling of wellbeing I had been carrying since kicking Ethan Cunning out of my car returned to shield me from the awful weather. Now that I had a place to go, the rain seemed to roll off me.

I looked around me with a newfound interest. The shops that were grey and forlorn a minute ago were now coming to life. Metal curtains were brought up, lights were turned on, though the doors remained shut, and a few perky young women fussed behind the counters.

An old lady farther down the street treaded the sleek pavement with caution. She managed to look dignified despite her deluge-tailored apparel. She was all clear plastic: clear raincoat on top of a woolen dress, clear shower cap to protect her curls, clear giant umbrella in her frail, small hand.

Across the street, a long legged man kept his head down as he walked in the same direction I did. I brushed the wet tentacles of my hair away from my eyes and stared more intently at him. For some reason his silhouette seemed familiar. So did the hooded khaki army coat that hid his face. And that dimple on his chin...

The nerve of that guy!

"You're following me now?" I yelled to Ethan Cunning.

"I told you I'd find you," he called back.

Desperate, desperate, desperate. The ugly word started ringing in my ears. I felt my lip begin to quiver as shame replaced my indignation.

"Please, leave me alone," I said, needing to get away from Ethan Cunning fast before he saw me cry.

"What did you say?"

"Leave me alone," I screamed above the traffic noise and the rain.

"What? No biting comeback?" he said, as crossed the street in my direction.

"No. I'm all out of those. Please—"

"Oh, come on! You can't still be worked up about this morning!" Beside me, he pushed down his hood so I could see his face. "I didn't mean it... I mean, you might be a kook, but I don't think you're desperate."

Was that supposed to make me feel better?

"I just said Varela would think you're desperate. It's a good thing," he said.

My feet accelerated their movement of their own accord. "Stay away from me!"

"Try to be reasonable," he said, attempting to keep up with me. "We have to talk."

My power walk turned into a clumsy jog because of how slippery the sidewalk was. I had to get rid of him. I thought of the teahouse mere meters away, but what would stop Ethan Cunning from following me in there? The picture of the hot cocoa cup in my mind burst into shards.

I scanned the street quickly to find a place to hide. A sweet diffused light shone from a front window two buildings down. I held back a cry of satisfaction as I realized what it was: Ginger and Honey Spa – massages, waxing, and nails. No way would Ethan Cunning follow me there!

I fought the urge to stick my tongue out to him. Instead I

shoved open the door. A sweet bell rang while I stomped into the amber-toned reception area. The cleansing smell of lemongrass mixed with the spicy aroma of warm tea washed over me. Meanwhile my shuddering amplified, my body overwhelmed by the contrast between the inside and the outside. An angel of mercy came to my rescue.

"You poor thing! You are wet," the woman in white pants and matching top informed me, sympathy etched on her porcelain face.

Really? I haven't noticed.

"Come!" She gestured toward her desk. "What can we do for you today?"

I wiped my face with my equally wet sleeve. "Uh…" I hadn't really thought further than getting rid of Ethan Cunning. "First, could you do something for me?"

"Of course!" she said with a smile.

"Could you see if there's a man outside? He's in an army jacket."

"Sure," she answered as if it were a common request from her clients.

She made her way around her desk toward the door. I buried my face in a treatment menu.

"Discreetly!" I hissed as I watched her press her face to the window.

The treatment list was longer than my arm. They must have an army of employees to provide all those services. I didn't need anything done but I felt bad leaving after asking the receptionist's help and ruining their carpet with all the rain I had brought with me.

I hated having my nails done and always ended up being talked into the weirdest designs that I hurried to remove as soon as I got home. A giant waste of my time and theirs.

A hot stone massage sounded divine with the cold settled deep in my bones. Only getting a massage in the middle of a school day, getting a massage at all for that matter, felt way too decadent for me. It wasn't something I'd ever do.

All that was left for me to do was to apologize for the disruption and leave a generous tip for her kindness. The thought of facing the rain outside depressed me.

The receptionist had been stuck to the window for ages.

"So?" I asked. "Is he here?"

"The cutie in an army jacket?"

"That's the one."

"Lucky girl! And he's waiting for you under the rain? He must be crazy about you," she said.

"No, crazy, full stop." I couldn't very well start explaining the whole story to her.

"Really? What a shame!" She gave Ethan one last glance then retrieved her place behind the desk. "Psycho?"

I gave the thought consideration. "Not that I know of."

"Stalker?"

No, that would be me. "Something like that."

"Well if he ever gets tired of stalking you, feel free to send him my way."

"Will do," I replied absentmindedly.

How long would I have to wait to come out? He was absolutely mad to wait for me with this rain.

"So have you decided on a treatment?" she asked.

I scanned the treatment menu to find the longest one they offered.

Turned out the longest treatment they had was a weird, slimming seaweed wrap. Definitely not as enjoyable as a massage, if not for the knowledge that *he* waited in the rain. I smelled like a dead fish and felt as sleek as well.

"You should be a therapist," I told Nala, the Thai beautician who had endured my rambling for the past hour and a half, as she walked me back to the reception.

She stared blankly. The petite woman in a white uniform didn't speak a word of English, which had allowed me to empty out my heart. I had told her every single detail about my life without fear of being judged. My only friend was Claudia and she didn't do heart to hearts. Not that Nisha did either, but I hadn't needed it so much when we were friends. I felt lighter now.

I tipped Nala, hiked my bag higher on my shoulder, and

waved goodbye.

"You should try a personal trainer," my non-English speaker beautician told me. "One of my other clients also felt self-conscious, so she did it and loved it. I like the gym better. Love the energy."

"Uh?"

"Not that you need it." For someone who didn't understand English just a few minutes ago, her accent was flawless. "You've got a great body. I'd never have guessed you had kids."

"Thank…thank you," I said.

I was beyond embarrassed and tried to recall the most shameful things I had told her during our session. Why did she talk about the gym? Maybe it was because I had compared my stomach to a tub of clotted cream or my thighs to Jell-O. I had told her about staking out Kate, I realized.

"Why? Why didn't you say? That you speak English?"

"Beauticians are like priests, you see? I take my job very seriously," she said with a proud smile.

"So you keep a vow of silence too?"

"Of course! Your secrets are safe with me." She winked.

The doorbell rang as a middle-aged blonde stepped inside. Her umbrella was closed and she didn't drip all over the carpet. This was a good sign. My own clothes were still damp even after hanging them to dry for over an hour.

"I have to take this client," Nala whispered to me. "You should dump the guy by the way."

"Who?"

"Tom, of course! He's a jerk." *So I had been told.* "And besides, the sea is full of fishes." She giggled.

With the way I smelled, I was pretty much over fish analogies.

The receptionist waved to Nala. I nodded goodbye then walked to the door.

"This here is Nala," I heard the receptionist say. "She will be performing your treatment today."

"Hello," Nala said with the thickest Thai accent she

could muster.

I considered telling the client about the sham but then decided against it. A benevolent ear was too rare to find. She might as well get to enjoy it as I had.

Outside, I had been expecting to find Ethan Cunning waiting for me. But he was nowhere to be found. Good, I told myself, overlooking the pang of disappointment in my chest.

The Waitrose a couple of blocks away was now open,. I took out my list of groceries and headed inside. As usual when I went to buy a couple things, I left with five overflowing bags. I juggled them down the street, my wrists screaming from the strain. I turned the corner to my street. It was way less crowded than Kings Road, the absence of shops keeping its attraction low.

"Here you are!" a voice boomed behind me.

Ethan Cunning jogged up to me, looking light and rested. "Had to take a lunch break," he said.

I, on the other hand, was panting as loud as a bull about to be released in the arena. My arms were three inches longer from the weight of the grocery bags, making me look like a gorilla. I shot him a vicious look.

"Here, let me help you," he said and grabbed the bags as if they weighed nothing.

I tried to say thank you but my tongue wouldn't yield. He didn't seem to be waiting for gratitude anyway. It was a surprise. Tom used to do a lot of things for me but he always expected a thank you. Like he did things just for that magic word. *Thank you, Tom, you are wonderful. Thank you, Tom, you are my hero.* He always needed to be congratulated. *Men's egos!*

"You really went all PMS on me today," he said. "Ready to kiss and make up?"

I pounced forward, my hands reaching for his throat. The playful smile hanging on his lips kept me in check. *Kiss…*

I shook myself. I'd rather punch him than kiss him. Besides, the only man I wanted to kiss was Tom.

"For an IRS agent, you're awfully cocky," I said instead.

"Don't go dismissing my job like that. We IRS agents are badass."

"What? You hit people with calculators?"

He paused in the middle of the street. I stopped a few steps farther when I realized he had stopped following. When I turned my head to see what the holdup was, I caught him looking at me. *No, not looking – staring.* As if he was trying to figure me out.

"What?" I asked. "Have I upset you? You can't take a few jokes?"

I hoped I hadn't hurt his feelings. I may be a *new me* today but *new me* wasn't cruel. At least I hoped she wasn't.

"You're different than I expected," he said at last, catching up with me as he did.

There was a spring to his steps, the way a teenager walked. My gaze lingered too long on his distressed jeans.

I didn't dare ask how different I was. Desperate was enough of a descriptive for the day, thank you very much.

"And you're different than what I would have pictured an IRS agent to be."

"I know, I'm way too good looking for the job."

"You're way too conceited."

"Well, that too." He chuckled.

With all the bantering, we made it to my house so fast I blinked a few times to make sure we were really there.

"So you'll help me?" he asked.

"No way," I said from the steps of my house.

I held on to the ramp and lingered just a little. What was I doing? I was behaving like a flirty teenager. Even with my honorable height of five foot seven and standing two steps higher than him, our faces were level. The corner of his mouth twitched with a smile.

He started climbing the stairs toward me. When he spoke next, it seemed that a switch had been turned on.

"I could make it worth your while…"

His voice was husky and his stare burning, making my toes curl. *Oh boy!*

I tore my gaze away from him. *Get a grip!*

"Goodbye," I stuttered and dashed to the door.

I heard him chuckle.

"I'll find you!" he called from the stairs.

I slammed the door shut, and then slapped my forehead when I realized I had blown my only chance to come into the house undiscovered.

"Sloane!" Bizzy said, coming out of the living room. "Where were you? It's lunch time already!"

Lunchtime? My bags! I hurried outside. The grocery sacks were all stacked neatly on the doormat.

"You forgot your groceries on the doorsteps?" Bizzy asked, her chin jutting above my shoulder to see.

I leaped.

"Why do you always need to scare me?"

"Why do you always get scared?" She countered. "Really, Sloane, you don't live in a cloak-and-dagger novel. No reason to be so jumpy."

If only she knew.

"Will you help me bring this in?"

"Can't, dear." She waved her flaming nails at me. "Just did them." She turned toward the living room. "Claudia? Will you please be helpful for once in your life?"

"I can't hear you. Sloane, are you here? I've got a weird illness. I'm deaf when it comes to your mother."

"Why do we keep her?" Bizzy asked.

"You don't do anything. I do. She's great."

"The house is always a mess."

"She's my friend."

Bizzy sighed before leaving me stranded in the doorway. I waited a couple minutes, but then realized Claudia wouldn't come. I ended up lugging the groceries to the kitchen on my own. Claudia was polishing the toaster thoroughly.

"I think it's clean enough," I pointed out.

The living room, on the other hand, looked like a crime scene. Or a war zone, more accurately.

"Do you mind tidying up the living room before you go?"

"I'll do it later. I can stay longer today. If I go home, Michal wants me to clean the house. I'm better here."

Apparently 'not cleaning' was what she meant. I pretended I didn't see the irony.

"We can go spy on Kate later," she offered.

I considered this. After Ethan's comment, I wouldn't give him the pleasure of seeing me there anytime soon. *Desperate!*

"Not today."

Claudia stared intently. "Are you okay?"

"Yes, why?"

"You come home late. You don't want to spy on Kate. You look different." She scratched her bright pink hair. "You're over Tom?"

"Of course not!"

She looked disappointed. "So what is it?"

"I just thought it was time for a change." I lied because I couldn't talk about Ethan. "I don't want to be depressed anymore," I said, realizing I meant it whole-heartedly.

"Good," Claudia said. "So how do you plan to do it?"

"I'm thinking of getting a personal trainer."

"That's a great idea!" Bizzy said, joining us in the kitchen. "What will you do? Yoga? No, you should do Pilates; it's perfect for your body type."

"And what type of body is that?" Claudia glared, feeling protective of me.

"Soft," Bizzy replied matter-of-factly. She turned to me. "You're slim; you don't need to lose weight. You've got my blessed morphology."

Claudia pretended to gag.

Bizzy looked good for almost sixty but she had gained a couple sizes since her twenties. I envied her self-confidence. And she was right about me. I was lucky. I never really put on weight. But the lack of exercise had indeed turned me mushy. It was time I got in shape. I just couldn't rely on my good metabolism forever.

"I don't know what kind of exercise I want to do yet. I'm going to my room to hop on the Internet." And change into dry clothes before I caught my death.

I closed the door with relief and walked to my closet, stripping along the way. I put on black skinny jeans and a silk shirt, a fine improvement to my previous 'take-out-the-trash' outfit.

I fired up my laptop that sat on the dressing table and brought it with me to bed. I propped myself against the pillows, the computer resting on my extended legs.

I typed 'Private Instructor London' in the search engine. As private instructors of everything and anything under the sun, or rather the London rain, popped up in my browser, I realized I hadn't been precise enough.

Teaches Mandarin, burlesque, ballet, the dark arts of esotericism, tennis, and *Kung Fu.*

The way I saw it, I had three choices – scroll to the next page and get more of anything, type in a new search with the words 'fitness' or 'sport' included somewhere, or believe in fate and pick from the one page before me. Admittedly, I was a bit afraid of what the next page might reveal, but mostly I was in the mood to listen to the universe for once. This sounded like something *new me* would do – something bold, spontaneous.

I narrowed the decision to the only three sports advertised. Tennis was too dangerous. Put a racket in my hands and a concussion wasn't far away. I had an unfortunate thing with throwing rackets rather than balls across the court.

Only two left. Ballet was a bad fit. I was still traumatized from my one and only class a quarter of a century ago. Miss Valérie had kicked me out of her class mid entrechat for – these were her exact words – "…being as graceless as an elephant in a ceramic shop."

I rubbed my forehead for a moment, eyes closed. Could I be the Kung Fu type? It seemed more like something Claudia would enjoy – give her fists a chance to catch up with her sharp tongue.

I was too weak. The way I had reacted yesterday when Ethan had invaded my car was proof enough. I'd thrown a cookie at him! *A cookie!* I had never felt so vulnerable before in my life.

The feeling of frustration took over me as I remembered it, which was precisely why I needed this class. So when it happened next time – correction, on the off chance it ever happened to me again – I would be prepared, capable of defending myself. And wouldn't it be nice to be a badass for once?

My fingers hovered above the link to the Kung Fu instructor. I thought of Tom's patronizing voice, of how much he would tease me if he heard of this plan. This only made my decision more appealing. I right clicked to the website. It was high time I kicked some ass.

Grabbing my computer, I went to the living room to get my cellphone. I dialed the contact number for Sven, the Kung Fu instructor. Before I could change my mind and hang up, he picked up, promising to be at my house the following Thursday at 4 p.m. I did a little victory dance in the middle of the room.

"What is wrong with you today?" Bizzy materialized in the living room, startling me again. The woman was too sneaky! I was starting to suspect she had superpowers.

"I'm happy?" I mumbled apologetically.

"Did you find a teacher?"

"Yes, I did."

"And?"

"And what?"

"What does he teach?" Bizzy sighed.

I already knew she wouldn't like it.

"Kung Fu," I said.

Her mouth gaped open, like a fish out of sea. "You? Kung Fu?"

I retreated to my bedroom to escape her criticisms. Apparently, *new me* didn't extend to my mother. When it came to her, I was still behaving like a middle grader.

A middle grader who was about to learn to kick some ass.

Chapter Four

"Fancy meeting you here!" Ethan Cunning's voice boomed behind me, startling me out of my lookout position.

Crouching behind a van, I landed on my knees in the gutter, muddy water soaking my jeans. At least I hoped it was water, and not a smelly present left by the Labrador sniffing around earlier today.

I muffled my cry of frustration and stared at Ethan hovering above me. His five o'clock shadow teetered on seven, masking his dimple almost completely. He grinned.

"You again! Why won't you leave me alone?"

"Can't," he replied while helping me back up on my feet.

I crouched again, afraid Kate might see me.

"Besides this is too much fun."

"Harassing me, you mean? I could call the cops, you know."

"No, you wouldn't." He tugged at my hair teasingly as he brushed off my threats.

He was right not to be afraid. Ethan had now been following me for a week and I hadn't reported him. He showed up everywhere, popping up at the grocery store, the dry cleaner, the fishmonger, helping me select ballet shoes for Rose, and a birthday gift for Poppy's friend's birthday party – all the while attempting to change my mind about helping him. My phone now counted more text messages from Ethan than from any other person in my life although I still hadn't figured out how he got my number.

At least he had the good taste to never show up around my daughters and after a week, my anger from the day he had insulted me had faded away. I could agree to help him. I wanted to help him. But I couldn't say the words.

As soon as he was in sight, an imperious need to annoy him overtook me. Like a teenager disagreeing with her parents on principle, I couldn't grant Ethan Cunning the satisfaction of giving him what he wanted.

"You stayed away a whole week! Not bad." He whistled appreciatively.

I considered biting him, I was so annoyed. I hated that he believed I had stopped myself from spying on Kate because of him. That I cared what he thought of me – he was absolutely right, of course.

"I've been busy."

He tilted his head to the side and raised an eyebrow. He knew my past week's schedule better than I did. I could have come to spy a thousand times but I had stretched my willpower to its limits – at least I had to be grateful to Ethan for finding my pride in the deep ditch Tom had hidden it.

I slapped his hand away from my hair, making him laugh.

"Where's your car?"

"I couldn't find a parking spot," I fibbed lamely.

Half of the parking spots in the street were vacant. I had come on foot in the hope he wouldn't see me. *Great thinking, Sloane!*

Activity by Varela Headquarters made me forget about Ethan momentarily. Judging by his silence, he had lost interest in teasing me too. He crouched next to me.

I hoped and dreaded to see Kate all at the same time, like a child looking through spread fingers at a horror movie. I had a compulsion to see her, to face her perfection, but I had no idea what I could gain from it. Perhaps I had become masochistic sometime during the divorce. Either that or I hoped to find her fatal flaw. Like every deity, Kate must have one, the Achilles' heel that would help me slay the dragon and conquer Tom again.

Instead of high cheekbones and two-meter-long legs, I saw two shady looking men dive into the revolving door and be spat out of it almost instantly, a security guard at their backs.

The shorter one, with dirty blond hair and a patched up jacket, jumped at the guard's throat with the obstinacy and lack of good judgment of a tiny Jack Russell. The guard's giant fist gathered him by the collar of his jacket and dangled him at a distance.

Instead of coming to his rescue, Shorty's sidekick snarled something at the guard, his arms folded against his scrawny chest. When the guard didn't respond, he kicked the building's glass walls a couple of times like a child throwing a tantrum. Then he walked back toward the two men and said something to the guard who finally let go of Shorty.

Shorty waved his fist before the guard's face then pivoted on his heels and followed his friend across the street. I held my breath as they hit our side of the sidewalk, but then they took the first left away from our hiding spot. I let out a sigh of gratitude. I did not want to cross paths with those men.

They had been standing close to us just long enough for me to notice Shorty had a tattoo along one side of his chin – some vine leaf, intricate motif or a tribal symbol of some sort.

Ethan didn't share my relief. His attention was focused on the building in front of us. His jaw was clenched hard and his furrowed brow gave his stare a hawk-like quality.

A bald man, in his mid-sixties, I guessed, stood before the revolving doors with the security guard. The man had a protuberant stomach, showing under the silk of his shirt, and a satin black suit straight out of Tony Montana's wardrobe. He twirled his mustache as he talked to the guard. Despite his lack of elegance, his attitude said he was the man in charge. Mustache man walked back inside Varela's global headquarters, but instead of being able to relax, a presence very near me demanded my immediate attention.

From his unfortunate height, Shorty loomed over me. I mustered all the resolve I could find not to tremble as my eyes found his tattoo. A snake – at least my curiosity was satisfied.

Where had he come from? Instinctively I turned around

toward Ethan for reassurance but he had vanished. *Some sort of white knight.* I felt incredibly small and lonely from my pitiful crouching position. Shorty must have waited for mustache man to return inside before coming out of his hiding spot. His sidekick was gone, apparently.

"What the hell are you looking at?" he growled.

Small dogs were the most vicious. They were the ones that bit. Possible answers escaped my brain faster than I could conjure them up.

"You have a problem?"

"N…no."

"What's fucking wrong with you?" He gestured toward the ground.

I tried to look impassive and playful at the same time – a colossal feat.

"Hide and seek," I murmured.

Terrible liar!

"Yeah? You think I'm a clown or something?"

He stepped closer to me and grabbed the collar of my shirt. I folded my arms over my face to protect it from the blow that surely would come.

I peeked through the barrier of my arms. I had never received a beating. Not even by a brother or sister – possibly the best part of being an only child. How much would it hurt?

Apparently, the universe decided to spare me the discovery today. Just as fast as Ethan had disappeared, he now rematerialized behind Shorty. He was at least three heads taller than my assailant was, but for a second, I feared for him just the same.

That was, until he launched himself onto Shorty. With one swift, circular move of his leg, Ethan swept up the vicious mutt from the ground while elbowing him in the ribcage. The blow was so sharp I heard a crack on impact. Shorty let out a painful wheezing sound before going limp. With a speed that left me dizzy, Ethan managed to grab Shorty by the shoulders and cushion his fall to the ground. The body connected with the pavement without a sound.

"Come on!" Ethan urged me, pulling my hand.

I jumped to my feet and hurried in his wake. After seeing him fight, I didn't know whether I was safer with him than with Shorty but hanging around for the thug to wake up seemed like a worse option. I kept glancing sideways, trying to match lethal Ethan to the cool, laid back guy I knew him to be.

"What was that about?" I asked when he finally conceded to stop, two streets down.

I reclined against a wall, pressing my hand to my chest to control the furious beating of my heart. *Not a runner*. Ethan pulled off the hood that had concealed his face during the altercation.

"Sorry I didn't act sooner," he said, instead of answering. "I couldn't risk being discovered by Hector."

"Wait... What? Who's Hector?"

"Varela's chief of security."

Mustache man!

"I thought you had left me behind," I said.

"I was hidden between the cars."

"Well, I guess you *did* protect me after all," I said.

Ethan took a step closer. The thought of what could have happened to me if he hadn't stepped in made me tremble. Or maybe the shivering came from him hovering over me. There was virtually no space left between our bodies.

I gasped as he leaned in against me. His lips move closer to my face. I closed my eyes.

His warm breath tickled my ear as he whispered, "Anytime—"

Then he pushed himself away from me, leaving me panting and sorely disappointed. *So close!*

Ethan stuck his hands in his pockets and took a few steps down the street. I jogged after him.

"Did you know the guy who threatened me?"

"No. Must be some punk looking for trouble," he answered.

"In the middle of the day? In an office building?"

Something didn't add up. They looked more dangerous

53

than kids looking for mischief. Thugs, more like.

"Maybe they were drunk. Or high. Or lost," he said.

My gut told me otherwise but it was known to be wrong more often than not and I had no other explanation at hand.

Maybe they were secret admirers of Kate.

He picked up his pace. I trotted to keep up with him. I realized I had yet to thank him for saving my ass.

"Thank you."

He winked at me. "Don't mention it."

Seeing that playful Ethan had returned helped me forget my big scare. I felt strong enough to tease him, which was a good sign.

"So, Karate Kid, is this standard IRS training?"

"Just a hobby of mine."

"What is that move you pulled called?" I needed to ask my Kung Fu trainer to teach it to me.

"Fly-by-the-seat-of-my-pants." He grinned.

"Good name!"

I doubted my teacher would have it in his inventory. *Such a shame*. Ethan stopped to look at me. His shoulders shook with laughter.

"What's so funny?"

"Hide and seek?" he asked.

I blushed.

"What was I going to say? I told you I'm an awful liar. See? You don't want my help. Worst spy material."

"Nice try," he said. "Stop dreaming. You're not getting rid of me so easily."

I huffed.

"You're crazy," he said. "You know that, right?"

"So you keep telling me." I sighed, walking away from him. "Not that I don't enjoy your company, but I'm late to pick up the girls. And trouble seems to follow you."

Way to ruin a perfectly pleasant stake-out session! Once again, I'd missed Kate, defeating the whole purpose of my morning.

"Please stay away from me," I said above my shoulder.

Ethan followed me now.

"No can do. Varela is expected to land in London anytime now. Next week, according to my sources. Only you can keep tabs on him for me without getting noticed. I need your help." He ran a hand in his tousled hair as he said so.

I fought the urge to rearrange his hair.

"I'm going now," I warned, averting my eyes from his.

His slender fingers grabbed mine.

"Sloane. It's important."

Ethan sounding serious was a rare occurrence. Rare enough that I felt compelled to stop and answer him.

"I know. I'll think about it."

Why couldn't I just say yes? I was like those bullied men that once given the smallest amount of power turned into tyrants. Ethan was the only person in the world who needed me – besides my daughters, obviously – and instead of aiding him, I made him squirm.

"Well, okay then." He chuckled. "See you later." He wriggled his fingers in a mock girly goodbye.

"Ugh!" *Could he ever be serious?*

I held the front seat flat down while Poppy and Rose fought their way inside the car. I helped Poppy into the child seat and locked the security belt. She dropped the paper she had been holding onto the floor.

"Mummy! My drawing!"

"We'll get it later. Okay, honey?"

It had fallen under the seat on Rose's side and I wasn't in a mood to play contortionist.

"But mummy! It's a pony!"

I kissed her forehead, closed the door, and sat behind the wheel. Rose's face disappeared from the rearview mirror.

"It's okay, Poppy. I'm going to find your drawing," she told her little sister.

Rose pestered against the security belt hindering her movements, but not her willpower. She kept at it for a couple blocks then came back up, a triumphant smile on her face.

"Here!" she said. "Got it!"

"But that's not my pony," Poppy said.

Rose stayed silent for a second.

"What is it honey?" I asked. "What did you find?"

"A picture!" she exclaimed. "He's handsome! Is he your new boyfriend, Mummy?"

"My boyfriend?" I asked as I stopped at a red light. "What are you talking about?"

"Mummy has a boyfriend?" Poppy giggled. "Mummy and her boyfriend sitting in a tree…" she sang.

"Him," Rose said as she passed the picture to me.

I mentally slapped my forehead. It was Gabriel Varela's picture. I had completely forgotten about it. And to think I wanted to keep the girls out of this whole mess. *Good job, Sloane!*

"It's no one, baby."

"But why do you have his picture in the car if he's no one?" Rose asked, disappointment seeping in her voice.

Since the divorce, finding me a boyfriend had become her life mission. She'd tried to set me up with every man she found remotely attractive. Unfortunately, there were many. Her sensible judgment took a hit on all romance-related subjects.

Lucky for me, Poppy didn't share her passion for my love life and had moved on from our conversation already. She twirled a lock of hair around her pinkie while humming to herself.

I lied to Rose. "He's a friend of Claudia's, baby. She forgot the picture in the car."

In the rearview mirror, I saw Rose's little forehead crease with questions. But, thank god for kids' trust, she shook her suspicions quickly and instead started telling me about her day.

At the house, the girls rushed to the kitchen. They tried to climb on Bizzy's lap, who sat at the counter, reading a magazine.

"What are you? Monkeys?" she asked, affection hidden under the apparent harsh words. "Careful, Poppy. Do not

56

spill my lemonade."

I checked my watch. 3 p.m. and already drinking. She was the most efficient social drinker I had ever seen. As if alcohol transformed into water when it hit her system. Great liver, I supposed, which I'd not inherited. I was a lightweight. Two drinks and I would make out with a lamppost.

"Girls, sit on your stools. You don't want to wrinkle these pants. They are linen, impossible to iron," she explained as if the girls might care.

They did as she asked though. Bizzy had some kind of natural authority when it came to the girls. She never had to scream or punish. She treated them as equals and in return they strived to be worthy of her trust. Unlike me who threatened, bargained, and occasionally bought their cooperation. I grabbed a few cookies for the girls from the jar on the counter and handed it to them. Then I placed two glasses of apple juice before them.

"Where's Claudia?" I asked Bizzy.

"Not working. Clearly. She hasn't shown up today."

"Again!"

"It's the second time this week. Can we fire her?"

"No, Mom," I said as I looked for my phone.

I dialed Claudia's number. She couldn't stand me up all the time like that. I rehearsed my speech while the phone rang.

"Hello," she answered, her voice furry.

"Are you sleeping?"

"No. I'm in the bus. I'll be there in thirty minutes."

"You were supposed to be here five hours ago," I said.

"I had a fight with Michal."

"I'm sorry. Are you guys okay?"

"Yes. He was just being an ass. Anyway, we ended up drinking a bottle of vodka between the two of us. Polish-style make up."

"Sounds painful," I said.

"Tell me about it. I've been popping Advil all day."

The doorbell rang. I checked my watch. 3:45 p.m. Damn

Kung Fu teacher was early and I hadn't had time to change. I popped my head in the kitchen.

"Do you mind taking the girls out during my class?" I asked Bizzy.

"No problem. There's an exhibition at the National Portrait Museum I want to see."

"Not something too grim, okay?"

Last time they went, Freud drawings had traumatized the girls for ages. Claudia's muffled voice called my attention.

"Sorry," I said as I put the phone to my ear. "I completely forgot about you."

"Gee! Thanks!"

"Not like that. I forgot you were on the phone."

The doorbell rang again. I pulled on the collar of my sweater. Did I already say how much I hated being late? Bizzy saw my panic rising.

"Sloane, you go change. I'll get the door."

"Thanks," I yelled while jogging toward my bedroom. "Sorry, Claudia, gotta go. I'll see you soon." I hung up the phone and changed into hot pink shorts and a matching sports bra. But as I watched myself in the closet's mirror, I hurried to shrug the shorts off and find something more appropriate. I wasn't Pilates Barbie today. I was kickass Sloane in sweatpants and a Brown University oversized t-shirt. Still more student-y than Kung Fu-y. *Baby steps…*

"Sorry I'm late," I hollered as I slammed my bedroom door shut.

I power walked down the corridor. From the top of the staircase, where I stood, I could see four mats arranged in a square behind my couch. A man's voice rang from somewhere inside the room.

"If you want to use your own mats we can. I assumed you weren't equipped yet."

"You assumed well," I replied halfway down the stairs.

Bizzy sashayed out of the kitchen and into the living room holding a tall glass. Even though I was mere meters away, she looked completely oblivious to me.

"Mom? Mom?" I called. "What are you still doing here?

Where are the girls?"

"Change of plans! They're playing in their bedroom."

"But why?"

"Someone had to play host to Sven."

Only now did I notice the stupidest grin on her face.

"Have you been abducted by aliens? Where's my mom?"

"Very clever, Sloane," she said without dropping the smile. "Here, Sven! Your lemonade."

I followed in her wake. When I saw the man she handed the glass to, I understood her newfound motivation to stay home. Sven gave her a toothpaste commercial smile as he grabbed the glass. I waved my hands and mouthed a warning but we were not tight enough, Sven and I, for him to understand the danger. He drank a big swig of the lemonade and his pale skin turned Tabasco red. He nearly choked before retrieving his placid expression. I was impressed at how fast he regained his cool.

"Thank you, Bizzy," he said.

So they were already on first name basis. Bizzy didn't waste any time.

I stepped around my mother and extended my hand to shake.

"Sloane," I said.

"Sven," the Scandinavian god standing in my living room answered.

He held his lemonade glass like it was poison, with two fingers, keeping it as far away from him as possible.

"Here, let me help you."

I took his glass and set it down on a bookshelf.

"I'm going to get some water. Want some?"

Sven winced.

"Just water," I specified.

"Yes. Please." He nodded eagerly. "Thank you."

I ran to the kitchen. When I came back, Bizzy hovered dangerously close to my poor Kung Fu teacher, who, despite his giant stature, seemed to have shrunken to the size of a troll. She had him cornered against the couch, her hand feeling his biceps through the kimono.

"Water," I said as I raised both glasses.

Bizzy acknowledged my presence reluctantly.

"Sven is telling me all about his regimen. Did you know he won the European championship two years in a row?"

"I haven't had a chance to talk him yet, Mom. You've quite monopolized him."

"He's also a holistic massage therapist. Tibetan monks trained him as a teenager."

"Fascinating. And you got all that in the time it took me to pour a couple glasses of water?"

"And when you were getting ready. Sven is a resourceful young man."

"I love all this," he said. "But my real passion is modeling." His ice blue eyes turned dead serious. "It takes a lot of discipline, you know?"

More than Kung Fu? I bit my lip not to laugh.

"Your parents must be very proud," Bizzy said.

Dear Mrs. Robinson!

"They don't approve. They think it's not good enough."

You had to admire his honesty. Here he was, in his early twenties, a man in all his glory, with the honesty and dreams of a child.

"I'm still waiting for my big break. When they see me on posters for Calvin Klein all over town, they'll have to admit I was right." He turned to Bizzy. "Underwear modeling is the most difficult, you see? Your body must be perfect."

"I'm sure you're on the right track," she answered.

"Just a second," I told Sven.

I grabbed Bizzy by the elbow and dragged her out of the living room.

"If you tear off his kimono, I'm pretty sure the class will be canceled. You should be ashamed of yourself! What about dad?"

"What about him?"

"You've been drooling all over Sven since he's got here."

"I don't drool, Sloane. It's not proper. And your father has been hunting big game for the past five months."

Not a code name for whores, my dad had actually

transformed my divorce into a sabbatical hunting year around the world.

"Besides, I'm just looking," Bizzy said. "There's no harm in looking."

"Well, okay. Can I start my class now?"

"Okay" she said reluctantly. "I'll go check on the girls."

"Would you mind keeping them upstairs till the class is done? I don't want to be interrupted," I said as I turned my back to her.

"Sloane? Sloane?" she whispered urgently.

"Yes?"

"He's not a gigolo, is he?"

I did not dignify her question with an answer.

Chapter Five

On Friday morning, I dragged my poor aching body to the kitchen for my ritual coffee. I nearly died of a heart attack when I found Claudia, dressed in an oversized, fluffy turquoise sweater and ripped jeans, standing before the coffee machine. I checked the clock on the fridge. 7 a.m. Nowhere near the time she started working. She was meant to start work at nine, which usually meant ten-thirty, eleven, and sometimes, like yesterday, five p.m. But never, ever earlier.

"Did someone die?"

"You're hiding something from me." She waved her finger threateningly. "I've been up all night thinking about it. The Kung Fu teacher – he's kept me awake too. The size of his arms… I bet he could fuck me standing up," she said.

Anyone could; she weighed less than my handbag.

Her blue eyes focused again.

"You don't obsess about Tom so much, you've stopped spying on Kate—"

"I was there yesterday."

"Without me?"

"You were late," I reminded her.

"And who is this boyfriend of mine in your car?"

A man in my car? I think I would have noticed.

"Rose told me about my handsome boyfriend when I got here yesterday. Apparently you have a picture of him in your car."

Gabriel Varela. *Mental slap.*

"I doubt you have a picture of Michal. Beside he's ugly as a cow's arse. Even Rose has better taste than that."

"I don't have a picture of Michal in my car."

"I know! Who is he? What are you hiding?"

"He's no one. Just a picture I found in the street," I stammered. "I've been pretending he's my boyfriend."

Claudia's face fell. "*Kurva*! It's the saddest thing I've ever heard."

I should become a writer, or a spy. I was getting good at making up believable lies. Albeit ones that made me look even more pathetic than I was.

"You can't have fake relationships. You know what you need? You need to get laid."

"Well, Tom is neither available, nor interested."

"Someone else. I was going to call dabs on Sven…"

"Dibs. Call dibs."

"Whatever. But as I was saying, if you want, I'll let you have him."

I pictured my gentle Kung Fu teacher slash model. As a bonus to the class, where the only butt getting kicked had been mine in the manner of unending abs and leg moves, he had read my aura by having me stand still against a door for ten minutes. Apparently, my aura was blue. Bizzy's aura was red. Go figure, I would have guessed black.

"Thank you, but I'm okay. And what about you? What about Michal?"

"If I drink one more bottle of vodka, I'll die. The man is a screw-up. I think it's time for a change."

"Doesn't he live with you?"

"Yes. So what? He'll find a couch elsewhere. That's already where he's been sleeping most nights at my place."

Practical Claudia. Life must be so easy when you knew you were always right. So different from mine. I tried to picture Sven's two hundred pounds of muscles holding Claudia's frail silhouette. This made me oscillate between a smile and fear for him. No doubt she would eat the sweet giant alive.

"So I keep dabs on Sven. But we need to do something for you."

"What about going to spy on Kate? Will you tag along today?" I asked.

Going alone had been a stupid move. At least with Claudia there, Ethan would have to keep his distance, secrecy and all.

"Okay. I want to be a good friend. If you need me to come with you, I will."

Her offer sprung from one of two places. Either she honestly felt bad for me, or it was her day to clean the oven – her most dreaded task, because of the mess I made when I cooked. Possibly a combination of both.

"Okay. I'm going to get ready now," I said. "Then we'll drop the girls at school and go."

"Go where?" Bizzy asked, sporting the same beatific smile since meeting Sven – who was really Steven, I had learned yesterday. The name change was for modeling reasons.

"Grocery shopping," I lied. Was my nose getting longer?

"Well, be sure to be back at eleven," she said while pouring herself a cup of coffee.

"Why?"

"We're having a class with Sven," she said.

"What?"

"I asked him to come every weekday. My treat," she said to end the argument. I definitely couldn't afford private lessons every day.

"You're going to do Kung Fu?" Claudia hooted.

"Yes. Why the surprise?"

"Because you're as old as Mama Klaus. No. Old as dinosaurs. No. That's not right. Old as the Big Bang."

"Hilarious. I will have you know I'm in tiptop shape. It will be a breeze."

"Well, don't mind if I watch," Claudia said.

"I do. I would rather have you clean something," Bizzy snapped back.

"Good thing I don't work for you then."

"Sloane?" Bizzy asked me hopefully.

"No firing Claudia, Mom."

Bizzy sighed and took her coffee to the living room. Claudia opened the broom closet and extracted the Hoover.

64

"I'll be upstairs. You should get ready before the girls wake up," Claudia said.

It was my turn to sigh now. Between Bizzy and Claudia, my only alone moment of the day had come and gone.

"Mummy! Poppy's making me smell her feet!" Rose shouted from my bedroom.

And now they were awake.

"Coming!" I hollered as I ran upstairs.

Our stake-out session was another bust, with Kate a no-show.

Bizzy wasn't home when we got back. We both poured ourselves cups of coffee and sat at the kitchen counter, enjoying the gift of her absence.

Half an hour later, we heard the door open.

"I need a hand," Bizzy called from the hallway.

"Your mother," Claudia said.

Boy, did I wish to forget! Bizzy loved a grand entrance. She wore oversized sunglasses, a red, knee-length raincoat, and held two huge plastic bags from a sports company proudly. She looked like a Broadway actress poised for her lead act. I half expected her to break into a song and tap dance her way to the living room.

"What's this?" I waved at the bags.

"Our kimonos of course!"

"Why?"

"Didn't I tell you a thousand times already? It's essential to always look the part."

She handed me both bags and walked away. I hunched over their weight.

"What are they made of? Chainmail?"

And how did I end up doing all the lifting again?

"I might have overdone it a little. The salesman was nice. Very polite."

Reading between the lines: hot. I dropped the bags on the living room's wooden floor. Bizzy sat on the beige linen couch and encouraged me to open them. In the first one I found two black silk kimonos trimmed with red. In the

65

second one, about thirty silk scarves that I assumed were belts. They ranged from white, which I knew were for beginners, to black, the highest level.

"You're planning to become a Kung Fu master?"

"If it keeps Sven here, yes," she answered.

Claudia nodded. "For once, I'm with the old hag."

"You're both nuts," I said, keeping the white belts out and stuffing the rest back into the bags.

"I'm nothing like her," Claudia said.

"Thank God for that!" Bizzy exclaimed.

I left them together and went to change in my bedroom. I might want to become a Kung Fu master too, I thought as I slipped on the kimono. This was the most comfortable thing I had ever worn.

I stayed put till the doorbell rang. When I arrived downstairs Bizzy had already hogged Sven.

"Look, we're matching." She giggled. "Want some lemonade?"

"No. Thank you," Sven hurried to say. "Water maybe."

"I'm on it!" Claudia called from the kitchen.

Claudia being helpful? It was a first. Perhaps what we missed in this house was testosterone to keep all the females in check. I should ask Sven to move in. I ogled the couch. Alas, he would never fit there.

Claudia strutted inside the living room. She looked uncomfortable doing it, like you could see she wasn't used to the flirting. Claudia was more of a 'shut up and kiss me' type of girl.

"Here," Claudia said, handing him a glass of water. Was she batting her eyelashes? It looked painful.

"Thanks," I muttered, realizing I would have to fend for myself. I went to the kitchen to get a glass too. I didn't offer one to Bizzy. She would probably act offended at the very thought of water touching her lips.

When I returned Sven was trying to set up the mats behind the couch. He had brought two more to create a bigger practice space for Bizzy and me. She and Claudia were elbow-to-elbow, trying to get as close as they could to

Sven.

"Down," I whispered to them both.

They didn't look the least bit ashamed but went their separate ways. Claudia sat on the couch's arm and Bizzy waited by the mats.

The class started with a hundred ab crunches on the floor. I gritted my teeth while lying down. Every single muscle in my body hurt – even some I'd no idea existed. By number twenty-three, Bizzy threw her hands in the air. She was as red as her nails and she looked fresh out of the shower.

"When does the hand-to-hand part of the training start?" she asked.

Sven gave her question great consideration. Thinking so hard didn't seem to come naturally to him. I could almost hear his brain sizzling.

"A couple of weeks? Maybe less if you keep practicing every day."

"That long!" Bizzy exclaimed. "Well, I guess I'll just wait for that part to start. In the meantime, I'm going to fix myself a drink. Anyone interested?"

"Me," Claudia said.

"Anyone but the housekeeper? May I point out that she isn't cleaning, yet again?"

Claudia hissed and folded her arms. Sven stared at the ceiling uncomfortably. I wheezed painfully, hoping I would live to see Poppy graduate to primary school.

On the Saturday, I was in so much pain I considered amputation. Every single limb in my body hurt.

A furious rain lashed against the windows all through the day. For once, it played in my favor. We couldn't go to the playground where I would have needed to run after the girls, and instead stayed home and played board games.

By the end of the day, Poppy had turned into a caged lion. It was like watching Bruce Banner turn into the Incredible Hulk, a fearsome thing to behold. She was just ripe for Tom to arrive.

Kate was in for her money tonight. She wanted my

husband? Let her deal with the full, frightful package then – the most frightful, sweetest package there ever was, I amended. She did not deserve them, even at their worst.

While the girls packed their bags for the night, I changed from my sweatpants to a wool midnight blue dress Tom had gotten for me a few years ago. It was perfect for my mission – feminine yet casual. I didn't want to look like I was trying too hard.

Waiting around was getting me nowhere. It took me long enough to see it. *New me* was proactive. She did Kung Fu and made a hot IRS agent squirm. *New me* would get her husband back.

"You look pretty, Mummy," Poppy said, as she met me downstairs. A pink pony ear stuck out of her tiny backpack.

"Do you have a date?" Rose beamed.

Weren't my daughters supposed to want me back with their dad? Mine were pimping me out way too willingly.

"No, honey. Sorry."

"It's okay," Rose said, snuggling against me. "You'll find someone."

I struggled to keep my smile in place. This was unfair to Rose. She shouldn't have to worry about me.

"I'm fine. I promise, baby."

The doorbell rang.

"Daddy's here!" I said, trying to lift Rose's worries.

The girls fought to be the one getting the door.

"Don't pull your sister's hair," I reminded Rose. She grudgingly let go of a golden curl.

On her tiptoes, Poppy tried to reach the bolt on the door. Her tongue stuck out between her lips in concentration. In the end, my daughters reached a compromise. Rose got the bolt while Poppy turned the doorknob, their faces radiant as their dad appeared on the front steps.

"My flowers!" He beamed. "What took you so long?" he asked me, folding his umbrella. "Days like these I really miss New York."

Clear blue sky, crisp cold air – a wave of nostalgia washed over me.

"But you forget about the blizzards and the heat waves."

"Yeah. But this damn rain!" He remembered the girls. "How are you, my flowers?"

"Blooming!" they chorused proudly.

The girls stared at him with such admiration, their hero, their dad. They could barely contain their excitement at spending the remainder of the weekend with him. They were literally skipping on the spot.

"You better get going," I told Tom.

I didn't want to see them go but I was afraid they might self-combust otherwise. I hugged them both, smelling their hair deeply to get a fix that would last me till the next day.

"Have fun, okay?" I ruffled Rose's hair.

While they put on their coats, I stepped closer to Tom. He noticed my dress at last.

"You look good, babe. Got a hot date tonight?"

Judging by his smirk, he thought this as improbable as him growing a third eye.

"No. But I could," I said.

"I remember that dress," he said, while gawking blatantly at my legs.

I blushed. All those classes spent trying to hit a bookshelf were finally yielding results.

The girls demanded their father's attention.

"Ready!" Rose said, as she put her tiny fingers in Tom's hand.

"Ready!" Poppy echoed, grabbing Tom's other hand.

She wore her coat like a pinafore, buttons in the back. I strived to keep a serious face. Looking at Tom who was ready to leave, I asked, "Why don't we have dinner tomorrow?"

"Dinner?" He paused to consider it. "Sure. Why not?"

Butterflies fluttered in my stomach. I had a date with my husband! *Ex-husband*. I squashed the nagging voice and smiled instead. He bent toward the girls.

"What do you think? Should we have a pizza party?"

"Yeah!"

No!

There went my date night. I tried to spin this in a positive light. Maybe a family night was what Tom needed to come back to us. Maybe he needed to be reminded of what he was missing. I started a new imaginary checklist as I watched them go.

Operation 'A Pizza to His Heart' was launched.

Chapter Six

I looked forward to having the house to myself. I had a cozy mystery picked out, pasta from my favorite Italian caterer heating up in the oven, and a chilled bottle of Chardonnay with my name on it.

Bizzy had gone to the theater with an old roommate from sailing camp and would undoubtedly stretch the night into dinner, reminiscing about Cape Cod and the time when their breasts had yet to meet their bellybuttons.

Claudia was probably kissing and making up with Michal over gallons of vodka, and my girls were hanging out with my husband and his Kate.

A lump the size of a fist lodged itself at the base of my throat. I pictured Kate's fist stuck in there – and it was giving me the finger. Katherine Stappleton was dead set on ruining my life. First, she had stolen my husband, and now she was making a move on my daughters. She wouldn't stop until she'd robbed me of everything.

The lump grew bigger, making swallowing that first sip of wine difficult. But new and improved Sloane wasn't a quitter. I coaxed myself through the first glass of Chardonnay then persevered to glass two.

By that time, Kate's fist had receded to a waving finger and the clear liquid trickled effortlessly down my warmed up throat. Optimism returned just as my appetite flared up. I staggered on unsteady legs, surprised to find them so wobbly, to the kitchen.

Kate should enjoy her luck while she could. The tramp might have my family tonight, but tomorrow we had a pizza date. In the end, good people always won. Tom would come back to me.

Armed with checkered mitts, I sprang the oven door open

and deftly moved the pasta container from the oven to the kitchen counter. On my second attempt, I managed to haul myself on a stool and poured glass three all the way to the rim. Then I picked a couple pastas from the aluminium tub, juggling them from palm to palm, waiting for them to cool down.

As soon as the girls were out, I tended to eat like a college girl. No crockery, no plate; souvenirs of a girl who had lived without dishwasher for a few years and attempted to keep cleaning to a minimum. I loved forgetting I was a mom for a few hours; pretending I was careless, a rebel, and eating straight from the container embodied all those ideas. Sometimes I even fell asleep with the TV still on.

But tonight this wouldn't cut it. I nursed my half-emptied glass of wine, looking for my next act of rebellion. Should I have a dance party in the living room? Sleep naked? Message an ex-boyfriend on Facebook? Or that teacher from Brown University I always fantasized about?

No, I needed something more, something real, something to annihilate the last remnant of the lump called Kate in my throat. Alcohol had cut my appetite so I had barely grazed at the pesto. I pushed aside the pasta dish and stood up.

It seemed like a waste to wear a dress so pretty and have no one see it. Let alone once you thought of the leg shaving, moisturizer slathering, and pantyhose stuffing it had taken to get into that dress.

I could go out, I thought with a thrill. I could catch a movie, all by myself, like the confident, independent woman I had now become. I could get popcorn – the corners of my mouth connected with my ears. This was a grand idea.

I downed the rest of my wine. The bottle standing close to me on the counter was nearly empty already. Had someone drunk my wine? Probably the ghost of my ancestors partaking through me in the libations.

My head was quite clear for having drunk so much. Maybe I had always worked under the wrong assumption that I couldn't handle alcohol. Maybe I wasn't such a lightweight after all. To celebrate my new discovery – and because wine wasting seemed like a capital offense – I poured the last of the wine and gulped it greedily.

Only then did I march out of the kitchen, toward the front door. I had no idea what movies were on at the theater close by but it added to the thrill of the night. I would catch a random movie when I got there. Tonight, I was spontaneous and brave. I shrugged on my navy raincoat and grabbed my purse from the floor. Then lifting my head high, I stepped outside.

Just as the door slammed shut behind me, the lump reappeared, inside my chest this time. The cool breeze made my legs shake just as my head regained some of its steadiness. What the hell was I doing outside?

I sat on the front steps and tried to fight off the bile rising up my throat. I was so pathetic. Tom was probably snuggled up comfortably on his new white couch, Kate's mile-long legs resting lasciviously on his lap, while our daughters slept like angels in their brand new beds.

I, on the other hand, was so lonely I considered going to the movies alone on a Saturday night. I had no friend to call, no lover to meet, no place to be.

I pictured the crowd in a movie theater at night. Surely, there would be a few teenagers traveling in packs, oblivious to me except for when one of their popcorn projectiles knocked my head. And couples, loads and loads of cute, snuggly faces covered with drool, lovers looking for the dark room's cover, reveling in being together while getting lost in a crowd.

I raked my hands through my hair, trying to fight off the panic. I wasn't strong enough for this. I would unravel if I went. Remembering respiration techniques, I stuck my head between my knees and inhaled deeply. Now that I was out, maybe I could go meet up with Bizzy and her friend.

I scraped the floor with my running shoes. No, I couldn't go meet Bizzy anyway. A night with her was worse than anything else. Registering the shoes at my feet, my heart leapt with joy. I had forgotten to change my shoes. I simply couldn't go out wearing sneakers and a dress. *Let's face it.* I had to call it a night and go back home now.

The gloom lifted immediately and I managed to pull myself up. Keeping one hand on the door for balance, I used the right one to look for my keys. I banged my head against the wooden surface as I realized I had left the keys on the hallway console.

"Come on!" I shouted, cursing my bad luck.

Would this night ever end? I kicked the door a couple of times for good measure, preparing myself for the phone call to Bizzy I now had to make.

"Why? Why? Why?" I chanted over and over again.

"I can't answer without knowing the full question," a familiar voice boomed behind me.

I swirled around to discover Ethan on the sidewalk, hands in his army coat's pocket, and cocky grin blasting.

"Fancy meeting you here," he said again.

I buried my face in my hands.

"You must be kidding me!"

What did I ever do so wrong to deserve such bad luck? What deity did I offend and what could I do to make amends? Please unjinx me, I prayed silently. I turned to the door and fumbled with the doorknob. It didn't move one bit.

"Open, goddammit!"

"I take it you're stuck?" Ethan stated rather than asked, a smile in his voice. "I must be in luck; I was actually hoping to talk to you."

Really? He wasn't roaming a deserted street on a Saturday night for fun?

"Thank you for stating the obvious. Now leave, pretty, pretty please."

As usual, he pretended he couldn't hear me.

"You still haven't given me an answer. You know you want to help me," he said, treading on my doorsteps. "Say that you will and I might do something about that door."

My eyes lingered on his full lips etched in a smile. I

swayed toward him slightly, his dimple working as a magnet. Alcohol might be clouding my judgment a little bit. I shook out of my dimple-induced trance and looked for a snappy remark to restore the order of the world.

"Are you telling me you're a locksmith on top of an accountant?" I snorted. Clearly, he must be pulling my leg. "I don't want you near my door, my house, or me, for that matter," I said, pointing at the sidewalk.

Without ever parting with his nonchalant smile, Ethan obliged me. Even standing three steps higher than him, I was still barely taller.

"No can do. And since it doesn't look like you're going anywhere, why don't we have a chat about it? I can be very persuasive."

Frustration raged inside me as I realized he was right. No matter how much I wanted to storm back inside my home and leave him behind in the street, I was stuck. Ethan Cunning was way too persistent and way too lucky for me to ever think I could win this argument.

I tried to sit down to collect my thoughts but missed the step I had aimed for, landing hard on my butt on the lower step. Tears brimmed in my eyes – part annoyance, part pain. My ego, as usual, took the major blunt of it all.

"Please, not tonight. I'm tired," I argued feebly, angry for sounding so whiny.

Ethan dropped the cool guy act. "What's wrong?"

"What isn't?" I sighed.

"Your keys?"

"My keys, my ex, his Kate, my life," I listed. "Nothing is as it should be."

"Well, isn't it a good thing? Predictable is boring," he said.

"Boring sounds great right about now."

"Better than sitting on your doorstep with a man as handsome as me?" He grinned.

"Way better," I answered, the ghost of a smile curling my lips.

A cool draft of wind made me shiver. June had brought

us summer at last but nights were still chilly.

"You'd better get inside before you catch a cold," Ethan told me. "But just so we're clear, this conversation isn't over."

"Ah. Inside. Very funny."

I shook my purse to remind him of the keys' situation then wrapped my arms around myself to keep warm.

"I told you I could—"

"Please, I'm in no mood to be teased." I choked on a sob. "I have to wait for my mom to come back."

The words tasted sour. Tonight I'd wanted to prove I was a mature, independent woman and instead I sounded like a needy five-year-old. No wonder I had self-esteem issues.

"Okay," he said, lifting his arms in the air in surrender. "If you insist on being stubborn, there's a pub one block away. Why don't you come with me while you wait for her?"

I scrutinized his face wearily.

"I swear I won't talk about the case. Not tonight anyway," he said, amending his previous statement.

Didn't seem like I had more thrilling things on my agenda. Considering my past with Ethan, I just shrugged, refusing to look desperate.

"Let's go."

Standing up, I spent all my focus on maintaining balance. Glass four hadn't been necessary. Noticing my swagger, Ethan kindly offered his hand for support but I walked straight past his peace offering, pride fueling my every step.

"It's the other way around," I heard him say, struggling to keep the laughter bottled up.

I pivoted toward the right direction, intent on not looking at him.

"Oh! Don't thank me…" He chuckled.

We made it to the pub in less than five minutes. A bunch of stinking drunk people were huddled outside, a cloud of smoke hovering above their heads.

I got the door, refusing to give Ethan the gentleman's role. Inside, the smell of stale beer hit me with a vengeance, resurrecting all the glasses I had consumed tonight. I turned around, hitting Ethan square in the chest.

"Move! Out—"

"What?" I heard him say behind me.

I ran past the pub crowd and their nasty cigarettes, and then kneeled straight on the pavement, my head hanging above the sewer. My chest throbbed heavily from the nausea but I miraculously managed not to puke. From the sound she made, the girl hidden in the semi-darkness close by wasn't so lucky. Brits simply couldn't hold their drink.

I kept grinding my teeth till the queasiness receded. I was quite proud of my self-control, but thinking of Bizzy, I knew she would be beyond appalled if she heard about tonight. I had forgotten the WASPs' cardinal rule when it came to drinking: pace yourself. Alcohol always hit with a delay and I now had a full bottle of wine punching me right in the gut.

Footsteps rang against the pavement. I turned around, squinting to lose one of the two Ethans facing me. As far as I could guess, rather than see, he was concerned…and relieved. Happy?

"How are you?"

"Take a wild guess," I muttered, feeling grossed out as I remembered I was on the pavement.

The tights needed to be burnt tomorrow. Unfortunately, my hands I would have to keep. Loads and loads of soap might do the trick.

"It all makes so much sense now! Let's take you home. A woman in your condition should rest."

"My condition?"

"The bad mood, the nausea, your obsession with getting your loser ex back. I should have seen it sooner. Every time my sister gets pregnant—"

"You're an idiot," I slurred through clenched teeth.

As an accountant, couldn't he do simple math? Since Tom left me six months before, that would make me at least seven months pregnant.

"I'm not pregnant, I'm drunk," I said, throwing a hand at him so he could help me up.

"All the time? Because since I've met you—"

"Careful," I said.

Ethan wrinkled his nose and took a step back.

"You're drunk all right. You smell like a bum."

I glowered.

"I hope there really isn't a baby in here." He pointed at my stomach. "Otherwise he might be growing a second head."

I tried to let go of his arm. My brain was screwing up commands, because instead of walking backward, away from him, the spinning threw me straight back into his arms. Ethan beamed.

"Can't get enough of me, right? Who could blame you? I'm irresistible."

"You're an ass," I mumbled against his flannel shirt, careful not to breathe too close to his face.

The evening was a total bust. If only I could do something fun, something to make this night unique in a good way. I scanned the street just as a double-decker bus slowed down before a stop.

"That's perfect!" I exclaimed, pushing Ethan away.

I jog-limped toward the bus.

"What are you doing?"

"I've been in London eight years and I've never been on a double decker. So now I'm gonna do it! See the city from the roof of a bus."

Plus the fresh air was bound to sober me up.

"But—"

"Come on! It will be fun!"

"I'm sorry to tell you—"

"Oh! Stop being a party-pooper! The night is young and so are we." I twirled my way to the bus stop then skipped inside the red British icon.

I popped my head out of the door and waved.

"Are you coming?"

Ethan dragged his feet to the bus.

"Yeah. But just because you need a chaperone," he said, as he bought tickets for the both of us.

Tickets. I had quite forgotten about that.

"This is so not how I pictured my Saturday night," he said, as he handed me my ticket.

I stuffed it inside my purse. The doors closed with a *woof,* and the bus started. I felt claustrophobic, and the movement of the bus made me feel queasy all over again. I did my best to hide it from Ethan.

Instead, I tried for a perky voice as I suggested, "Let's go upstairs, onto the roof."

"Sloane, there isn't—"

I didn't hear the end of the sentence because I was already climbing the stairs, holding onto the banisters on both sides, lips blanching from concentration. As I made it upstairs, all I could see were the same rows of seats and large windows, but most annoyingly, a solid roof above my head. I scanned the floor to detect other stairs leading outside but with my faulty eyes, it was a total waste of effort. I moved aside to give way to Ethan.

"Where are the stairs?" I asked him.

"If you only let me finish one sentence once in a while, you would know there aren't more stairs. Open-top double deckers are for tourists and they only run during the day. This is a regular bus." His dark eyes bore into mine. "I know you're spoiled, but have you never taken the bus?"

"Of course I have."

Just never when I was drunk as an ass. I slumped on a seat nearby and stared outside the window to tame my violent urge to hurl. Ethan sat down, his long legs crammed against me.

"There are plenty of empty seats, you know?"

"You're a mean drunk." He chuckled. "Five minutes ago you were dragging me into an adventure."

His shoulders shook with laughter. I crossed my arms against my chest, pouting.

"How long till the next stop?"

"Not long," he replied as his mirth quieted down.

We might have been in a regular bus but the nocturnal view of London was breathtaking. The pale artificial light highlighted the three-story buildings huddled close together, watchful giants in a dark as ink sky. The bus came to a stop but neither of us made a move to stand. Although I was looking out, I could feel Ethan's gaze in my direction. Whether he was looking at the view or me, I couldn't have said.

The quiet pace of the bus, its gentle sway, rocked me gently. Ethan's silent company, a miracle in itself, soothed me. My eyelids began to feel heavy, to the point where I had to close them.

"I'm lonely," I whispered just as sleep enfolded me. "Can you hold me?"

I plopped my head against Ethan's shoulder and drifted off to sleep.

Chapter Seven

I woke up with a jolt, recalling a red bus and a warm shoulder under my cheek. Had it all been a dream?

I tried to stand up in my bed but a massive headache nailed me back to the pillow. *So not a dream!* But why didn't I remember calling Bizzy to get inside?

Eyes shut, I felt for my phone on the bedside table. I slid an eye open, just enough to scroll through my contacts then dialed Ethan's number.

As I waited for him to pick up, ear screwed to the receiver, my foggy brain started making connections. The last thing I'd asked Ethan yesterday was to hug me and now I was in my bed, with no recollection of what had followed. My alcohol-clouded brain was more than eager to supply pictures of what I'd forgotten. Blood rushed to my cheeks as if my face was stuck in an oven. Perhaps I was wrong.

"Hello?" Ethan's sleepy voice answered.

Did he sound like a man who just got laid? It would be so unfair, if I finally got some action and could not even replay it for all the lonely moments to come.

No, I couldn't have done it. Tom was coming tonight; we were about to patch things up. Soon my inner sex goddess would be freed and launched on my husband. Just to be sure, I asked the dreaded question.

"What happened last night?" Realizing I sounded frantic, I breathed deeply. "Did we?"

"You're still wearing your shoes."

Forcing both my eyes open, I lifted the comforter. *Yep.* Sneakers, tights, and dress. *Yuck!*

"You could have removed the shoes—"

Now the heat in my face was fueled by crimson humiliation. Of course, we didn't have sex. I'd thrown myself at Ethan and he was obviously not interested. And who could blame him? After all, I was just another desperate housewife.

"Is this an invitation? I'll keep that in mind next time."

"Yeah, right," I replied bitterly.

He could flirt all he wanted, but I knew the truth now.

"Generally speaking, I like my conquests awake." He paused. "Definitely not snoring."

"I don't snore!"

"You do too. You snored all the way from the bus stop to the cab then through your entire house." He laughed. "You sounded like a tractor. Nice place, by the way."

"You came inside?"

"How do you think you got into bed? Sleepwalking?"

"But how did we get in?" My mother would make me pay hell for this. "You had to call Bizzy, right?"

"I don't know who that is." He yawned.

I let out a long sigh of relief.

"But how?"

"I told you I could work my way around closed doors."

"Handy! IRS training?"

"Let's just say I've not always been on the right side of the law. I picked up a few things growing up."

"What did you do?"

"Just the regular. Killed a few gangsters, cooked meth, bombed my old high school—"

My jaw went slack before realizing he was pulling my leg.

"God, you're so annoying!" I stopped his wild imaginings. "I don't care anyway."

Ethan went silent. Did I offend him?

"I guess I should thank you anyway, for bringing me home."

"You're welcome. It was kind of fun."

I thought I could hear his smile through the receiver. I closed my eyes and pictured his dimple and warm eyes, slowly drifting back to sleep. Ethan's gruff voice pulled me back briefly.

"Can I go back to sleep now?"

"Sure. Good night."

"It's nine a.m. already. Bye, crazy girl."

Good thing the girls were out today. I needed to recuperate. I dropped the phone on the pillow next to me and passed out again.

"Mummy! Poppy's putting candies on her pizza!" Rose said, holding her heart-shaped face between her hands in despair.

"Daddy said I could," Poppy replied before resuming her work of art.

"Candies on a pizza?" I asked Tom. "You know I can't put this in the oven. We'll have to throw the whole pizza away."

"We never eat Poppy's pizza anyway," he said. "At least it keeps her from ruining the kitchen. Remember the flour debacle?"

We both laughed. How could I not remember? The ceiling had never recovered.

Tom was in a particularly good mood tonight. Pizza nights had always been his favorites. As a little boy, he used to garnish pizzas with his mom. One of the rare memories he'd shared from his childhood.

Not that his childhood had been sad or that he had suffered a trauma of any kind. His parents were now dead but had been good, loving, and hardworking people. He still had two brothers and a sister living in Jersey and as many nieces and nephews as the olives on my pizza. The girls rarely saw them all.

Tom was ashamed of his family. He feared that the simple fact of seeing them would make him poor again.

He brushed my forehead with his thumb. This simple gesture sent chills throughout my whole body, making my toes curl.

"Tomato sauce," he said as he sucked his thumb. He clapped his hands. "Time to show your creations!"

Rose's, Tom's, and my pizzas went into the oven. We

deemed Poppy's so beautiful it sat as a centerpiece on the dining table.

Tom and the girls played in the living room while the pizzas cooked and I cleaned the kitchen.

Then we all ate together, our three pizzas and the candies on Poppy's creation. Tom went to put the girls to bed.

I was supposed to clear the table but instead I ran to the guest bathroom to check out my appearance. My hair looked great, golden and lustrous thanks to my visit at the hair salon the week before. Bronzer gave me a healthy glow, and my mascara hadn't run despite the oven heat. I popped open one button of my silk white shirt and returned to the living room.

I sat on the couch for a few minutes, almost shaking from anticipation. It was strange because a night like this felt so natural, boring almost in its normalcy, and at the same time, it was all new. Here I was, hoping to seduce my husband.

Bizzy wasn't back from the movies yet and my husband was putting my daughters to sleep. I couldn't believe that we weren't meant to get back together. It all just seemed so right.

I watched Tom come down the stairs, propping myself in what I hoped was a seductive pose against the arm of the couch. His shirt's sleeves were rolled above his elbows, showing the olive skin on his strong forearms. I handed him a beer as he sat down next to me.

"Thank you, babe," he said, patting my thigh.

I crossed my legs tighter to control the tingling in my hooha. Tom reclined in the couch, farther away from me. I sighed.

"Thank you for coming tonight. It's great having you here."

"Yeah. It was fun. I miss having the girls around all the time."

"You could see them more often if you'd like," I offered.

"Thanks. Seriously, Sloane. Thank you for letting me come over whenever. I know it mustn't be easy."

I put on a brave smile. "It's okay. I'm fine. We're fine."

Pitiful wasn't sexy. I scooted closer to him and tried to bend in a way that I would show some cleavage. Boobs didn't a cleavage make, right?

"You could come more often, you know that? You could come every day," I suggested, hoping he would hear the real meaning behind my words. *Come back home. Move back in with us. Marry me again.*

"No. Kate would have my skin."

Clearly, I had been too subtle. In my offer, Kate was out of the picture.

"And we might have to reduce the nights where I have the girls to one night a week," he added. He looked pained. "I wanted to be the one to tell you. I'm moving in with Kate."

My face fell. "What?"

"She has a huge apartment. It just makes more sense than me staying in my flat. We see each other every day anyway." He ran his hand in his hair. "Problem is, she's not big on kids. I can't impose two little girls on her twice a week. You understand, right?"

I understood I wouldn't get laid tonight. I apologized silently to my disappointed hooha. How long did it take to become a virgin again?

I also understood Kate was a giant pain in my butt. She was like a wild vine, impossible to get rid of and crawling over everything. This left me but one option – the thought alone made me wince. I had to help Ethan.

After walking Tom to the door a few minutes later, I climbed the stairs to my room and lounged on the bed. My fingers drummed against the bedstand for a while before finding the courage to grip my phone.

"Hello Ethan? I'm in."

Chapter Eight

"We have to clean the car tonight," I said, looking at the mess lying at our feet.

The Mini had turned into a constant reminder of the Tom and Kate dilemma. Empty bottles of water, Starbuck's Styrofoam, cans of soda, and cake crumbs were so many remnants of the long hours spent staking out Kate.

Twelve days since Tom had announced he was moving in with her, and I was no closer to getting rid of the witch. I had twenty-eight days left to prevent doomsday. They had set a moving date of the first day of summer break.

My life felt like a long journey across the desert – no adventure, no sex, and no man in sight. Tom flew in and out of the house like a breeze, Gabriel Varela was still a no show, and Ethan had completely disappeared since I'd agreed to help him.

"Don't say *we. You* have to clean the car," Claudia said, a tiara dangling on her head at an odd angle. "I'm a housekeeper remember? House, not car."

"Okay. Sorry." I raised my hands apologetically.

I dropped the magic wand I was waving on the backseat, worried Claudia would interpret it as a threat. It landed next to the Sleeping Beauty costume we'd gotten for Rose earlier that morning.

I grabbed a can of Diet Coke instead and shook it. It sounded hollow. I sighed miserably.

"Okay, Miss Sunshine," Claudia relented. "I'll get the drinks this time. Besides, I need to pee. What should I get you?"

I didn't care. I was depressed.

"I'll have whatever you're having."

"Great answer!"

Claudia tossed the tiara on top of the pink mess in the backseat, grabbed her anime printed bag, and left the car. I laid my head on the stirring wheel, praying for a sign from the stalker god that my luck was about to turn.

The only answer I got was from a pigeon pooping on my windshield. Was it supposed to be a good omen? *Note to self: avoid parking under the tree.*

Now I really needed to wash my car.

A gleaming black Mercedes stopped before Varela Global, distracting me from the green goo. The driver got out and walked to the passenger side. He held the door open, a worshipping expression on his serious face. I craned my neck to see who the illustrious passenger was. Judging by his height and his white shirt, he was a man. My heart began racing.

Turn around damn it!

"Got you a green juice." Claudia's voice startled me.

She stomped into the car, slamming the door behind her, and handing me some liquid resembling the pigeon's poop in a bottle.

"A pigeon shat on your car," she said.

"Thanks," I replied, both for pointing out the obvious and for bringing me the worst drink ever.

Dear Claudia, always worrying about my health; if only I could convince her that a regime of stale cookies and Diet Coke was perfectly sustainable.

I took the drink from her before returning to the Mercedes's passenger. He was almost through the revolving doors, and with him, my only chance of confirming my suspicions would be gone.

An older man stood next to him. As soon as I saw his big belly and mustache, I recognized the man from the thug incident, Hector. He said something to the mysterious VIP, who turned around. He looked at something straight before him, somewhere close to where we were parked. *Bingo!* Gabriel Varela in the flesh. The picture Ethan had given me did not do him justice.

"Who's the hottie?" Claudia asked, leaning to my side to get a better look.

"Gabriel Varela," I answered absentmindedly, too busy thinking of all the kinky things I would do to the man.

"You know him?"

Foolish me!

"Of course not! He's Kate's boss," I lied. "I checked it online."

Claudia's clear stare bore heavily into me, reminding me I really had to be more careful around her. We watched Gabriel Varela and Hector turn around and walk inside the building in silence.

I waited what seemed like a reasonable time before offering, "Why don't we go home? I can drop you. Then I'll go pick up the girls."

And then I could call Ethan at last.

My butt burnt from the need to extract my cell from my jeans' back pocket and dial him. You miss him, a tiny voice murmured in my ear. *Damn irritating conscience.*

"Hello," Ethan answered his phone.

"Varela's here!" I said, driving away from my house.

"Now?"

I paused.

"I'm not sure. But he was there thirty minutes ago. I saw him step inside Varela Global."

"And you only tell me now?" he yelled.

My knuckles turned white around the cellphone.

"I'm telling you as soon as I can. I wasn't alone before," I said. "I just dropped off Claudia."

"Sorry," he said, his temper seemingly in check. "It's just… One month I've been waiting for him to arrive."

"I know," I said back. "But now he's here."

"Can we meet up?"

We met a block away from my daughters' school. Ethan's five o'clock shadow was turning scruffier by the minute and he had dark circles under his eyes.

"Been busy lately?" I asked as a way of greeting.

I had to bite my tongue to stop myself from reproaching him for his silence of late. I waited patiently while he fumbled with the passenger seat command to give his lean legs more room. Then he sighed contentedly, arms above his head to stretch. My breath hitched as his grey tee hiked up, showing golden abs. I almost slapped my own hand to stop my itchy fingers from wandering onto the hard, tantalizing surface.

"You can say that," he replied, without caring to elaborate.

Apparently, we weren't so close he felt compelled to share his schedule with me. Besides, it must be super boring, like filling up Excel sheets, so he might be doing me a kindness by keeping me out of the loop. I let it go.

"Who was with Varela?"

"Hector and the driver."

Ethan took out a few pages from his pocket and handed them to me.

"Here," he said, waiting for me to unfold them.

A few pictures, a couple of pages of undecipherable script. The content of the file but more wrinkled.

"I need you to keep tabs on these guys," Ethan said. "When they come, when they leave, who they talk to, those kinds of things."

"That's it?" I asked, without managing to mask my disappointment.

"What more did you want?" Ethan asked. "Thwart a terrorist mission in twenty-four hours? Maybe it's too safe for you now."

"So these guys, and Varela?" I asked.

"Every time you see Varela come and go, I want you to call me immediately."

"What about Claudia?"

"Your faithful sidekick?"

I nodded.

"Send a text when she's here."

His tone had been brash, a small notch below mean.

"Sorry, I might be grouchy today. I haven't gotten much

sleep lately."

"You look awful," I said.

"Guess I deserve that. Sorry for being a jerk." He scratched his head. "And thank you for helping me out. It means a lot."

I decided to let it slide and returned my attention to the pages. One picture was Hector, another one was of a man aged about thirty with arms like tree trunks – Varela's bodyguard according to Ethan – and another one was unmistakably the scrawny driver I'd seen earlier. I recognized the flaming red hair. The last one seemed oddly familiar.

"Who is he?" I asked, taking in the dirty blond hair and appallingly crooked teeth in an otherwise handsome face.

From the picture, you could see his clothes were expensive but looked out of place somehow. New rich most probably.

"Yuri, one of Varela's major clients."

"What does he buy? Prostitutes?" I joked.

"Flowers," Ethan answered.

"Flowers? Very funny."

"Orchids to be precise." He didn't seem to be joking. He looked rather dismayed in fact. "Seriously. After all that stalking, you never checked Kate's employer online?"

Well, when he said it like that...

"You're kidding me, right?" I asked.

"Sloane, Varela Global is the second biggest flower distributor in the world."

"So let me recap to see if I've got it right. You can correct me any time." *Please correct me.* "My special super-secret government mission is to help an accountant imprison a florist?"

What a thrilling life I led!

In Belgravia Prep's lavish conference room, the ritual introductory tea was dragging longer than usual. Fourteen women including myself waited for Alina Alexeyev, head of committee for the International Awareness Gala, to launch the festivities. The Gala, held every year, was the school's great pride, and careful preparation was key to its success. To me it was the same old party, held every year, but saying it out loud would surely get me burnt at the stake by the other mothers.

"Where is she?" Keira whispered. "I have to pick up Malcolm by noon."

"She'll be here in a minute," Nisha said, assuming Alina's role in her absence. "Family crisis."

"Oh?" Miss Stevenson, who served as a secretary to those committees, asked. "Will she be all right?"

It was just enough propping to launch Nisha into confidences.

"It's her stepbrother. A real trouble maker."

All voices faded away in the grand room. We were fourteen gossips but one ear.

"He was about to go on trial in London, but Alina's husband sent him back to Russia to escape a conviction."

"What for?" Miss Stevenson asked again.

"Drug charges. One can't blame Alina. Most families have their lot of screw ups," Nisha said, beaming for the chance to show her compassion. "You would be surprised at how many lords do drugs."

Here went the name-dropping. Nisha and Vijay, her husband, had made befriending powerful and rich people a national sport. They were socialite groupies.

Tom and I had been the exception. Our friendship had been made possible by how much we had in common. Tom and Vijay worked together while our daughters frequented the same schools. They had charitably shut an eye to the fact that we didn't belong to the Fortune 500.

"Someone has to sell them the drugs," she continued.

Just then, the door slammed shut.

"That's quite enough," Alina said with her delicate Russian accent.

Her pretty brow was furrowed with worry as she walked to the head of the conference table.

"But I was defending your brother," Nisha stammered.

There were just a few people on this planet able to make Nisha lose countenance. Alina was on top of that list.

She ranked higher than Nisha on about every social scale. She was richer, more powerful, and more elegant; besides gorgeous outfits only loads of money could buy, she had a ballerina silhouette from her past career worthy of a queen. She was more beautiful too – if Grace Kelly and Audrey Hepburn had a daughter together, she would have Alina's heart-shaped face and silky pale hair. Above all these things, she was kind, something Nisha could never best.

"Nisha," Alina warned. "I told you this in confidence. You have no business discussing it."

Nisha looked like she had swallowed the rest of her sentence along with her arrogance. She bowed her head while Alina stated the objective of today's meeting. Teatime was over and we gladly spent the rest of the hour discussing the upcoming party. We were just happy we didn't get caught in the crossfire.

I gathered my stuff at the end of the meeting. As usual, I was the last one ready to leave. Alina and her posse had already exited the room, abandoning me with Nisha and Miss Stevenson. I kept my head down, grateful they pretended not to see me.

Miss Stevenson slithered toward Nisha, an eager smile on her lips.

"And do we know this brother you were talking about? Alina's brother?"

Harpy.

Nisha beamed to the vicious secretary, glad she was offered a new opportunity to spit her venom. This was the smile that made you foolish enough to seek her affection. The smile that made you feel special, chosen – the one that brought you back to a time when you were the last one picked for the teams at school. This smile had made me act like a complete idiot around Nisha, following her like a puppy and trying to mold myself after her.

I watched Miss Stevenson hang onto Nisha's lips with idolization and thanked heavens I wasn't under her thumb anymore. Lonely was better than stupid.

"I'm sure you've seen him. He's come around a few times, waiting for Alina outside of school."

From Miss Stevenson's frown, it was clear she had no idea who he was.

"Short, blond guy," Nisha continued. "Ah! He had a snake tattoo on his jaw," she exclaimed, sure this detail would do it for Miss Stevenson.

"Oh yes," the secretary lied to please Nisha. "Vaguely…"

This description might mean nothing to Miss Stevenson but it was too close to the thug who had threatened me to be a coincidence. What did a drug dealer have to do with Varela Global?

I clasped my phone as I made my way out of the room, impatient to text Ethan about my findings. Nisha beat me to the door.

"Sloane! Hello!" She flashed her most dazzling smile at me.

For once, I didn't swoon over it. I was too preoccupied to care, or hope she had regrets about the way she'd treated me. I tried to go around her but she sidestepped in front of me to block the exit.

"How are you?"

"Fine. Thanks."

The phone keyboard burnt my fingers. As tactfully as I could, I nudged Nisha to the right. Graciously, she decided to let me go.

"I've been worried about you."

Wait. What? I almost forgot about Alina's brother.

"It must be hard. With Tom and Kate becoming quite the item, I mean."

Here it was! Nisha grinned as she delivered her poisonous dart.

"Vijay and I had a lovely dinner with them yesterday at the Arts Club."

"That's fantastic, Nisha," I answered before scurrying out of the room.

Judging by the disappointment on her gorgeous face, it

wasn't the reaction she had in mind. *Good. One point for me.*

I texted Ethan as soon as I exited the school. Fifteen slow minutes later, my phone vibrated on the passenger seat.

Just a coincidence, he'd texted.
Seems too big to be a coincidence, I typed back.

I made my way home, checking my cell a thousand times in the next couple of hours. Out of patience, I sent Ethan another text.

Can we meet up?
Can't. Too busy, he fired back.
Please, I'm a bit spooked.
I promise on my mother's head that Varela has nothing to do with drugs. How's that? he texted.
Good, I guess.

For two weeks, I couldn't shake him off and now he didn't have five minutes for me? I swallowed the frustration, resolute not to beg.

I promise I'll find you soon, he wrote as a goodbye.

And what if I needed to find him first? The man was always one step ahead from me. He knew where to find me, who I saw, what I liked, but I knew absolutely nothing about him except that he had the most boring job in the world.

I buried my head in one of the couch's pillows and moaned loudly.

"Should I worry?" Bizzy asked from her favorite armchair.

"Nooo."

"Good," she said, taking a sip of her lemonade while turning to the fashion magazine on her lap.

God forbid we would have a heart to heart.

Chapter Nine

"I am B-O-R-E-D!" Claudia yawned.

She stretched her arms above her head, then to the right, hitting the passenger window.

"Are the walls closing in on us? It feels like they are," she said, waving her hands in front of her to generate some air. "I'm supraventilating."

"Hyper," I corrected. "Hyperventilating."

"Whatever. I'm panicking. I think I'm going to faint."

It didn't take a genius to figure out Claudia's claustrophobia was really her hangover talking.

"Why don't you go home and rest?" I offered, tired of her playacting.

"Maybe I should... You're sure you don't mind?" she asked, hand at the ready on the door handle.

At any rate, the car had begun to feel too small. I didn't mind seeing Claudia go.

"Sure."

"A hundred percent?"

"A thousand," I replied.

I was too weary to speak in full sentences. I took a sip of tepid Diet Coke.

"Damn," I said as some Coke fell on my blouse, splashing into some sort of exotic flower shape. "I have to change now."

"No great loss here," Claudia said as she exited the car. "You look like a Stepfuck wife—"

I was pretty sure she meant *Stepford* wife. Although Stepfuck might be an interesting place to visit. She waved her hand up and down toward me. "These clothes! Ridiculous!"

I wore a pencil skirt and grey silk blouse.

"I'm channeling my inner Kate. Tom's stopping by later tonight to pick up the girls," I explained.

"And you thought cloning his girlfriend was a good idea? Besides, she has massive boobs. You don't."

"Weren't you leaving?"

"Oh! I am. Let me know when my friend Sloane decides to come back."

"See you tomorrow?"

Claudia slammed the door and left. I stuck my forehead to the cool window, trying to catch a break from the unduly heat inside the Mini. It was a beautiful June day. The kind that rarely came about in rainy London. Instead of enjoying it, here I was, stuck yet again inside my car, doing nothing. I must be crazy.

A knock on my window caught me by surprise. I shook like an epileptic when I realized Gabriel Varela stood next to my car. He was bent down toward me, his face leveled with mine, his smile dazzling. He gestured for me to roll down the window.

I considered locking the doors and driving the hell away from him but then I figured the chances that a florist would off me in the middle of the street in broad daylight were slim to none. I looked for his bulky bodyguard from the picture. He would gladly shoot me dead. No one in sight. My hand shaking, I opened the window.

"Hello," Gabriel Varela said, extending a manicured hand to me.

It was a beautiful hand, delicate yet powerful, with long pianist fingers. The hand of an intellectual, its skin soft, as I shook it feebly. The hand of a real man all the same. A hand that swallowed mine completely and made me feel small. A hand that invaded my car like a threat.

I plastered a smile on my face as he continued.

"I just had to introduce myself."

I searched for the faintest trace of an accent but couldn't find it. I knew from his file and his level of hotness that Gabriel Varela was Colombian, but I could have never guessed it from hearing him speak.

"I think I've seen you quite a few times around here. Am I right?"

Could I lie and get away with it? *Doubtful.*

"Yes…yes," I said.

"You work in the neighborhood?"

Was he pulling my leg? I looked around again, half expecting Ethan to be hidden behind him, ready to announce it was all a joke. *No such luck.* How much did Varela know?

"Not exactly. I'm here to see a friend."

"A friend? Does he work here?" he asked, gesturing toward his building.

"She," I corrected him before cursing myself for saying too much.

How was I supposed to get myself out of this? I was utterly screwed. Now I had to come up with an imaginary friend. Sweat trickled down my back as I tried to make up a name – any name.

Ethan's words came rushing back to me: *You'll fly under his radar*, he had said. Great analysis of his opponent! Three days in and Gabriel Varela had already made me.

"Do I know her?" he asked, making me feel like my head was about to explode in a thousand pieces.

I had not enough brain left to craft another lie. His green eyes were planted firmly into mine, making it impossible for me to come up with a coherent thought. *No time.* Under panic's debilitating influence, I blurted out Kate's name.

"Do you know her?" I asked pitifully.

From pathetic to even more pitiful. I was now pretending to be friends with the woman screwing my husband. This was all Ethan's fault. If I ever got my hands on him…

"What a coincidence!" Gabriel smiled. "Kate works for me. I'm Gabriel Varela."

He pressed my sweaty fingers in his cool palm. How did he manage to look so fresh? No sweat stain on his navy polo, no glistening upper lip. Meanwhile I could feel beads of sweat rolling down between my nonexistent breasts.

I tried to get my hand back but he wouldn't let me. The

pressure on my fingers was frightening but sexy at the same time. The way his thumb lingered on my palm, the strength of his grip. *He's a bad guy.*

"And you are?"

"Sloane. Sloane Harper," I said, blood rushing to my cheeks.

I had no idea why I'd given Gabriel Varela my maiden name, but it felt good, cozy, like stumbling upon an old favorite jumper and finding out it still fit.

"Sloane Harper," he repeated as if he were testing its ring. "Nice to meet you."

He let go of my hand and leaned in. Half his body was now inside the Mini. I shifted uncomfortably, partly from fear but mostly because of my body's reaction to him. The man oozed sex appeal.

From the playful smile that lifted only one corner of his mouth to his smoldering green eyes, everything in his appearance seemed designed to attract the female gender, and certain men, no doubt. Added to this his aristocratic stance, perfect manners, and wavy hair, and you had a man straight out of a woman's fantasy.

His stare made me burn hot so I fanned myself with my hand. Then realizing how it must look, I said, "It's really hot today."

Meet him in the middle of the winter and it would still feel like the Fourth of July in your hooha.

"Why don't you come inside?" Gabriel Varela asked.

I left the realm of fantasies and resurfaced into reality with a crash. "With you? Inside? No. No, I can't."

"Why not? You've come to see Kate, haven't you?"

"No." I waved my hands in refusal. "She's busy."

"Weren't you supposed to meet?"

"Well she obviously forgot. It's okay... I'll come back later."

"I'm sure she'll be thrilled to see you. I insist," he said, nodding for me to follow him.

I watched as he turned around, hand oscillating between the handbrake and my car keys. What would running away bring me? Gabriel Varela had me trapped. I had to play it out and see where this led. I had to know what he knew to assess the danger. The danger to which I might have subjected my daughters. Guilt squeezed my heart with an iron grip. I was such an idiot to think I could play spy without any consequences.

After inwardly stomping a few times, I grabbed my bag and left the car. The beeping sound of the car door closing sounded sinister as I followed Gabriel Varela inside the building.

What did the lair of a dangerous florist look like? I pictured a giant, carnivorous orchid as a watchdog or vines as far as the eye could see, ready to entrap the trespasser. Instead, I found a glass desk standing before two steel elevators. The hostess standing behind the desk batted her lashes furiously as we stepped inside the building.

"Hello again, Mister Varela," she cooed.

He shot his million-buck smile at her and I feared she would faint. Hell, I feared I might too.

"Kate must be in my office right now. She's almost finished with the redecorating."

"How wonderful," I mumbled, stomach in my heels and self-esteem running away in shame.

"Have you known her long?" Gabriel Varela asked.

I stepped behind him inside the elevator. In just a few minutes, he would learn I didn't know Kate at all. It was a wonder I still bothered to lie.

"No. Not long." I paused to think. "Three weeks give or take."

"She's quite the number, isn't she?" He chuckled, bringing Columbia's sun into the elevator that now felt like my pride's coffin.

If only we could get stuck! I toyed with the idea of Varela and myself locked inside the small cabin. Which naturally led to another hot flash. I suddenly had much more compassion for Bizzy and a newfound respect for her. Menopause must be like going through a sex drought. But at least her period was gone. I, on the other hand, had nothing to show for it.

"You can say that," I replied.

This was the understatement of the year. Many adjectives came to mind when I thought of Katherine Stappleton, but a 'number' wasn't one of them. I shushed the potty mouth inside my head. I was a WASP, this kind of vocabulary wasn't proper for girls like me. Sure felt good, though.

"Here we are," Gabriel said, gesturing toward the sliding door.

I left the elevator in his wake, giving it one last, longing stare. I braced myself for the humiliation to come while walking down a long corridor carpeted in a plush emerald green – my own green mile. This was pride's death row or better yet, the place where pathetic ex-wives such as myself came to die. Tom would never let me forget this once Kate told him.

"What do you think?" Gabriel asked.

"What?"

He pointed to the walls where a few lovely paintings were hung. They struck me as bizarre, just like the carpet, at odds with the modern structure of the building.

"Beautiful," I said politely.

"But?" Gabriel said.

"They look out of place somehow. I love them but I'm not sure they belong here."

Was I really discussing interior decorating with the man I was supposed to spy on? And about to meet the woman I was stalking, my conscience reminded me. *God forbid I forget that!*

"My thought exactly." He beamed. "Your friend Kate is helping me remedy that. This was my father's," he said, making a wide arm gesture, encompassing everything around us.

From looking at him, I placed Varela somewhere close to forty-five years old. His dad must have stepped down as director of the group a while ago, if he was still alive, but the decoration had remained the same up until now.

"Your father used to run the company?"

"Yes. And so did his father. I'm fifth generation," he said.

"And your kids?" I asked, my curiosity strong enough to make me forget about the upcoming disaster. "They will be the sixth generation."

"No kids," he said. "And no wife," he added, his gaze intent. "What about you? Husband?"

I felt myself blushing. Was he flirting with me?

I started to say "yes," but then remembered that just this once I could tell the truth – whether I liked the answer or not.

"No. No husband."

"Good." He smiled, making my toes curl. "And now that we've cleared this out of the way, after you, if you please," he said as he pushed open two massive glass doors.

"I hope Kate is still here," he added.

I plastered a brave smile on my face as I looked around his office.

"Oh! It's beautiful!" I said.

The contrast with the corridor was flagrant. Rows of books in steel bookcases, a leather beige and grey recliner, a delicately woven ash rug, and a massive glass desk paired with a tanned leather armchair. Behind the chair stood Kate, her back to us, busy hanging a canvas that looked uncannily like a Jackson Pollock on the wall. I wondered if it was genuine.

"Whoever you are, I'm glad you like it," she replied without turning around.

Only after she had adjusted the painting to perfection did she pivot to face us. I held my breath for the scene to come. Kate looked at her boss then stared dumbly at me. Eyes round as marbles, lips parting slightly, she looked stunned, like she had just woken up from a deep slumber. I refrained from snapping my fingers in front of her face to break the daze.

"Kate, you were right! The Pollock does belong here!" Gabriel exclaimed and moved closer to her to kiss her cheek. "Great job."

The way he said the last part along with the kiss

suggested history between them. Either that or Varela went around kissing all his employees, in which case I wanted to be part of the payroll. Except that he would despise me in a few seconds.

"I found your friend Sloane Harper waiting for you downstairs. Apparently, you've forgotten her." To me he said, "I do apologize for holding Kate longer than I should have. She's all yours now."

Kate and I stared at each other in silence. My cheeks burned even hotter as I remembered my outfit was a picture of hers. I was the liar here; the least I could do was give my husband's mistress permission to speak first. She pulled her long, wavy brown hair in a ponytail.

"I'm so sorry about that. You know me with work," she said as she came forward and air kissed me on both cheeks.

My jaw dropped. Why did she cover for me?

"It's okay, I guess. It happens."

"How forgiving of you, Sloane!" Gabriel said with a warm laugh. "I'm curious. Won't you tell me where you both met?"

I shot a desperate look at Kate. Whatever her reasons for lying for me, she might as well continue to make the lie believable. After all, she owed me big.

"At an art auction," she said.

Next to Katherine Stappleton's cool composure, I looked like a naïve farm girl.

"And what did you buy, Sloane?" Varela asked, manifestly entertained by the conversation.

"Noth... Nothing," I answered. "Kate snatched what I wanted to buy."

"Pity," he said to me. "Ah, Kate, as fierce in business as in love. At least your bad manners have allowed me to make the acquaintance of your lovely friend."

He turned to me and kissed my hand. Delicious shivers ran along my arm.

"I've got a few more details to oversee here," Kate told me. "Do you mind rescheduling?"

Thank heaven!

"Sure! No problem. I'll just go," I offered. I could feel Gabriel's smoldering stare on me. "Goodbye," I said as I air kissed Kate again.

Ugh! I'd rather have kissed a toad. I turned to Gabriel.

"I'll escort you downstairs," he said. "I can't have a gorgeous lady lost in my humble palace."

"There's no need." I waved my hands dismissively.

"I insist," he said, pressing his palm to the small of my back. "Keep up the good work, Kate."

My ears were buzzing as we left the office. No matter how I looked at it, my brain simply couldn't wrap itself around the way Kate had reacted. This could have gone so much worse, I admitted as I replayed the whole scene. I really hoped she didn't believe I owed her one though.

When the doors to the elevator opened up on the glass hallway, I finally allowed myself to breathe again. During the short ride down I had worried Gabriel Varela might plan to take me to his dungeon downstairs for questioning.

He walked me to the doors under the envious scrutiny of the receptionist.

"It was lovely meeting you, dear Sloane," Gabriel said, taking my hands between his.

My knees turned to jelly while the only answer I could come up with was mental stutter. At last, I grunted in acquiescence.

Gabriel loosened his grip slightly and turned my hands, palm facing up. His thumbs ran up and down the soft flesh, as if trying to read my fortune. He gazed at the discolored band where my wedding ring had once been.

I had stopped wearing it a while back in an attempt to salvage my dignity. Both my engagement ring and wedding band were stashed in my bedstand's drawer, ready to be taken out of oblivion and restore order in my family.

If it surprised or intrigued Varela, he didn't comment on it. Instead, he applied a few insistent kisses on my folded fingers before planting his green eyes into mine.

"*Ay! Que estuviera afortunado de zozobrar en estos ojos de cristal,*" he recited in his smooth baritone.

"Uh?"

"How lucky would I be to drown in those crystal eyes," he translated with a grin. "You need to have dinner with me."

Yes. No. Worst possible idea.

"I can't. It's complicated," I said.

Not that he must care so much about it. A man like Varela must have thousands of women lining up at front of his door.

"I happen to love complicated." He took out a card and slipped it in my hands before letting go of them. "Call me. You've just made me want to prolong my stay."

"I can't."

"Goodbye, *divina* Sloane," he said before returning to the elevator at the back of the room.

The receptionist shot me a murderous look. I hurried outside, worried I might make a mortal enemy of her.

I left half a dozen messages for Ethan on my way back home, their content ranging from fear to threats to downright feverish nonsense.

At the house, I slammed the door open, threw my bag on the floor by the console, and marched toward the stairs. I ran into Bizzy and Sven on the way.

"You're late," Bizzy pointed out from her favorite armchair.

I had no clue why she bothered with the kimono. She hadn't participated in the class since day one. Mostly she drank while watching Sven's butt when he showed me kicks.

"Where were you?" Claudia asked from the couch.

"I thought you were going home," I told her.

"Yes. Home to rest. This is *a* home, your home. And you've got cable."

Made sense.

"You shouldn't make Sven wait," Claudia said, taking a sip of her drink while batting her lashes at Sven.

Had Bizzy and Claudia become one and the same

person? Everyone was getting on my nerves today. Not dignifying her comment with an answer, I stomped up the stairs.

"No worries," Sven said. "Take your time changing. I'll wait for you."

"Not now!" I yelled to poor Sven, whose face fell as I ran to my bedroom.

"I'm sorry for my daughter's behavior. I can assure you I taught her better than that," I heard Bizzy say downstairs.

I picked up my laptop, threw it on my bed, and then sprawled next to it, belly down. I fired the search engine between frantic glances at my phone's screen, desperately blank. I typed *Gabriel Varela* into Google. While the Wikipedia page downloaded, I resumed texting:

What the hell? Call me back right this minute!
Then again, *I need to talk to you! Now!*

I decided to gather all the info I could about Varela, hoping to assess whether he posed a danger to my family. I should have done it ages ago.

Gabriel's bio was pretty standard for a hot socialite. The names of the boarding schools and colleges he went to – not a good student apparently, considering the number of schools mentioned – a longer list of his many conquests, including several famous models and actresses, and then a descriptive of Varela's Global.

Ran by Gabriel's father, Cristian Varela, up to his death in a car crash five years ago, it owned massive flower farms all throughout Colombia. The company charted, marketed, and sold the flowers on a worldwide scale on top of growing them.

Apparently, Gabriel had taken the commands just after his father's death but seeing him in his office today, I figured there must have been a real employee somewhere running the company in his stead. Otherwise, it would have gone belly up five years ago.

My findings didn't give me any motive to worry. So much so that halfway through my lecture, I was so bored I stopped to check my phone again. Fury rose inside me as I realized Ethan was still MIA. I had to bring out the big guns.

Varela has asked me out on a date!!!!!!!!!!!!!!
At last, that got me a response.
??? Are you drunk? I'm busy.

Even Ethan thought that a man asking me out was unbelievable. I punched my pillow before answering him.

Too bad. We need to talk NOW. Varela stopped by my car today. I waited a beat before adding, *If I don't hear from you right this minute, I'm out.*

My phone vibrated in my hand a mere second later.
"Hello," I barked.
"You don't sound drunk. You sound pissed off."
"No kidding, Sherlock. You're such a dumbass. You said I would fly under his radar. Moron!"
I might suffer from a disease where people shouted insults without knowing it. I forced myself to breathe to regain a semblance of calm.
"Varela knocked on my car window an hour ago. He invited me over to meet Kate."
"He did what?" Ethan exclaimed. "Is that for real?"
"No, I was just bored and made it up," I snapped. "Of course it is!"
He finally started catching up with what I was saying.
"What did he want with you?"
"I don't know! He said he had noticed me hanging out in the neighborhood. Then he asked me to dinner. He was…"
"Wait a second… Didn't you say you saw Kate? I assume it's Katherine Stappleton you're talking about?"
"Yes. She—"
"You mean the Katherine Stappleton who's dating your

ex?"

"Yes. Yes. You've turned into a gossip now? I thought you cared about Varela."

"Yes. Of course. Why don't we meet up so you can tell me about it?" Ethan offered. "I'm in the middle of something right now. Text me the address and I'll meet you in two hours."

"Okay."

He hung up and I mentally browsed for a meeting place.

My eyes fell on my alarm clock. In two hours I was supposed to pick up the girls. This felt like an electroshock. For the first time in my life, I had forgotten about my daughters for a few hours. The catastrophic proportions this afternoon could have taken crashed down on me, fear pinning me down to the bed.

Playing super spy was ridiculous. I'd behaved like a careless teenager and was in way over my head. Look at the facts: first Alina's brother and his drug business, and now Gabriel Varela coming up to me. I wasn't sure whether he had made me or not but I couldn't chance running into him again. Taking his card out of my pocket, I threw it on the bedspread. I typed one last message.

Can't meet you. I'm out. Sorry.
Ethan's answer came fast.
You can't. Too late to turn back now.
This is too dangerous.
What about Varela? You're in now.
I can't.
That will make him suspicious.
I paused, fumbling to retrieve my initial resolve.
Don't call me again.
You've got it, he typed back.
That's it?
Yep. I'm done too. You're a basket case.
That's harsh.
I don't have time for your shit. You don't know what you want. Keep running from everything; you're so good at it.

107

I'm done.

No more beeping from my phone. Once again, Ethan had managed to turn the tables on me and have the last word. I stared vacantly at the screen. This was over.

Chapter Ten

While Sven went to the bathroom upstairs, I lay on my back on the living room floor, panting. A contented smile loomed on my lips as I relished the sweet ache in all my muscles. I brought my arms above my head to stretch. This had been the most intense session we'd had since beginning classes.

Without men in my life, I figured training was the closest I would get to sex. Besides, fighting helped me get rid of my frustration toward Ethan. I still couldn't fathom the ease with which he'd cast me aside. He wasn't in love with me, but between all the teasing and bantering, I'd thought we were becoming friends. *Stupid, lonely me.*

Kung Fu helped me clear my head. I hoped that if I trained hard enough, I might understand what had happened with Kate the other day.

I had two possible explanations for her behavior.

One, she'd covered for me out of guilt.

Two, she hadn't realized who I was. She couldn't possibly know my maiden name was Harper.

Then why would she pretend she knew me? Had she been afraid to upset me? I might have reacted the same way if I thought a psycho was standing in my office. She might have pretended to know me to get rid of me faster. Or perhaps she didn't want to make a scene in front of her boss.

Despite the giant holes in this theory, it made more sense than my husband's mistress, who I'd been stalking for weeks, covering for me.

"Are you planning to lie here all day?"

I watched Bizzy's face hanging over me and accepted the neat, French-manicured hand she extended.

"Thank you."

"Perhaps I should have trained with you. You're getting good," she said.

"Mom? How's your head?"

"Don't start bragging. I didn't say you were great," she chided. "Besides, I don't need Kung Fu lessons to defend myself."

"Yes, you can always claw your way out of a fight."

Or freeze her aggressors with her contempt. It certainly worked on me.

Sven stumbled down the stairs, checking constantly behind his shoulder like a hunted deer. I was about to ask what was wrong when I saw Claudia descend the stairs behind him. From her drooping eyelids and huntress's grin, it was easy to make out the situation. Claudia had finally decided to make a move on poor Sven, and the Kung Fu trainer was trying to decide whether he liked it, or feared it.

"See you Monday, okay?" Sven asked me, dashing to the front door.

"Sure." I did my best to keep a straight face.

"You might need help finding your coat," Claudia said. "Let me give you a hand."

Sven shot me a desperate look.

"Have a good weekend, Sven." I giggled despite myself.

When they left the living room, Bizzy turned to me.

"Did I miss something? What's so funny?"

"Nothing, Mom. It's nothing."

"As you wish." She sighed. "Let's go out tonight. It's Friday and I'm bored out of my mind."

"I'm not sure I feel like it. Besides, I have the girls tonight."

"I can babysit," Claudia offered as she returned to the living room. "M is moving out this weekend and I'd rather not be there when he does."

"Aren't you afraid he'll take your things?" Bizzy asked.

"What? My dingy couch or piece of shit TV? Honestly, the things I worry most about are my makeup and hairdressing tools but even Michal isn't metro enough to steal them."

"What hairdressing tools?"

"Claudia studied to be a hairdresser, Mom," I explained.

"Then why is she a housekeeper?" Bizzy sounded completely dismayed.

"I'm here, you know?" Claudia waved with both arms. "Better pay, less hours. Plus, I keep hairdressing for fun. I'd hate it as a real job.

Bizzy rolled her eyes. This was the kind of concept that flew right above her head.

"I'm going upstairs," Bizzy said. She looked at Claudia. "So that's settled then? You're babysitting tonight?"

"Sure. Then I'll sleep on the couch."

"If you must," Bizzy said. "Sloane, why don't you book something for tonight? Shall we say 8 p.m.? Something exotic. Chinese. No better yet, Indian," she added as she disappeared on top of the stairs.

Why didn't Bizzy book it then? She had done everything else. That was so like her – pretending I was in charge while refusing to relinquish control over anything. Good thing my father was so laid back. If he had been a control freak as well, they would have killed each other years ago.

"Will do, Mom," I said before returning my attention to Claudia. "So you and Michal. You're officially through?"

"Good riddance! Anyway I've got a better option now." She winked at me.

"Sven? I've noticed," I whispered. "When did that happen?"

"Wednesday, when you came home in a fury."

The fact that she didn't ask me why I was so angry showed how distracted Claudia was. *Thank heavens for pheromones!*

"Where?" I asked.

"Kitchen. Against the fridge, and the sink and the door."

"Sex?" I cried.

"Of course not! Kissing!" Claudia snapped. "I never have sex before the second date."

Well, that made a huge difference, then! *My bad*. Not like

111

I had a rule. My first time had been a one-night stand in Cancun, my second had been my boyfriend all throughout college; I might have made him wait a few times but then again, I had never been known for showing restraint. And then Tom – I blushed just to think of it – halfway through our first date. It had helped that the date was a candlelight dinner at his place, the bed a door away from us.

Claudia with her two dates policy was a prude next to me. Good thing I had been a serial long-term dater. Otherwise, my list of lovers would make Madonna feel lacking. I wasn't ready for the world of dating. I had to have Tom back!

"So what qualifies as a date? Not hanging out at my place, I assume?"

"Dinner…and vodka."

"And when are you planning to do that? Has he asked you out?"

"No. Not yet. I think I intimidate him."

Put the fear of God into him, rather. "Maybe you should be a little less forward? Let him do the work?"

"Nope. Not for me. I tried the girly flirting. It's embarrassing!"

It did look like she had something in her eye when she batted her lashes.

"It's just not my style. I'm a doer, that's what I am."

"So will *you* ask him out?"

"Are you crazy? That's a man's job. You Americans, you're like Brits, you don't understand anything. Feminism is crap. Men ask you out. Men pay the bill. We put make up on and eat lettuce." Polish dating 101.

"But didn't you pay the rent in your flat?"

"Exactly. Momentary lap of judgment."

"Lapse…?"

She pretended not to hear me.

"One of the many reasons he's going. If I want to pay for someone, I'll just become a lesbian."

Life 101 by Claudia. Poor Sven was in for a ride.

"You could have picked someplace more lively," Bizzy said as we parked in front of Bombay Palace.

"Indian restaurants aren't trendy. If you wanted a party, you should have asked for sushi."

"We could still go?"

"It's London, Mom. You have to make reservations weeks in advance." I exited the car. "Bombay Palace is nice. It's quiet and the food is great."

Also, it used to be our secret place with Tom, and I was in a nostalgic mood. I pushed open the nondescript door to the building. Behind it, the restaurant was hidden on the right side.

"A terrace, at least. It's summer outside and you lure me into a dark cave," Bizzy grumbled.

"We can go have a drink later if you want to sit outside."

I looked for the maître d', but he was nowhere in sight.

"Table for two for Gennaio, please," I asked a waiter by the entrance.

"Right this way, ma'am."

Two meters in and I was already overwhelmed by the smell of spices. My stomach growled loudly as I saw silver platters on white tablecloths. Even Bizzy's reluctance melted into a smile.

"Mrs. Gennaio, hello," the maître d' said, bowing. He was walking back to his station at the entrance of the restaurant. "It's good to see—"

He did a double take and pivoted on his heels.

"Kumar. Kumar you should sit the lady and her *mother* over here." He waved toward a table in back.

"But, sir, the table is over there." The waiter gestured somewhere across the room.

"Mother? Mother?" Bizzy choked on the word.

"I've looked on the chart. Table nineteen. There," the waiter repeated.

There was a mix-up. The waiter looked young; he must be new at this. He also seemed eager to prove himself because he completely refused to admit his error and dragged us along where he thought our table should be. I found the whole scene extremely amusing, the maître d's face so red he was close to apoplexy, so I followed anyway.

Poor Kumar dropped his confident expression when we arrived to the table he thought was assigned to us to find it already occupied – by a couple making out shamelessly, no less.

"But...table nineteen."

"It's okay." I put a hand on his shoulder. "Everyone makes mistakes. Mister Mahesh, would you be kind enough to show us to our table, please?"

The maître d' looked beyond relieved.

"Of course. Right this way."

By now, we'd caused quite a commotion. Bizzy was still echoing the word *mother* like a mad woman and young Kumar was scratching his head in confusion, mumbling something about switching tables. We were loud enough that the couple unglued their lips for a moment to stare at us.

Nausea hit me while my head began spinning uncontrollably.

"T... Tom?"

"I'm so sorry, Mrs. Gennaio. Mister Gennaio. Ladies." The maître d' looked at Bizzy and of course, at Kate sitting across from Tom. "It's an honest mistake. I apologize sincerely," he said.

"After all, two tables for two for Gennaio – quite a coincidence, right?" He tried to make light of the whole situation.

My eyes locked on Kate's icy gaze. The contempt behind the almond-shaped eyes fringed with long thick lashes was enough to make me unravel.

"Come, Sloane." Bizzy pulled at my arm. "Let's sit over there."

"I... I can't," I answered, my voice reedy.

It felt like I had swallowed a tennis ball that was stuck right in the middle of my throat. I had to hide before it dissolved into a torrent of tears. I ran to the bathroom.

Just as the door slammed shut, the waterworks started. The pain was so intense it made me stoop across the sink. I pushed my arms against it to stay upright.

Seeing them together made it all more real somehow. It pried my eyes open to the truth of the situation. Tom and Kate were happy. Tom had brought Kate to Bombay Palace. *Our* place. Since the divorce, he had never spared me but this was worse. Out of all the Indian places in London, he had to bring her here.

With this small act, he'd defiled everything that had made us special, unique.

The pointlessness of it all hit me with a staggering force. I now realized my one-woman quest was a hopeless one. Tom had gone too far in trying to erase us. He'd left me nothing to salvage.

I grabbed a few paper towels from the dispenser and attempted to wipe away all traces of my meltdown. I was defeated, wounded beyond words, but I didn't have to give Tom and Kate the pleasure of witnessing my downfall. They must be holding hands, snickering about the whole incident right this moment.

"You!" a voice boomed inside the bathroom.

My first instinct was to run but instead I figured I might as well face the music. Kate's beautiful face, appearing in the mirror next to mine, was frozen in a mask of scorn. I turned around from our mirror reflection. Kate and I standing next to each other wasn't an image I enjoyed.

"I'm done with you and your craziness!" Kate said, pacing back and forth in the bathroom. "I didn't sign up for this!" she exclaimed, more to herself than to me, apparently. "You are daft!"

"I—"

"Shut up. Just shut up," Kate said. "I never want to see you again! Do you understand me? If you follow me again, I'll call the police. Do you hear me?"

"Yes. Yes. But I didn'... I didn't know... I didn't know that you were here."

She snorted.

"Yeah. Of course you didn't. Like you didn't know where I worked the past month? You just happened to park there day after day after day by accident?"

"You knew?" I exclaimed.

"Of course, you loon! You are quite possibly the worst stalker in the universe," she said, putting her pacing to rest for a while.

My head spun frantically. I should have worn a wig!

"But why? Why didn't you say something? With Gabriel?"

She breathed deep, trying to keep her anger in check. "First, he's my boss. I worked hard enough not to let you ruin my reputation. I don't bring my love affairs to the office."

"You certainly did with Varela," I muttered.

"Stay out of it." Her tone raised a few octaves as her fury escalated. "And yes, stupidly enough, I felt bad for you. Your husband did leave you for me. I tried to spare you further humiliation."

"How kind of you!" My lips quivered from fresh tears trying to break through.

"It's very magnanimous of me. No one else would have put up with your madness for so long," Kate said, waving a finger at me. "Would you rather I told Gabriel that you're a deranged stalker? Or Tom? I'm pretty sure he could win full custody of your girls if he brought this to a judge."

The full stupidity of my actions crashed over me.

"Please. Don't—"

"I won't," Kate said. "But if I see you lurking around me, or my workplace again, I'll tell Tom. Are we agreed?"

I nodded like a guilty child, the pitiful remnants of my pride stuck so deep down my throat I feared I might never speak again.

Kate turned toward the mirror. She fumbled in her purse and brought out some lipstick. I watched in dismay as she applied the dark red color on her full lips then rearranged her lush, chocolate-colored mane, like nothing had happened. As if I were already gone, both from her life and her thoughts. I took this as my cue to leave.

Obviously, dinner was out of the question now. I simply couldn't sit and eat across from Tom and Kate and pretend everything was hunky-dory. I skimmed the wall on the opposite side to where Tom sat. I couldn't face him again tonight. In the half-light, it took me a few seconds to spot Bizzy. She sat at a small round table in a corner, her nose buried inside the maroon leather menu.

I walked over and tapped her shoulder. "Let's go. Please, Mom."

"But Sloane…"

"We can eat somewhere else. Or order a pizza. Please…"

"I don't care what we eat. I didn't want to eat here in the first place. But you can't leave."

I spied Kate coming out of the bathroom. Her threats concerning the girls echoed in my mind.

"Mom—"

"You are a Harper. You can't let them chase you away."

"I don't care about our name."

"That's not what I meant," Bizzy said. "You…"

Kate bent to Tom's ear and whispered something. They both chuckled. Tom caressed Kate's hand as she sat down in front of him. Bile rose at the back of my throat.

"I'm going," I told Bizzy before turning around toward the entrance. "Come with me…or don't come. I don't care."

As I pivoted on my heels, my arm connected with something. The massive silver dish on Kumar's serving tray went flying. He turned bright purple as *murgh makhni* chicken poured all over me. Tears streamed down my cheeks. It hurt like a bitch but not nearly as much as the shame that came with the pain.

Apparently, today wasn't Kumar's day – or mine for that matter. Snickering erupted behind me. I pictured Tom and Kate pointing in my direction, tears of laughter pooling in their eyes. Without a second look to Bizzy or the happy couple, I ran out of the restaurant.

I ran past my car, past the next block then the next. After

three weeks training with Sven, I was in the best shape I had ever been.

I ran and I cried till I was so tired I couldn't cry anymore and my shoes felt like they were filled with lead.

How many times would I have to be dragged in the mud before I learned my lesson? My ego had been trampled too many times to count and now I risked losing my daughters. I couldn't let that happen. If Tom took them away from me, I would die.

I reached a dimly lit square. A man played guitar in its center. He had a black velvet cap upside down before him on the ground. From its meager contents, it mustn't have been a great night for him either, but he smiled anyway. I sat on a bench to listen to him and give my legs a rest – a one-person audience.

Ever since Tom had left, the ground shifted constantly under me and all I could do was hang on for dear life. I'd been stripped of all sort of control. Like a pinball, I got kicked around, praying I wouldn't fall but knowing it was imminent nonetheless. Tom, Kate, Ethan, Gabriel – they were the players. And apparently, they had all outgrown their use for me.

"Bad night?" The guitarist startled me.

"What makes you say that?" I made a jaded arm movement encompassing my whole fabulous self, covered in *murgh makhni*.

"That to me could mean the start of a great night." He chuckled softly. "Want to tell me about it?" he asked while putting his guitar down and taking a cigarette out of his pocket.

"Sorry…but thank you. I'm all talked out."

"No worries, darling. I'll just smoke a fag before calling it a night."

"You look awfully happy," I told him, watching his grin as he lit a cigarette.

"Fancy this time of night. Thoughts are clearer for some reason. Must be the quiet."

My thoughts were one huge, screaming mess. I tried to

focus on the silence, spruce out my scrambled brain.

Could Kate really take my daughters away from me? She would need proof of my stalking – pictures, witnesses. I doubted she had photo surveillance on me but it wouldn't be too hard for her to get proof. London had cameras installed at every single street corner. Surely, one must have caught me on tape.

She might have the means to trap me but why would she want to do it? Didn't Tom tell me he had to reduce his nights with the girls because Kate didn't want the kids around? If she truly wasn't a kid person, then her threats had to be a bluff.

She might tell Varela and Tom about my spying on her but she would never help Tom get full custody of the girls. Because then, in a couple of weeks, they would live with her, and that must sound like some sort of nightmare to Kate.

The gloom lifted. My daughters were staying with me.

Kate could humiliate me all she wanted. I didn't care any longer. What I cared about was payback.

I fished my phone out of my bag, took a ten pounds bill out of my wallet, and stood up. I gave the bill to the guitarist sitting on the ground next to his cap.

"Thanks, love. See the night cleared your head too." He nodded toward my grinning face.

"It did. Thank you."

He winked at me before closing his eyes to enjoy his last drag. I walked away into a side street, waiting to make sure I was alone before making the call.

"Hello… Changed my mind. I'm in after all… Where can we meet?"

Chapter Eleven

Ethan's hotel was just a short taxi ride away. The cabbie had made me sit on old newspapers in an attempt to preserve his impeccable leather seats.

Now as I knocked against room 107's door, I patted my sticky butt to hunt any leftover pieces of paper. I had too much respect for literature to let it meet this tragic end. My ass could not be the place where the written word came to die. Besides, I wouldn't give Ethan more ammunition than I already had to make fun of me.

He rolled his eyes as he discovered me in the doorway. "Should I ask?"

"Not necessary." I shook my head as I stepped inside. He closed the door behind me. "It just isn't a good night for me," I said, before turning into a blubbering mess for the umpteenth time tonight.

Ethan put a hand at the nape of my neck and pulled me into his arms. He patted my dirty hair till I finally reined in the flow of tears. I lingered a while longer in his embrace, relishing the feeling of strong arms encircling me, and my cheek resting on Ethan's muscular chest. My eyelids closed as I inhaled his clean scent: soap and nothing else. Real men didn't need cologne. He just smelled like Ethan, his own particular brand of aphrodisiac.

On this worrying thought, I tore myself away from his hug.

"Your t-shirt, I'm sorry," I said as I noticed the mess I'd made.

Once white, now it was soaked with tears and smudged with creamy pink sauce.

"Who cares?"

Ethan stripped off his tee and threw it in a corner of the

room.

"You might want to take these off as well," he said as he waved toward my matching navy skirt and blouse.

"What?" I exclaimed, bringing my hands to my cheeks to hide their crimson hue.

The thought of being naked next to his perfection was terrifying. My mosquito bite breasts, the faded stretch marks on my thighs from my pregnancies – these would only be more acute next to his ripped abs and carved, lean arms.

Then it struck me: why would being imperfect be the thing that bothered me in his proposal?

"Wait what?" I asked again.

"I'm not letting you sit on my bed like that. I can lend you some clothes."

"Oh, sure," I answered, slightly disappointed.

As usual, my sex-deprived mind had conjured up a whole tale out of nothing.

Ethan crossed the whole two feet separating him from a closet on the opposite side of the room. His jeans fell low on his narrow hips and his strong back muscles rolled under his skin as he searched the top shelf. He turned around with two similar inscription tees and sweat pants. He threw one tee and the pants at me and nodded toward a door on my right side.

"The bathroom," he said as he shrugged on his own tee. *Goodbye, happy trail*. The Budweiser logo hid it now.

I scurried inside the bathroom. That it would be called a bathroom was quite a stretch. It was so small that I had to stand inside the shower to change, and when I dropped my soiled skirt on the floor, it almost fell inside the adjacent toilet. This layout must be a great time-saver in the morning. Ethan could pee, brush his teeth, and take a shower all at once.

I should have taken a shower but I didn't feel comfortable doing so with Ethan in the next room. Instead, I cleaned up my face as well as I could manage in the sink and pulled my dirty hair into a messy ponytail.

I rolled the sweatpants three times around the waist to

keep them from falling. Even so, it looked like I was wearing a parachute.

"Like beer much?" I asked Ethan when I came out of the bathroom. The t-shirt he had lent me advertised Coors.

"Private joke. With my sister."

That was the second time he'd mentioned his sister. The other night when he'd believed I was pregnant, and now.

"You too are close, right?"

"Well, it's only her and me, so yes," he answered.

I should have dropped the subject. Talking about his private life obviously made him uncomfortable, but I was way too curious not to pry further.

"And she has kids?"

"I've got three nephews." Judging by Ethan's smile, he was quite fond of them all. "They live in Florida. Miami."

"That's where you live?"

"Yep. I grew up in Boca. True Floridian mom." His eyes smiled before they turned cold. "Met my dad on his way from Ireland to jail."

He looked puzzled as if wondering why he'd confided in me. Knowing Ethan, I doubted he went around telling his family story to everyone. My chest swelled with pride at the vote of confidence.

I felt sad for him. Having a criminal father must have made growing up hard.

Ethan had told me he hadn't always been on the right side of the law. Maybe his young, rebellious self had tried to emulate his father. Once again, I pondered how he had ended up in the IRS. It was quite an achievement really, to rise above the example that your family set for you.

Silent as a vault now, Ethan plopped down on his unmade bed and gestured for me to sit next to him. The offer was quite innocent but I had fantasized enough about him and me in a bed to hesitate. I froze before the bed, flashbacks of the best scenarios assailing me.

To top it all, I could now match these fantasies with Ethan's shirtless vision. It seemed hard to believe but he looked even better than the already flattering picture my mind had conjured up for him. The light trail of hair on the perfect abs, the Ken doll muscles hidden partly by the distressed jeans. I fanned my face to keep from self-combusting.

Fortunately for me, Ethan was too exhausted to notice my embarrassment. Instead, he patted the bed again as if I hadn't seen him the first time. I nodded and sat on the opposite corner of the bed, as far away from him as possible.

The comforter was thicker than I thought, so soft I bounced when I sat on it and lost my balance. Ethan's fingers grasped my wrist right before I could dive head first on the shabby carpet. After he helped me up, I found myself sitting much closer to him than I would have wished. I was tired as well, and I was tempted to rest my head on his shoulder for a while. I shook myself out of it.

"Charming place," I lied.

To be honest, I wouldn't have believed the IRS to be so cheap.

"Piece of crap hotel. I'll be glad to head back home."

"And when will that be?" I asked, surprised to feel sad at the thought of him leaving.

"Depends whether you help me. The sooner, the better."

Without standing up, Ethan grabbed us two beers from a mini fridge. I laid the chilled bottle against my cheek then downed half of the bottle in one long swig.

"So what brings you here, Sloane?" he asked. "What made you change your mind? You're quite the rollercoaster, you know that?"

I told him all about my night, sharing even my humiliating conversation with Kate in the bathroom and her threats. That should put my fears to rest of things getting out of control between Ethan and me tonight. *So not sexy.*

Then, I recounted my meeting with Varela.

"So what do you want me to do about it?" I asked Ethan.

He was silent for a while.

"I'm not going to lie. If you accept Varela's invitation, it might go a long way in helping me solve my case."

123

"So it's settled then—"

"But as you told me time and again, you have responsibilities, Sloane. You must do what's best for you and your girls. At the end of the day, it has to be your decision."

"I'll do it." I tried to control the quivering in my voice. "I'm not doing it only for you if that's what you're worried about. I can't let Kate get away with it. If there is the slightest chance I can get payback, I need to take it. What kind of example would I be to my daughters if I don't stand up for myself?" I put on a brave smile. "And after all, how dangerous can a florist be?"

Ethan's bright eyes turned cloudy for a second. I put my hand on his, feeling uncharacteristically bold.

"Trust me, Ethan. I'll be fine. And I won't back out now. I'm all in."

One corner of Ethan's mouth lifted in a grin.

"Look at you all proud and ready to kick some ass," he said as he picked a sticky strand of hair away from my lips.

His eyes locked on mine as he rolled the strand between his thumb and forefinger. My breath caught in my chest as his face drew closer to mine, stopping mere whispers shy of my mouth. All sounds around were drowned by his soft rhythmic breathing, and the wild fluttering of butterflies' wings in the pit of my stomach.

Ethan laid his forehead against mine.

"You're so damn cute," he muttered as if it annoyed the hell out of him.

Yet he kept his head against mine. I blinked, trying to sift through the haze in my thoughts. Could he possibly find me attractive, or was it another game for him?

We'd been this close a couple times already, but this time felt different. The way he looked at me, intently and almost greedily, startled me. For once, I believed that if I vanished, someone would notice.

I leaned in, overpowered by the urge to keep being seen, to be touched. Ethan kissed my forehead first before slowly ambling his lips toward mine.

"And you taste great," he added.

Before I could help myself, my chest heaved in uncontrollable sobs.

"What's wrong?" he asked, his eyes widening in surprise.

"*Murgh makhni....* Why I taste so good." I sniffled unattractively. "My favorite... They've ruined *murgh makhni* for me!"

Ethan rolled his eyes and settled for a bear hug instead.

"Come here," he said with a sigh. "Everything is going to be okay."

Chapter Twelve

I staggered home in the wee hours of night – well, at 2 a.m., but to the mother that I was, it felt like I had pulled an all-nighter. I felt drunk, both from the endless tears I had shed and the tumbler of whisky Ethan had made me drink to settle my nerves. Who knew I was so attached to Indian food?

I had hung around the studio apartment for as long as I could to see if Ethan would try to kiss me again. When it was clear I had missed my chance, I'd asked Ethan to walk me to the street, hailed a taxi, and returned home. I ran a finger on my lips, recalling the fiery intensity in his eyes and his raspy voice.

I stared at the mirror in the hallway. Did he really say I was cute or had I dreamt it? Between my red eyes and runny nose, I looked like a hamster, and my hair was glued to my scalp. Bizzy's reproaches to me rang hollowly in my ears – if only I had taken better care of myself, Tom wouldn't have left me; I couldn't expect to catch men with vinegar; I should treat my body like a temple if I wanted a man to worship it.

Yet I'd been looking my worst tonight and this was precisely the night Ethan had tried to kiss me. Was he part of this rare breed of sensible men who saw through appearances? Or did he pity me so much he tried to raise my spirits by hooking up with me?

Biting disappointment warred with relief inside me. *We'd dodged a bullet here.* Not that a make-out session wasn't exactly what the doctor prescribed, but it would have significantly complicated our relationship, and I had enough complications in my life right now. Give too many balls to a juggler and he'll be bound to drop them all eventually. I'd never been too agile to begin with anyway.

Then again, maybe he had been teasing me per usual and never intended to kiss me. Which would mean I hadn't messed up anything by behaving like a psycho. Which in turn meant Ethan was the biggest jerk alive, and I was still as unattractive as ever. *Oh, so many questions!*

I crept past the living room, careful not to wake up Claudia. She slept like the dead, one leg hanging from the couch and her chin resting on the armrest. Her tiny butt in Hello Kitty shorts rose rhythmically as she snored like a rusty truck engine.

On the first floor, I held my breath till I made it to my bedroom. I dreaded coming across Bizzy. My head was already threatening to explode and I was pretty sure a sermon from her would finish me off. I exhaled thoroughly as I closed the door and rested against it for a second. Then I remembered my mission. I scurried to the bathroom and sat on the cool tiles in front of the bin. Under a gigantic pile of paper tissues, Gabriel Varela's calling card rested intact. Three days after I had thrown it here, the garbage still waited to be emptied. *Thank heavens for Claudia's poor housekeeping skills!*

I almost kissed the card before recalling where I'd fished it. So instead, I just put it carefully next to the sink and dragged myself into the shower. There was nothing more I could do tonight. Might as well sleep and try to recuperate. I would call Varela tomorrow morning.

Claudia peeking through the doorway startled me awake. Which in turn woke up Rose and Poppy nestled against me.

"Good. You're awake," Claudia said, as she strode across the room and sat at the foot of the bed.

"I am now," I said.

My eyelids felt like they were held shut with Krazy Glue and I felt queasy, as if suffering from a hangover. Rose yawned and scooted farther down under the comforter, hoping to resume her night. Poppy stretched her arms above her head, sticking her tiny fist in my eye.

"Ouch." I blinked.

Poppy hummed the theme to Princess Sofia, unaware that she'd come very near to blinding me. She turned her lovely face to me and laid her plump little hand on my cheek.

"Hello, pretty mummy. I love you!"

I took her tiny hand between mine and kissed it four or five times.

"Hello, my angel. Love you more."

"Ugh!" Claudia pretended to barf.

"Don't be jealous," I teased Claudia. "We love you too."

"Yes. I love you, Claudia," Poppy said.

"Go away!" Rose moaned from her hiding place. "Sleepy…"

Eight years old and already behaving like a teenager.

"You're sick. You know that?" Claudia said, but smiled. "All this love makes me want to puke."

Poppy raised a curious eyebrow.

"She doesn't really mean it, baby. Claudia's just being silly."

"Are you planning to sleep with them till they are eighteen? If I recall correctly, they were sound asleep in their beds when I passed out yesterday. Your couch blows, by the way."

"I can't help it. I just love snuggling with them."

"Mummy! I want to sleep!" Rose whined again.

"Sorry, baby." I left the warmth of my bed with a sigh. "Come, Poppy. Let's go make French toast downstairs. Your sister needs to sleep a little longer."

"Yes! French toasts!" Poppy danced her way out of the room.

I stared longingly at the bed.

"Are you coming?" Claudia tapped her foot.

My eyes drifted to the alarm clock on the nightstand. 6.30 a.m. No wonder Rose was still tired. I shrugged on a light sweater.

"It's twenty-five degrees outside and you wear a sweater?" Claudia asked.

I waited to shut the door before answering.

"You woke me up too early so yes, I'm wearing a sweater, because I'm exhausted and it makes me cold. Why?" I pushed my hair away from my face with both hands. "Why would you wake us up so early?"

"I couldn't sleep. I was bored. And I was too curious to wait. What happened yesterday?"

"Nothing."

"Bizzy stormed in at 9.30 p.m. and when I fell asleep at midnight you were still out of the house. You can tell me. I can keep a secret." She followed me down the stairs. "Come on! I'm dying here!"

I had a feeling she would nag at me till I said something. "We ran into Tom and Kate."

"*Kurva!*" She bobbed her pink head in disbelief. It was so bright it hurt my sleep-deprived eyes.

"Your hair is really pink. But really, really pink."

"So?"

"Just saying. I should wear sunglasses." I massaged my temples.

"Are you drunk?"

"Of course not! I never got to drink. Kate and I had a discussion. Well, she spoke-barked and I listened mostly."

I hurried as I recalled that Poppy was alone in the kitchen. God knows what mess I would find there now.

"Can I tell you the details later? I'm exhausted. Bottom line is dinner was canceled and I ended up roaming the streets till 2 a.m.," I fibbed.

"That great a night, huh?"

"Yep." I pushed open the door to the kitchen. "Poppy! Come down from the table this instant!"

My youngest stood straight on top of the kitchen counter, feet wide apart and arms forming an arrow on top of her head.

"But mummy! I'm the Eiffel Tower!" She giggled.

"The Eiffel tower? Like in Paris?" Claudia said behind me.

I struggled not to burst out laughing. Poppy had been very impressed by the giant metal tower on our trip to Paris last summer.

"Yes, like in Paris," I answered Claudia. To Poppy I said, "You're the Eiffel Tower because we're making French toasts. Very clever, Miss Poppy."

Poppy beamed proudly as she extended her arms to me. I picked her up, kissed her soft curls then put her down on the wood floor.

I rummaged through the fridge for eggs and milk then sliced white bread for everyone. With such a full house, I used the whole loaf. The first batch was sizzling in the pan when Bizzy came downstairs. I cast my eyes on the stove to avoid facing her.

"Hi, Bizzy Granma," Poppy said.

"Hi, Mom," I said without turning around.

"I'm not saying hi," Claudia said. "It's way too early to talk to her."

"For once we agree on something," Bizzy replied. "Sloane, I'm glad to see you're alive and well."

The biting irony in her words made me bend my head in shame.

"I'm making French toasts. Want some?" I asked by way of an apology.

"No. I'm going out for a powerwalk."

The only times Bizzy powerwalked were when she was beyond mad. Good thing I hadn't run into her last night. If she still was so angry in the morning, she would have crushed me yesterday.

At least, if she refused to talk to me, I wouldn't have to lie to her about going to Ethan's hotel. Every lie I was spared was a blessing. I pretended not to see how mad she was.

"Okay, then. Enjoy your walk."

"I don't walk. I powerwalk. One is idle ambling; the other one is exercising determination. Something you know nothing about apparently," she snapped before storming out of the kitchen.

"Ouch!" Claudia exclaimed from her bar stool.

"Ouchy!" Poppy mimicked, whirling tirelessly in the

middle of the kitchen. With her arms extended to the side, she looked like a spinning-top: a happy, giggling, blonde spinning-top.

I set up three plates on the counter just as Rose emerged in the kitchen.

"Morning, Rose baby," I said. "Perfect timing."

I poured maple syrup on Poppy's toasts then handed it to Rose. Claudia wolfed down her toasts as well as Bizzy's portion. I nibbled straight from the pan, nervous about the phone call on my agenda this morning.

When the girls were finally settled in front of their cartoons and Claudia took a shower in the girls' bathroom, I locked myself in mine. I dialed Varela's number on my cellphone. My lips were dry and I had to fight the urge to hang up before he could answer. I quickly rehearsed what I would say to him.

"Hello, Gabriel?" I said as soon as he picked up. "Sloane Harper. I'm Sloane Harper. I don't know if you remember me…"

"Ah! Yes. Divina Sloane. I've been waiting for your call."

His husky voice sent my toes curling instinctively. I fanned myself with my hand, trying to come up with something intelligible to say next.

"I…"

"Have dinner with me tonight," he said, saving me from further humiliation.

"Tonight?" I stammered.

"How does 8 p.m. sound? I'll pick you up."

"Uh… 8. I guess…"

"Text me your address," he said before hanging up.

"Great. See you tonight," I told the dial tone.

Claudia knocked on the bathroom door.

"Can I come in? I need to use your blow-dryer."

I unlocked the door and waved her in.

"Are you all right?"

I nodded.

"You look like you've seen a ghost."

"Stranger than that," I replied. "I've got a date tonight."

"A date?" Claudia asked, scratching her head wrapped in a white sponge towel. "I think I need to sit down." She slumped on the edge of the bathtub.

I sat down next to her.

"Yeah, me too."

"Who with?" Claudia asked as soon as she recovered from the news.

"Remember Kate's boss? Gabriel Varela?"

"As in Varela Global, Varela?"

"Well, yes."

Claudia whistled. "Nice! Hot and loaded."

"How would you know?"

"He has his name on the door; he has to be disgustingly rich."

I pictured the Pollock above his desk, the expensive furniture in his office, and his designer clothes. Even his immaculate teeth screamed money.

"Yeah. Probably."

Claudia searched the cupboards under the sink for my blow dryer.

"Here." I helped her find it.

I started recounting my encounter with Varela from the other day, shouting above the blowing sound. Then I told her the details of the night before, leaving only Ethan out of the narrative. It felt great telling the truth for once, albeit a partial one.

"So you're going on a date with Varela to piss off Kate?"

"In a nutshell, yes."

"Prince Charming knocks on your door and you still want your sleazy ex-husband back. I try to understand you, Sloane, but sometimes you make it impossible."

I didn't quite understand myself either. My father always said I was too stubborn for my own good. Every particle in my body yelled for me to let go of Tom. He was in love with someone else. Worse, I wasn't even sure he was a good person. But my pig-headed brain wouldn't accept this. Getting Tom back had been my sole purpose for the past six months. I couldn't just walk away now.

"I just require a break from it all," I said. "Maybe a date is exactly what I need."

Ethan's face popped into my mind. *Not a date.* Tonight wasn't a date. I was on a mission.

"I'll do your hair if you want."

Double-edged sword. Claudia was a moody hairdresser. I could end up with a Mohawk if the muses inspired her that way. Now that her hair was dry, I could see white and purple streaks among the pink. I was pretty sure they weren't there last night.

"You like?" she asked.

"I do. But I don't think that would—"

"Don't sweat it." She held a hand, palm up, to shush me. "It's your first date in a century. I'll do something classic. A bland, neat brushing. Something resembling you."

Bland? Ouch! I winced painfully and stood.

"Thank you. We probably should go downstairs and check on the girls."

"Yes. We'll do your hair later this afternoon."

"You're staying over again tonight?"

"Yeah. I might sleep in Rose's bed though. I can't stand the couch."

"No problem."

Tom had the girls tonight anyway. And Claudia was so petite, she would fit into my eight-year-old's bed easily.

We came downstairs to find two furies zigzagging around a dizzy-looking Bizzy.

"How long have you let them watch cartoons?" she asked me. "They were staring at the TV like junkies when I came home. And when I turned it off, they started behaving like wild animals. I think they might be having a psychotic break."

Always one for exaggeration. I checked the grandfather clock on the mantelpiece; I'd gone up one hour ago. More than I usually let them watch TV but nothing that would lead to a mental condition. Mostly they were in dire need of fresh air.

"Girls, go get ready."

"Where are we going, Mummy?" Rose asked as she climbed down from the couch.

"To the playground, honey. As soon as you're dressed, we'll go."

"Come on, Poppy," Rose said as she dragged her little sister out from under the coffee table.

How the heck had she managed to crawl into such a tiny space?

"I'll help you get dressed," Rose told Poppy.

"Can I wear the pink dress with flowers?" my youngest asked her idol as she followed her up the stairs.

"Only if you're very nice," Rose told her sister.

She gave Poppy her hand to hold.

"Thank you, Little Mummy." Poppy used my nickname for Rose.

I watched their small silhouettes on the staircase. Poppy's plump, babyish body in teddy bears printed pajamas, and Rose's slight shoulders and serious stance in a liberty nightgown. *Serious love overflow.*

At 6 p.m., I slumped down on the sofa, legs on the coffee table before me. Saturdays were the longest days. As if three days had been crammed up in the one. Especially when your friend slash housekeeper woke you up before 7 a.m. My weekends started on Mondays when the girls went to school. Their weekends were my longest working days.

"Let's do your hair." Claudia clapped her hands to kick me into action.

"In a minute," I said.

I didn't want to go on a date tonight – shave my legs, wear something uncomfortable, do my hair. What I wanted was a hot bath, a good book, and ugly sweatpants. The girls had gone to Tom's place. I should be resting tonight.

"I might cancel. I think I'm getting sick."

"No. No way," Claudia said. "This date is a miracle. You don't turn down miracles."

"Date?" Bizzy's nose came up from her book.

She had been giving me the silent treatment all day but apparently, the word 'date' had magic powers. All was forgotten and she beamed at me.

"Who is she going on a date with?" she asked Claudia.

The supernatural influence of the word 'date' extended to Bizzy and Claudia's relationship as well. They found a truce while Claudia got Bizzy up to speed on my romantic status. They were cordial to each other as they got me ready.

I dozed through Claudia's brushing and sat obediently on my bed while they picked my outfit. They did not tear each other's throats even though their tastes couldn't be more different. Claudia wanted me to wear a tiny red number that left nothing to the imagination and Bizzy tried to dress me as a sexy Quaker.

Gazing at my closet, I realized I had no taste of my own. The whole wardrobe attested to that. Most of the black had Claudia's name on it, the designer pieces came from Tom, and the numerous silk blouses screamed Bizzy. A couple pink accessories were gifts from my daughters. If you were what you wore, I was no one but the conglomerate of the people in my life. *Actually, scratch that – the sweatpants and Uggs were mine – I was a Jersey native.*

Claudia and Bizzy found a compromise in one of Tom's dresses. It was a deep burgundy color, with a demure round neck and mini skirt. Black, four-inch sandals completed the outfit. They tried to play makeup artist but my head was spinning and I needed a break from their constant chatter. I sent them downstairs and applied a touch of bronzer and mascara in front of the mirror. Excitement bloomed inside me. I squashed it immediately. This wasn't a real date.

It didn't stop me from rushing down the stairs when the doorbell rang at eight sharp.

"I'll get the door," Claudia hollered from the living room.

I hurried the pace, hoping to get to the door before her. Who knew how she would manage to humiliate me if she got there first? When I finally reached the landing, my heel caught in the rug, sending me flying head first in the living room, just in front of the entrance door that opened at the exact same moment. I buried my face in my hands. *Why? But why?*

"Are you all right, Miss?" a man's voice asked. Not Varela's.

"You're not her date," Claudia commented.

He shifted from one foot to the next under Claudia's scrutiny, and Bizzy's, who had just joined our party.

"I'm the chauffeur."

"Hello..." Bizzy waited for the chauffeur to say his name.

It took him a few seconds to realize what was expected of him.

"Jimmy, ma'am," he answered, wringing his hands like a schoolboy called to the blackboard.

Bizzy flashed him the smile of a woman used to getting her way.

"Jimmy, please, be a dear and don't tell your employer about this." She waved toward me – I was *this*, the mess to sweep under the rug. "You look like a gentleman. You wouldn't want to embarrass my daughter. Am I right?"

"Yes, ma'am. Uh, no ma'am. I mean..."

"It's okay, Jimmy," I told the poor driver drowning in my hallway. "I just fell. No reason to cower in shame." I scrambled up to my knees.

"You finally have a date! Try not to ruin it," Bizzy said as she ushered me toward the door.

Like I fell on purpose. I knew I should have worn sensible heels. I dusted my scraped knees and finger brushed my hair.

"Try to get laid," Claudia whispered in my ear.

On the doorstep, Bizzy gave me a not so gentle nudge toward Varela's car. Eager to marry me off much? *Meet Sloane, Bizzy Harper's charity case of a daughter!*

"And Sloane? Do me a favor, please? Watch where you step," she said before shutting the door in my face.

Hope she doesn't change the locks while I'm gone.

I followed Jimmy to the car. The driver seemed to breathe better now that he was on neutral ground. I did too –

there were way too many pheromones in my house. I looked for Varela, to no avail because the car had tinted windows. Jimmy opened the back door of the Mercedes for me.

I lifted my chin high for courage, stepped inside the car, and sat on Varela's knees. The surprise made me jerk backward. I knocked my head against the car's roof while Varela scooted to the right side of the passenger seat. He struggled to hold his smile but quickly gave up, beaming as I rubbed my bruised skull.

"*Divina* Sloane, are you all right?" Gabriel asked me while kissing my free hand.

"Dangerous," I muttered.

"What is?"

"Dating."

Varela chuckled. He held onto my hand as Jimmy put the car in motion. Hector, chief of security, sat next to the driver. He nodded curtly at me before returning his attention to the road ahead. Gabriel's laughter was infectious and soon I joined him, forced to admit the humorous turn this evening had taken so far.

Fifteen minutes later, we parked in front of Chiltern Firehouse. The red brick, rehabilitated firehouse was London's hottest place to be these days. I knew it from hearing Nisha and the other moms boast about their latest soirees there. The waiting list was a couple of months long at its shortest. With my extravagant social life of late, I'd obviously never set foot in the fancy restaurant.

I buzzed with excitement. This was the kind of place I went to every week with Tom, although I dreamt of a cozy restaurant or a simple night at home. Then, from one day to the next, I had been granted my wish and I found myself missing a little bit of the glitter and decorum Tom fancied so much. *Bet Katherine Stappleton appreciates it more than me.* I banished her quickly from my thoughts.

Varela circled the car to help me out of my seat. I held onto his arm for dear life as we walked into the burgundy hallway lit by hundreds of candles. *Great choice of outfit. The restaurant and I are matching.* Like I was trying to be even more invisible than I usually was, I could now blend in with the walls.

As if on cue, a tall amazon in a white silk jumpsuit swayed our way. Between the stark contrast of her dark skin and the white fabric, and her extravagant Afro, she was everything but invisible. She greeted Gabriel with a dazzling smile and a lascivious pose. Me, she didn't see. One doesn't pay attention to the wall.

"Mister Varela, good to see you again."

"Hello." He smiled mildly while circling my waist with his arm.

Her envious sneer told me she must have noticed. I scooted closer to him. The restaurant's manager came our way, kicking the hostess into action. She walked us to a secluded alcove accommodating a small table for two, and handed us menus.

"If you need anything, please let me know," she told my date, trailing her thumb on her full lower lip as she spoke.

Thank heaven this was all fake. Dating Varela was way too cutthroat for me. Ethan's image hung before my eyes for an instant, reminding me I was here on a mission.

"Sloane?"

I snapped out of my Ethan thoughts to find Gabriel smiling at me.

"Where were you just now?"

I shook my head for nowhere.

"Good. I want you with me. You made me wait three days, cruel Sloane Harper."

I raised an eyebrow.

"No woman's ever made me wait so long," he said matter-of-factly. He was lost in thoughts for a second. "Come to think of it, no woman's made me wait at all. Ever."

He stared at me wide eyed, the blue of his shirt complementing their deep green color nicely. No wonder no woman ever made him wait. Varela was drop dead gorgeous.

"Must be nice," I said to cover my embarrassment. "I

138

wasn't playing hard to get. Things in my life are just complicated."

I buried my nose in the menu.

"I know," Gabriel answered. "You've been busy lately..."

Ethan. Gabriel knew. I gripped the menu tightly, my knuckles turning white. My voice sounded alien, croaking grotesquely when I spoke next.

"What do you mean?"

Perhaps I had it wrong. I was making mountains out of molehills. He hadn't said anything about Ethan. I was just being jumpy.

The right corner of Varela's mouth lifted in a grin.

"You're quite the little spy, aren't you?"

Shit! Not my imagination then. I dropped the menu on the table, resulting in a resonant bang. How did I ever believe I could pull this off?

I assessed the situation.

Chiltern Firehouse was way too public for me to worry about my safety. The alcove we sat in might be secluded but at least ten people had seen Gabriel on our way in, none nearly close to forgetting about him. Even wearing casual chic clothes like tonight, he looked like a dream.

Most likely I was in for a not-too-friendly lecture and a slap on the wrist. None of which sounded too appealing right now.

So instead of hanging around for the inevitable, humiliating sermon to come, I summoned the little courage I had left and made a move to leave. I grabbed my clutch and tried to stand up from my chair but the sommelier stepping inside the alcove, impeded my exit.

I huffed impatiently as I waited for him to leave. A persistent smile still floated on Gabriel's lips while he listened to the sommelier's recommendations, but it didn't quite seem to reach his eyes. There was a cold glint in the stormy green eyes that boded ill for my near future.

Apparently, under his mellow charm, lay a man not to be trifled with, and my skull thrummed as I pictured my

139

conscience clubbing me over and over on the head for being so stupid.

The sommelier beamed as he left with an order for a bottle of outrageously expensive champagne. Evidently, the evening wasn't over yet for Gabriel. Well, it was for me.

"I'm sorry. I'm going to go now."

Gabriel grabbed my wrist and began shaking with laughter. The warm chuckle echoed against the arched ceiling and made my cheeks burn with hot humiliation. Was that the punishment he had chosen? Mocking me? He was right; I was the most ridiculous spy after all. I squirmed on my chair, hoping to escape his sneering. When Gabriel saw I didn't share his glee, he sobered up at last.

"Forgive me, *divina* Sloane. I didn't mean to embarrass you. I find your dedication quite endearing."

He kissed my fingers softly.

Good thing my jaw was firmly attached to the rest of my face because it would be somewhere on the table otherwise. I was utterly stunned.

The waiter returned with a transparent bottle in a silver ice bucket. With a flourish, he opened the bottle and poured the gilded liquid into tall champagne flutes. I stared intently at the minuscule bubbles' ascension in the glass before me.

"*Salud*," Gabriel said, raising his glass and knocking it against mine.

I took my champagne glass and emptied it in one long gulp. *Liquid courage.*

"I'm sorry I ambushed you with Kate the other day. It was childish of me." Gabriel smiled. "I simply couldn't pass on an occasion to tease Kate. That was so unlike her. It was such great fun!"

I tried to speak but my tongue was tied. So Gabriel didn't know about Ethan? *Phew! Close call.* But he knew about me staking out Kate. I blushed all the way to my hairline.

"You've been parked almost every day this past month in front of my building. You raised a red flag and my chief of security had you investigated," he explained.

I waited to see if there was more but Gabriel didn't

mention a cute IRS agent. I still held my clutch in my free hand. I figured now was as good a time as any to leave and kill myself by taking a dive from a sidewalk.

"Thank you for the champagne."

"Please stay. I don't want you to go."

"But why?"

The good thing when you're beyond humiliated is you can afford total honesty. *Almost total.*

"You know about my husband then. You know I want him back."

"Yes. That was my understanding," he said while studying the menu. "Very admirable of you, trying to keep your family together."

"So you just want to be friends?" I asked.

I masked my disappointment by burying my nose in the menu.

"Absolutely not." Gabriel waved me off.

I looked up to see if he was teasing me.

"I think it's adorable that you went to these lengths to give your marriage a chance."

"You do?" I blurted from the effect of surprise.

"Yes. Such loyalty is rare," he answered without a trace of irony. "Where I come from it's downright unheard of. The women I date are usually fickle things, more devoted to my money or status than to me. As for my parents..." his voice trailed off. "They never showed such devotion to one another."

"Are they divorced?"

"Divorced? Ah! No. They are Catholics. But they have an understanding."

"That must have been hard, growing up."

"It is what it is," he said, waving my concerns away. "Anyway, I sometimes wish I held the love of someone worthy. Someone like you, *divina* Sloane."

Gabriel's honesty took me aback. I had pegged him to be a superficial playboy yet here he was, genuinely confiding in me. It took a real man to show weaknesses and the mother in me felt compelled to take him into a close embrace. I refrained though, confident it wouldn't sit well with his ego. As if reflecting my thoughts, Gabriel gave me one of his dazzling smiles.

"All this to say that I'm certain your ex isn't good enough for you."

"Have you met him?"

"No need. How could he be good enough when he passed on a woman like you for one like Kate?"

"You don't like her?"

"I do. Very much. She's a great friend actually."

"So?"

"She's not the relationship type. Kate is business or fun. She usually chooses married men to avoid commitment. I was quite surprised when I heard she was dating someone seriously." He shut the menu and nodded to our waiter.

I let him order for both of us, not caring much for food tonight. For the second night in a row, something had cut my appetite.

"But your ex's loss is my gain. I should send him a thank you basket." He smiled.

"I love him."

"You think you do. I'm quite confident you'll soon fall head over heels in love with me and forget all about him."

"You're awfully cocky," I said.

"I told you I love a challenge. Be prepared to be romanced, beautiful Sloane."

His gorgeous eyes locked with mine and he planted another kiss on my wrist. I drank some more champagne and let myself relax for the rest of the evening.

When Gabriel asked for the check a couple hours later, my head buzzed pleasantly and a comfortable warmth spread through me. True to his words, he had applied himself to prove that romance wasn't dead. Spanish poetry – made more lovely by the fact that I couldn't understand a single word of it – long staring matches, and showers of compliments made me worry I wouldn't make it through the doors, my head had grown so big.

Here I was, sitting in London's trendiest restaurant,

across from the handsomest man in town, when yesterday I'd been roaming the streets covered in *murgh makhni*. *And almost kissed by Ethan.* I had to admit, that part had been nice.

To my surprise, Gabriel was much more than an idle playboy. He was cultured, sensitive, and well traveled. Prince charming in the flesh – every little girl's dream come true.

Hector came at the same time as the waiter carrying the check. He whispered something in Gabriel's ear.

"Stop being paranoid," Gabriel answered him.

His eyes looked drawn and his smile began flickering.

"No need to bother with the back exit. Tell Jimmy to bring the car out front."

Hector mumbled in disagreement but did as he was bid. He left without ever acknowledging my presence. Surely, I was one in a thousand girls he'd seen with his boss, I concluded sourly.

"Sorry about Hector," Gabriel told me, his tone curt. "He's very intense when it comes to my security."

My date, on the other hand, looked like he had not a worry in the world. Maybe Ethan had it wrong. Apparently, it was Hector and not Gabriel that was paranoid. I was curious.

"Hector's the one who did the background check on me?" Humiliation came flaring back but I squelched it in the bud.

"Yes. I told him it wasn't necessary but there's no stopping him."

He rubbed the back of my hand with his thumb.

"If he had his way, I would sleep in my panic room." He chortled.

"You don't think he has reasons to worry?"

"In South America, maybe. Kidnappings are common currency and I would make for a handsome ransom," he said matter-of-factly. "But here in London? I'm just another businessman. Yet another charm of this city." He gazed intently at me.

143

Gabriel Varela was many things but certainly not *just another* anything. I took in the way his jet-black waves caressed his pale skin and the two green gems peering under perfectly arched brows. No wonder women swooned over him.

I wasn't impervious to his charms either, no matter how many times I reminded myself this wasn't a real date. My brain knew it, but my hormones stubbornly rejected the truth. "Take us home!" they yelled like groupies at a rock concert.

Chapter Thirteen

Disappointingly, Gabriel turned out to be a gentleman. He took me home and kissed my cheek chastely before bidding me goodnight. My hormones tore their hair in frustration. My brain did a victory dance. I was too tired to care either way.

I tiptoed in direction of the stairs, hoping I wouldn't stir Claudia. All I aspired to were white fluffy pillows and cozy sweatpants. The number of empty martini glasses on the ground made me stop. Claudia slept on the couch, fully dressed, drool running down her chin and pooling on the beige fabric.

A snore loud enough to make the walls shake resonated from the armchair by the window. Was there a man here? I craned my neck as far as it would go to see who my loud houseguest was. I stifled a giggle when I realized it was Bizzy making this ruckus. She too was still dressed, passed out. This was quite a feat. Bizzy Harper had finally met her match in the brazen Polish housekeeper. I was far less careful about noise as I climbed the stairs up to my room.

I brushed my teeth, changed, and jumped into bed. I stretched leisurely across the white sheets, rubbed my head in the pillows, happy like I hadn't been in a long while. I felt giddy.

Tonight's fake date had been a good one – minus the drama at the beginning of the evening – and for the first time since Tom had left me, I was capable of enjoying having the whole bed to myself. As if tiny grey pebbles had been dislodged from my chest, I could breathe again at last.

I should have called Ethan to debrief him about my night

but instead I decided I would treasure the feeling a while longer. I put my phone on vibrate, plugged it to the charger, and drifted to sleep.

Next morning I was the first awake. I scurried to the kitchen to make myself a cup of coffee. While I waited for it to brew, I checked my phone. Seventeen new messages blinked on the screen. I immediately worried about the girls and decided to cut lost time by calling Tom before checking the messages.

He answered with a sleepy voice.

"Hullo?"

I heard cartoons behind him.

"How are the girls?" I demanded, bordering on hysteria.

"Fine. Active. Ahhh…" He yawned. "What's gotten into you?"

"I received a thousand messages. I thought maybe they were from you. About them, I mean."

"Not me, babe." He chortled. "Must be your secret admirer."

Jerk. I started gathering the empty martini bottles lined up on the kitchen counter. Claudia and Bizzy had held quite a bash without me yesterday.

"So the girls are fine?"

"I told you they're great. We're eating breakfast. Kate's gone out to the gym."

To go to the gym at 8 a.m. on Sunday, she must really be desperate to get out of the house. *Good girls.*

I tried to recall precisely what Gabriel had told me about Kate. She chose married men to avoid commitment. Couldn't she have done the same with Tom? Use him for sex and send him back home to me?

Wow! I mentally slapped myself for even thinking it. Wishing to be lied to and cheated on was a new low, even for me. I remembered Tom was still on the line.

"Okay. Great."

"Is that mummy?" I heard Poppy ask in the background.

"Let me talk to them for a sec."

146

"See you later, babe. Here…" Tom passed the phone to Poppy.

"Mummy?"

"Yes, baby?"

"Why don't you come here to play? Kate has a hundred lipsticks – orange, red, pink," she said.

"And she doesn't want you to play with them," Rose said. "Give it to me, Poppy."

"Mummy?" Rose said, now in charge of the phone. She turned on the speakerphone. "Poppy's being cheeky. She put on Kate's lipstick yesterday. And she spilled gold eye shadow in the bathtub."

She sounded positively outraged.

"Thank you, little mommy. Don't be too hard on your sister, okay? She's still a baby, you know."

"I'm not a baby!" Poppy cried out. "I'm…" I could picture her counting her chubby little fingers. "Four and a half."

"Very true. You're not a baby anymore. I'm sorry. But you're *my* baby? Right?"

"Mmm," she said carefully, obviously giving this great thought. "Fine."

"Okay, girls. Mommy has to go. I'll see you tonight. Have fun with your dad."

An avalanche of kisses hit the receiver.

"Love you," I said before hanging up.

I should have said something to Poppy about Kate's makeup but the small revenge on Kate was too sweet.

I unlocked my cellphone and scrolled through the messages. There were five texts and twelve missed calls. The missed calls were all from Ethan, as were the texts except one from Gabriel. I started with the latter.

You are a singular woman, divina Sloane. Looking forward to Tuesday night. Hope to get to know you deeper. Dream of me, hermosa…

It was stamped at 1 a.m. I was already fast asleep by then. Whether Gabriel had used the word *deeper* on purpose or as an unfortunate Spanishism, a heat wave hit me from head to toe. I *deeply* regretted I wouldn't have a chance to know him that well.

That reminded me of Ethan and my mission. I moved on to his texts. The IRS agent was far less wordy than my Colombian suitor was.

So? 12.30 a.m.
Are you at his place? 12.53 a.m.
Did you find something? 1 a.m.
Sloane, what the hell? Answer me. 1.02 a.m.

I poured myself a cup of coffee, hovered over it to inhale its rich scent, and then tasted a first sip. Only after completing my morning ritual did I call my voicemail.

The first ten messages were white noise and the click of Ethan's phone.

"Received, today at 1.30 a.m.," the robotic feminine voice stated.

"Sloane," Ethan grunted on the other line – then the click. *Great voicemail.*

"Received, today at 4 a.m.," the recording machine said again. So far, she was way chattier than Ethan.

"Sloane! I told you to search his house. Not to sleep over. If you don't call me back in five minutes, I'm coming to get you."

Oh, shit! I peeked in the living room to make sure Claudia and Bizzy were still sound asleep. Just in case they woke up, I decided to take this discussion outside.

I grabbed my coffee and stealthily crept out of my house. I closed the front door as quietly as I could manage and sat on my doorsteps. It occurred to me that I might run into a neighbor while wearing pajamas, but I didn't care. The weather was warm already and the sun on my face was worth all kinds of humiliation. *And let's face it; I should be immune to it by now.*

148

I put my cup down on the step next to me then dialed Ethan's number. The five minutes he gave me to call back had been over five hours ago, but surely I would have heard from Gabriel if Ethan had forced his door looking for me.

"Ethan?"

"Yeah!" he barked.

"Don't tell me you barged in on Gabriel last night?"

"You would have noticed, wouldn't you?"

"Uh? What?"

"Where are you anyway? Hidden in his bathroom? Huddled under his sheets?"

"In my—" *Kitchen,* I started to say.

Then again, who did he think he was to ask such private questions? I decided to turn the tables on him. "Where are you?"

"In a car. Parked in front of Varela's house."

"What are you doing here?"

"I came for back up. In case you needed me. I was worried. Foolish me!"

"You have a car?"

"A friend lent it to me. What the hell, Sloane? I thought I could count on you. I thought you were serious."

"You slept in the car?" I asked again, trying to process the info.

"Yes. Who cares? I can't believe you had sex with him!"

"It's sweet. That you cared enough about me." *Oh, fine.* I chose to stop toying with him. "I'm home. I never went to Gabriel's house."

"You didn't?" His relief was short lived. "What about our plan?"

"Delayed, I guess. To Gabriel, yesterday was a date. If I'd asked him to take me home, what do you think he would have expected?"

Ethan stayed silent.

"I'm seeing him Tuesday. I'll try to search his house then."

"No, it's okay," Ethan said. "Most probably, the proof I need will be in his office. Don't bother with his home."

"But you said—"

"I was wrong. Trust me, Sloane. You don't have to go to his house. Ever."

Ethan was becoming very touchy on the home subject.

"I guess I could start with his office…"

"Great plan."

"Anything else?" I asked after a minute listening to him yawn.

"Let me know when you plan to search his office. And Sloane?"

"Yes?"

"Keep your distance from Varela."

Ethan hung up in my face.

"Have a good day too, jackass," I told the silent receiver.

The guy had some nerve. How was I supposed to keep my distance from Varela while dating him? He could just as well have asked me to go take a swim without getting wet.

I cast my phone on the step below me. Then I oriented my face to the sun and reclined on my elbows. Boy, I needed a vacation.

The front door banged open behind me, making me start.

"Here you are!" Claudia said, sitting down next to me. She took a sip of my coffee and sighed. "You mind?"

I did. Coffee theft was high on my list of capital offenses, next to forgetting to put the toilet seat down and eating the last piece of pie.

"Not really," I lied because above all these horrid things, what I minded most was an argument.

Claudia took another sip then held her head between her hands. She grunted.

"That bad a night, huh?"

She looked up ever so slightly.

"Actually, that good. Wait…weird—" She bent her head again, as if she was about to hurl.

I scooted further to the left to avoid being in the crossfire. My pajamas were clean.

I couldn't say the same of Claudia's clothes. Her black

fishnet tank was totally rumpled and pink smudges covered her jeans. Her pink bob stood on her head like an Afro.

"I'm okay. I'm okay," she said, more to herself than to me. She looked up again. "How was your night?"

"Fine." I dismissed her question; I had a more pressing matter to discuss. "Let's rewind to the part where you said you had a good time. Shall I remind you that you were locked in a house with Bizzy Harper? You hate her."

"Well, yeah. I did. But she's pretty cool, actually. *Kurva!*" Claudia shook her head in disbelief. "If you tell her, I'll kill you. Mafia style."

She waved a threatening finger at me. I wasn't sure what mafia style entailed or whether Poland even had a mafia, but I knew Claudia and I didn't want to get killed by her – whatever style she chose to accomplish the deed.

"Your secret's safe with me. I need a shower," I said as I stood up.

I helped Claudia to her feet and pushed open the front door. Bizzy was coming around as we reached the living room. She blinked a few times then stood up on shaky legs. When she spotted us, she straightened herself as best as she could – *Image is everything, my dear.* Despite her slept-in clothes and hazy gaze, she did her best to look collected. A WASP's very own superpower. Inherited from settlers to mothers to daughters. Too bad it had skipped my generation.

Bizzy glanced timidly at Claudia. She had the smile of a smitten, teenaged girl. Claudia returned her smile. *What the heck?*

My mom turned to me. "Good morning, Sloane. How was your date?"

"Great. Gabriel took me to Chiltern—"

Bizzy emitted a sound between a hiccup and a gagging noise. When we saw her shoulders heave, Claudia and I stepped backward in unison. Bizzy managed to rein in her nausea.

"If you'll excuse me, I'll go refresh myself now," she said, power-walking her way to the guest bathroom.

"Empty herself more like," Claudia said when she had

disappeared.

I tried my best to keep a straight face.

"What did you do to her?"

"Nothing! We just drank a few martinis."

"More than a few. You emptied two bottles!"

"One and a half. Your mother had already nicked the first bottle earlier in the day."

"Should I worry about her?" I asked Claudia.

"Nah." She shook her head. "She's okay. You, on the other hand, are a sissy."

The sound of the toilet flushing made me drop the subject. At least Bizzy could still be hungover. She wasn't totally immune to alcohol yet. A terrifying grunt emanated from the bathroom.

"Mom? Are you alright?"

Claudia moonwalked toward the kitchen.

"Where are you going?" I asked her just as the bathroom door flung open.

In the short time between me looking at Bizzy's mask of scorn and turning back toward the kitchen, Claudia had disappeared.

"Where is she?" my mother demanded. "I'll kill the little vixen!"

Just then, I noticed the motive of her anger. Bizzy had untied her messy bun so I could see her hair loose for once. The tip of her shoulder-length blonde hair was dyed in the same pink sported by Claudia, across a surface of about three inches. I gasped.

"Look at that! She ruined me!"

Claudia bravely stuck her head out of the kitchen.

"You asked for it!"

"I would never!" Bizzy said.

"You did too. You said you wished you had taken more risks when you were young-"

"I am young!" Bizzy snarled.

"And you thought my hair was cool and you wanted the same," Claudia continued, retreating farther behind the door.

I could see recognition registering on Bizzy's face. Her anger remained unaltered all the same.

The young housekeeper spoke again. "You asked for the whole head but I figured *this* might happen when you sobered up. This way you can hide it in your boring buns."

"Classic. Buns are classic."

"I think it looks good," I said, trying to diffuse the tension.

"Sloane!" Bizzy said.

I retreated toward the kitchen and Claudia.

I had to give her credit. As far as it went, the kitchen was a clever holing up spot. If we had to hide away from Bizzy for a while, at least we would have enough coffee and food to sustain ourselves during the siege.

Bizzy observed my not-so-subtle recoil with exasperation. She grunted again then stomped away from the living room and up the stairs. Her disheveled hair swatted her shoulder blades, resembling a gliding pink and golden bird.

"I knew she couldn't be that cool," Claudia mumbled behind me.

The right corner of my mouth lifted of its own accord; the order of my house was restored.

I finally got around to taking that cool shower I desperately needed. Then I sat at the dining table to fill in the girls' paperwork that needed to be turned in before the end of the school year, just a week and a half away from now.

As usual since my daughters had entered my life, I asked myself the same question: *Where had the year gone?*

Every end of the year, birthday, and Christmas, time came nagging at me, reminding me of life's fleeting quality. The girls grew, seasons changed, and I stood in the midst of the constant swirl, baffled at how unseeingly the new year had crept up on me.

This year's pace had been very strange. Since the divorce, time seemed to have slowed down to a torturous halt while I waited by the phone for Tom to call and apologize. But from the moment I decided to take matters in my own hands and started staking out Katherine Stappleton, it had felt like my life was stuck on fast forward.

In two weeks, Tom would move in with Kate and my chances at reuniting my family would go down the drain. Now was the time for Hail Marys. Although not a spiritual person, I found myself praying for a miracle.

The doorbell saved me from my depressing thoughts – mortality and the end of a love story. *What a cheerful Sunday morning!*

Bizzy's face appeared in the staircase. "Who is it?"

Claudia recoiled behind the couch, dropping her novel on the rug as she did.

"I haven't the faintest idea," I replied, walking to the door.

I looked through the peephole and discovered Tom holding each girl with one hand on my doorstep. I stared at the sky; was this the divine intervention?

I gave myself a once over. I wore ugly cut-off shorts and Ethan's *Coors* beer tee.

"Claudia," I hissed. "Claudia!"

The third attempt got her out of the living room. She scanned the hallway, probably afraid to run into Bizzy. When she realized it was safe, relief flooded my housekeeper's features. I gestured toward my outfit then pointed at the stairs. Claudia's eyebrow hitched in a question mark.

"Get the door. I'll go change," I translated into words before running to my bedroom.

Halfway up the stairs, I heard the bolt unlock.

"And my day just went from bad to worst!" Claudia said.

I could picture Tom correcting her grammatical mistake and the argument that would surely ensue. I had to stop it before Claudia tore his throat.

Foraging through my closet for something more feminine to change into, I fell head first, literally, on a sky blue jersey dress, took it as a sign from heaven, and shrugged into it. The fabric draped prettily at the shoulders and flowed down to my knees. The color would complement the bruise I felt flourishing on my forehead from the dive in my closet. I slipped on jeweled sandals, patted my hair hopelessly, and then ran downstairs.

Tom's head peeked out above Claudia's shoulder. His eyes that crinkled at the corner with a perpetual look of amusement now drooped down as if he were utterly exhausted; probably Claudia wearing him down with her usual verbal joust. With her fists on her hips, she looked like a miniature, pink-headed bouncer.

I rushed to Tom's rescue but got captured by my girls on the way.

"Mummy!" they cried in unison.

Poppy's chubby arms circled my bare leg while Rose interlaced her slender fingers with mine. I kissed my eldest's cheek while ruffling Poppy's curls.

"You look like a princess, Mummy." Poppy clapped.

Rose looked more dubious. I was about to ask what was bothering her but Poppy dragged her to the kitchen.

"Let's bake a cake!" Poppy suggested enthusiastically.

I swallowed painfully. It would take me hours to clean up her mess. But I couldn't be the one that turned her lovely dimples into a frown. Maybe if Claudia supervised, we could keep the havoc to a minimum. Rose seemed to read my mind.

"Don't worry, Mummy. I'll help." Her little forehead creased as she considered the herculean task ahead.

"Thank you, little mommy. I'm sending Claudia as backup."

Rose nodded in dismay. "Claudia, Mummy? Really?"

I watched my friend's frail silhouette in a shimmery pink, cropped tee and black leather pants. With her platform shoes, Claudia barely reached Tom's chin, who wasn't that tall anyway. Rose, in her dark blue leggings and liberty blouse, looked more adult than Claudia did, if not for the height and baby face. I suspected she was the most mature person in my packed house.

I smiled apologetically to Rose then headed for the door.

Tom barely stood his ground on the doorstep before Claudia in full bull mode.

"Hi, babe." He grinned.

"What are you doing here? I wasn't expecting you for hours."

Tom shifted his weight from one foot to the other like a little boy.

"Yes. What is he doing here?" Claudia asked me.

"I could return the question," Tom said. "Has she finally decided to work? Making up for all those hours she owes us?"

"I don't work for you. This is not your house anymore. Thank God!"

"Claudia's spending the weekend over," I said.

I nudged Claudia to the side, so we ended up shoulder to shoulder.

"You still haven't told me," I said. "Was something wrong?"

Tom glared at Claudia but she stood her ground. To me, he said, "No. Nothing. Kate had a last minute lunch plan." *Still avoiding my daughters, apparently.* "And the girls missed you."

I raised an eyebrow.

"They've been awake for ages already," he said. "My apartment is a mess and the fridge is empty. I'm in over my head without you to help."

In those rare moments of total honesty, Tom was the most adorable man alive. I fought the urge to smooth the lines of worry from his forehead just like I had with Rose earlier today. Rose was a mini-me, but right now her father looked so much like her, it was frightening. Tenderness wrapped around me like a shawl.

"First smart words that ever escaped those lips," Claudia said, breaking the spell.

I channeled my bad-cop/mommy glare.

"Enough. Can you go check on the girls?"

"I would rather stay here."

"Claudia, please. They're baking."

156

She rolled her eyes and lifted her palms to the sky.

"Okay. Okay. But you owe me."

"Sure."

I turned sideways to make sure she'd left then looked back to Tom on my doorstep. I noticed now that he wore tennis shorts and a matching polo.

"Sorry about that. I guess you have somewhere to go," I said.

Tom took a step to my right side and kept staring at me in silence.

"Tom?" I snapped my fingers in front of his nose. "What?"

I looked down and remembered the reason why I had never worn the dress before. On both sides of my body, the dress had slits that went from under my arms all the way to my panties. Claudia had insisted I get the dress and I had relented, thinking I would wear it with a slip underneath. Instead, I had no slip, no bra, and okay-looking white cotton panties.

I was basically naked – something that was reflected in Tom's narrowed pupils and dumb silence. My ego enjoyed his attention very much but then I remembered Rose's skeptical expression and I couldn't wait to change into something less revealing. I was a respectable mother after all.

"I have to get back inside. Have a good game."

Tom tore his gaze away from my bare right boob and blinked a few times.

"Game? What game?"

"Well, tennis, obviously," I gestured to his clothes.

"Oh! That! We're playing later with Nisha and Vijay."

The 'we' made me angry.

"I bet Kate plays better than me," I said.

"Babe. A racket alone plays better than you."

I smiled despite my best effort. There was no denying it; I was the worst player ever.

"Have fun," I said, still sulking a little bit as I closed the door.

Tom blocked it open with his hand. I held my breath.

"I was thinking—"

That he wanted to come home? That he loved us – me and my tiny, naked boobs – madly?

"Well, Kate has her lunch and I'm not meeting her before 2 p.m."

He wanted to be fed, I substituted rightfully. Clearly not the love declaration I had hoped for but I tried to see the positive anyway. Didn't they say that the key to a man's heart was his stomach?

I mentally reviewed the contents of my fridge. Was there a recipe on Google to mend a marriage? A dish to dish Kate? Something so sweet Tom would stick at home?

Tom didn't bother to finish his question. Instead, he went around me, stepped inside the hallway, and emptied his pocket on the console. At least he still felt at home here.

"Tom!" Bizzy walked to him, arms extended and burgundy lips puckered for a kiss.

They air kissed, barely touching cheeks.

"It's good to see you. With Sloane's hectic weekend, you're in luck our cook *extraordinaire* doesn't have other plans."

I stared at Bizzy. What was she up to now?

"She's a busy girl, you know."

Tom laughed. "Friday night was definitely thrilling. I'm sorry about that, by the way," he told me in passing.

Better than nothing. Yet he couldn't believe I might have a life outside of him. Coming from the guy who had been married to me for almost a decade, it stung. I blinked to keep from crying.

Bizzy's eyes had turned even chillier than usual despite her courteous smile. My eyes bulged out of my face in a silent plea. Tom thinking I had no life played in my favor.

"I don't know what you're talking about, Mom. My weekend has been utterly boring."

Tom raised his shoulders and pointed at me. *You see? I'm right*, the gesture told Bizzy.

For some reason, Bizzy chose to ignore my wishes and

kept going.

"Only if you consider going on a date to Chiltern Firehouse with a Colombian magnate boring," Bizzy said.

"Hot!" Claudia pitched in from the kitchen. "Super hot," she added before growing quiet again.

Tom downright laughed at that. Then he grew thoughtful. "Seriously? You had a date?"

"Not really. It's complicated…"

I waved Tom in, resolute to save the day despite Bizzy's best effort at sabotaging me. Instead, Tom seemed to change his mind and picked up his wallet and keys from the console.

"Come to think of it, I'm gonna go. I'd rather have lunch at the club."

"You're sure?"

Bizzy answered for him. "Sounds good. Girls! Come say goodbye to your dad!"

Poppy rushed in, covered in chocolate from head to toe. Rose followed, eyebrows knotted.

"I did my best, Mummy." She shook her pretty head in defeat.

I hugged her close. "Thank you, baby. I know you did."

Tom kneeled down and opened his arms for a group hug, careful to keep Poppy's chocolaty paws at a distance.

"See you later, Tom," I said, while holding the door for him.

As soon as he left, I pinched Bizzy's arm.

"Ouch! What—?" she asked as she followed me into the living room.

"What is wrong with you?" I hissed, trying my best not to burst from fury.

"Wrong? I thought you would thank me." She looked truly surprised at my reaction.

"Thank you? You're dead set on ruining my life and I should thank you? Why don't you want me to be happy?"

I realized my voice had grown louder so I forced myself to calm down.

"Stop your nonsense, Sloane. The man requires a push.

A good dose of jealousy is exactly what he needs."

"You're trying to sabotage my marriage!"

"Sabotage?" She sniggered. "There's nothing to sabotage! You're not even married anymore!"

The nerve of that woman! I looked for a clever response, but to no avail. Shoving away the tiny voice whispering to me that she was right, I stormed out of the living room, my dignity in shreds.

Chapter Fourteen

"Hit it," Sven challenged me on Tuesday.

"You're crazy. That's way too high. I can't—"

"Hit it," Sven repeated.

I stared at his hand, level with my nose and just a few feet away from it.

"You do it," I said.

"Sloane," he warned.

How sweet, sheepish Sven could turn so confident and authoritarian on a tatami was a mystery to me. I sighed in defeat and focused on his hand for balance. Without moving an inch, I lifted my right leg and kicked it toward his hand with all my might.

"Aaargh!" I screamed as I missed the hand by a whole head and my heel connected instead with Sven's shoulder. My leg curled at an odd angle around the giant's body and brought us both down to the ground. I fell on my back with a loud thump against my Kung Fu teacher.

"Are you all right?" I asked as soon as I recovered from the fall. "Are you breathing?"

"Well, he wouldn't be able to answer you if he wasn't," Claudia said from the kitchen.

Sven grunted, reassuring me that he was still alive and well. Claudia came strolling in the living room and hovered above us.

"What did you do to him? My warrior, are you okay?"

I laughed at the ridiculous nickname and the feat I'd accomplished.

"I brought you down! I made you fall," I chanted.

More grunting. The doorbell rang then.

"I'll get it," Claudia said. "Move away from my man,"

she added with a smile.

I wished I could, but it was harder than it looked. I rolled myself from left to right to find enough momentum to slide off Sven. When I did, I landed face down next to him, my hand resting on a very awkward part of his anatomy.

"What the hell are you doing?" I heard Tom ask.

Startling me in this position wasn't the greatest idea. I pressed on my hand instead of removing it, resulting in another painful grunt from Sven.

"If you hurt the goods, I'll kill you," Claudia threatened again, this time dead serious.

I extended a hand to Tom who helped me to my feet.

"So that's the handsome Colombian magnate?" Tom sounded a little on edge as he pointed to Sven.

I took in Sven's white blond hair and clear blue stare. Colombian? *Really?*

"How observant of you," I said, chuckling. "No, he's not my handsome anything."

I turned to Sven, afraid I might have hit his susceptibility. Looks were everything to the underwear model. "You're undeniably gorgeous; you're just not mine," I explained.

A wide smile blossomed on his young face.

"Tom, this is Sven, my Kung Fu teacher. The kimonos might have given us away."

"You? Kung Fu?"

I sighed loudly. Could people's reactions be less redundant?

"Yes, me. Why are you here so early?"

"My last appointment got canceled. I figured I might as well come pick up the girls directly."

This, or he was still hung up on the news about Gabriel. Perhaps he cared…

"I'm sure they'll be thrilled to see you. I packed their bags already so they're set to go. Girls!" I called out as I climbed the stairs toward my shower. "Daddy's here!"

I remembered Sven in the living room. "Bye, Sven! See you tomorrow."

Poppy barreled down the stairs, pink backpack in tow. I

held onto her shoulders long enough to give her a hug then let my tornado resume her descent. The culprit for her excessive energy was most certainly the box of chocolate cookies I had left in her room before Sven arrived. Confirmation could be found in the large chocolate stain she had just left on my kimono. I congratulated myself for the success of my cunning plan. *Good luck, Kate!*

I met Rose on the landing. She muttered to herself, looking utterly spent as she held onto the straps of her backpack as if it were the Earth on Atlas's shoulders. I leveled my face with hers and pushed a strand of her hair behind her ear.

"Everything okay, baby?"

"I tried, Mummy. I tried..." She lifted delicate hands above her head. "I told her only two cookies but there was no stopping her." She brought her hands down in defeat. "I even ate half of them to make sure she wouldn't. Oh dear!" She sighed, clutching her stomach.

Her skin had taken on a greenish hue. Apparently, my master plan was backfiring on me. I took the bag away from Rose and scooped her up in my arms.

"Let's get you some soda water, baby. You'll feel better in a jiffy, you'll see," I promised as we descended the stairs.

"No shower?" Claudia raised a thin eyebrow when we stepped inside the kitchen.

Tom was washing Poppy's hands and face in the sink.

"There's no way you're stepping inside my car like that. Do you know how much it costs to have the seats cleaned?"

Poppy giggled and squirmed, leaving wet stains all over Tom's pinstriped shirt. He held on tight and proceeded to dry her hands with kitchen towels.

"What is wrong with her?" Tom asked me under his breath. "She's possessed!" he exclaimed before releasing his hold on our youngest.

Rose moaned in my arms. I dropped her on a kitchen stool and went to grab a soda water from the fridge.

"Coke," she murmured. "I think I need Coke."

Not so sick apparently. It was a rule in the house that

Coca Cola could be had only as a remedy. As a result, the girls used the sickness card to its maximum.

"What's up with her?" Claudia asked, pointing her chin at Rose.

"Cookie overdose."

"Chocolate cookies!" Poppy chimed happily before diving under my legs as if they were a bridge.

She tried to do the same with Claudia.

"Oh, no you don't. I'm not freaking Gymboree."

The toilet flushed next door. I expected Bizzy but it was Sven instead who strolled into the kitchen. He sat next to Rose, whose heart-shaped face turned crimson. She gazed up at him, all thoughts about her upset stomach apparently forgotten.

"Should I worry?" Claudia asked me with a smile in her voice.

"Oh, definitely!" I whispered. "Big crush! Huge!" I mimicked by opening my arms wide.

"I thought you had gone home, Sven—"

"He's waiting for me," Claudia answered for him. She blushed like a little girl, a surprising expression on my tough-as-nails housekeeper's face. "He's taking me on a date."

"Second one?" I asked, hoping that at least one of us might get laid tonight.

"First." She gave me a knowing nod.

"Well, I guess I'm not going anywhere tonight," I said. "I can't leave Rose like that."

"And I'm not taking her home with me. If she throws up on the curtains, Kate will be super pissed," Tom said. "I knew you had a date!"

Why did he care?

"It's too bad you have to cancel," he continued, though his voice clearly said otherwise. He sounded triumphant. "I really want to spend time with the girls. I have an idea. Why don't we all stay here tonight?"

I scratched my chin as I studied the face I had come to know so well during our marriage. What was Tom up to?

Did I detect jealousy under the light tone and cool attitude? Excitement pulsed in my chest before a not-so-happy realization doused it. If Tom was indeed jealous, then that meant Bizzy had been right and I'd been out of line the other day.

Despite that major setback, my enthusiasm returned along with hope for my family. Maybe my plan had indeed been genius and like chess players, I had calculated each moves up to this one. Maybe my subconscious was brilliant but I was too blonde to realize it. I could make spaghetti and meatballs marinara and –

"You have a date, Mummy!" Rose exclaimed, dragging me away from my planning and crashing me back down in a mess. "You can't cancel it! It could be your one and only chance!"

Melodramatic and flattering. Tom chuckled beside me.

"He could be your true love, Mummy. You have to go! You can't cancel for me!"

"It's okay, baby. It's not really a date. He's just a friend."

"So a date," Claudia whispered in my ear.

"You have to go!" Rose grabbed my hand, her eyes becoming suppliant. "I'd never be able to live with myself if you missed out on your true love because of me."

What the hell did she read? I made a mental note to give her library a much needed spring-cleaning. She talked like a Barbara Cartland heroine.

I tried to change the subject but to no avail. Rose was dead set on sending me out on a date with Gabriel.

"I can't leave you here alone."

"Bizzy is here. And Daddy will stay with us. You said you wanted to spend time with us, right?" She smiled expectantly at Tom.

Hanging out with Bizzy might not have been what he had in mind, but Rose's hopeful eyes were impossible to resist.

"Of course I'll stay." He kissed her forehead and walked to me. "I can't believe you're going out when your daughter's sick," he said under his breath.

Great. Not only did I miss out on a romantic dinner with

Tom but now I was heading to a guilt party instead. I sighed and stared into Rose's eyes, green and grey glimmers dancing in the iris's light azure that were the exact replica of mine.

"You're sure you'll be fine?" She nodded solemnly. I lifted my arms in the air, palms turned outward in surrender. "Okay…you win."

"Yes!" Rose said.

"Go get ready," Claudia said.

"I love you, Mummy," Poppy said.

I kissed Poppy's delicious cheek swiftly before leaving my overcrowded kitchen to jump into the shower. When I came out, clean and wrapped in my favorite robe, Rose, Poppy, and Claudia were waiting for me on my king-sized bed.

I modeled a few outfits before we all came to an agreement over the black dress I was admiring in the mirror. The V-neck plunged low, stopping somewhere at the base of my breasts. That was the one good thing about having no boobs. No décolleté on earth could appear vulgar. That, and not having to wear a bra all the time . . .

The dress made me look slimmer, mostly because of the contrast between the tight waist and the knee length skirt that flared at the hips. A rare occurrence for me, I was quite content with the way I looked. I even twirled, to the great delight of Poppy who was obsessed with swirling skirts.

Rose ceremoniously picked out high heels to complete my outfit. To her, they must have held the same significance as Cinderella's glass slipper – the key to my true love's heart. Poppy tried to impose her pink bunny backpack on me. In the end, we convinced her that the black beaded clutch, half-forgotten under my bed, was a way more suitable option.

"Black is not happy," she had commented sadly.

"You make me happy, little bunny," I'd whispered into her warm curls.

At 7.45 p.m., I downed the last drop of my white wine while waving goodbye to Sven and Claudia. Tom was only too glad to see the Nordic god go.

"Goodbye," he said, squaring his shoulders to look buffer than he actually was as he shook Sven's hand. I was surprised he didn't growl or do something equally stupid to prove his manhood.

Like most small canines, Tom felt compelled to bark louder than the larger species in the room. Sven's mere existence was a threat to my ex's virility, especially once he mentioned his career as an underwear model. Like all big dogs, though, Sven was oblivious to Tom's snide remarks.

"Careful with your man there," Tom told Claudia with a sly smile. "Looks like he's got his panties in a bunch."

Claudia gritted her teeth, her eyes set on me as if to say she let Tom live only as a favor to me. Two hours of dumb jokes about underwear was more than we could all take.

Unaware of how petty he sounded, Tom couldn't resist dropping one last joke.

"What's wrong, Claudia? Cat got your thong?"

Bizzy, who sat quietly in her beloved armchair, huffed impatiently.

"Tom dear?"

"Yes, Bizzy?"

"Why don't you shove it?" She asked, staring into her half-emptied martini glass. "You're being crass."

I snorted unattractively, her outburst so uncharacteristically funny. She answered my bout of hilarity with a silencing glare. Since our fight two days ago she had been avoiding me and apparently she wasn't ready to forgive me yet. I'd tried to corner her in the kitchen earlier in the evening to present my apologies but she'd artfully eluded me.

Poppy had insisted she stay up past her bedtime and she now sat with her sister by the window. They had their noses pressed against the glass panes to make sure they wouldn't miss my date. For the past half an hour, every time a man walked past the window, Rose swooned over his good looks and Poppy repeated her sister's comments. And each time, Tom grunted in response but glanced outside all the same.

The sight of Claudia and Sven walking side by side toward the entrance door lifted my mood. His arm dangled close to her, as if he wanted to hold her hand but was too shy to try it. Claudia had borrowed a dress from my closet. It really was more of a tunic for me but it fit her. It also was the only piece of clothing that belonged to me that didn't look like a parachute on her. She had made a concession on the dress but not on the shoes, so between the loose dress and heavy platform shoes, her legs looked even more fragile than usual.

From the back, she could have been fifteen, and her smile when Sven opened the door for her was just as juvenile. I waved goodbye once more, then stared back at my empty glass, contemplating refilling it one last time.

"Incoming!" Claudia yelled from the door, before disappearing in the street.

She left the door open. I walked swiftly to the girls and hugged them goodnight. They didn't care one bit about me, too mesmerized by Jimmy the driver to give me the time of day.

"He's dreamy," Rose said with a sigh as she rested her cheek against her hand.

"He's—" Poppy stopped mid-sentence and pursed her lips as she saw Jimmy more clearly.

No matter how much she wanted to emulate her big sister, the driver's red hair, sail-shaped nose, and crooked teeth stopped her short. Tom joined us and craned his neck to see outside.

"That's your hot Colombian?"

His chest began heaving with deep laughs and tears pooled at the corner of his eyes. Jimmy disappeared from our angle of vision and rematerialized in the doorframe. He knocked at the door.

"Hello?"

"No, Tom, dear. That would be the driver," Bizzy said.

Tom's good humor died instantly. With a hawk-like gaze, he stared outside again, spotting the Mercedes with its black tinted windows.

"But, Mummy, I want to see him!"

Rose held onto her stomach and made a show of being sick even though she hadn't mentioned her stomachache all evening; my little actress. I would have obliged her had Tom not been here. But at this point, asking Gabriel to come in felt like dousing a fire with gasoline.

"Sorry, baby. Maybe next time. Hi, Jimmy," I said just as Rose began moaning. "I'll be there in a minute."

"Sure, ma'am. No worries."

The chauffeur sauntered away from the front steps. Tom, who had closed the distance between us without me noticing, grabbed my arm a tad too strongly. He released his grip as soon as he noticed me wince.

"Just don't come home too late, okay? I'll be waiting for you."

I stared into his puppy dog eyes and smiled back at him. This was precious. Seeing Tom vulnerable was too rare an occurrence not to appreciate it. My heart leapt in my chest as I recognized jealousy. If he cared, then things were definitely not hopeless.

Tom quickly shrugged it off. If there was one thing Tom hated above all, it was being pitied. Unfortunately, he often mistook concern for pity when it was bestowed upon him.

"I have things to do, you know?" he said to inflate his ego.

"Oh!" Rose exclaimed from her lookout post.

I turned toward the window just in time to see Gabriel exit the Mercedes. Rose would be granted her wish after all.

My date was as handsome as ever in blue slacks and a white polo. He leaned against the car, an amused expression on his face. Not a date, I chided myself for the hundredth time.

"I'd better go," I said, blowing kisses at my daughters who clearly didn't care one bit about me leaving.

Tom had returned to his observation post, next to the girls. I dashed outside. As I crossed the threshold, I heard the girls sigh.

"He's dreamy," they swooned in unison.

"Yes, Rose, honey. For once you are right," Bizzy replied. "But I think the right word for him is *yummy*."

I almost backtracked. How many martinis had she had already?

But then Gabriel's eyes lit up for me and his lips curled up into a seductive smile. I reminded myself that a very sober Tom was with the girls and I leaned in for a kiss on the cheek. Gabriel lingered just a second too long before pointing at the window and the two tiny faces contorted against the window so hard, they looked like pugs.

"Yours, I presume?"

"Yes." I smiled apologetically before cracking up.

Rose was kissing the window by now, imitated by Poppy. Gabriel waved to them, his bleached white teeth gleaming. They eagerly returned his wave.

Tom's cross face hovered above theirs.

"The ex?" Gabriel asked, as he nodded toward Tom.

I sighed. Tom folded his arms in front of his inflated chest. Gabriel's eyes turned glassy but his lips still curled up in a smile. He touched his forehead with two fingers then moved them toward Tom in a salute. Tom glared back.

Yep. Not awkward at all. Great.

"Shall we?" Gabriel asked as he opened the car's door for me.

"Yes please," I said as I waved one last time myself, then rushed into the car.

Chapter Fifteen

A short ride later, we stopped in front of the Arts Club.

"But I thought you weren't a member?" I asked as Jimmy let me out.

Gabriel came up next to me and circled my waist with his arm. The tingle that shot through my body made me flinch. Maybe I should see a neurologist. There must be something wrong with me, the way I reacted so strongly to the merest touch. Or maybe you should get laid, the mischievous voice in my head suggested quite cleverly.

"I am now," Gabriel said as he ushered me in.

I watched Hector's stern attitude that clashed with the red and gold silk skirt he sported, as he scoured the reception then the dining room before giving us the green light.

"But the membership waiting list is one year long. At least!"

"I've got my ways," he said, a childlike grin etched across his beautiful face.

New receptionist, same reaction. The red-haired hostess looked like she might self-combust when she spotted Gabriel.

"Mr. Varela," she purred. "Your table's ready."

Our table was on the terrace, by the large mirror that covered the whole wall and made the outside space appear twice as big as it actually was.

Maybe Ethan's landlord could use this trick. It could make the rooms almost human sized instead of catering only for Oompa-Loompas.

I hated it when Ethan popped into my head like that. I shoved him out of my thoughts quickly and returned my attention to Gabriel who was just done ordering an expensive bottle of white wine.

Gabriel squeezed my hand. "Is she here?"

I scratched my head. "Who?"

"Your nemesis, of course. Nisha. Why do you think I brought you here?" His eyes twinkled with mischief.

"You're hoping for a catfight?"

"That would definitely make the evening interesting but that's not exactly what I had in mind." He chuckled. "You said she cast you aside since the divorce and has been snubbing you ever since. I thought tonight could be payback."

"How?"

"Well, using me, of course." He winked. "What better revenge than parading your extremely attractive and filthy rich lover in her club?"

The word *lover* made my heartbeat race and my cheeks turn feverishly red. Conceited as Gabriel may sound, his intentions were sweet. My own knight in shining armor, standing up for me. I couldn't remember when was the last time someone had gone to such lengths to make me feel good about myself. We might only be fake dating, but this was proof that he truly cared.

"So is she here?" he asked again.

I scanned the terrace, using the mirror to be more inconspicuous. Sure enough, Nisha was sitting on the opposite side of the patio, in the lounge area, having drinks with an attractive couple. Vijay, her husband, stood a few tables away, talking animatedly to an older looking man smoking a cigar.

They were working the crowd separately as was usual for them, trying to make the most out of the exorbitant membership fees.

As if she could feel my eyes on her, Nisha stood up and looked in our direction. She caught my reflection in the mirror and paused when she spotted Gabriel next to me.

Confusion danced in her lovely eyes as she probably wondered what a man like him could be doing with me. I would have been upset at her reaction had I not known she

172

was totally right. I still couldn't comprehend why Gabriel paid me any kind of attention.

Nisha wasn't the type of succubus – *uh, woman* – to stay puzzled for too long. She thrust her lovely chin up and smoothed the silk of her orange blouse before fending off the crowd in our direction.

"She's here," I hissed. "And she's coming."

"Ah!" Gabriel rubbed his hands in anticipation. "Let the games begin!"

I trained my eyes on Gabriel and left them there till Nisha's posh accent forced me to turn around.

"Sloane!"

I flailed my arms awkwardly to feign surprise at seeing her here, which only made me look like a giant, crazed chicken. Gabriel's grin grew wider but Nisha remained impassive. After all, she had been my friend for years; she knew the dramatic extent of my acting skills.

"Won't you introduce me to your friend?" Nisha suggested with her sweet, evil smile, her own version of arm-twisting.

"Yes," I stuttered.

As usual, Nisha brought out the teenager in me. I couldn't help being impressed by her radiating confidence.

"This is my friend, Gabriel Varela." I pointed at him. "Gabriel, meet Nisha Kothari."

"It's nice to meet—" Nisha started as she hovered over our table, apparently waiting for Gabriel to stand up and air kiss her.

But instead Gabriel seemed absorbed by my hand, kissing the palm with fervor.

"*Divina*," he said, as he applied one last kiss on my wrist before finally acknowledging Nisha.

He shook her hand across the table in a very un-European fashion.

"Hello, Nisha."

His gaze bore through me as he scolded me kindly.

"Really, *mi corazòn*. We are more than friends, aren't

we?"

What the heck?

To avoid answering the question, I took a huge gulp of water. It went into my airways, making me choke. I dried the tears that had sprung to my eyes while trying to figure out what his declaration made me feel.

I had to admit it – some tiny part of me was ecstatically glad that Gabriel thought of me as his girlfriend. He was handsome, kind, worldly, and he seemed to find me attractive. I never thought anyone but Tom could like me, let alone profess to be my boyfriend after just two dates.

But for the most part, he was putting me in a world of trouble. Didn't he know that Nisha was the most notorious gossip in London? I was sure I had told him.

Now she would run her mouth and tomorrow I would graduate from lonely, dormant potential danger, to full-fledged menace to the male population. No man at school would be allowed less than twenty feet away from me.

And how would Tom react? He might get more jealous, which would be good for me, or super pissed and that would be bad. The problem with Tom was that his ego always took precedence over his heart. I was pretty sure he wouldn't enjoy hearing that his wife paraded her new lover at the club. Not that he ever showed any reservation about doing the same with Kate.

Nisha looked like she had swallowed a sour pill.

"How lovely for you two," she commented drily before retrieving her fake enthusiasm. "Let me ask the waiter for a chair. Then you can tell me all about the way you two met. I'm sure it's fascinating!"

A timely phone call saved us from Nisha's invasion. Gabriel's eyes looked drawn as he stared at his cell's screen. His tone turned metallic as he let go of my hand and stood up.

"*Sì?* Hold on," he said into the receiver. Covering the phone with his hand, he added. "Ladies, if you'll excuse me."

Nisha stopped him before he could dash, her small hand

pressing insistently against his bicep.

"It was nice to meet you, Gabriel. I do hope I'll see you Thursday at the Gala!"

Oh no! Please god! I had completely forgotten about the stupid gala. I closed my eyes, refusing to watch the metaphorical car crash about to happen. Showing up at my daughter's school gala with Gabriel would be far more damaging to my reputation than mere rumors of a relationship. I would become Belgravia Prep's official pariah, dethroning even Slutty Stephanie.

And there was no way Tom would come back to me after what he would perceive as being publicly humiliated at the gala. I crossed my fingers and toes for good luck.

Gabriel's lips twitched impatiently.

"Sure. I'll be there," he said before leaving the terrace, phone screwed to his ear.

Had I been alone, I would have knocked my head against the table, again and again till I gratefully passed out. Actually I would even have done it in public. Just not in front of Nisha. Instead of finding relief in passing out, I stood up straighter and took a sip of the chilled white wine the waiter had served when I wasn't looking.

"Thank you for that," I muttered between clenched teeth.

"You're welcome," Nisha smiled sweetly, pretending not to hear the sarcasm in my voice. "I'd better let you get back to your romantic date, then," she waved goodbye.

Sure. Now that you've ruined my evening.

I opened my mouth to speak but decided against it. Whatever reproach I could serve her would be useless. In the end, Nisha wasn't a good person that had behaved badly toward me. She was a bad person through and through, with no redeeming qualities and no aspirations for ever doing the right thing. She was happy being superficial and vain. No matter how lonely I sometimes felt, I didn't need someone like her in my life.

"Goodbye, Nisha," I said, happy to be left alone with my thoughts.

Life was full of surprises these days and, although I still

hoped that there was a chance left for Tom and me, for our family, I now carried the deep certainty that I would be fine either way.

After thirty years of being transparent, I finally believed I might have some substance and it might be worth finding out who I could be. If Tom had done one good thing in leaving me, it was teaching me I was stronger than I ever suspected I could be. I couldn't help being grateful for that.

I also was grateful for Gabriel. However strange the circumstances of our meeting had been, it felt incredible knowing I had someone in my corner. His arrogance was only a mask hiding a kind, attentive man.

I considered thanking Kate for sending him my way. Without her, I would have never met Ethan, who in turn would have never asked me to spy on Gabriel. A flashback of Ethan's burning stare the other night, before our almost kiss, made my insides churn with desire for him and, at the same time, with guilt for Gabriel. The man was sweeter to me than anyone had ever been and how did I repay him? By spying on him.

As if he could hear my train of thoughts, Hector materialized at the edge of the table, startling me. I pushed against the back of my chair, in the vain hope that I could fuse with the lacquered wood and disappear. The security guy scared the hell out of me.

Hector sat down before me with a grace that was surprising for someone so overweight. His red satin shirt with yellow leaf motifs made me wish I hadn't touched the wine. Between the loud colors and his bushy mustache sprinkled with – *were those chip crumbs?* – I was beginning to feel seasick.

"Is there a problem?" I stuttered in an inaudible voice. "Where's Gabriel?"

I began to worry. Had something happened to Gabriel? Otherwise why would Hector feel comfortable enough to sit in his place? Why wasn't he prancing around the club, subject to his usual paranoia?

"*Mister* Varela is fine," he rolled the *r* in Gabriel's name with reverence while his eyes darted to the door of the restaurant, as if he were worried to see his boss. "You, *aunque*, will not be if you stick around him too long. I know you. Girls like you. You're no good. You're up to trouble. I can smell it," he said, pressing his oily, ugly nose with a stumpy index finger.

Instead of cleverly defending myself, my brain went on strike and my windpipes shut off. I shook my head no while wheezing awkwardly. The frightening thing about all of this was, Hector wasn't completely wrong about me.

He glanced again toward the door then stood up swiftly. In the mirror, I spotted Gabriel stepping onto the patio.

"*Acuerda te*," Hector whispered with a pleasant smile that didn't reach his eyes. "I'm watching you. You should disappear. *Poof*!" He popped his fingers open before his chest like a magician.

"Mister Varela," he said as he pulled Gabriel's chair out for him.

Gabriel sat down and apologized for the phone call. I blinked a few times, trying to tear my eyes away from Hector, who stood beside his boss, a benevolent smile on his face.

"Do you still need me, boss?"

Gabriel waved him away.

"Nice chat, Miss," Hector nodded to me before returning to his bodyguard duties.

"I'm very sorry about this," Gabriel apologized, circling my wrist with his long pianist fingers.

I stared blankly. Did he know what Hector just told me? Did Gabriel send him over to me?

"Business never sleeps." Gabriel sighed.

So he was referring to the phone call, not the lovely threats from Hector. Which meant that Hector probably came to see me behind his back. I considered telling Gabriel about it all but then again, I wasn't exactly beyond reproach myself. This could all blow up in my face.

"It's ok," I said too slowly.

Gabriel interpreted it like I was mad at him.

"Why don't you let me make this up to you? Come have lunch with me tomorrow. I'll leave my phone at the office so nothing comes between us again."

"Don't you need to work? You're leaving soon. You must be very busy." I spoke hurriedly, Hector's threats still fresh in my mind.

I was already seeing Gabriel on Thursday, so having lunch with him tomorrow might get his right-hand man riled up.

Gabriel smiled. "Don't worry; the office runs itself. Thank god for that! I just need to make an appearance once in a while to justify my substantial paycheck."

"Are you hiring?" I teased. "I wouldn't mind a job like that."

"Are you looking to be hired?" His eyes turned playful. "Cause I've got a few jobs for you in mind…"

My fingers fiddled with the napkin on my lap as I tried to recover from the innuendo's effect on my starved libido.

"Come have lunch with me. I'll head for the office in the morning, make a few rounds, pretend I care about business, and then you can meet me."

His description of work was precisely what was wrong with nepotism. I was about to point out how unfair it sounded toward his employees who actually did their jobs but he didn't give me a chance.

"I like you, Sloane. You're the most important thing in my life right now."

All reproaches about work disappeared, replaced by a goofy grin on my face. Every time Gabriel came close to annoying me, he said something so sweet it knocked the air right out of me.

"You know I'm supposed to leave at the beginning of next week. I want to get to know you better before that and figure out if there's a reason for me to extend my stay." He leaned in and kissed me below the ear, sending shivers down my spine. "Say you'll be mine until Sunday…"

Oh dear! Was I in trouble!

Chapter Sixteen

Per Gabriel's command, I drove to Varela Global the next day for our lunch date. I pretended my motivations were purely professional and had nothing to do with the butterflies fluttering in my stomach every time his face popped into my mind. Spending thirty minutes looking for the perfect outfit was only a necessary part of my quest for justice.

To clear my conscience, I'd decided to use the date as an opportunity to search Gabriel's office. It would also get Ethan off my back.

I parked two blocks away from Varela Global, hoping to make a discreet entrance inside the building, which would give me enough time to fulfill my mission. I was half an hour early. Plenty of time to get inside, and out, unnoticed.

I reached the sleek office building, cursing my choice of shoe apparel. Who wore stilettos in the middle of the day?

Me, the idiot with blisters.

I waited for a delivery guy to get near the revolving doors to hide in his wake. As soon as he stepped through the revolving doors, I jumped behind him, my gaze trained on his bald head while I struggled to take my hands off his ass in the cramped space.

Instead of serving as decoy, the delivery guy emitted startled noises that attracted the receptionist's attention. Very poor strategizing.

The receptionist's pretty blonde head snapped in my direction, a question mark hovering in her hazel eyes as she tried to situate me. A thirty-something-year-old man in a suit approached the woman.

"Brittany! How is the most beautiful woman in the world

doing today?" he asked.

She giggled as she twirled a blonde lock around her pinkie. The man bent over her desk.

"What do you have for me today, love?" he asked.

I used the distraction to make my way round the receptionist's desk, in a wide circle, keeping my eyes trained on them as I went. Brittany leisurely started sifting through the pile of mail before her, clearly enjoying the attention. I couldn't blame her. With his dirty blond hair and square jaw, her suitor was very cute. Was it company policy to hire only good-looking people? Just then, Hector's gross mustache popped into my mind and made me rethink the theory.

This man was a godsend; I'd almost made it to the elevator unnoticed. Apparently, there wasn't enough space in Brittany's head to fit both her suitor and me, the intruder. Then my shins hit an armchair set up in my way and I tumbled head first against the cushions, legs up and skirt hiking all the way to my waist.

I placed a hand against my butt in an attempt to salvage some decency while the couple at the desk erupted in laughter. *Note to self: throw away all ugly granny panties and make a pit stop at Victoria's Secret on the way home.*

I pushed myself back up, patted my hair back in place, and faced the receptionist. My cover was blown now.

"I'm meeting Mister Varela," I stammered before running to the elevator.

This statement seemed to sober her up. A mean sneer distorted her pretty features. I pressed the up button frantically.

"Wait, I need to call him," she said.

"No need. I know the way to his office," I told her as I jumped in the elevator cabin and pressed the penthouse button.

"Love? What about my mail?" The handsome angel of mercy distracted Brittany once more.

She bent over the mail, looking distraught. His flirting might have bought me a few minutes to search Gabriel's office and I was planning to make the most of it. No way was I going back to Ethan empty handed. If I did, I would never hear the end of it.

When the doors opened, I hesitated. Had I been mistaken on the floor? Gone was the ugly green carpet, replaced by a tasteful steel grey one. The furniture was sparse – a couple of lounge chairs by the elevator, a bronze folding screen with lace-like patterns all over its length, and a small glass side table with magazines stacked artfully across the surface. The paintings on the walls were the same as before, but in the new, understated décor, they glowed like prize gems.

I stepped gingerly out of the elevator, testing the carpet as if it were ice water ready to swallow me at the first wrong move. Ten feet in, and voices emanated from an office to my right.

"What if he finds out?" a woman asked anxiously.

"He won't. Gabriel is never here," a male voice answered, one I was pretty sure I recognized, and didn't like one bit.

The door was open so I couldn't scurry past it without being spotted and my mission compromised. Instead, I backtracked to seek refuge behind the folding screen.

"We've been keeping this secret for years and he's never suspected anything," I heard Hector say.

"Yes, but he's never come to the office as much."

"It's just a phase. He's bored."

The voices paused and I waited restlessly, sure I had stumbled upon something important. *I knew Hector was up to no good!* After just a couple of minutes that felt like ages, he spoke again.

"Trust me, Isabella, once he's over the dumb blonde, we'll never see him near the office again."

I could only assume I was the dumb blonde. *Jackass*.

"I hope so." The woman sighed.

I heard her heels click against wooden floors then her head popped out of the door, into the corridor. Although I was cleverly hidden behind the screen, I stopped breathing for fear of being discovered.

The woman, somewhere in her mid-fifties I presumed, twisted her neck left and right to make sure they were alone. She had shoulder length caramel hair and doe eyes. Clad in a navy skirt and white silk blouse, she looked beautiful still, and confident despite the worry that made her bite her lip.

We were alone in the corridor, and I was well concealed, but she closed the door on her way back anyway. I wished I could have heard more about their big secret but the door was thick enough to muffle their voices.

So instead I returned to my initial plan, praying the time I had lost waiting around wouldn't sign my demise. Creeping up the corridor, I looked at the plaque on the office door.

Isabella Munoz
Chief Financial Operator

I kept walking, a new theory blooming in my head. By the time I reached Gabriel's office, I was even less eager to search the premises. With my new belief in place, I was more certain than ever of Gabriel's innocence. To me it was clear his only sin was to be a lousy businessman.

I knocked lightly against the door, just in case Gabriel was inside although I didn't expect him to be. I counted to three then when no answer came, I edged my way through the massive glass doors.

Sure enough, there was no Gabriel in sight. As he'd told me yesterday, his job was to make rounds to remind his employees they had a boss, not to sit in his new beautiful office. But he would most probably stop by anytime soon, if only to come looking for me. I had to hurry.

Behind his desk, next to the sleek computer tower, stood a small cabinet with drawers. The key had been left in the hole, making my investigation way too easy.

If he had indeed been a crook, wouldn't he hide incriminating evidence instead of leaving it for everyone to find? This again comforted my gut feeling about Gabriel. Or maybe the loud pleading from my libido masked the sensible voice of reason. I decided to check the file cabinet to be sure.

I walked swiftly toward it then flung open the drawer. I had to stifle a laugh as I saw it was even emptier than my own at home. For a big import export magnate, he sure didn't store much. I wondered if apart from the decorating and socializing, he ever did any kind of work. Most probably he let his highly skilled management team do the job for him – Isabella Munoz, with her big, impressive title, at the top of the crew.

It made sense considering the management offices were in London and the guy lived halfway across the planet for most of the year. I doubted Gabriel helped his workers farm the greenhouses so that left him to have fun and reap the benefits of his employees' work. How could Ethan ever think he was the big brain behind a money laundering empire when the rare files in his cabinet were titled 'May in Harbour Island', or 'Fortieth Birthday Bash in Oslo'?

The files looked more like bored housewife planning than CEO strategizing, and certainly didn't contain scamming-the-government documents. Not that I was an expert.

Just to be on the safe side, I moved on to his desk drawers. I sat in the giant armchair I'd longed to try since my last visit and pulled on the top drawer carefully. Staples, staples, and more staples. No stapler in sight. Maybe hidden inside one of the boxes of office supplies lay illegal documents? The thought made me smirk and because I was bored, I toyed with a box while continuing to search the bottomless drawer.

My thoughts returned to Hector. *That backstabber!* I boiled with a sense of betrayal on Gabriel's behalf. I wished I could staple his ugly, oily face to avenge the sweet man who trusted him with his life. Gabriel was a good, decent man. He certainly didn't deserve having Hector go behind his back.

The selfish jerk embezzled money with that Isabella, I was sure of it. What other secret could he share with the elegant CFO? And who better to doctor the books than the woman in charge of all financial aspects of the company? It made me sick to my stomach.

If only I could find proof of their guilt, I could get Ethan to drop his case against Gabriel. The office I should scour was Isabella's, but I had no idea how to get access to it without being discovered. *And until then, guilty till proven innocent, right?* It just was way too easy to pin the embezzling on Gabriel.

"You're kidding me!" Kate's voice boomed inside the office, fright forcing me to drop the entire contents of the staples box in my hand.

Lost inside my feeling of indignation, I hadn't heard her come in. The tiny office supplies hit the floor with a metallic sound. I hid behind the desk, pretending to pick the staples up, as Kate marched up to the desk and slammed her hands onto the glass surface.

"You must be bloody mad! I told you to stay away from me." She shook her head vehemently. "But more importantly, I should have said to stay away from him."

"You already have my husband. What more do you want from me?"

"God, you sound like a broken record. Screw Tom! You can have him back." She bit her lip as if she realized she had made a mistake. "Just a figure of speech. I can't hand him back like that. Sorry," she mumbled as she walked around the desk to where I hid.

She extended her hand toward me, making me cower farther under the desk. I cursed the glass when it made contact with my head.

"I'm not going to slap you. I just want to help you up."

"I'm okay. I can stand up by myself. Thanks," I said, waiting for Kate to step back before daring to leave my shelter.

When she spoke again, my husband's mistress sounded exhausted, like all the fight had left her.

"Listen, Sloane. I've heard people talk about you."

I braced myself for the insults and list of my many flaws.

But Kate surprised me instead.

"You're a great mother and a good wife. A good, honest person." My chest swelled with pride but I reined in the smile trying to break through my tight lips. "But Gabriel is trouble."

"You're jealous."

Her humorless laughter was cut abruptly by the sound of footsteps outside the doors. Fortunately for us, Gabriel was way less inconspicuous than Kate had been coming in. We both retreated into sour silence as he stepped inside the office.

"Here you are! The receptionist told me I could find you here. I hope you didn't wait too long?"

I forced a smile on my face.

"Not at all. Kate was keeping me company," I said.

"Thank you, Kate." Gabriel nodded to her.

He walked round the desk and grabbed my hand.

"Come on. I want to take you to my favorite Italian restaurant. You'll love it!"

"That sounds great! I'm starving."

I nodded goodbye to Kate, my cheeks hurting from a forced grin and locked arms with Gabriel's. I had the upper hand for once and I wasn't going to let Kate's comments get under my skin.

Two hours later, Gabriel vanished through the revolving doors of Varela Global as I sighed in relief. My fingers were instantly on my skirt's waist button, snapping it open. At this rate of one date a day, I would outgrow my entire wardrobe in less than a week.

I pulled my tank top out of the skirt to hide the small, fat rubber ring hanging from it then made my way back to the car, cursing myself for parking so far.

All the way home, I fought against the food-binge-induced drowsiness that made my eyelids heavy like metal curtains.

When I spotted my favorite parking spot at last, right in front of my house and welcomingly empty, relief washed over me. But then I spotted a familiar silhouette sitting on the bench nearby and cussed like an old sailor.

Despite the six foot three of rugged male perfection awaiting me, I considered driving past and looking for another parking spot. Ethan stood between my desperately needed siesta and me. I could always sleep in the car elsewhere, rather than be questioned by Ethan for hours.

Hands gripping the steering wheel, eyes darting from Ethan to the road ahead, I tried to make a quick decision.

He wore the usual jeans and a short sleeved, V-neck tee that clung to his chiseled chest. His lean, muscular arms were crossed against him and his eyes were closed as he soaked in the sun. He was so perfectly immobile I let myself hope he was sleeping. With luck, I might be able to pass right by him.

I angled the car toward the curb and parked. I turned off the ignition and concentrated, trying to channel my inner ropedancer – graceful and quiet. Surely, there must be a small part of me that wasn't clumsy as a clown. Hopefully, there was…

While I concentrated, I watched Ethan's resting form. He must spend a lot of time outside these days because honeyed highlights were now weaved in his hair and stubble while his skin had taken on a darker hue. The tan was really flattering and most probably what he was used to, living in Florida. Ethan Cunning, Miami's smoking hot IRS agent. My jealousy extended to all Floridian women momentarily before I remembered that our relationship was strictly professional.

Seeing that he still seemed to be sleeping, I cracked the door open carefully, hoping to make it to the house unnoticed. But before I could even set a stilettoed foot out of the car, Ethan's tall body pounced away from the bench and he blasted the door wide open for me.

"Hello, Ms. *Makhni*," he said, chuckling at his own joke.

"Very funny," I said, recalling the night of my Indian food disaster.

Then I remembered we were standing right in front of my

house.

"Come in, quick!" I hissed, as I stumbled backward inside the car and closed the door in the same move.

Ethan jogged to the passenger side.

"Why so cramped?" he said, his chin resting on his knees as usual.

"Why so tall?" I replied. "What brings you here, Ethan?"

My eyes surveyed the sidewalk and my house's front steps.

"I thought our dealings were meant to remain secret. So let me point out that standing five feet away from my house isn't discreet. Not at all."

Ethan shrugged.

"After your phone call this morning, I had to see you. So what did you find?"

I had indeed called Ethan before heading to lunch to let him know I planned to search Gabriel's office. I just thought he would phone me later in the afternoon for debriefing.

"The search was a bust. The office was as empty as a bimbo's head." I smiled. "Sorry," I added as I read disappointment on his face .

His teeth were clenched and so was his fist. He slammed the latter against his thigh. I leaped in surprise.

"Damn it! Of course they must be hidden somewhere safer," he muttered.

I moved my hand tentatively toward his arm to comfort him, but then, seeing as he was seething, I decided against it. Better keep your distance from the awakened volcano.

"To be perfectly honest, I doubt Gabriel has files anywhere."

It was a miracle the man had learnt how to write between his unending parties and constant travels, let alone read a firm's annual report. I had learned more about his company from Wikipedia than in all our dates put together.

"What do you mean?" Ethan shot back at me.

"The man doesn't work. His title as CEO of Varela Global is purely honorary. Other people run the company," I explained, my infatuation for Gabriel crumbling off ever so slightly as I admitted what I knew to be true. "People who might be less scrupulous," I added, thinking of Hector and the mysterious Isabella Munoz.

"And do you have someone special in mind?"

"I do. I just can't prove it yet. I need to find more proof that Hector, you know, his chief of security and—"

Ethan ran his hand through his short hair while he laughed without humor.

"You think Hector, Tony Montana's wannabe, is the mastermind behind Varela Global's operations?"

"Not just him. Isa—"

"You might have a crush on Gabriel Varela, but come on. Even you can't be that naïve."

Because Ethan looked desperate, and I did, truth be told, lack any kind of solid proof, I bit my lip hard and quit arguing. His anger was understandable with his job probably on the line here. Although it wasn't my fault he had the wrong suspect in his line of sight, I decided to take the high road this time.

"Gabriel's escorting me to my daughters' school gala tomorrow. I'll try to get you more info then."

"Sure. When you're not too busy socializing, drinking champagne, or flirting with Varela," he said.

I struggled hard to keep my temper in check. Ethan truly had a talent to bring the worst in me.

"I'm *not* dating Varela. I'll remind you that you asked *me* to get close to him and by seeing *him*, I'm doing *you* a favor. Besides, what I have with Gabriel can't be real because I believe Tom might be coming around, and as my husband, he is my priority."

I took a second to breathe and collect myself. When I spoke again, my voice had ceased quivering.

"And for that I have to thank *you*. If you hadn't asked me to throw myself at Gabriel, then Tom wouldn't have been jealous and my marriage would still be over."

I put a hand on Ethan's knee and forced the regret I felt at realizing I was a married woman once again to the back of my head. My eyes lingered on his dimple, his lips. I strained them up to meet his eyes that looked clouded.

"So thank you," I said, hoping I sounded more convinced than I actually was.

"I can't believe you're that stupid." Ethan looked bewildered as he pried my hand away from his knee.

My jaw went slack.

"I'm sorry?" I asked.

"Tom is an absolute jerk and after the way he treated you, you still want him back? He's your priority?" he mocked in a girlish voice. "Are you brain dead?"

"What have I ever done to you?" I squeaked, all the air sucker-punched from my lungs.

"To me? Nothing." He laughed before frowning. "What are *you* doing to yourself?"

Ethan let me muddle his question while reorganizing his features into a mask of cool composure. The total control over his facial emotions made me think of Tom. Were all men I was attracted to chameleons?

No. At least Gabriel was genuine. He was good tempered, constant, and honest. Or so I hoped. Ethan's scorn was making me lose faith in the male species all over again.

When he spoke again, Ethan's voice had regained its original steadiness.

"I guess my initial assessment was right," he said, as he reclined as best as he could in the narrow space between the passenger seat and the dashboard.

Ethan locked his arms behind his head to relax further. His voice came out as a breeze.

"You truly are desperate." He yawned and stared ahead as if what he said wasn't slicing my soul like a knife.

My mouth opened and closed like a fish washed upon the shore, but no sound escaped my lips. My air pipes were sealed shut, crushed by the familiar insult and the wound it ripped open once more.

Ethan glanced my way before returning his blank gaze to the road. He repeated the operation a few times.

If he was waiting for a clever comeback or a biting

repartee, he could wait forever. I was damn well resolute never to speak to him again till the day I died. I stared at my lap to avoid his judgmental glare.

That he had categorized me into the desperate divorcee clan before meeting me was something I could forgive. After all, the evidence was against me. But after weeks knowing each other, working together, hanging out, and teasing one another, the blow was unforgivable. It was cruel, unjust, and just plain assholish.

Couldn't Ethan see how much I had grown and changed since I'd met him? I was Sloane 2.0, a better, more confident version of my old self. I went on dates, did Kung Fu, and I'd stood up to my mother only last weekend – true, I'd been wrong and had to apologize about that, but that shouldn't remove anything from the heroism it had taken to face Bizzy.

The tiny, nagging voice inside my head stopped my best attempt at ego boosting. What if Ethan was right? Maybe my updated version was still not good enough. Maybe I was lacking somehow. Was I ready to take Tom back after what he'd done to me, to our family?

The answer came instantly, irrevocably. *Yes, absolutely.* If Tom came back then I would mend my family. I would take much harder decisions for my daughters' sakes. So long as it kept them happy, I could deal with an unfaithful, two-faced husband.

Would I ever learn to trust Tom again? Only time would tell, but it was my problem, and my problem alone. Children shouldn't carry their parents' emotional burdens. For Rose and Poppy, I would greet their father with open arms and plaster a brave smile on my face every morning till one day, hopefully, I wouldn't have to fake it anymore.

After all, I'd been stupid in love with Tom once upon a time. That kind of love could be rekindled, *surely*.

Ethan glanced my way once more, launching me into action. I was so bitterly disheartened by his reproaches, the simple idea of sharing the air he breathed was too much to endure. I gathered my stuff and propped open the door.

Tears of betrayal broke my voice in painful shards as I spoke one last time to a man I'd thought I knew and respected.

"What I do with my life is in no way, near or far, your business."

My words sounded metallic, sharp. They seemed to echo from some faraway place, muffled by the buzzing in my ears. That single dreaded word – *desperate* – repeated, distorted, and amplified till it encompassed my whole mind.

"Never try to contact or see me again," I warned Ethan before slamming the door behind me and heading toward the house.

I didn't once look back. This time I was well and truly done with Ethan Cunning.

It took emptying my pockets on top of the hallway console to realize I had forgotten my car keys, and Ethan, inside the Mini Austin. After getting locked out of the house the other night, I had come up with the brilliant idea to separate car and house keys on two separate key chains. *Great move, Sloane!*

Well, screw it! I would wait for him to leave then I would go outside to retrieve my keys. The car was most probably safe in the street. Who would steal a baby blue Mini and think they could get away with it? As Ethan the Jerk had pointed it out to me, it wasn't exactly *inconspicuous*.

The house was quiet for a change, a miracle, which I took as the wheel of Fate turning in my favor. I let the silence soothe me and nurse the wounds inflicted by Ethan to my psyche.

Inside the kitchen, I ran into Bizzy. She sat on a kitchen stool, her back straight as a ballerina's, her signature French twist pinned firmly to her head, and a silk, eggshell tank top showing toned arms that defied gravity.

The absence of a drink before her surprised me just as much as the contemplative expression I spotted in her grey-blue eyes as I rounded the kitchen counter to face her. For the first time in probably ever, it was Bizzy's turn to be startled by my sudden appearance.

"I didn't hear you come in."

I refrained from gloating.

"Where's Claudia?" I asked instead.

"She just left."

I remembered my fight with Ethan right in front of my doorsteps. What if Claudia had seen us?

"Just left? As in an hour ago?"

"How does that qualify as *just*?" Bizzy wondered. "She left five minutes ago. Maybe ten?"

"Could you be mistaken? You seemed lost in thought when I came in."

"Thoughtful, yes. Not comatose. Why is that important anyway?"

If I attracted Bizzy's hawkish attention to this, I would never get rid of her. I decided to drop it.

"No reason." I shrugged.

I hoped my reticence didn't show when I spoke next.

"You were right about Tom. He's jealous."

Bizzy crossed her right wrist – adorned with three rows of pearls locked together with a ruby and diamond clasp, one of my Grandmother Harper's only pieces of jewelry left – on top of her left wrist against the counter. She kept silent but raised an eyebrow keenly. She clearly enjoyed this.

"Anyway, thank you for giving him a push." I concluded my semi apology quickly.

"I'm glad things are working out for you, Sloane," Bizzy said.

"Gabriel is coming with me to the gala tomorrow."

Bizzy hummed absentmindedly.

"It's a mistake, isn't it?"

I was such an idiot! I should have uninvited Gabriel the minute Nisha had left our table yesterday. Tom might be jealous but his ego was way larger than whatever feelings he might still have for me. He would never forgive me.

"I can't go parading Gabriel at school, in front of all of our friends. I've ruined everything!" I started hyperventilating.

"Breathe, Sloane," Bizzy said. "Is Tom bringing his

harlot?"

Well, he was taking her everywhere else. I didn't see why he would pass the chance to flaunt her around yet again. "Yes."

"So now you'll be even," she stated.

She stood up and began fretting over unfolded napkins.

"I talked to your father this morning," she said.

"How is Africa?" I asked, while pouring myself a glass of water.

"Cold apparently. It's winter over there. He's heading back to New York."

"This soon?"

"Yes," she replied, examining her reflection in the silver wedding dish propped by the window. "I'm meeting him next Tuesday," she added quickly.

I almost dropped the glass in my hand.

"What? Tuesday as in next week?" I counted in my head. "As in six days from now?"

Bizzy nodded slowly as if communicating with a child or an idiot. Probably the latter in my case because she'd never treated me like a child.

"I bought my return ticket home this morning."

"But what about me? What about the girls?" I demanded. "How can you leave us?"

What happened to our plans? We were supposed to wait a couple weeks in London after the end of school, and then head to New York together for the summer holiday. I struggled to breathe, as I understood all that her decision implied.

"So does it mean you're not coming back in the fall?"

Bizzy stared at her blood red nails intently.

"I miss him. He's my husband---"

"Are you coming back?" I asked again.

"I'll visit," she said.

Never in my life had I heard Bizzy sound so apologetic. But instead of calming me, it annoyed the hell out of me. If she had resolved to desert us, she should at least own up to it.

193

"You seem to be in a good place right now. You have Gabriel, and Tom is coming back. I can see Claudia is a great friend to you even though she drives me insane, and the girls are doing great. You don't need me anymore. I'm always in your way."

I stomped the kitchen tiles like a four-year-old throwing a tantrum.

"How dare you?" I exclaimed, before charging out of the kitchen and seeking refuge in my room.

Yep, still behaving as a teenager over here. I was almost surprised not to find my favorite Bon Jovi poster on the wall as I slammed the door shut.

Why did everyone leave me?

I allowed myself twenty minutes of pouting before rushing to pick up the girls.

Outside, I looked for the Mini but it had disappeared from its parking space. *So much for my karma changing.* I flipped karma the bird and took my phone out while keeping an eye for a taxi.

As I texted the one person I had promised I would never speak to again, my teeth hurt with resentment. I was tired of being a punch line in that giant cosmic joke called life.

Do you have my car? I typed, bordering on hysterics.

I would much prefer having to report the car stolen than to contact Ethan but I had a nagging feeling he was behind my car's disappearance – probably because I had last seen him inside the Mini, with the keys on the ignition. *Clever me.*

Of course. You offered so kindly.

My mind conjured up Ethan's head plastered on a massive piñata. I took a moment to savor the fantasy, smashing the bastard's face over and again, before I began typing again.

I could kill you. I need it. Now!

Sorry, can't do. I have errands to run.

Another text popped on my screen soon after.

By the way, you could never kill me. You could never hit me, little girl.

The nerve!

I could too.

Could I? I should. Otherwise, what was the point of Sven's training? I glanced back at my butt. I had traded my date skirt for tight jeans I hadn't worn since the 'Before Rose' era. A satisfied smile played on my lips. I might not be *Kung Fu Panda* yet but there was a point all right.

At last, I dragged my eyes away from my shrunken booty and remembered my daughters waiting for their vain mother in a cold, desolate school.

Down the street was a taxi driving away from me. I ran after it like a hen chased by a fox, arms flailing above my head to attract the driver's attention.

Only when I was seated inside the cab, did I return my attention to solving my car's theft.

You're a jackass. I have to pick up my girls and I have no car.

Good thing London is full of buses. Heard you love them.

That's low. Even from you.

Why don't you just thank me? I'm offering you an adventure.

I pictured Ethan smirking behind *my* car's steering wheel. Throwing back my drunken stupid words at me was cruel. I looked for a good, unequivocal comeback.

London is full of cops too. And they LOVE looking for car thieves.

Don't. I'll drop the car later tonight, came Ethan's response in a matter of seconds.

So he was afraid of cops? Why? He was IRS after all, appointed by the American government. He must have immunity or something. Maybe it was an ancient fear, from when he was on the wrong side of the law, like he'd said.

These things tended to linger. I had stolen glitter eye shadow once when I was fourteen and I still feared shops' security guards when I found them looking at me. To this day, they manage to make me feel guilty somehow. Sometimes I even wanted to confess the glitter theft, the pressure was so much to bear.

Fine. I hate you.

Chapter Seventeen

Thursday morning, I watched Poppy rearrange her raspberries into a smile on her maple-syrup-glistening pancake, while listening to Rose's romantic advises. Apparently, Gabriel would fall in love with me if I put on cherry lipstick and wore an ankle bracelet with a heart charm clasped to it. *Good stuff.*

Bizzy was holed up in her room, still digesting our latest epic fight. I couldn't blame her. I needed time myself, and in fact, had spent the previous evening coming to term with her leaving us.

I might have overreacted to her news. I would go further and admit I had behaved quite selfishly. She had, after all, left her life for six long months to take care of us. Well, 'take care' might be too much of a word; be with us, boss us around, rather. Nonetheless, she had showed up when she didn't have to do so.

I shouldn't feel abandoned. I was thirty-two, not twelve. And I had bitched so much about Bizzy staying here. Shouldn't I be elated to hear she was leaving? Logic would have me burning candles in church to celebrate this miracle, throwing the bash of the year, wearing my bra as a hat, and tapping a jig.

But as odd, and frankly, as frightening as it was, I would miss having Bizzy around the place. She had been a shoulder to rely on in these trying times, not a cuddly mom but an ally, and all this without ever a word of gratitude coming from me.

Oh god! I needed to apologize to her. *Again!* The thought made me queasy.

It would have to wait anyway. I had the girls to get ready

then drop to school before that. At least I had my car back.

True to his word, Ethan had returned the Mini to the curb sometime between 7.30 and 8 p.m., while I was giving the girls a bath. The bastard hadn't bothered to call, or ring, or text me, to return the keys. Instead, he had broken in behind my back and left the sheep-shaped keychain smack on the console.

Maybe I should have called the cops. That would have served him right. *Selfish carjacker, housebreaker, hot-as-hell jackass. Urgh!*

I downed my tepid second cup of coffee then began loading the dishwasher. The sound of the front door opening lulled me out of the kitchen. Had Tom started using his keys again?

"Poppy, eat your pancake, baby," I urged my youngest as I crossed the threshold.

In the hallway, the sight of Claudia with dark purple hair startled me.

"You're not Tom," I said.

"And I thank my lucky star every day for that!" She raised her arms in the air in gratitude.

"What are you doing here so early? And what happened to your hair?"

It had been a long time since she'd had a major hair change. Usually Claudia's need to transform herself was proportional to her emotional upset. Judging by the new color, something big had happened.

"Did you break up with Sven?"

She blinked.

"No, he just gave me a lift."

"A lift at 7.30?" I beamed. "So how was it? Yesterday was date two, I gather?"

"No. We haven't yet… He starts working super early and he has a car. Nice change from Michal and his lousy bus Oyster card." She snorted then shook herself.

When she spoke again, her finger was pointed threateningly at me and she sported the ferocious look of a hunting dog homed in on its prey. Not good.

"Don't change the subject. I haven't come to talk about buses with you."

I'd talked enough about buses for a lifetime. In fact, I loathed buses with a fiery passion.

"Who's the man, Sloane?" she demanded.

"Who?"

"In your car?"

"There's a man in my car?" I asked, surprise making me slow to catch up.

Ding-dong! Ethan in my car, of course. She was talking about yesterday.

"I saw you two together. I knew something was up. What the hell were you doing with him? Who is he? Are you cheating on Gabriel?" She took a second to breathe. "I was so pissed that you hid him from me, I had to dye my hair purple. It's such a bad color on me!"

As opposed to pink?

"Please keep your voice down," I begged, remembering that my daughters were next door. "I am not cheating on Gabriel. I would need to *be* with Gabriel to cheat on him. And even so, I would not be cheating on him because I despise E—" I lowered my voice. "The man in my car."

Claudia took a step backward and crossed her arms defiantly.

"So if you're not shagging him, why are you hiding him?"

I bit my lip. Maybe I should have said he was my lover. After all, knowing Claudia she would have patted my back and congratulated me for getting justified revenge on mankind. With a fake affair, her curiosity would have been quenched.

If I'd lied this argument would be over, whereas now I had no answer to offer my nosy best and only friend. Not if I wanted to protect Ethan's secret.

Despite how much I hated him right now, I just couldn't betray Ethan's trust. Contrary to him, *I* had principles.

Unfortunately for me, Claudia wouldn't take my silence for an answer.

"Who is this man to you? And don't tell me he's your accountant because I won't believe you."

My jaw dropped to the floor as I wondered if she had psychic powers. As far as wild guesses went, Claudia was pretty spot on. What had tipped her off? Did she have a mental vision of spreadsheets?

"I'm sorry but I can't tell you. I promised," I explained.

"Is that Claudia?" Rose asked from the kitchen.

"Hi!" Poppy exclaimed, barreling in, her sister at her heels.

My curly tornado threw herself at Claudia for a hug. My Polish inquisitor returned her embrace, her eyes seething behind a plastered smile. She waited for Poppy to wander away from her grasp to speak again.

"You can't or you won't?" she hissed angrily. "*Kurva*! I thought you trusted me."

"Claudia!" I gasped. "I asked you not to use curse words in front the girls."

"It's not like I said *whore*. They don't speak Polish, do they?"

Rose tiptoed our way.

"What's a whore, Mummy?"

I glared at Claudia.

"Nothing, honey."

"But you said it was a bad word. What's whore?" she demanded once more, a frown marring her smooth forehead.

"Not whore, Rose. Horse." I grasped the first semi acceptable idea that crossed my flustered mind. "You know Claudia has a weird accent sometimes."

Claudia looked like she was about to go all Polish mafia on me.

"I don't have an accent," she said.

"Yes, you do." Poppy giggled. "It's funny."

"Why would horse be a bad word, Mummy?" Rose insisted. "I don't understand."

"In Poland it is."

Claudia seemed like she was about to burst but I

wouldn't apologize. I was too busy fixing up her mistake. So faced with her temper flaring, I just shrugged and hoped she could control herself a while longer. Anyway, what was the harm in one more tiny lie?

"They don't like horses."

Poppy emitted a high squeak and buried her face in the folds of my navy pants, sniffing wildly. It took a promise of Oreo cheesecake to coax her into ungluing her runny nose from my leg.

She gestured for me to kneel by her side so she could reveal what had bothered her. Poppy kept a wary eye on Claudia as she spoke in my ear – not whispering, as one should for a secret. Poppy thought it was the act of speaking directly in one's ear that preserved the secret, no matter the volume of your voice.

"Claudia doesn't like horses, Mummy?"

Tears brimmed in her sky blue eyes and her sweet voice quivered. What had I done?

To my four-year-old, hating horses was up there with yanking fairy wings and coloring rainbows black. Poppy loved horses with a passion, from stuffed animals to the real ones in Hyde Park. Her last birthday had a *My Pretty Pony* theme. In her pink, fuzzy world, only evil witchy witches hated her spirit animal. I worried that I might have scarred her relationship with Claudia for life.

"Of course I like horses," Claudia answered.

Poppy's eyes looked like two full moons as she tried to figure out what witchy talent Claudia had used to hear her secret question.

"Yes, honey. Claudia is very special." I smiled crookedly at my friend, hoping she would forgive my wild imaginings. "She loves horses despite being Polish."

The way Claudia glared at me, I was far from forgiven.

"I'm happy," Poppy screamed in my ear before throwing herself at Claudia for the second time that day.

We'd lost precious minutes having this stupid argument and now I had to rush the girls to school. At least that would save me from Claudia's nagging questions.

"Seems like we have to run." I pretended to be disappointed. "Girls, go brush your teeth, please."

Rose ran up the stairs, Poppy on her heels.

"Whore." Poppy giggled, tapping her big sister on the shoulder.

"Whore yourself." Rose turned around to tickle her as payback, her crystalline laugh filling up the staircase.

"Horse, girls! *Horse*, not whore. Claudia meant horse!" I shouted loud enough that they had to hear me.

"We know, Mummy." Rose could hardly breathe she found the word so hilarious. "But it's funnier with Claudia's accent."

"Look what you've done," Claudia said.

"I wouldn't have to if you didn't have such a potty mouth."

Bending in front of the girls' backpacks lined up against the wall, I checked their insides thoroughly, making sure they had everything for the day.

"I'm sorry I can't stay and chat but I'll see you when I get home, okay?"

Maybe I could stay away all day. Claudia might get selective amnesia by tomorrow.

"I won't let you set a foot out the door till you tell me his name," she warned me.

"Then we'll be here all day. I told you, I can't say."

Disappointment made Claudia's lower lip pucker. Angry Claudia, I was used to dealing with, but this sad version of her took me by surprise.

"Why do you care so much anyway?"

"Why wouldn't I? Friends aren't supposed to keep secrets from each other." She laughed without humor. "But we're not *really* friends, are we? I'm just the maid you trail along when you're feeling lonely."

"Of course not! You're my friend." I planted my eyes on hers to show I was sincere. "I swore I'd keep his secret. It's not like I told someone else."

"That, I believe. You have *no one* else to tell," she

snapped.

That stung. I went from apologetic to pissed.

"I'll have you know I have plenty of people!"

I did, didn't? I rifled through my head for one friend other than Claudia but came back empty handed. There was always Nisha. I was pretty sure she would be my friend again, if I stayed with Gabriel – well, probably.

Just then Poppy came charging down, Bizzy's silk Hermes scarf tucked in her mouth. Her big sister was two steps behind, holding onto both sides of the scarf as if they were reins.

"Look at my whore, Mummy!"

A massive migraine exploded inside my skull and it was only 7.45 in the morning. I massaged my temples slowly, wondering if I should correct Rose again or not. Finally, I decided against it. Somehow, it felt that every time I tried to rectify the situation, I threw fuel onto the fire instead.

"Okay, time to go. Grab your bags, fast." I clapped a few times to get them in motion.

Poppy dropped the scarf on the floor. If Bizzy saw that it had drool all over, she would have a stroke. I picked up the silk heap from the floor and snatched my keys from the console.

"Do you think you can fix this?" I tried to hand the scarf to Claudia.

Instead of grabbing it, she stepped back.

"No, this maid needs a break." Her voice was cold as ice. "I'm taking a few days off."

She walked past me, stopping to ruffle the girls' hair, before storming out of the house.

I did not see this one coming.

"Mom! Can you take the girls? I'm running late!" I yelled from the hallway.

I charged up the stairs. I'd no idea where Bizzy was, but hopefully she'd heard me. Otherwise, based on past experiences, I might return to a pillaged kitchen or a giant tent erected in the center of my living room. It was a chance

I was willing to take.

Gabriel was supposed to pick me up in thirty minutes and I was far from ready. I would have been, had I not been called to Ms. Giles's office on my way out of the school.

Apparently, Poppy had nearly caused a *diplomatic* incident earlier today when she had accused Eva, her Polish classmate, of being a horse hater. Eva's father might be a diplomat of some kind but it seemed to me that the headmaster's reaction was blown out of proportion. Especially when my youngest could have accused Eva of being a *whore* hater instead.

I pulled my blouse over my head and threw it across the room. I kept walking till I reached the bathroom, stopping short in front of the mirror. From the drawer I picked two identical red elastic bands and set them before me. I brushed my hair energetically, leaving a few knots here and there that hopefully no one would notice, and parted it in two in the middle. Then I made two neat braids that I tied up with the red elastic bands.

With the light freckles scattered across my nose from the sun, I looked like an older, blonder version of Pippi Longstocking.

Next, I applied a light touch of bronzer on my cheekbones, penciled my eyes in black, tried to conjure up some lashes with mascara, and then spent five good minutes dabbing black smudges away from my forehead and chin. I winked at Pippi Longstocking's slutty lookalike in the mirror before heading to the bedroom.

Time to dress.

My costume was spread across the bed, enjoying its annual outing. To my greatest satisfaction, I didn't need to hold my breath to zip up the mini denim skirt. Last year I'd allowed myself one tiny fried shrimp and the zipper had caved in, almost blinding Vijay Kothari, Nisha's husband.

I buttoned up my most prized star spangled shirt, bargain hunted in a thrift shop in Malibu in the summer of 2002. It had a red gingham print with navy blue shoulder pads and white stars over the breasts. *Classic.* It was also super tight, managing to make even my microscopic boobs look rather impressive.

I raided the girls' room in a hurry, holding my cowboy boots in one hand. I found a ruler in Rose's desk drawer and used it as a shoehorn. My feet screamed in agony, stuck in their tight leather cage. They had grown a size between my two pregnancies and the boots unfortunately predated that change. I clenched my teeth and dropped a couple plasters in my horse-embroidered clutch. If I ever managed to remove the boots without the help of a crowbar at some point during the night, I could use the Band-Aids to relieve the pain.

I checked my reflection in the mirror. My cowgirl costume was honed quite skillfully after five years of the same end-of-the-year-party theme.

It wasn't as elegant and sophisticated as some of the other countries represented at the gala, like Nisha's wonderful saris, or Freija's snow queen dress. Freija was the only Finnish mom at school, and she swore that all her compatriots wore white mink from head to toe.

But it was way sexier than the French costume with the beret and *baguette* bread stuck under the armpit, no matter how short the dress.

At least cowgirls were fun and hotheaded. I decided to take a page from my avatar's book and be more audacious for once. After all, if I managed to make Tom jealous enough tonight, this might be my last outing ever as a single woman. I should make the best of it.

My heart fluttered excitedly when I heard the doorbell ring. I rushed down the stairs, praying that I wouldn't find the bottom part of the house in shambles. I exhaled deeply in relief when I found the girls playing with dolls in the living room, Bizzy sitting before them in her beloved armchair, sipping a martini.

"Mom, thanks for babysitting tonight." I stopped on my way to the door, hoping she would hear the apology behind my words.

That would be too easy.

"It's fine. That's why I'm here, isn't it?" Resentment seeped through her tone. "It's not like I have a life, or a husband to consider. Just my daughter, Sloane, and *her* needs."

I gave up. Obviously she was too mad to listen to me and justifiably so. I tipped the brim of my Stetson as a farewell gesture.

"Well, have a great night." I blew the girls a kiss. "Love you, my flowers!"

In an attempt to get back into my good spirit before answering the door, I tried to picture Gabriel dressed up as a gaucho. I was excited as a teenage girl doodling her secret crush's name in a notebook, knowing that we would match. Like destiny was setting us up together tonight.

But instead of a gaucho, Jimmy the driver awaited me awkwardly at the door, and inside the car, my steaming hot date looked nothing like a farmer from the Pampas.

"Why aren't you dressed up?"

"I didn't realize I was supposed to."

He lied. I clearly remembered telling him half a dozen times on the way back from our lunch date to Varela Global. I took in his sharp navy suit that made his eyes spark like sapphires – eyes that showed no remorse as he lied to my face. I swallowed a resentful sigh.

Maybe Gabriel's impossible confidence was a front. Perhaps he was one of those people who felt self-conscious dressing up. No reason to ruin our evening for a tiny white lie.

I fiddled with my Stetson. Next to his elegance, I literally felt like a cowgirl fresh off her ranch. Delicate silver cuff links tied the white sleeves of his shirt. From the cuffs, my eyes strayed to his slender wrists then to his powerful hands. The thought of what those hands would feel like against my skin sent shivers down my spine.

"I'm certainly glad you dressed up tonight," Gabriel whispered with an appreciative smile.

His gaze had fallen to the tight fabric across my chest, making my hooha hula-hoop merrily in anticipation.

I curled and uncurled my toes a few times in the tight cowboy boots to try to get rid of the pent up sexual tension that made my muscles jolt as if I had been thrown in a bathtub while holding a blow dryer.

I prayed that we would make it to Belgravia Prep before I self-combusted on the backseat of the Mercedes.

Belgravia Prep's greatest pride was its nineteenth-century grand hall, with stained glass windows and delicate ceiling moldings. This was where the school held all social events, from parent reunions to spelling bees.

The school PTA held about five fundraisers a year, all the stay-at-home moms craving a chance to feel useful and generous – although the signatures on the checks were usually their husbands. The biggest check ever donated in the history of the school had displayed five zeros, courtesy of Ani Minassian, who celebrated her divorce by depleting the soon-dismantled couple's shared account, in favor of bonobos' preservation during Quiz Night.

We stood by one of the exquisite windows, its stained glass designs glowing under the diffused light from the massive chandeliers above our heads. As could be predicted, Gabriel was an instant hit with the posh crowd, women gravitating around him as moths to the light and men trying to figure out how to turn his acquaintance into a fruitful relationship.

I should have been on cloud nine. Just like Cinderella, my pariah curse had been lifted till midnight, and Gabriel, despite dispensing his compliments charitably to every woman around, only had eyes for me.

But these social evenings bored me to death. I was always worried I might say something stupid or trip over my own feet, or do something equally embarrassing, so I held onto my date's arm and smiled affably to the other parents, praying I didn't have a shred of lettuce stuck in my teeth.

My stomach growled like a grizzly bear in the spring. Silver plates with tiny skewers and microscopic tarts waltzed around the room, but like in a nightmare, every time I tried to grab something, the dishes danced away from my reach.

Champagne didn't shy away from me, though, and I showed my gratitude by downing glass after glass after glass of the golden nectar of the gods. Realizing my flute was empty, yet again, I left Gabriel in the good hands of Freija – the Finnish mom in her winter fantasy dress. The ex top model tossed her silvery blonde mane over one shoulder, trailing slim fingers along her alabaster neck suggestively, as I made my way to the bar. Apparently, I wasn't the only one planning to take Gabriel home tonight.

I made a note to add a glass of champagne for my rival. Covered in fur like she was, it was no wonder she behaved like a bitch in heat. Champagne would cool her off. Whether I gave it to her to drink or poured it on her head had yet to be determined.

I waited in line behind a tall man whose son was in Poppy's class but whose name had escaped me. Before him was a woman collecting two tumblers full of sparkling clear liquid with a wedge of lemon – gin and tonic. The woman turned around, her expression deterred as she surveyed the crowd. Apparently, kids were not the only people Katherine Stappleton couldn't stand. Parents didn't seem to be her thing either. I was with her on that one.

"You," she said with puckered lips.

"Hi."

I'd seen Kate so much recently, my hatred for her had started to erode to a slight annoyance. I hated that Tom had left me for her but I had begun to believe her when she said she'd not meant for this to happen. Anyway, she hadn't forced Tom point blank to choose her. He was the one to blame for our divorce, not her.

"Of course, you're not dressed up," I said.

"Neither is your boyfriend. Besides, I'm British. What should I dress up as? The queen? Or a bobby maybe?" she answered drily before taking a large gulp of her gin and tonic. "Sorry. I abhor fancy dress parties."

Yet another reason we could never be friends. Costume parties were fun.

"Is Tom around?" I asked, pretending I didn't care either way.

"Yes. I guess I have to go find him." She sighed and nodded goodbye.

I nodded as well, and then a waiter took my order. Next to me, I noticed that Alina was waiting to order a drink. I smiled shyly and waved.

No matter how old I got, the school queens always had the same attraction to nerds like me. The Russian ballerina kindly smiled back.

"Good evening, Sloane. How are you?"

She rolled the *r* delicately, making the simple conversational starter sound poetic and graceful. I felt privileged she had cared to ask.

"I'm fine, thank you. You look beautiful," I said, pointing at her outfit.

"Thank you. I'm a *matryoshka*." She giggled lightly. "You know the Russian dolls?"

"Yes, of course." If I remembered correctly, they were short, stout, and old looking, as far from the svelte, adorable tsarina facing me as could be.

"Do you want this?"

I offered Alina the champagne glass intended for Freija. I would much rather share it with someone I liked than the minx flirting with my date.

"Oh, thank you. That's very kind," she said as she accepted the glass from me.

She gestured to the man standing before her. A wide tray was set on the bar and the bartender kept filling it up with various drinks.

"It seems Hugh is ordering drinks for the whole party," she whispered. "He's monopolized the bar for so long, I was beginning to consider flirting my way into one of his awful cocktails."

She blushed delicately at her own brashness as she stepped away from the line. I thought we would part ways then, happy for the simple friendly exchange we'd just had, but instead she hung around. I shifted my weight from one foot to the next, unsure what was expected of me.

"My husband's not here yet," she said after a while.

"Do you want to join us for a drink?" I offered a bit too eagerly. "Although I'm not sure I still have a date." I chortled awkwardly.

Alina raised a pretty eyebrow.

"I've left him with Freija," I said.

"Oh! We should hurry then," she said mischievously. "Where have you left this date of yours?"

I scanned the crowd. When I spotted Gabriel, holding his ground a good two feet away from Freija, I exhaled sharply.

"Over there." I nodded.

Alina locked her arm with mine and let me lead the way. Her closeness worked like a soothing balm on my Nisha-inflicted wounds. I didn't even care that she was the most beautiful, elegant woman I had ever seen, or that she was the toast of the school. She certainly didn't behave like she was.

I just enjoyed the closeness to another woman, the hope of friendship her easy companionship sparked.

"I'm glad to know you've brought someone." She sounded apologetic. "I know the past year has been hard for you. I'm sorry about the way you've been treated here. I should have done something."

What could she have done? Obviously, she was a leading figure at school but faced with a mob of gossips, I doubted her influence would have changed a thing. I was just glad they seemed to be over picking on me. No one seemed to give me the time of day tonight and it was damn fine with me. They were too busy drooling all over Gabriel to notice me.

"Thank you." I squeezed Alina's arm to show I truly meant it.

Now if only Tom could behave, I might enjoy myself tonight.

Gabriel's face showed immense relief as he spotted me. I

introduced Gabriel to Alina then the Russian ballerina went to chat with Freija, leaving me free to reach my date.

"Are you okay?" I asked with a smile.

"She's intense," he replied, circling my waist with his strong arm.

My beautiful escort using me for protection; the thought made me smile as I relaxed in his embrace.

"Are you having a good time?" I asked.

"Yes. How about you?"

"Actually, it's going pretty great." I smiled as I realized I didn't have to pretend.

Then, catching a sight of the one person I wanted to avoid most, I was forced to amend my answer.

"Well, it was so far. I'm sorry about him," I whispered as Tom zeroed in on us, a long-suffering Kate in tow.

"Look at you two, all cozied up," Tom slurred as he shook Gabriel's hand.

Considering how red his face looked, I could only guess he was putting all his strength into this handshake. If he was crushing Gabriel's fingers, my date was man enough not to let it show.

"Tom." Gabriel smiled coolly.

"So you've heard of me." Tom looked smug, sticking his thumbs in the loops of his cowboy pants.

I should have gone with the Roaring Twenties this year rather than match his sheriff outfit. I was almost tempted to tear off my cowgirl shirt or my boots. Or maybe that was just my poor, aching feet talking.

Instead of answering my drunk ex-husband, Gabriel kissed Kate's cheek.

"How are you, Kate? If there's one place I would have never pictured you, it sure is here." He laughed.

"Me either," she replied. "I also would not have pegged you for the school fundraiser type."

"The things we do for love," he said, kissing my hand.

"Love, or a good game," Kate replied, her spirit livening up by the second.

Tom tugged at her arm and French kissed her sloppily.

We all made disgusted faces, Kate included.

"Behave yourself," she hissed before hastily wishing us a good evening and walking away.

"I'd better see what's put her panties in a bunch," Tom said, readjusting his Stetson over one eye.

I took mine off and held it at arm's length, as if it were contagious.

"I'll catch you later," he said to Gabriel, trying so hard to stare him down that it made him squint.

"Please forgive me," I begged Gabriel.

He laughed it away as if Tom was nothing more than a fly landing on his bacon. Slightly annoying, but considering the way he traced my hip with his long fingers, not gross enough to make him lose his appetite.

Alina came to meet us then and began chatting cheerfully. I never would have guessed that she was so easygoing underneath her stately bearing. She was kind, and had a quirky take on people and situations that made us roar in laughter a couple times. Her voice on the other hand, never rose above a gentle breeze; making us sound like a couple of ruffians.

We were chatting about her son, Andrei, and his latest stunt, when Alina's husband stepped inside the grand hall. A pink glow suffused her high cheekbones while her smile turned demure and tentative.

"Yuri!" she exclaimed happily, extending her delicate arms toward him.

He marched toward us, his ice blue stare seeing his wife only. The man walking by his side, hand in his jacket pocket, was scoping out the rest of the party. No one really knew what Alina's husband job was, but they all agreed that it must be dangerous and mysterious. Poor nine-year-old Andrei had a security guard waiting for him in the school's corridor, day in, day out.

As they kissed, I decided there was no couple more mismatched than these two lovebirds. Alina was so fine, aristocratic, even in these poor woman clothes, whereas Yuri was tall, wiry, patched up from head to toes – from his many scars and tattoos that peeked out from a sleeve or the collar of his shirt, to his clothes that were most certainly expensive but looked at odd with his strange physique.

Despite looking peculiar, he was quite handsome, just not right for the tsarina on his arm, like pink stilettos on a cosmonaut or black army boots paired with a ball gown. This one princess seemed passionately in love with her combat boots, I realized, as Alina's eyelids remained closed while she savored her kiss.

When they finally came up for air and Yuri acknowledged us at last, I gasped in recognition. Same name, same hawkish eyes, same crooked teeth that made his smile look scary as hell. Alina's husband was the orchid dealer from Ethan's secret file. No wonder he'd looked familiar. Our kids attended the same school.

I almost gushed over what a coincidence it was that they worked together, before remembering I wasn't supposed to know that. So instead, I grinned, waiting for the men to announce it themselves.

It was too perfect to be true. I seemed to have made a friend in Alina, and our boyfriends slash husbands knew each other.

Except I was going back to Tom, if he wanted me back, so this perfect set up might be short-lived. The thought of Tom's gross tongue-lapping Kate's face made my skin break into goose bumps. It would take us years of marriage counseling for me to get over that. *Absolute yuck!*

"Yuri Alexeyev," Yuri said as he shook Gabriel's hand.

"Gabriel Varela. Nice to meet you," Gabriel answered impassively.

My smile froze on my lips. This was far from the warm greeting I had expected. Why did they pretend not to know each other? My gaze went back and forth between the two men as an uneasy feeling settled in my stomach.

Refusing to listen to my suspicious conscience whispering tauntingly in my ear and letting it ruin a perfect evening, I searched for a logical explanation. Considering how little time Gabriel spent at the office, it was very plausible he'd never met Yuri. Odd but possible.

I just didn't understand why Ethan had asked me to keep an eye out for Yuri if the two men had indeed never met. From my own discoveries, Ethan's Intel sucked – *big time*. Which shouldn't surprise me because so did he. I was still reeling about my car and the offensive way he had spoken to me yesterday. *Jerk*.

"I need a drink," Yuri said, his accent so thick I could barely make sense out of it. "Come with me," he told his wife.

Alina's glass was still half-full but she complied happily. Before leaving at the arm of her scary husband, she touched my wrist softly.

"Let's have tea sometime next week, all right?"

"Definitely." I smiled gratefully. "Have a good evening."

"See you later." She waved.

My karma was unequivocally changing. Claudia's taunting resounded in my ears – *you have no one else*. Just the same day, here I had made a friend. And not just any friend, the coolest friend ever.

But it didn't stop me from regretting my fight with Claudia. I hoped she would forgive me soon, and all would be forgotten. She wasn't just a stand-in for Nisha. She had been great in these trying times and I wanted to keep her around in better times too.

In truth, she was the greatest friend I'd ever had. Funny, brutally honest, caring, and kind even if she would have slapped me if she knew that's how I saw her, loyal. Ethan had put me in an impossible situation when he'd chosen to burden me with his lies; yet another reason to resent him dearly. If push came to shove, I would betray his secret. Claudia's friendship was more important to me than his crazy theories.

"I need to talk to Hector for a minute," Gabriel told me, jolting me out of my thoughts. "Do you mind?"

I shook my head *no*. "I need to use the ladies' room anyway."

Before Gabriel left, I held him back.

"Why do you think Yuri isn't dressed up?" I asked.

It was meant as a joke but I was quite curious. Everyone but Kate and Gabriel were dressed up tonight.

"Oh! But I think he is. He's a Russian mobster." He winked.

I watched the long black cashmere coat and the diamond ring glistening on his pinkie from afar. It certainly fit the cliché. From what I recalled though, Yuri dressed this way every day. Did he try to emulate a mobster or was he the stuff from which mobster movies drew inspiration?

And then I remembered his true job. Nothing like the wild theories than ran through school. He wasn't KGB or a women trafficker. He was an orchid trader, which was possibly the least badass job that ever existed.

Chapter Eighteen

I blew my concerns about Yuri and Ethan from my mind and listened to the pressing demands of my bladder instead.

The reception hall didn't have a private bathroom so the parents had to use the students' stalls, all the way across the ground floor. I walked down the long corridor dedicated to music instruction, past the hallway with the administration offices, and into another corridor with doors labeled French and Spanish, when suddenly someone grabbed me from behind, shoved their hand over my mouth, and dragged me into a dark room to my left.

I kicked like a demon, fueled by fear and all those mock fights with Sven. My eyes couldn't see a damn thing in the freak obscurity but my teeth could sink in the hand that gagged me, and my feet could hit my assailant's legs, which I made the most of. I barely experienced panic, too busy making sure I wouldn't be the only one going down in this fight.

"Stop it," my captor commanded. "You're going to hurt yourself."

What the fuck? I kicked some more, bending my leg from behind to hit him straight in the nuts. He grunted but didn't release his hold of me. It was like being held between the jaws of a mutant robot.

My breath became frantic as it dawned on me I might not make it out of this dark hole alive. And the questions began: *Why? Why me? Why here? Why now?* My brain felt like a butterfly caught in a net, batting its wings wildly against unyielding walls.

"God, woman! You're impossible," the voice in the dark spoke again, this time sparking a flicker of recognition and a fresh wave of anger.

I sunk my teeth into his hand, resolved to draw blood. Well, not really, I was way too squeamish to bite that hard, but I did make sure I hurt the hell out of him. He tried to get his hand away from my pit-bull clench but I held on for dear life, enjoying the payback. Once I was satisfied he would never pull something like that on me again, I let go.

"For fuck's sake, Ethan! If you ever do that again, I'll kill you," I spat.

"You're nuts," he muttered, flipping on the light.

I blinked a few times, trying to get accustomed to the harsh brightness. A naked light bulb hung in the janitor closet into which Ethan had dragged me.

Yep, the guy was definitely a smooth operator. Kidnapping me and stashing me in a closet full of brooms, mops, and buckets was everything a woman's heart could desire. Although it could have been worse; I could have woken up in a gym.

Ethan lounged against the cleaning product shelves, leaving as much space as he could between us, while nursing his hand. The bite marks were visible from the short distance separating us, filling me with pride. Now he knew not to trifle with me.

"What are you doing here?" I demanded, a hysterical edge to my voice.

After all, I'd been pretty sure I was going to die just a couple minutes ago. I was allowed a meltdown.

"Getting marred by you, apparently." He frowned.

I tapped my foot and waited for him to speak.

"I wanted to make sure you were okay," he admitted.

My heart melted ever so slightly. The method was crazy but the intention behind it was kind of sweet. I noticed he wore a waiter get up – black slacks, white shirt, and white jacket.

"You're pretended to be a waiter? That's how you got in?"

"Yes. The parents in your school are arrogant pricks, by the way," he said. "Security is air tight. It was the only way

I found to slip through the net."

Ethan stepped toward me.

"You can't go home with Gabriel."

"Are you jealous?" I teased.

"No. I'm worried about you."

Bam! In the face! My ego retreated to its niche to nurse its new wounds.

"Gabriel is a perfect gentleman—"

"No. He's dangerous, Sloane."

"How?"

"Uh?"

"How is he dangerous?" I demanded. "If you expect me to trust you, you might as well tell me. Other than allegedly embezzling money he doesn't need, that is. Because the only one who feels shady to me right now is you."

"I can't tell you. If I did, I'd risk screwing up the whole operation. It's a chance I simply can't take."

"So that means you don't care if I'm in danger, as long as your *operation* runs smoothly."

"Yes. No," he huffed. "If I told you the truth, you would be in danger."

"So? I'm not in danger now," I said.

"You can't see Varela," he barked.

"Without more information, I'll be making my own decisions," I replied coolly, white arctic fury coursing through my veins.

I wanted to hurt Ethan for lying to me over and over again, leading me to believe he cared for me one second and the next dropping a bucket of ice water over my head, making me like him so much and using me in return. I should loathe him, I hated him, but hearing the worry in his voice and seeing the desire in his eyes when he looked at me, made my knees buckle every time. I didn't care what he said, no matter how many times he assured me of his indifference toward me, I knew he wanted me. *Coward.*

"You should be happy. I might get to search his room tonight at last," I said.

Apparently, I finally made it through his barrier. One

second I was standing defiantly before him and the next Ethan had me pinned against the door, his whole length melting against me while his lips captured mine. My arms were above my head as Ethan held both of my wrists in one hand, the other cradling my head firmly in place. His kiss was neither sweet nor gentlemanly but rough and passionate, and it sent shivers straight from my lips to my core.

At this precise moment, I didn't care whether we were in a janitor closet, or that this closet was in my daughters' school and someone could walk in on us at any time. I had fantasized about kissing Ethan a thousand times and this was even better than all I could have imagined. I wasn't letting go.

His tongue did some deft exploring and I moaned against his mouth, thrusting my hips against him, daring him to take his exploration one step further. But instead of giving me what I needed, he tore himself away from me and pressed his hands against my shoulders as if he was worried I might tackle him. He might not be completely wrong.

My legs trembled and my lips felt cold as I tried to understand what had made him stop.

"Stay away from his house," he said sternly, readjusting his white jacket.

Had he viewed our kiss as a chore? Something he had to do to keep a desperate, lonely woman in check? Did he really believe it would suffice?

"So you expect me to swoon over your kiss and obey you like a lobotomized automat?" I asked, angry that it was precisely what my hooha wanted me to do.

Anything to get Ethan under this miniskirt of mine. What was I to do? My hooha was a total slut.

"No. I expect you to be intelligent." His voice was hoarse with desire.

There was no way he was that good an actor. He wanted me as much as I did him.

"For you. For your girls." He shook his head. "I hope I won't regret this. I am not IRS, Sloane. And Varela isn't an embezzler. I work for the Miami PD," he said, his red-hot stare fixated on my lips.

I shook out of his hold and retreated against the door. Betrayal made me see stars, as if I had run smack into a wall of bricks. If what he said was true, I didn't know Ethan Cunning at all. Not the first thing about him.

"What are you saying?" I croaked.

"I'm a cop—"

It certainly did make sense. Ethan was the least likely IRS agent I had ever met. Not that I knew any others. I didn't let him finish his sentence.

"Show me some ID! Now!" I snarled. "And not your stupid driving license."

"I can't. I left my shield at the precinct," he explained as if it all made perfect sense. "I don't have jurisdiction in the UK. I'm on an unofficial capacity here. But the Brit—"

"Shut up! Just shut up!" I yelled, slithering away from his grasp. "You're a psycho!"

He had to be. This whole story simply didn't make sense. Just like Gabriel being a crook.

Ethan tried to grab my wrist but I shoved him away.

"Let me go! Now!" I grabbed the door handle. "Or I swear I'll call the cops. The real ones!" I spluttered hatefully, rushing out the door without one last glance at Ethan.

My eyes burnt from growing tears as I hurried toward the bathroom and its anonymity. My fingers ran across my swollen lips manically just as my mind reeled with Ethan's revelations.

Disoriented as I was, I landed in the staircase leading to Rose's classroom instead of the bathroom. I swallowed back a sob and pivoted on my heels, but voices nailed me to the wooden floor. Life had a strange sense of humor. Spying on Yuri and Hector on the second floor landing, I had to admire how getting lost had brought me exactly where I was supposed to be.

I crouched under the stairs, listening avidly to their

argument. Yuri's voice crackled with contained violence.

"What's he doing here?"

"Nothing. I told him he shouldn't come," Hector answered.

"This is my son's school. I don't mix family and business. Do you hear me?"

Yuri's *r* rolled like thunder across a restless ocean. I cowered behind the stairs, praying they were enough to conceal me.

"Neither do we," Hector replied. "Don't worry. After Saturday, you'll never hear from us again."

What was happening on Saturday? I worried about Gabriel's safety.

"Nothing's changed?"

"Everything's set up. The crates are being flown to Rotterdam as we speak."

"Good. You're sure they'll transit here safely?"

"No problem. Customs won't bother us. I've got someone inside to make sure it runs smoothly."

"It'd better." Yuri didn't bother to veil the threat behind his words.

"I told you it would. The delivery is set for 11, just as we said."

Steps resounded on the staircase. Yuri was coming down now. Shaking myself up, I cursed him silently. Didn't he have any manners? He should have said bye. When people said bye, it gave you time to make a quick exit. Now all that was left for me to do was run because the staircase wouldn't hide me from him once he reached the ground floor.

I launched myself out of the staircase before Yuri reached the first floor. A few people hung out in the corridor. I slowed down just enough not to attract attention, switching from a sprint to a powerwalk on speed. I still needed to pee but couldn't afford to go to the bathroom. I had been gone too long; if I went now, Hector would be onto me for sure.

As I came hurtling inside the grand hall, Nisha's deep, throaty laugh made me flinch.

"Where have you been? You've missed an episode of

your own show! What a scene!"

She pretended to dab her eyes, as if whatever she was alluding to had made her shed laughing tears. I was too busy looking behind my shoulder to pay her any heed.

I tried to walk past her but Nisha was a hard one to get rid of. She stepped right in front of me, blocking my way. Yuri was coming up the corridor so instead of fighting with Nisha, I decided to use the little energy I had left to hide I was out of breath. Yuri's shoulder grazed mine in the crowd without seeing me.

Cold sweat ran between my shoulder blades and beaded on my upper lip. I waved my hat as a fan. Hector strolled in soon after, glowering as he passed by me. For once, I was grateful to Nisha. She gave me a great alibi in case Hector wondered where I had been for the past ten minutes.

"Tom was—" Nisha started recounting merrily.

I pushed her aside. She stared at her bold yellow sari indignantly, as if I'd ruined the precious fabric by merely touching it. After reflection, she might be right; there probably was a wrinkle somewhere in the many folds that could be attributed to me.

"You'll have to excuse me, but my date is waiting." I winked at her.

The chance for payback was too good not to savor fully. Without waiting for her answer, I left Nisha behind, her words still suspended in the air, and went to find Gabriel. He grabbed my arm and pulled me to him.

"Where have you been? You were gone forever."

"I got cornered by Nisha," I said. "I thought I would never get rid of her."

"That bad, uh? You sound exhausted."

"Well, that's Nisha for you." This party was endless and my brain was full of cryptic information. The swirling was incessant, enough to make me faint. "Is it okay with you if we go?"

"Of course." Gabriel kissed my cheek, his lips lingering.

He waved to Hector, standing against the wall by the door.

"Hector will have the car out in a minute."

I breathed better as I saw the security chief slash backstabbing bastard exit the room. For a moment while we walked down the corridor, I wondered whether I should tell Gabriel about what I'd heard.

But what had I heard really? I needed time to unscramble everything before I told Gabriel. Right now, all I had sounded way too much like Ethan's conspiracy theories for my own tastes.

I was convinced Hector was working with Isabella, and that they did something illegal with Yuri. But other than this certitude, and the fact that it couldn't be embezzlement because money scamming wasn't something you could deliver like a pizza, I was lost. What did Yuri possibly want from Hector?

For once, I was pretty sure the gossips were right. Yuri didn't only deal orchids. I suddenly remembered Alina's brother, the thug with the snake tattoo. My selective memory had managed to annihilate him from my thoughts for the past weeks, but now my brain was making connections. It was all about drugs, it had to be. What it had to do with Varela Global was something I had to figure out.

I couldn't wait to be home, in the privacy of my own room to decipher the clues laid before me. Unfortunately, this didn't fit into Gabriel's plans. The time for courting was over and Gabriel was launching the offensive.

"*Eres divina*," Gabriel whispered in my ear as we climbed inside the car.

"To the lady's home?" Jimmy asked from the front seat.

Gabriel pushed aside one of my braids, leaning against my neck as he answered. "Not tonight, Jimmy. It's time I showed Ms. Harper my house."

My body froze as his breath caressed my skin and I processed his directions to Jimmy. There was only one thing he would want me home for, and the mere thought of it knocked the air right out of me. I stared outside, trying to fight off the panic. I didn't know what upset me more – that he planned to take me home, or that he didn't bother

223

consulting me about it. This was what I wanted, right?

Instead of parrying with something equally flirtatious, I squeaked, "The girls."

"I'll have you back home before they wake up." He kissed my neck.

I wriggled out of his wandering hands' reach.

"I can't. I have to go home."

Gabriel's jaw clenched into a tense smile while his eyes turned glassy.

"Sloane, I told you I like a challenge, but don't toy with me."

"I'm not. I wouldn't—"

I could never play Gabriel. If he had to know one thing about me, it was that I was no player. All my life I had been the one getting played, never the other way around.

But even if I'd never intended to toy with his feelings, I might have led him on all the same. Although Gabriel knew about my situation with Tom, he might not realize that if I were given a choice, I would always choose Tom, if only for the sake of my daughters.

I owed Gabriel the truth.

"Tom, my husband. I think he might be coming back."

"Is that why you want to go home?"

Was Tom the reason why I was passing on sex with the hottest man alive? I stared at his glossy black waves, his Caribbean sea green eyes, his lips that were still tight from my rebuke. No, that wasn't it. Tom might be the reason I'd never considered committing to Gabriel – him, and Ethan the liar – but Tom's infidelity gave me a free pass for a one-night stand. It made it my constitutional right.

"I'm just not ready yet," I told Gabriel, realizing how much these words were true.

I still hurt too much to jump into a new love affair lightly and although I could pretend it was just sex, I would just be lying to myself. I was a hopeless romantic. Despite the disillusions that came with my divorce, despite the voice of reason shouting in my ear that no man could be trusted, it would be way too easy for me to fall for someone else.

My chest still throbbed from Ethan's deceit. I knew from the start I had to be weary of him, and yet I'd let myself be lulled by his lies. When we'd kissed, I had dropped all my barriers, standing bare and vulnerable before him. And he'd crushed me in return.

"*Cara* Sloane," Gabriel said, his pleasant smile back in place. "I understand why you want your husband..." he puckered his lips as if the word tasted sour, "...back. But I'm here now, and I like you."

For a Latin man not afraid of overstatement, the word *like* sounded oddly flat and empty.

"When you make your decision, remember I've never hurt you, or lied to you."

Give it time, the nagging voice in my head whispered. I shushed it down. I couldn't let Tom and Ethan spoil all men for me. Not every man lied and manipulated, not all of them toyed with women's feelings. My past bad luck shouldn't penalize Gabriel. He deserved the benefit of the doubt.

"You can trust me, Sloane," Gabriel said, bending over me for a kiss.

I let him kiss me. I folded my arms around his neck as his mouth pressed against mine, parting my lips when he decided to take the exploration further. Our lips worked well together, responding to each tug and pressure naturally, like a beautifully orchestrated ballet. Just like Gabriel, it was a perfect, flawless kiss.

Miles away from the rough, sometimes clumsy kiss Ethan and I had exchanged in the janitor closet. There had been some teeth banging, and plenty of lip grazing, just like what someone would expect from a first kiss. There had also been a marching band in my head, drowning all thoughts except that of Ethan, me, and the kiss we shared.

In opposition, while I kissed Gabriel, faint classical music resounded in my ears, like the background music in an elevator or most probably, the music coming from the car radio. I jerked backward. It infuriated me that thoughts of Ethan could invade even moments like this. It felt like I was cheating on Gabriel, which made me turn crimson with shame.

"Look how beautiful you are when you blush." Gabriel ran a hand on my cheek.

The car parked in front of my house.

"Here you are, *princesa*. Home before midnight." He kissed me once more, a self-satisfied smile hovering on his lips as he let go of me.

"Thank you," I stuttered to Gabriel's intention while Hector opened the door for me.

"You're welcome. I won't be so gentlemanly this weekend though," he said, his words sounding like a sensual promise.

"This weekend," I repeated, placating a smile on my face to pretend I looked forward to it.

I ran inside the house without giving Hector time to walk me to the door. I was in enough turmoil already not to let him reiterate his threats.

I turned around long enough to catch the loathing in Hector's eyes; someone wanted me dead.

In case Hector decided to pay me a visit later, I made sure all the bolts were locked. As I climbed the stairs, I turned into a jittering mess, the events of the night taking their toll on me.

I shook under my comforter for ages before sleep embraced me at last, making my worries vanish for a few precious hours.

"Mummy!" Poppy hurtled in my bedroom at full speed, jumping smack in the middle of my chest and knocking the wind out of me. "Daddy's here!"

My eyes snapped open as I gasped for air, my instincts tuning into flight mode before realizing I wasn't being mugged by Hector but squeezed by my baby girl.

"Poppy!" Rose stepped in after her. "I told you not to wake up Mummy."

"What time is it?" I mumbled.

"7.30," my eldest answered.

"What? We're going to be late!"

I settled Poppy next to me, and sprang in a sitting position like a Jack in the box.

"Poppy and I are ready, and Bizzy said she would take us to school this morning and to let you sleep. She said you must be tired from the party."

She didn't know the half of it. My eyelids felt like they weighed a ton and a half each and I shivered though I wore two sweaters and we were in July. More sleep was exactly what I needed so I really hoped I'd dreamt Poppy's words.

"Poppy, did you say your dad was here?"

"Yes! He's waiting downstairs. He looks mad," she said.

"Bizzy said to brush our teeth and wait upstairs while you grownups talk," Rose said. "Come on, Poppy." She took her younger sister by the hand and led her to their bathroom.

I dragged myself out of bed, keeping the two sweaters on and adding yoga pants. I brushed my teeth hastily, my heart almost giving out when I caught my reflection in the mirror. I looked like a braided raccoon. I hadn't bothered untying my braids last night and they stuck awkwardly on both sides of my head while the dark circles around my eyes were so big, they threatened to swallow the rest of my face.

For months, I'd been dressing to the nines every time Tom visited but today, Sloane *au naturel* would have to do. I ran downstairs, curious as to what could have brought Tom here so early.

He was pacing back and forth across the living room, his fists clenched tightly.

"Tom? Why are you here?" I asked as I reached the last step.

"Why? Why?" he asked. "That piece of shit!"

"Keep your voice down," I growled.

"I'll do as I please," he retorted like a petulant child, his voice shifting a couple octave lower even as he claimed to do otherwise.

Bad husband, bad person, but good father – hence my personal dilemma.

"Who are we talking about here?"

It seemed evident he was referring to Gabriel but I couldn't understand why the sudden vehemence.

"Who? Your stupid Latino lover, that's who!" he hissed. "First he screws my wife and then he has the nerve to have me kicked out from my girls' school!"

I shook my head from side to side, as if this could unscramble the bucket load of info Tom had just dropped on me. First, he seemed to be working under the false assumption that Gabriel and I were having sex. I thought I might correct his mistake but then it seemed like an easy way to get payback so I let it slide.

"Ex-wife," I said coolly. "And kicked out? What's that all about?"

"Don't act like you don't know."

I stared blankly, convincingly enough that Tom cared to elaborate.

"The coward had me kicked out of the gala yesterday by some mustached goon."

So this was what Nisha was gushing about yesterday. Thinking about why I missed the scene, my knees turned weak and my lips jutted instinctively. Flashbacks of the dingy janitor closet and the man inside assailed me. I removed one of my two sweaters.

"What did you do?"

"What did *I* do?"

"Come on, Tom. He must have had a reason to get you kicked out."

"My fist might have slipped accidentally against his cheek," he admitted reluctantly.

"Slipped?"

I thought of Gabriel's face yesterday. There was no sign he'd gotten punched – not a bruise, not a scratch, not a single blemish.

"You were so drunk you missed him, right?"

"I wasn't drunk," he said.

Either he'd lied, or he'd switched from Armani to gin cologne this morning.

"I'm pretty sure I nicked his jaw before falling down."

I fought to repress a smile.

"I want you to call him, and tell him to screw himself." Tom stomped his foot.

"Tom, there's no way I would do that. From the sound of it, you deserved what you got."

I wasn't mad at Tom, or happy, or sad for that matter. His stunt left me indifferent. The way I spoke to him, I sounded more like a mom than a wife – *ex-wife*.

Tom was raging in front of me, bewilderment distorting his features.

"Sloane, I won't stand it much longer. If you want to get me back, you'll stop this nonsense immediately and stop fooling around with that asshole."

What a conceited bastard! If *I* wanted him back? What I wanted was to kick his butt out of this house, all the way to Jupiter. But then the deep certainty that my daughters needed their father kept me in check.

Only the slightest tremor in my voice betrayed my true feelings when I spoke next.

"As far as I know, you're the one who left me. And the one supposed to move in with Kate tomorrow. Has that changed?"

"It could."

"Are you still with Kate?" I demanded.

"Maybe, but that's not the point."

"It's exactly the point. Unlike you, Tom, I'm no cheater."

"What? Are you taking her side now? She's your new BFF?"

Apparently, this conversation wasn't going as Tom had planned. Like most people used to always getting what they want, there was nothing that made Tom lose his composure as much as being denied his whims. I enjoyed knowing I was the one making him squirm, savoring the newfound power. *Revenge is sweet.*

"Don't be stupid," I said. "I don't like Kate."

Tom perked up for a nanosecond before I elaborated.

"But she deserves your respect anyway. If *you* want to get me back, you'll do the decent thing for once in your life and break things off with her properly."

I realized that applied to Gabriel as well. Since our talk and kiss in the car yesterday, he probably thought we had become an item.

I was relieved that Tom's declaration got me out of the sex with Gabriel but dreaded the awkward conversation to come. I'd never broken up with anyone before. I complained constantly about getting dumped but in truth, looking back at my short romantic curriculum, the men who had left me had done me a favor. I was so chicken to leave, I would be married to that German dude from Cancun if he'd called the day after taking my virginity.

Realizing I could have done much worse than Tom made me look at him in a softer light. Despite his numerous flaws, there were things I loved about him; things that if I concentrated on exclusively, could hopefully make me love him again. I wasn't the queen of denial for nothing. If one person could resurrect the ghost of our marriage from ashes, it had to be me.

"So if I break up with Kate, I can move back in, right?" Tom asked, his stance nonchalant now, as if he didn't care either way.

"Probably," I answered, incapable of saying a definitive yes.

I wanted to but my voice simply wouldn't yield. The nagging, teeny person in my head congratulated my voice for its smart answer. I think she might not like Tom much. And who could blame her really?

"That's not good enough. I need a definite answer for the movers."

Who said romance was dead?

"Well, you won't get one today," I snapped.

It might've been childish, but I enjoyed the power too much to relinquish it so fast.

"Now the girls have to get to school, and you have to talk with Kate."

"What about your Gabriel? Are you going to talk to him?"

"I will. Not that it's any of your business. Let me call the girls down so you can say goodbye."

"I have to run; I'm late for my next appointment. I didn't expect you would be so difficult."

My jaw clenched so hard it hurt. I knew exactly what he'd expected – that I would roll over and act beside myself with gratitude. *Well, guess again, you moron.*

Tom was already at the door, his briefcase in one hand, and the other one on the handle.

"Kiss them for me," he said as he propped open the door. "And call me with your answer today. I won't wait around forever," he warned before leaving without a last glance for me.

I exhaled sharply a couple times before peeking into the kitchen. Bizzy sat at the counter, pretending to be busy with her magazine. I was pretty sure she had heard every single word but I didn't have time to discuss it now.

"You're ready?" I asked.

Bizzy stood up and stacked the magazine neatly on one side of the counter.

"I am. Where are the girls?"

"I'll ask them to come down now," I said on my way out of the kitchen. "Thank you for taking them, by the way."

"You're welcome."

I knew I still owed her an apology but it would have to wait for after she dropped Rose and Poppy at school. They were already late as it was.

"I'm calling the cab," Bizzy added.

I stuck my head in the staircase.

"Girls! Time to go!"

Poppy and Rose came running down the stairs, elbowing one another to be the first to reach the bottom.

"No running in the stairs! And no fighting," I scolded them, putting a stop to their quarrel.

"Sorry, Mummy," Rose said.

"Where's Daddy?" Poppy asked, hugging my legs.

"He had to leave, sweetie."

I rearranged her wild curls with my fingers.

"He's with Kate?" Poppy asked again.

"No, silly," Rose replied. "It's Friday. Daddy works on Friday."

"Good. I don't think Kate likes daddy very much," Poppy continued while I picked up her backpack from the floor and handed it to her.

"Why would you say that?" I asked.

"They're always fighting. And they look sad," Rose answered in her sister's stead.

"Yes, like you when Daddy lived here," Poppy said.

"I did?"

"Yes. Your eyes didn't smile," Poppy mused aloud. "Just your mouth. Like now, Mummy."

I forced as much cheerfulness as I could in my voice as I lied to my daughters yet again.

"I'm not sad."

Poppy gave me a knowing look, while worry for me clouded Rose's thoughtful eyes. They looked so grownup suddenly.

"Would you want your dad to come home? Live with us again? Would it make you happy?"

"Would your eyes stop smiling again?" Poppy asked.

I thought about it long and hard.

"Maybe."

"Then I guess not. Besides, it's nice to have two houses," Rose said.

"Yes! We get to have two of everything!" Poppy giggled happily. "Two beds, two ponies—"

"Are you girls ready?" Bizzy asked as she walked into the hallway. "The cab is here."

"Yes." Rose ran to where her grandmother stood, picture perfect as ever in her grey uniform.

While Poppy hummed to herself, daydreaming, Rose began fidgeting.

"Poppy," she hissed. "We have to go! I don't want to be late. Take my hand," she said, waiting for her little sister to grab her slender fingers.

"Have a good day, my flowers." I waved goodbye as I

opened the door to let out my little troop.

I locked the door after making sure they were all fitted in the cab then returned to my bedroom. I plopped myself under the soft comforter and checked my phone.

Its screen was lit, indicating someone was calling but by the time I could answer, it was too late. The screen grew dark again. Dreading a call from Gabriel or Tom, I typed in my security code anyway to unlock the phone and check the missed calls.

The missed call along with two more in the past hour were from the third and worst man in my life: Ethan. I was surprised he'd tried to contact me and resented him for trying to reach me despite the fact that I had been very clear yesterday about never wanting to see him again.

I should get accustomed to it by now. No man ever listened or cared about what I wanted. There was no reason for it to change now.

There was a text from Ethan as well. I could only read the first line:

Sloane, I need to explain everything to you.

It was promising enough that I opened the text to read the rest.

Can't do it over the phone. Need to meet.

My curiosity was sorely disappointed. It was the most useless text in the history of all texts – a whole message full of nothing.

Knowing Ethan, he was only trying to lure me into helping him again while expecting me to be content with half-truths and full lies. I had fallen for his tricks too often to get sucked in again.

Instead, I erased his text, regretting the day we met, and then plugged the phone back to the charger before resuming my night. I was well resolved not to dream of him. As far as I was concerned, Ethan Cunning was dead to me.

Chapter Nineteen

Later that morning, rested and in a much better disposition, I settled on fixing a peace offering lunch for Bizzy and me. I hoped my karma would appreciate the gesture.

While I diced the eggplants, zucchinis, and onions for the ratatouille, I tried to come to terms with my decision. Getting Tom back had been my single obsession since the divorce, more than six months ago. To achieve my goal, I'd shown a dedication I didn't know I possessed.

I had suffered – from the sciatica resulting from the long hours spent staking out Katherine Stappleton in the car, to the constant humiliation beating my ego to a pulp.

I had hoped – without cause and beyond reason, that one day Tom would come back to me, and my family would be whole again, healed. I had never stopped searching for the silver lining, no matter how dark and stormy the cloud grew.

I had lived – in six months, I had lived more intensely than in the past ten years with Tom. I had faced my fears, grown more independent than in all my married years; I had met people on my own, I had flirted and was flirted with, I had learned how to kick ass.

All this I had done to get my husband back but now it felt like I had outgrown Tom somehow. My mind was made up already, and I'd decided to take him back, although it filled me with a sense of dread.

After our time apart, I saw our marriage under a new light. I had been content when we were married, much more than I had ever been since Tom had left me. But my marriage brought me no happiness. If not for my wonderful daughters, I would have been as dim as a flickering light in a cloudy sky. Fighting to stay alight but doomed to be stifled in the end.

Tom didn't really see me. He didn't live with me but alongside me. I was one of the fixtures in the house, useful, sometimes decorative, unchanging. Even as he asked me to welcome him back into our house, I was certain Tom hadn't noticed the transformations in me. Moreover, he didn't care. It would rather inconvenience him to realize I had found my voice after all these years.

How was I supposed to resume our married life, then? Was there a way to deaden my conscience so it would endure his constant oversight and condescension? Could I return to a bad marriage willingly and still preserve my sanity?

So long as I was sure it was the best course of action for my daughters, I never considered an alternative. But after my talk with Poppy and Rose, it now seemed like I had options. They said children were intuitive but I'd never realized how much. My daughters knew I was unhappy way before I did. No wonder they had never seemed rattled by the divorce. *My sweet, bright girls.*

If I decided to marry Tom again, I would have to protect my daughters better. I would never forgive myself if their vision of marriage was spoiled forever by their parents' bad one. I refused to steal their hopes.

The question was: could I force my eyes to smile even on the days I didn't feel like smiling deep inside?

I almost asked Bizzy as she joined me in the kitchen but then thought better of it. This was a question I had to figure out on my own. Instead, I ushered her to take a seat on a stool and slid a plate of ratatouille and fried egg in front of her before doing the same for me.

She looked at me wearily, probably afraid I would bite her head off if she opened her mouth. Brushing aside the feeling of *déjà vu*, I launched myself into a fresh wave of apologies.

"Mom, I'm sorry. I've been selfish."

I poured water in both our glasses and swallowed back tears. How did I transition from avoiding my mother like

235

the plague to sobbing at the thought of her leaving? Must be some hormonal imbalance.

"You're perfectly entitled to go back to Dad in New York. I should never have let you stay so long. I never stopped to think what a sacrifice you were making. I'm really sorry," I mumbled again.

Bizzy bit into a tomato then took her time chewing, her face as indecipherable as a mask.

"Sloane, you're making my head spin. For the past week, the only words I've heard from you have taken the form of an apology or an accusation."

I nodded, conscious that she was perfectly right. Except during my pregnancies, I had never before acted so erratically.

"I never considered my stay here as a sacrifice. You've been through a hard time and as your mother, there is no other place I should be than by your side. Plus, as you know, your father was grateful for the sabbatical."

As she smiled drily, my whole body relaxed, just like kids in the classroom when the bell for recess rings.

"I hope he doesn't bring too many trophies," I joked lightly.

"The only trophies that will cross my threshold are pictures. If he tries to bring any animal part into my house, they'll be sharing a bed with him in the basement."

Poor Dad. Just like me, he could never win an argument against Bizzy. But for once I was with her on the trophy thing. I was very fond of my dad but I found his hobby barbaric. What made him believe he was more of a man by hunting wretched animals that minded their own business? It baffled me. Perhaps it was because he was married to a predator. Maybe he needed to be the hunter, not the prey once in a while.

"Seriously, Sloane. I wouldn't head home early if I weren't certain that you were doing fine. You're in a much better place than when I got here."

It didn't feel that way. I was confused, and scared, and sure I would die alone.

"You have Gabriel, and if I heard correctly this morning, you have Tom as well. You don't need me anymore."

My future with Tom looked bleak, and Gabriel, despite saying he wanted to make this work, still felt flimsy to me. Maybe it was his past as a player that made it so hard for me to trust him. I couldn't quite picture him committing to anything, let alone a serious relationship with a mother of two. Besides, he was way too hot for me.

I kept my doubts to myself, refusing to burden Bizzy any more than I already had.

"If you play your cards right, you'll have Tom back in the house before I set foot on the plane home."

Her remark made my eye twitch. It had been a while since she had laid the blame on me for the separation but now it seemed we were back there. I attributed it to unfortunate formulation and let her elaborate.

"I'm glad to see you've learned from your mistakes."

My mistakes?

"You think it's my fault Tom left?"

"No. That's not what I'm saying. Just that in every divorce, there're wrongs on both sides."

She took a sip of water.

"But now you're different. If you keep paying attention to your looks and don't grow overconfident, I'm sure you'll do just fine."

Before I could help it, I stood up and slammed both of my hands against the kitchen counter. Bizzy dropped her composed look for a moment, her mouth gaping like she would swallow a fly.

"Stop making it like it's my fault!" I screeched. "I didn't make Tom leave me. He left because he's a jerk."

Bizzy shook herself out of her trance and tried to speak but the furious torrent bursting through my lips drowned her words.

"I might not have worn enough make-up to suit your taste, or dressed to the nines every damn morning but it doesn't mean I dropped the ball."

Violent tears sprang from my eyes, my stomach churning

from a sense of injustice. Why was she so prejudiced against me? My own mother, when everyone else, from Gabriel to Ethan to my four- and eight-year-old daughters even, saw how unhappy Tom made me feel and how unfairly he'd treated me. To Bizzy, I would always be the one at fault, no matter the situation.

"He dropped me! From one morning to the next – no thank you, no goodbye, no *you've been a great wife for loving me no matter what*, no *thanks for giving me two wonderful daughters*." I doubled over, a painful stitch in my side like I had just run a marathon, making it hard for me to breathe. "Nothing!"

The burning tears were turning into heavy, soothing sobs that I welcomed. They were purifying tears. They came with a realization that set me free.

"I did not deserve this."

This wasn't the first time I'd thought the words, but never before had I said them aloud. They ripped the heavy curtain of duty that hid all other choices from me and opened up a whole new horizon.

Faced to my dramatic reaction, Bizzy stood frozen on her stool, ghostly faced and tongue-tied. I was surprised she hadn't sought refuge under the table by now. I could have starred in *The Exorcist*, I was so frightening.

I left Bizzy behind, feeling nothing but resentment for the woman who had always brought me down unduly. But as I made my way out of the house, my anger collided with a strange sort of cheerfulness.

"I did not deserve this." I chanted the magic words over and over again.

They were merciful. They freed me from my obligations to Tom. Perhaps Fate was presenting me with a chance to be happy.

I stashed my keys in my purse and slammed the door to the house shut. The guilt I'd been carrying since the divorce exuded from my pores with every step I took, leaving room for a new host of possibilities.

It was as if my heart had been full with the ugly feeling

of shame, and my fight with Bizzy had cleared enough room for other positive feelings. I wanted to start fresh, to build something pure and good, to chase the gloom of Tom with radiant love.

I thought of Gabriel and what he'd told me the previous night. He was willing to give us a try, and as suddenly and unexpectedly as I had shied from his touch yesterday, I was now ready to give us a shot as well.

I wished I could talk to someone about all those new feelings that made my head swirl. Claudia would be so proud of me if she heard I was at long last over Tom. My hand closed around my phone, ready to dial her number before I remembered she wasn't talking to me. She'd asked for some time and as her friend, I had to respect that. Besides, knowing Claudia, she would ask me to grovel for ages before dropping the subject and letting me gush about my new life's prospects. I couldn't risk losing my mojo so soon.

So I went to see the second best person in line, who was also the first best listener in my entourage – Nala, the esthetician. I walked for ten minutes to the Ginger and Honey Spa before realizing my favorite confessor might not be there. Like kids who think their teacher lives at school, since meeting Nala, I had carried the silly belief that she was constrained to the beauty parlor.

My tongue felt heavy with words needing to be spoken and I almost cried from foreseen disappointment. But I made myself go in anyway, on the small chance she might be in today and also because if I wanted to take my relationship with Gabriel to the next step, I was in desperate need of waxing.

A different receptionist welcomed me from her desk.

"Hello, may I help you?" she asked with a nasal voice.

"Is Nala here?"

"Yes." She nodded. "She's with a client."

I breathed a little better now that there was hope.

"What do you need?"

"Waxing." I winced in anticipation.

I bent down to examine my bare legs in a skirt. They could do with a little sprucing up.

"Half legs and bikini."

I'd shaved my armpits the day before so the hair there would never be long enough to wax.

"Nikki can do it," the receptionist offered instead.

I waved her off. I was sure Nikki could take care of the waxing fine, but I wasn't about to confide in a perfect stranger. After our one wrapping session, Nala and I had developed a feeling of kinship. We were tight.

"I would rather wait for Nala, if you don't mind."

She raised an eyebrow but decided to humor me.

"Just sit here, please." She steered me toward the bench seat. "Would you like some tea? Water?"

"Tea would be nice," I replied, reclining against the silky cushions.

While I waited, I sent a text to Gabriel, feeling extremely bold.

Are you free tonight?

The girls were staying with Tom this evening for his last night in his bachelor pad. He would drop them tomorrow early, before the movers came but I could still make it back to the house before they even knew I had been gone.

Always for you, mi divina. Where would you like to go?

If we went out, I was afraid I would lose my nerve yet again. So did the sex-deprived goddess inside me, apparently, as she seemed to take over my hand and dictated the next message.

Want to show me your house?

Inner frustrated goddess launched herself into a *risqué* burlesque act. I worried my thumbnail, afraid Gabriel wouldn't take the bait.

Jimmy will pick you up at 8. Until then, I'll be thinking of you.

Major heat wave. I fanned myself with a spa brochure, crossing and uncrossing my thighs to control the pressure building up in my lower abdomen. *Six months!*

Nala stepped inside the hallway then, relaxed client in tow. She showed her to the desk where the receptionist waited with the bill. They spoke in Thai for a short while then Nala turned to me. I jumped on my feet, a warm smile etching on my face.

"Let's go," I spoke excitedly as I grabbed her arm and began dragging her toward the waxing rooms. "I hope you have time. Major crisis! I need a priest."

My confession session with Nala had left me sore all over and with even more questions than when I'd set foot inside her cabin. Should I jump head first into a new relationship with Gabriel, or should I take my divorce as an opportunity to learn how to be self-sufficient?

I was single for the first time in my life.

Should I explore singledom more thoroughly? Could something positive, some essential piece of wisdom, come out of it?

Or should I hang onto Gabriel for dear life and hope he would save me from a life of spinsterhood?

When Jimmy came to pick me up later that night, I was still trying to figure out what I should do. I wore a dress in case tonight was the night my inner goddess was finally let free, but it was demure enough it wouldn't look taunting if I went with door number two and chose to break things off with Gabriel. And even if I did have sex with Gabriel, I still didn't know what it would mean. Would it be a one-night stand or the beginning of a new relationship?

I sat inside the car, questions whirling wild in that head of mine. The pros and cons about dating Gabriel came flying fast, but no argument was strong enough to help me make a decision.

Mostly I wondered whether I would be capable of making it on my own. Could I handle it all? The girls, the house, school, the bills? Should I look for a job? Take up my studies? Suddenly the number of options laid before me was mind-blowing.

I could do anything. I could be anything. Would Gabriel let me be all that? Would he support me in my quest for inner growth and self-fulfillment?

Jimmy started up the car. As we drove down the street, I stared at my house, fondness filling me as I thought about the life I'd made there for myself, for my family. Tom leaving the house didn't make it less of a home.

The realization struck me that he'd never been essential to our life here. It was the girls, and me, even Claudia in her way, that made it home. We were the beating heart of the house. We were the core of our family.

"Stop the car," I heard myself tell Jimmy as fear washed over me.

The young driver turned around to make sure he had heard me right. Poor Jimmy, he looked lost in the face of the Harper women's fancies.

What would a new man do to my family? Could we survive another incursion in our life? Were we ready to welcome the change?

The universe shouted its answer clear and loud in my ear. It was too early. I was too wobbly still.

"Sorry, Jimmy," I said as I ran out of the car.

All along, it had never been about Gabriel. Only about me. I was a woman on a path to self-realization and I couldn't allow a man to divert my course. Not Gabriel, not Ethan, not Tom. I wasn't ready and neither was my family.

I'm sorry, I texted Gabriel from my front steps. *I can't.*

I didn't check my phone for an answer. Ever the coward, I prayed none would come.

Chapter Twenty

I woke up in Poppy's bed, the pillow soaked in tears. My sitting up was accompanied by a crunching sound from the cookie crumbs scattered all across the sheets. The cookie jar I'd dragged in bed with me yesterday night lay empty on the floor. I didn't need to worry about my weight anymore now that I had sworn off men.

Feeling fat and as empty as the jar, I hauled myself out of the tiny bed. My whole body screamed in agony from being cramped up in the small space all night. I just hadn't been able to face the solitude of my big bed. I'd needed to feel close to my daughters for the short hours sleep had descended reluctantly upon me.

My skin itched from sleeping with my makeup still on and I had chocolate tattooed on my hands and arms. I was in desperate need for a bath before the girls came home.

On my way to the bathroom, I stopped to check my phone charging on the nightstand. There was no text or call from Gabriel. I was glad to discover I was mostly relieved about that.

Ethan and Tom had tried to call me about two hundred times each. I ignored Ethan's calls just like I had been doing all of Friday but returned Tom's, just in case something had happened to the girls.

"Where have you been all morning?" Tom barked on the line.

I glanced at the clock on the screen. It was only 8.30.

"Hello, Tom. What can I do for you?" I replied.

"You never called me back yesterday. The movers are on their way. What address should I write on the boxes?"

"What address?"

Oh! So he thought moving back in was still an option. I almost laughed aloud at what a presumptuous prick he was. Then again, I might have led him to believe he had a chance. He couldn't possibly know what had gone on in my head since we last saw each other. That would require thinking of someone other than himself, and we both knew he was completely incapable of it.

"Tom, you and I are over. You can write Kate's address on your boxes. Or better yet, Alaska. Either way, I don't care."

"Is this a joke? Because let me tell you, Sloane, it's not funny," he said. "I've got twenty boxes to pack and two wicked daughters unpacking everything just as I close them. I don't have time for your shit."

I zoned out while he got himself worked up. All I could think about were the precious minutes of bathtub time I was missing.

"So I'm coming home, right?"

"Sure. And while you're at it, you should invite Kate over. Once Bizzy leaves, we'll have a spare room for her."

"Kate's not a problem anymore. We split up."

"Well, good for you. But you're not coming home either way," I retorted, the small reservoir of patience I still held for Tom about to run out. "Goodbye, Tom."

I hung up and threw the phone on my bed. I had probably less than half an hour before Tom charged in here. In the meantime, no one else would stand between me and my steaming, scented, bubbly heaven.

I stripped off my clothes in a flash, adjusted the water, and eased in the scalding hot water. The temperature was uncomfortable but I relished it, feeling as if it would burn my worries away. Mostly, I hoped I would be freed of my guilt toward Gabriel.

I had never been on this end of the stick and I hated it. As I closed my eyes and immersed my face in the water, I realized I would rather be the dumpee a thousand times over being the dumper.

I liked my conscience clean. This was the one thing I

had, my only pride. Up until yesterday, I had always been good, always tried to do the right things. When I looked in the mirror every morning, I might not like what I saw all that much, but at least I knew my soul was all right.

Now, I'd done precisely what Gabriel had asked me not to do. I'd toyed with his feelings and I didn't know how I would ever make it up to him. Leaving Tom and fighting with Ethan seemed futile in comparison to my behavior toward Gabriel. They deserved what they got, he didn't.

I returned to the surface of the water for air, feeling much more together. I knew what bothered me most and what I had to do. Now I just had to find a way to apologize. It wouldn't be today, or even soon – Gabriel probably needed his space – but I would eventually find a way to make amends.

"Sloane?"

"Mom!"

My arms flailed and I slipped, barely managing to stay afloat by gripping hard on both sides of the bathtub.

"You almost killed me!" I spoke between gritted teeth when I found my balance at last.

I craned my neck around and saw Bizzy standing in the doorway. Remembering I was naked, I crossed my legs tightly and collected foam from the surface of the water into a makeshift bra.

WASPs didn't do naked. Most of my family undoubtedly had sex fully dressed. They most certainly didn't expose their private parts to their mothers.

"Go away!" I waved her toward the door.

"I'm not going anywhere," she said, walking to the windowsill facing the bathtub.

Her silk wrap dress rustled has she sat down and laid her manicured hands on her lap.

"I'm busy," I hissed, feeling panicky.

This was a situation I was certainly not prepared to handle.

"Every time we talk, you storm out of the room before I can finish my sentence. Now, I'm your mother and you will hear me out. If it takes cornering you in your bathtub, then so be it."

"But I'm naked."

"Yes, you are. Just like the day you came out of me. Something you tend to forget."

The shine in her eyes belied the hard set of her mouth. She wasn't angry so much as she was sad.

"I am not the evil witch you make me out to be and my life's mission isn't to ruin yours. I love you, Sloane. Although from the look of it, sometimes ineptly."

"Can I at least get out of the bath? If you would just turn around for a second, I can grab my bathrobe."

"No. Please, stay. You know I don't do apologies well. I really need you to hear me out."

I sighed. I knew there was no arguing with Bizzy. I would just have to endure patiently.

"All right. Shoot."

Her mouth twitched at the colloquialism. I could picture her struggling with the need to correct me: "*You don't shoot anything, Sloane, you listen.*" She had enough sense to let it go, though.

"After our fight yesterday, I realized I've been working under the wrong assumption that you knew how I felt about you—"

"That I'm a lazy train wreck?" I offered with a dry smile.

"That I'm proud of you," she replied without losing her cool.

Surprise made my mouth seal shut. I surely hadn't seen this one coming.

"I never thought I needed to compliment you. As you know I've never needed anyone to make me feel self-confident."

I smirked. Yes, I knew that very well. "That's what people usually do. Praise their kids, tell them they love them—"

"So you think I don't? You truly believe your own mother doesn't love you?"

246

"I think I'm a big disappointment to you. You're quick enough to point out my many, many flaws."

"That's only because I care about you. I want to help you get better, stronger. Isn't that a motherly thing to do?"

"I guess."

Did she mean it? Could Bizzy possibly be proud of me?

"But then why do you always make it out to be my fault Tom left? Why can't you take my side once in a while?"

"I am on your side. I can't stand the little prick."

Utter dislike showed on her downturned lips. I stifled a laugh, taken aback by her outburst.

"You do?"

"Of course! First of all, I never thought he was good enough for you and second, he's broken my daughter's heart."

"Why then?"

"Why what?"

"Why do you take his side? You're all smiles when you see him. You're giving me advice on how to get him back—"

"I thought you wanted him back! I thought it would make you happy, though for the life of me, I could never understand why. I'm your mother, I want what you want."

"I told Tom we're over."

"Then I'm glad. But had you chosen to take him back, I would have pretended to like him for your sake."

She rubbed her forehead, rings flashing in the daylight streaming through the window.

"I'm sorry, Sloane. Since you were a little girl, you've always been good, sweet. Like your father. All I've ever tried to do is to make you stronger. I was afraid someone, like Tom, might take advantage."

"You don't take advantage of Dad."

"Your father and I are lucky. We love each other." She paused. "You were right when you said you weren't responsible for your divorce. Truth is, Sloane, you were dealt a bad hand with Tom. There's nothing you could have done to prevent him from leaving. He's a narcissistic little man with mommy issues. No amount of strokes to his ego or grooming on your part would have sufficed to please him. You deserve so much better."

My lips quivered and soon tears ran peacefully down my cheeks, rejoining the fast-cooling bath water. I'd pictured this scene so many times I couldn't quite believe it was truly happening.

"After yesterday I realized how wrong I was about you. All along I was trying to strengthen you, but you're already strong, Sloane. Much more than you give yourself credit for."

Her eyes lit when she smiled at me. Tears had been pooling in her eyes but she didn't shed any. Crying wasn't proper in Bizzy's book. I smiled back, my own tears coming to a halt. In the past months, I had cried more than in the rest of my life but these had been happy tears. I promised they would be the only one allowed for the times to come.

"I'm not scared about leaving you. I know you'll do fine," Bizzy asserted, sounding like herself again. "And now you can beat Tom to a pulp if he ever bothers you again."

"Thanks for the classes, Mom. It's really helped me. Although I think I might slow down on the cadence once you leave."

"You'll have to. Getting to watch Sven everyday was worth every dime but it quite depleted my bank account. Thank god your father spent most of our savings on his sabbatical! He's not in a position to give me a lecture on money. I would have been in a world of trouble otherwise."

"I could pay you back. It might take a while but—"

"Don't worry. We still have a few trinkets to sell. We don't want for anything, really. I don't know about your inheritance…" She smiled sheepishly.

"It's okay, Mom. You've done enough already."

Bizzy nodded.

"It's nice, you know, spending time together without bickering. I used to love your bath time. Remember we would sit like that every night while you told me about your day?"

I did, although I'd unfairly buried all good memories with Bizzy for many years. She was a good mother, in her own twisted way. There was a moment where we stared at each other, an instant so perfect I felt like giving her a hug. She must have felt it too because she stood up and took a couple steps toward me. Then recalling I was stark naked under the water, I said, "Maybe later?"

Bizzy chuckled and nodded. "Later."

She continued toward the door then backtracked to level with me.

"I almost forgot. Your phone," she said as she handed it to me.

I dried my hand quickly against the shower mat before taking it.

"It was buzzing when I came into your room then I completely forgot about it. I'm sorry, I hope it wasn't important."

"Don't worry, Mom. Thank you."

"I'll see you downstairs," Bizzy said before exiting the bathroom.

A smile played on my lips. For once, I looked forward to seeing her again.

I glanced at the screen. Three more missed calls and one text from Ethan. I looked it up wearily.

Stop screening my calls.

Fat chance for that.

Word on the street is something's going down tonight. Gabriel tell you anything?

I blew on a damp strand of hair that hung in front of my eyes. He must be referring to the mysterious appointment between Hector and Yuri. But how did he hear about it?

Ethan must be more connected than he had let me know. Too bad his sources couldn't get the right culprit straight. I suddenly worried tonight was a set up. Maybe Hector and Yuri were working together to put the blame on Gabriel.

Either way, this might be my chance to make it up to Gabriel earlier than I'd hoped. I had to use what I knew somehow to clear Gabriel's name. Perhaps I could find overwhelming evidence against the two of them to show Ethan he was harassing the wrong man.

I climbed out of the bathtub and shrugged into my robe, toes tingling from anticipation. This mission was exactly what I needed to change my mind from the men in my life and my fears for the future. I started reviewing the things I needed to do before tonight.

At the school, I had overheard Hector and Yuri say 11:00. Any TV show buff knew no evil deed ever happened in the morning so it had to be 11:00 tonight. Plus, otherwise, I was already too late. I would never figure out where to go in less than an hour.

There was no way I was involving Ethan in my mission or letting him know I'd broken things off with Gabriel. I send him a text only to get him off my back.

This is police abuse. Heard nothing. Leave Gabriel alone.

I walked into the bedroom with a new spring in my step. As I shrugged on a tank top and shorts, I bubbled with excitement, grateful for the chance to make amends.

Gabriel was a sweet man – his silence since yesterday a proof of his kindness. He was abiding my wishes, something no man except my father had ever done for me. I didn't change my mind concerning us. I knew with a profound conviction the time wasn't right for us. But I loved thinking I was acting as his guardian angel. Tonight, Secret Agent Sloane would unfold her wings and fly to his rescue.

Using my few last minutes of respite before Tom dropped the girls, I fired up my laptop and typed in a new search. I didn't have much to go on in my quest for justice but I trusted it would suffice. I was working on conjectures alone. Hopefully, chance would pitch in.

I thought back to the details of Hector and Yuri's conversation and tried to understand why Rotterdam had anything to do with their scheme. I was dead certain they cared nothing for flowers, but whatever was hidden inside the crates, wouldn't it be easier to fly it straight to London rather than add another stop in Holland?

I typed a search pairing "flowers and Rotterdam" on the laptop and discovered Rotterdam was the biggest flower platform in Europe. Except for flowers with extremely short life spans, they were all flown to the commercial port then dispatched all across Europe, either shipped or picked up by trucks.

If Hector diverted the shipment destination to London, he would risk attracting Gabriel's, and perhaps customs authorities' attention to their scheme. First question mark explained.

Also, Holland would make sense if they were trading drugs. Maybe the crates really carried flowers on their way in from Colombia before being filled with cannabis in Rotterdam.

Now I needed to find the right commercial port in London where Varela Global's crates were getting shipped. I hoped this was where Hector and Yuri were planning to meet.

I typed a new research and Fate rewarded my efforts by reducing my focus to one single port. According to Wikipedia, all docks in London had been shut down over the years, leaving just the one for me to visit, London's Royal Docks, east of the city. I knew the area a little bit because it was in the vicinity of London City Airport, London's smallest but most central airport.

The place seemed absolutely huge and I had no idea where exactly the delivery was supposed to take place but I figured the docks would be fairly empty at night, reducing the number of sheds I would have to inspect. I calculated the amount of time it would take me to drive to the docks and added an hour to find my way around the place.

Then I went downstairs to welcome the girls and face

Tom's inevitable tantrum.

At 9 p.m. sharp, I turned the ignition inside the Mini. The girls were tucked in bed already and Bizzy was on her third martini.

I was dressed in camouflage mode, wearing black from head to toes, including my undies in case they had a black light somewhere. Who said you didn't learn anything in nightclubs? "Push It To the Limit," *Scarface*'s theme song, blasted from the speakers. It belonged to my new 'Secret Mission' playlist that I'd put together earlier today.

On the passenger seat was a backpack with everything I might need tonight. My long stakeouts in front of Varela Global had taught me to bring snacks, a water bottle, and a thermos of coffee.

To that I'd added a flashlight to make my way through the deserted and dark docks, an extra pair of socks and a scarf in case they had AC in there – I mean, they must keep the flowers refrigerated somehow – my phone, and a can of hairspray because I didn't have time to get myself real pepper spray.

I really hoped I wouldn't need to use the latter, but as they say, better safe than sorry. All in all, I was pretty proud of my organizational skills. Mom spies had a great advantage over their childless counterparts. If you knew how to pack a diaper bag, a super-secret backpack in comparison was a walk in the park.

The headlights from a BMW parked farther down the street bothered me. I steered the car into the street to avoid their bright glimmer. Super-secret mission was a go.

The drive was pleasant at this time of night. I didn't have to wind through the Saturday night mess of central London, and I was grateful. In only thirty minutes, I arrived at the docks, my voice hoarse from singing along with the radio.

I had expected to find the parking lot completely empty but there were quite a lot of cars there. I wondered if they belonged to the few companies that had elected the commercial docks to set up their headquarters. Anyway, it made hiding the baby blue Mini Austin much easier. I parked behind a ginormous truck that provided the perfect cover for my car.

I took my time exiting the car, with thirty minutes ahead of me to find the appointed meeting place. I slid my arms into the backpack straps, slung my black hoodie across my forearm, and beeped the car shut. Then I crept stealthily across the parking lot, toward the docks.

The massive boats anchored to the wharf seemed to be a good indicator I was heading the right way. The sun had set just twenty minutes before, protecting me from inquisitive eyes, but it was light enough still I didn't need my flashlight.

Tiny silhouettes rustled about the first boat in view. Luck was definitely on my side. What were the odds other boats would be discharged so late in the night? I reached a shed at last, relieved I'd made it across the open space of the parking lot.

There seemed to be about two or three identical sheds in front of each boat. They were vast rectangles, their white paint fading where it hadn't peeled all together. Hugging the walls, I came as close as caution would allow to the boat. I squinted in the twilight to read its name but instead of a cutesy name like sailing boats usually carried or a simplistic name like Varela Global, it was crudely baptized VT-07985325.

Towers of crates were already stacked in front of the doors to the first shed. The light coming from inside was so dim that I couldn't read the name stamped across the wood without walking forth. My stare swept left and right then I held my breath and scuttled behind the towering boxes for shelter. Disappointment pinched my side. Whatever weird code name Varela Global might be using on its crates, I doubted it used Chinese. I didn't have to force a crate open to know these belonged to the wrong company.

For the first time today, I experienced doubts. Perhaps I had it all wrong. Hector and Yuri could be in Heathrow airport right now for all I knew. With no other option available, I decided to forge ahead.

I was less careful as I moved to the next boat, not worried anymore about this particular crew. That got me spotted by a few dockers with arms as big as me. Their t-shirts were damp with sweat despite the refreshing nightly breeze and they looked thirsty. The way their eyes glided down my bare arms in a tank top and my butt and legs – though very unattractively hidden under sweat pants – made me think no amount of water could quench their particular kind of thirst.

I hurried along, their whistles and crude remarks a great incentive for speed. The next boat was yet another bust, with yet another odd, multilingual crew that must have spent way too much time at sea to react so strongly at my sight. Their reactions made me teeter between vanity and fear all the way to boat three.

I was utterly mistaken when I'd thought the docks would be empty. Apparently, it reached its peak of activity at night. Under the cover of shadows, the place was bustling. Boat three was empty and its shed was dark. Boat four, PA-5429F had a very small crew working it, probably maintenance. They kept switching the lights on and off.

I'd thought I had plenty of time to spare but considering the long line of boats dragging in the horizon, I might never make it on time. Between the creeping and squatting it took to be discreet, I was ten minutes short of missing the appointment.

I hauled myself to boat five. It was eerily quiet. There was not even a bleep of the usual buzzing sound of the engine or the generator. The silence was so perfect, my mind conjured up sounds to fill the void – muffled footsteps, panting in the distance. But when I turned around, there was not a living soul. I pinched my hand hard to snap out of my paranoia.

The skin on my neck prickled from dread. I was almost tempted to skip my way to boat six but a strong instinct kept me there. Or maybe it was the massive turbine sticking out back of the shed, some kind of giant AC.

From my web search, I had learned flowers needed to be stored in cool sheds to keep them from wilting. So far it was the first cooling system I'd come across.

The light of the shed assigned to VG-90527 was on.

In case Shed 13 was the one, I went through the back and looked for a window to peek inside. I found two, just clear enough that I could see inside the shed despite the grime.

The sight of Hector standing beside about ten crates in the center of the room nailed me to the ground. Jimmy stood on his right side, looking as uncomfortable as ever as he shifted his weight from one foot to the next. To his left was a bulky, shaved man I recognized as Gabriel's bodyguard from Ethan's surveillance pictures.

I had never met him before so I'd assumed he didn't work for Gabriel anymore. Maybe he had switched allegiance and had since been recruited by Hector. Anyway that was one man I didn't want to know…ever. Something in his glassy, grey eyes and demeanor felt off. I retreated farther away from the center of the window, just close enough that I could see without risking being seen.

Hector gestured to the crates and both psycho bodyguard and Jimmy knelt on the floor. They hammered the lid of the first crate open without removing it, then moved on to the next. I glanced at my watch. It was 10.55. Yuri must be on his way. Because I didn't know which way he was coming, I pulled myself into a tight ball against the wall while waiting for him.

Our portion of the wharf remained silent for another fifteen minutes, making me worry Yuri would be a no-show. I shook my arms and legs every so often to stop them from getting numb and to keep myself awake. At last, footsteps echoed on the quay.

"Yuri."

I hauled myself up and surveyed the inside of the shed.

"Hector," Yuri replied without offering his hand to shake.

This wasn't a visit of courtesy and Hector seemed to be on the same page. He stared at the three goons forming a human fence before the Russian tulip dealer, then spoke.

"Do you have the money?" Hector asked.

"Yes," Yuri replied.

"Show me."

"First, the merchandise."

Hector nodded then turned to bulldozer man.

"Open it."

I held my breath as the bodyguard knelt again and worked on the heavy lid. I felt like a TV show contestant when the countdown is on. This was my last chance of getting the right answer by myself. The suspense was almost too much to bear and I feared I might pee my pants. What would be hidden in here? Weed? Cocaine? Meth?

The lid fell down with a loud thump and I pinched the back of my hand to make sure I wasn't hallucinating. The crate was overflowing with vibrant red and yellow tulips.

I looked in dismay at Yuri's face, waiting for shock or fury at the discovery, but he looked serene, like that's precisely what he had been expecting. *Sloane Harper: spy in the hot pursuit of a tulip smuggler*. Hysterical giggles came bubbling but I suppressed them before making a sound.

Bodyguard was still kneeling. He looked at Hector hovering above him and waited. Was he afraid of opening another box? Wild orchids stashed there maybe?

Instead, he scooped up armfuls of tulips and dropped them unceremoniously on the floor next to him. If I were Yuri, I wouldn't buy them now that they were damaged goods.

Under the tulips, about mid-level in the crate, was a wooden plank. He grunted as he lifted it and plopped it on top of the poor, ruined flowers. I pressed my face to the window, forgetting momentarily the dangers of my situation. My initial reaction was excitement – I had won! – immediately followed by panic; this was so much worse than anything I had imagined.

Bodyguard pulled out a large rifle-like weapon – a machine gun – from the bottom of the crate. It was followed by perhaps four or five of them, which, multiplied by the

256

number of crates stacked between the men, were enough weapons to arm a militia.

My first thought was for Gabriel. Were Hector and Yuri planning a coup against him? Or were they dealing weapons and planning to lay the blame on Gabriel? Anyway, I felt like I had to document this for later. I brought my phone out and took pictures through the window, my heart about to burst out of my chest.

One of Yuri's men picked a weapon from the floor and handed it ceremoniously to his boss. Yuri examined the long barrel, his face a mask of concentration as he fiddled with the trigger. He nodded for his man to bring the briefcase when a large boom came from somewhere very close to me.

I craned my neck toward the origin of the crash while keeping my phone trained on the inside of the shed. My finger was frozen on the shutter, jerking crazily as I spotted Tom about fifteen feet away from me, surrounded by fallen crates, his arm resting at an odd angle next to him.

"Tom?" I exclaimed in a strangled voice.

"My shoulder," he moaned.

"What are you—"

I slapped a hand on my mouth and peeked inside the shed, praying they had been oblivious to the commotion.

Hector's head was locked on my dirty window, his face distorted under raging madness. His fist was raised toward me while his other hand was lifted, palm out, in the direction of Yuri, as if he was trying to calm him down.

"This is a trick?" Yuri spoke, his *r* thunderous.

His men had gathered one machine gun each and retreated around their boss. Though the machine guns were probably empty, there was no doubt the guns sticking out of their pockets were loaded, making Hector sweat profusely.

"*Putana*," Hector spat at me before focusing on Yuri. "No. No, Yuri. It isn't what you think. The money—"

While he argued about payment, Hector stopped watching me altogether. I knew it was just a matter of minutes before he remembered he wanted to kill me so I decided to make the most of it.

I crept to where Tom was still lying and helped him up using his good arm. I gave him ten seconds to steady himself then whispered urgently in his ear.

"Run!"

Chapter Twenty-One

Tom slowed me down considerably. He had always been the worst patient and now he was provided with the role of his life: the injured fugitive. He panted and moaned so much it seemed like he was giving birth.

"Hurry!"

"I can't! I'm hurt."

"Not nearly as much as if they catch you. Come on!" I said as I steered him toward the wharf.

"Behind the sheds is faster to the parking lot," Tom argued.

"Yes, but the wharfs are busy. We can hide between the crews."

"I'm sure you'd like yourself a sailor," he hissed. "I heard their crass remarks on our way in. You must have loved it."

"So you followed me all the way. Why?"

"I wanted to see if you were going to Varela's. Ouch!"

He complained as I pulled his good arm to make him rush through boat four's deserted quay. I would feel much better once we melted into the swarming crowd of the docks.

"Tom, what's wrong with you?"

"What's wrong with me? What kind of crazy bitch hangs out on the docks at night? And you left me today! I had to know if it was for him."

"You left me six months ago. You divorced me! You have no right." I craned my neck behind for the hundredth time in five minutes.

No sign of Hector. Or Yuri. I almost let myself hope they had offed each other, and then I felt guilty for thinking it. I wasn't that lucky anyway.

"You're my wife!" Tom spat.

"Ex-wife. And I don't usually hang out here. I was looking for something."

"Yeah. Machine guns. Seriously? What the hell are you doing? I dislocated my shoulder because of you. I was so surprised I fell off the crates."

"What were you doing there anyway?"

"I was curious. And it was a great vantage point before the tower crumbled down."

"You shouldn't have been here."

Between sheds seven and six, I spied Yuri running in the direction of the parking lot. I stopped breathing while I watched him disappear behind the building then watched his men chasing after him, each cradling a machine gun in their arms as if they were babies saved from the flames.

We were right there in the open, an easy target had they wanted to shoot us but Yuri hadn't seen us, and his men seemed to consider us inoffensive. Thank god for that.

If Yuri thought this was a trap, he was probably afraid the cops were on their way. Hence the running.

I turned my jog into a full sprint as I realized Hector and his crew would soon come after us. Tom complained but I told him to shut up. I was saving his life here.

When we made it to boat two and its colorful crew, I slowed down a little. Tom's face was turning a sick shade of grey and I worried he might pass out on me. Tom wasn't tall, yet I could never carry his dead weight all the way to the car.

The sailors spotted us and their jeers burst forth through the night.

"Babe, leave the sissy!"

"If you want a workout, I know how to make you sweat!"

"He runs like a girl!"

I would have been scared had I not known there was way more danger coming for me. Between boat two and boat one, I spied Jimmy and the bodyguard. Behind them, panting like a bull in the arena, was Hector.

Jimmy snaked his way between the crew, his skinny body ideal for the task, while Bodyguard just shoved everyone out of his way. They were progressing way faster than we ever could with Tom half fainting from the pain. I kept my eyes ahead, trying not to waste any more time by looking behind, but Hector's voice forced me to look at him.

"You stupid American whore! I'll kill you!" he growled, one hand on his heart as if he feared an attack. Would serve him right. My stomach climbed into my throat as I succumbed to fear. There was no way out of this. I was screwed.

"What did you just say?" A man with a short sleeve tee and white blond hair advanced toward Hector, hands curled up into fists.

"He threatened the lady?" someone I couldn't see asked, his voice foreboding.

A couple other guys joined in the circle forming around Hector.

"Let's teach you how to speak to a lady," the blond guy suggested.

I almost ran back to kiss my white knight but my ex was hanging over my arm dangerously, and Bodyguard and Jimmy were still standing between us. They were busy watching their boss getting mobbed at the moment. I decided to take advantage of the situation. I shook Tom as hard as I could. His hazy stare struggled to focus on me.

"We just have this one chance. I need you to give it all you've got."

I breathed better when it was clear he understood me. Tom lifted his head up and angled his whole body in the direction of the parking lot.

"Go!" I urged him as we ran like the devil himself was at our heels.

We passed boat one in a breeze, my lungs burning like I had done ten shots of vodka but my hope flaming high. We just needed to make it through the large open space separating us from the parking lot then we would be safe. It felt like wings were propelling me forward.

We made it to the first truck when Bodyguard came barreling down on Tom. He snatched him from me, holding him down with one bulging arm then smashing his face against the side of the truck. A sinister crack resounded as Tom's face kissed the car and a terrified shriek escaped my lips. I stepped back, struggling with my backpack straps. My hand connected with the hairspray can just as Jimmy ran to give Bodyguard a hand.

I didn't worry too much about Jimmy. He looked more frightened than I was so I chose to help Tom first. He thrashed like a devil, blood spurting from his nose, helpless. Bodyguard wouldn't move an inch under his desperate assaults. Giving up winning this fight, Tom snarled at me.

"You fucking disaster! You're unfit to be a mother."

I curled up my fingers a couple times but fought the urge. Instead, I ran toward them, finger ready on the hairspray trigger.

"I'll sue you for custody!" Tom spat.

I would make him eat his genitals before he had the chance. I could leave him here, but then my daughters would be orphans and that wasn't an option.

"Shut up before I change my mind about saving your ass. Close your eyes!" I warned as I sprayed the whole can into bodyguard's face.

He doubled over, cussing and spurting, tears sprouting out of his eyes like a geyser. He let go of Tom who kept his eyes firmly shut, his arms flailing around him.

"Where do I go? Where do I go?" he mumbled.

Jimmy was now five feet away from me. He looked like he would rather be anywhere else. Before dealing with Tom, I decided to put the young driver out of his misery. I darted toward him and kicked him as hard as I could in the nuts, feeling every bit as shameful as a Kung Fu trainee ought to feel. All this careful preparation and all I could come up with was this. Talk about hitting below the belt. Jimmy fell in a lump on the ground, calling for his mom.

"Can I open my eyes now?" Tom whined.

"Yes," I barked. "The car, now!"

I sprinted toward the place where the Mini was concealed, Tom in tow. I almost cried when I found my beloved car still nestled behind the massive truck and beeped it open.

"My Bimmer!" Tom cried.

"Later! Get in!"

I shoved him toward the passenger door.

"You're going to drive?"

"Why? You think you should?"

He shut up then and did as he was ordered. I kicked the car into gear and drove the hell away from this nightmare.

When I considered we had put enough distance between the docks and us, I dialed Ethan's number on my cellphone. The sound of the prerecorded message made me curse. Weeks of harassing me and he couldn't answer his damn phone when I needed him?

All I could think about was Gabriel and how he might be in danger right now as I waited for the beep that allowed me to speak.

"Ethan!" I barked. "You were right. Something went down tonight. Hector and Yuri were dealing weapons. I saw the guns!" I yelled, saying the thing aloud reminding me how lucky I had been out there.

"I think Gabriel is in danger. I'm heading over to his house to warn him. If you're anything but a liar, you'll meet me there. This is serious, Ethan. I think they might kill him."

Not knowing what I could add to the message, I hung up and dropped the phone in the cup holder.

"We're not going to Varela's place. You're gone off the reservation. I need a hospital," Tom wailed, a bloody Kleenex pressed to his nose.

"We don't have time. Someone's life is at stake!"

"I don't give a flying fuck about your lover! My arm is broken."

"So is your nose, I think. Nothing that can't wait, though. We need to save Gabriel."

I fished my phone out of the cup holder and dialed

Claudia's number this time. The digital clock in the Mini indicated it was close to midnight but I had to try it.

"Hello," Claudia answered gruffly.

She was still mad at me but I didn't care. I almost wept in relief.

"Hi, Claudia? I'm so sorry, about everything. I don't have time to explain yet but I swear I will." I kept going before she had time to hang up. "You were right about the man in my car, something's up with him. I need you to try to get a hold of him for me."

"Sloane? Are you drunk?" Claudia asked, her anger replaced by worry. "It's the middle of the night. And I'm not alone." She'd dropped her voice to a whisper.

I whooped in my head for Claudia and Sven before recalling my urgency.

"I'm not drunk. Something bad is about to happen if you don't help me."

Tom rolled his eyes and I punched him in his good arm.

"The man in my car, his name is Ethan. I need him to meet me at Gabriel's house."

"This is fucked up," Claudia commented. "You want your lover to come to your boyfriend's?"

"No. No, he's not… It's not important, anyway. Gabriel is in danger."

"Varela?"

"Yes. Can you call Ethan and make sure he has his address? You have to tell him it's really urgent."

"Why don't you call him?" she asked, sounding suspicious.

"I tried. I don't have time. Please Claudia, do this for me."

I realized I sounded insane but I couldn't help it.

"Okay." She sighed. "You know how to ruin a good time, you know? What's his number?"

I gave her Ethan's number then Gabriel's address. He had shown me his house once when we drove past it.

"I'm not sure whether it's number 23 or 25. Tell him it's a white house. The largest one in the mews."

"Of course it would be the largest one," Claudia commented.

"Claudia, I need to go."

"Okay." She sighed.

"You'll call Ethan."

"Yes. I told you I would."

"Thank you! You're the best."

"I knew that already."

She hung up.

We were just ten minutes away from Gabriel's house now and I stepped on the gas, trying to drone out Tom's complaints to avoid getting into an accident.

When I parked in front of the house, all was quiet, letting me hope I wasn't too late. I snatched my phone that was frustratingly silent and threw open the door. Tom pretended that he was rooted on the passenger seat.

"What are you waiting for? Get out!"

Tom shook his head stubbornly.

"I'm not going in there. No way. You can go alone. I'll wait here."

No way was I leaving him here. I wanted to have Tom where I could keep an eye on him. Who knew what kind of trouble he could stir up on his own? I pretended that it was fine by me.

"Good. This way you'll be the first one Hector kills when he comes here."

I walked away from the car.

"Wait for me!" Tom hissed, closing the door after him.

I turned around and beeped the car shut. I skipped the large marble front steps in two long strides and pressed the bell.

"A bit tacky, isn't it?" Tom said next to me.

I looked at the house. It was an Italian style villa, with four large marble colonnades and renaissance carvings around the doorframe and the windows. Tacky to my taste, but I was sure Tom would eat his own arm to have a house like this.

A maid in a white apron came to answer the door. She

looked befuddled to find us here in the middle of the night.

"Is Mister Varela here? I need to talk to him." I grabbed her hand to convey my sincerity but she pulled her hand away from me and slammed the door shut to my face. Tom snickered behind me. I bit my finger to stop me from punching him. Thirty seconds later, the door opened again, this time Gabriel appearing behind it.

"Gracias. Io los conosco," he said to the maid hidden somewhere inside the hall.

His eyes were cold as he watched the pitiful pair Tom and I made waiting in front of his house. The corner of his lips curled upward in a mocking smile.

"Sloane. I expected you yesterday."

"He doesn't seem pleased to see you," Tom said.

"I needed to warn you," I said, my cheeks flushing from shame. "Hector—"

I scrutinized the dark mews before speaking again.

"Can we come in? It's not safe here."

Gabriel stepped back.

"After you."

I walked gingerly inside, followed by Tom. As soon as were both in the foyer, Tom fainted with a loud *thump* against the marble floor.

"Tough night?" Gabriel asked, nudging Tom's heaped body with his loafer.

That pissed me off. Tom might be a jerk but that was no way to treat a fallen man.

"Will you help me? He needs to rest."

Gabriel looked disappointed. If I left it to him, Tom would probably have served as a doormat till morning. I grabbed Tom under the armpits and Gabriel held his feet. We dragged him to a large living room next door. I found a comfortable enough looking sofa and dropped him there, my muscles crying with relief. Gabriel sat across from Tom in a blue velvet covered armchair without offering me to sit. It bugged me but I was too wired to sit down anyway.

"So what brings you here?"

"I had to warn you." I stopped and looked around the

place.

If Hector was planning a coup, he would be here any second. Even now that the money was lost to him, he still had the machine guns, enough gun power to overthrow a clueless playboy.

And if he had just wanted to use his boss's company as cover for his illegal dealings, he now knew that I knew, and it wouldn't take him long to suspect I had come to alert Gabriel. At the very least, he would come to take revenge over me, if he didn't decide to attack his boss in the open and get rid of us both. Us three, I corrected as I watched Tom's passed out shape on the sofa. His sleep was fitful, his eyelids twitching as if they wanted to snap open. I felt sorry for him. He'd had quite a night already.

Gabriel slapped his thighs to hasten me.

"I'm sorry. Does Hector have the keys?"

Gabriel rolled his eyes. I took it as a yes.

"Is there an alarm system that you can set up to keep Hector away? Otherwise, I believe we should go. It's not safe—"

"I'm not going anywhere. And now I want to know why I should hide from my staff."

He stood up and took a couple strides toward me. Something in the set of his shoulder made me cower, until the back of my shins hit the armchair behind me.

"Sit," he ordered.

It could have been a kind invitation, the way he gestured toward the armchair, without ever parting with his charming smile, but there was no mistaking the command in his cold stare. I sat down abruptly, recoiling further into the thick pillows, hoping to fuse with the gilded silk. Gabriel scared me and for once, I wished Tom would wake up.

Then I scolded myself for the irrational fear. The man had every right to be upset. I had dumped him via a text message and the next day I came charging in his home with accusations against the man to whom he'd entrusted his life. That didn't make him dangerous. That made him normal and perfectly entitled to his anger.

267

"Now. Talk. Please," he added as he began pacing the room.

I wrung my hands, trying to figure out where to start. I figured the 'peeling off a Band-Aid' approach would be best – fast, without time to think about the pain, so that it could be over before you realized it had started.

"Hector's smuggling weapons using Varela Global's shipment. He's selling them to Yuri Alexeyev."

Gabriel froze in the middle of the living room. He stayed silent for a minute before erupting in laughter.

"Wow! Sloane! That's a wild story you've concocted. If you wanted to kiss and make up, you could just have called."

"I'm not... It's not—"

"You expect me to believe that Hector – old, stupid Hector – is scheming against me?"

"He is!"

"Of course." He laughed some more. "And what proof of this conspiracy might you have?"

"I saw them! Tonight. They were on the docks."

Gabriel's smile faltered for the briefest moment. My heart swelled with hope. I was getting through to him at last. If I could just make him hear me, I could protect him.

"Where did you hear that?" he asked.

"I was there! So was he." I pointed at Tom on the sofa.

Gabriel's features softened a little, easing my breathing as it did. He walked over and knelt beside me.

"You saw them?"

His voice was soft as he took both my hands between his. I hadn't realized the slight tremor that made my limbs shake till he held me. I relaxed in his touch. After tonight's events, I was more shaken than I had let myself believe. With Gabriel looking straight into my eyes, I felt safe for the first time since I'd left my house.

"I did. I heard them plotting at the gala. I knew they were up to no good so I tracked them to the docks. I was afraid for you. I thought they might try to incriminate you in their stead," I blabbered away.

"Did you tell anyone about your suspicions?"

I thought about Ethan but I figured it was best to keep him out of this conversation. I needed Gabriel to trust me if I was to protect him from Hector.

"No one. I came straight here."

"Good," he said.

My eyebrows shot up.

"I mean, we should try to gather proof before going to the police. As you said, they might be trying to use me as a scapegoat."

I nodded. This was exactly what I feared.

"So they were smuggling weapons, you said?"

"Yes."

"And you watched the transaction take place?"

"Actually, it didn't. I guess I stopped it from happening," I said, a sense of pride lifting me up.

I thought I saw Gabriel's mouth twitch. Then his reassuring smile was back in place and I figured it was my mind playing tricks on me. No wonder the events of the night were taking their toll on me. Secret missions were exhausting.

"So it was all for nothing. We have nothing against Hector, or Yuri," he said.

"Oh no! We do!" I exclaimed as I retrieved my cellphone. "I took pictures."

I unlocked the phone and scrolled through the shots. I had documented most of the failed exchange, with a couple of portraits of Hector's distorted face as a bonus.

"Can I?" he asked.

I handed him the phone gladly. He looked at the pictures distractedly.

"Anything else?"

I scratched my head then said, "No."

"Good." He stood up and slipped the phone inside his jeans back pocket. "I guess I'll be holding onto that," he said as he dropped the smile all together.

My jaw went slack.

"Don't you want to call the police?"

The doorbell rang. Instead of answering me, Gabriel went to answer the door.

"Wait! What if it's Hector? You can't open the door," I argued as he left the reception room.

Hadn't I made myself clear? Were the pictures not clear enough? Why would he welcome Hector after all that? I prayed that it was Ethan at the door and just in case it wasn't, I tried to come up with an exit strategy. There was a window just behind me. I stood up and crept silently toward it, my hand on the latch in case I had to make a run for it, yet again.

"Just in time," I heard Gabriel say in the hallway.

He couldn't sound glad to see Hector. Surely, it was someone else at the door. I tapped my foot against the Persian rug, the suspense killing me.

"We have company," Gabriel said again.

When I spotted Hector's ugly silk shirt coming through the door, I flipped the window open and readied myself to jump. And then I recalled Tom sleeping on the couch and my muscles froze mid extension. I couldn't leave my daughters' father behind. Who knew what Hector would do to him in retaliation?

Hector's sadistic sneer welcomed me as I turned away from the window.

"Sloane was kind enough to come and warn me about what went down on the docks. I heard the transaction was a bust."

Why didn't he sound angrier? Or shocked at the very least?

"I'm sorry, boss. The bitch screwed it up."

"And the money?"

"Gone. Along with four machine guns."

Blood pounded under my temples, making me fear I might faint. I stumbled to the armchair and held on to it. Bodyguard on steroids stepped inside the room, eyes red and watery still from the hairspray, and Jimmy followed him, his mouth contorting in fright as he saw me there. His right hand moved protectively in front his slacks' zipper.

"Sorry, Mister Varela," Jimmy said, keeping his eyes to the ground.

Bodyguard just grunted. Gabriel resumed pacing the room, glancing at me from time to time, as if he were trying to figure out what to do with me.

"Gabriel. What is this? How? Why would you know?" I asked, tears making my voice break.

He snickered coolly. "Do you really believe my employees could pull off something like this? Behind my back?"

"But Hector! He said he was keeping a secret from you. I heard him with Isabella!"

His chuckle sounded sincere for once.

"You thought he was plotting with Isabella? Sweet, naïve Sloane. But they do share a secret."

I looked at Hector. Shame flushed his sweaty face bright red and he began mumbling. Gabriel raised a hand to shush him.

"Isabella is slumming with the help," Gabriel said with a vicious thrill. "She was my father's mistress for many years, and now she's fooling around with him." He waved in direction of Hector and sighed. "What grief would do to someone! But dear, old Hector has a code of honor, you see? Out of respect for my father, they've kept their affair a secret."

His laughter was cruel and a small part of me felt bad for Hector. That is, I would have if he didn't want to twist my neck so badly. How could I never see this part of Gabriel before? I had been so sure he was a good guy, but now I realized he was the worst of them all. I'd been dating a full-on psychopath all along.

"Now, sit down, Sloane."

I did as he asked. I was out of options. If Ethan didn't show up soon, I had a feeling both Tom and my life would be considerably shortened. Poppy and Rose's faces swam before my eyes and tears came in violent sobs.

"It's a little too late to cry, don't you think? Look what situation you've put me into. You could have had everything. You could have had me. But instead you dump me and then you put your filthy little nose in my business."

He ran his hand on the back of his neck.

"Now what shall I do with you, Sloane? How do we make this go away?"

"I won't... I won't say anything. If you let us go, I'll keep your secret," I said.

"See? I'm having a hard time trusting you. You haven't been very reliable, have you? Pretending you're a sweet, lost housewife yet using me to get back at your ex. I must say you have an awful sense of timing. Dumping me yesterday didn't exactly put me in the right frame of mind toward you."

"Please. I didn't mean it—"

"Shut up," he snapped. "Don't worry, I won't hurt you. I'm not a violent man."

Relief washed over me.

"Thank you! Thank you!" I cried.

"I think it's time for me to leave." Gabriel grabbed his sport coat from a loveseat by the door and shrugged it on casually.

Wait. He was taking me with him, right?

"Hector, take care of this," Gabriel said flatly as he turned around. "I'll be at the Claridges."

Pure, unadulterated fear twisted my guts. Hector rubbed his hands eagerly. I could see he had been praying for this outcome all along.

"Gabriel! Please! Don't... My daughters—"

He kept walking away, leaving me with the three men and my ex on the couch. Hector took his time walking toward me. He stopped by the coffee table and put down his gun. My hope was quashed almost immediately.

"I want to make this last," he said as he closed the distance between us in two fast strides.

The back of his hand hit my cheekbone with such violence, I staggered from the armchair and landed on the rug. The pain radiated across my entire face, so intense it muzzled my tears for good. I had never been hit before in my entire life.

Hector kicked me smack in the stomach, making me retch emptily. Just as the pain receded, he hit again, this time the tip of his shiny leather shoe connecting with my hip. I howled in agony.

My eyes fell on Tom's still form on the sofa and I dared to hope. He had to help. But even my cries weren't enough to wake him up. Resentment against Tom lodged itself in the pit of my stomach while a storm of kicks landed on me.

I tried to make Hector fall but he pared every one of my attempts by crueler hits. It all seemed hopeless.

I curled into a ball and brought my arms tight against my face to work as a shield. Once again, my salvation depended on a man. If Ethan didn't show up soon, Hector's vicious blows would end me. I hated that I was so weak and the shame rendered me even more helpless. *All that training, useless*. The pain clouded my thoughts and I wished I would faint.

The doorbell rung, miraculously preventing Hector's heel from crushing my hand against my face. He stopped hitting me just long enough to give Jimmy a command.

"Go get the door."

I tried to get away again but he smashed my stomach. Dots danced before my eyes. When they dissipated, I thought I was hallucinating.

"They said they wanted to see Mister Varela. Should I call him?" Jimmy asked the man in charge.

"*Stupid*! Who are these people?" Hector demanded. "Why did you let them in?"

I looked at Claudia in a knee length t-shirt that she had clearly borrowed and leggings. Her hair was blue now. Evidently, the pain was giving me visions. A disheveled Sven towered over her, his arm draped protectively around her shoulders. She shoved him away. Perhaps it really was her.

I used Hector's distraction to catch my breath and come up with a way to get away from him. So far, it was useless.

273

Claudia's piercing gaze fell on my crumpled form on the ground and I swore I could see tears brimming in her eyes. This lasted only a second, soon replaced by a defiant thrust of her chin and a caustic smirk.

"Wow! You're a terrible teacher." She turned to Sven.

My heart went to her as I discerned the concern behind her sarcasm. I must look terrible.

"Thought you might need some back up," she spoke to me directly.

If she was here, I feared that meant one thing. To confirm my suspicions, I raised my eyebrows in a question mark and nodded discreetly toward the door. Her face turned somber as she shook her head in a silent *no*. Just like I thought, she hadn't been able to contact Ethan. He wasn't coming.

This here – Claudia and Sven – was the only cavalry I would get. I pushed away the fear and sense of hopelessness and instead let fury fuel me. I stared at Hector hovering over me and experienced the full potential of my hatred for him. I wanted to kill the motherfucker.

Time to make my teacher proud.

Howling with rage, I grabbed Hector's pants hem and towed him down to the floor. He yelped in surprise as he fell then landed a new blow against my ribcage. The bone splintered with a sinister crack but I shoved away the throbbing pain. I dug my nails deep inside his arm instead. Claudia and Sven made their ways toward me to help.

"What are you waiting for?" Hector barked. "Get them!"

As I ducked Hector's fist, I watched as Bodyguard came charging straight at Claudia who dodged his assault effortlessly. Jimmy, who was trying to get away, found himself in Bodyguard's path and got knocked full force by the brute's body, sending him soaring toward Sven. The Kung Fu teacher reacted automatically, throwing a kick so high that the driver landed on the wall opposite from them.

Bodyguard changed his stance and aimed for Sven. He managed to kick the Viking in the shoulder before Claudia broke a Ming dynasty vase on top of his head. Bodyguard fell to the ground with a defeated *humph*.

I used the distraction to sink my teeth deep into Hector's arm, feeling the tendons hard beneath my clench. He howled in surprise and let go just long enough that I managed to roll away. I hauled myself on my knees, exultation making me buzz with victory. We were three against one now.

Hector was on all fours, heading straight for me. I jumped and ran to where Claudia and Sven were clustered close together. Their triumphant smiles faltered.

Never before had I seen Claudia looking shaken, let alone terrified as she did now.

"What's wrong?" I asked as I held onto Claudia's arm and turned around to see what scared her so.

Her arm was limp under mine as I spotted young, awkward Jimmy holding a gun in his quivering hands. My eyes darted to the coffee table – Hector's gun.

"Don't move!" he warned, sounding like he was about to cry. "Or I'll shoot. I swear!"

I made an appeasing gesture and tried to take a step forward. It was Jimmy holding the gun. He couldn't possibly mean it.

"Jimmy—"

"Stop! Stay where you are!"

"Shoot them, Jimmy," Hector said, using the coffee table for support.

"Jimmy, don't," I reasoned. "You don't want to—"

"Don't tell me what I want! Stop fucking talking!" he yelled, the gun jerking dangerously in his hands. "I'm done being told what to do!"

He was two steps away from a total mental breakdown. That made him dangerous.

"Now!" Hector barked, adding to the driver's tremor.

"Shut up! All of you! I need to think," he said, wiping a sleek palm against his slacks.

Hector bounded forward, making a move for the gun. We all ducked down as it fired.

A loud *boom* coming from the hallway echoed the

gunshot. I pressed my hands to my ringing ears, awash with panic. I didn't know what happened to Jimmy, or Hector, but Claudia and Sven seemed unharmed. Glancing into the hallway, I watched as a dozen men wearing black Kevlar vests and helmets teemed inside the house. Behind them came Ethan, also wearing a vest and holding a police scanner in one hand, a gun drawn in the other. His features were tense, as if he feared the worst.

When he spotted me, his eyes lit up, reflecting the relief in mine. The armed troops scattered around the living room, forcing all of us down on our stomachs at gunpoint. From the floor where I lay, I smiled at Ethan standing over me. I didn't care that it was embarrassing to be forced on the ground like a criminal or that I looked like a pathetic mess. The nightmare was over. He had shown up.

As a white rain of plaster from the shot ceiling fell softly on top of my head, I smiled. I never thought I would be so glad to see Ethan Cunning.

Chapter Twenty-Two

We all sat down in different corners of the room while the agents took our statements. Claudia had retrieved her usual nerve as she answered the questions curtly, her chin jutted in defiance of the authorities. Sven spoke like a robot, still shocked by being held at gunpoint.

My breathing had grown way easier since Jimmy and the bodyguard had been led in handcuffs into the vans parked outside. I tried not to delve too much on Hector's limp body on the floor, a button size crimson stain blooming on his shirt. Nor did I linger on the way his glassy eyes had locked with mine before the paramedics zipped him up in a body bag.

I waited for the guilt to hit me but mostly I was relieved. At least Hector wasn't a threat to me or my family if he was dead. I did feel remorse toward Jimmy, who had become a murderer tonight and whose young life was ruined because of it.

A squad had been dispatched to the Claridges after receiving my testimony. Hopefully Gabriel hadn't had time to get rid of my phone. They needed the pictures I had taken in order to arrest Yuri as well.

Tom had finally stirred and was being administered first aid by the paramedics. It had taken Jimmy's gunshot to wake him up. Surely, it was the same neurological deficiency that helped men sleep through fistfights as well as crying babies.

Ethan had been coordinating the whole effort and had barely spoken two words to me since walking in the house. When the MI5 agent who had taken my whole statement left, Ethan planted himself before me.

"Come," he said, grabbing my wrist and leading me upstairs.

We wandered into the first room to our right, the master bedroom, if its size was any indicator. Ethan closed the door and my legs shook all over again. I made an encompassing gesture toward the whole room.

"I finally got to visit the bedroom," I joked, trying to diffuse the tension.

Ethan barely managed to smile back.

"I thought I'd lost you. When I heard the shot—"

"Poor ceiling," I said, refusing to face the reality – I could have died back there. "You came—"

"I was waiting outside with the squad. I got your message straight away. Sorry I didn't call back. I was busy gathering everyone." He ran his hand in his messy hair.

"It's okay. I was worried you wouldn't show up."

"I told you I would always find you," he answered, his stare fixated on my lips.

I closed my eyes as his mouth crushed mine. The fear, the rage, the despair all combined into an all-consuming need to be touched, held, grasped. I locked my arms around his neck as his slender fingers dug into my bruised hip. The broken rib made it more difficult to breathe but mostly, it was the passion of his kiss that left me breathless.

I held on tight to the back of his head as he lifted me off the floor, without ever breaking off our kiss. It seemed like I could never get enough of it and I returned every stroke of his tongue with an equal fervor. The world stopped spinning while he held me, the endless flow of questions quieted as he laid me against the mattress, the weight of his body against mine putting my mind to rest momentarily.

I'd almost died tonight but the only thing that mattered this instant was Ethan and his healing caresses. Ethan leaned in deeper against me, against my splintered rib, sending a jolt of pain through me. A moan escaped my lips while my body tensed instinctively. Ethan broke the kiss and sat me down.

"You're hurt?" His brown eyes were full of worry as they searched my face.

"My rib." I winced, trying to bring him back toward me.

I needed to be close to him. When he held me, I was safe.

"No," Ethan said, sounding every bit as disappointed as I felt. "You need to see a doctor."

"Later." I waved him off, putting on a brave face. "First I have questions."

Ethan nodded, his fingers resting just a hair shy of mine on the coverlet.

"Did you know? About the guns?" I asked shakily.

Ethan's embarrassment answered before he had to open his mouth.

"Yes."

"So why didn't you arrest him before?"

"I almost did. In Miami. But he escaped before I could. I had to build a completely new case against him if I wanted MI5 to make the arrest. I have no jurisdiction here."

"That's where I came in. Right?"

He didn't dare meet my eyes.

"You almost had me killed," I said, sounding oddly detached. "My daughters—"

My daughters could have become orphans tonight. And he had done this. He had known my responsibilities and yet he had been far too willing to sacrifice me.

"Sloane, I'm so sorry. You have to understand. I investigated Varela for almost a year in Miami."

Ethan tried to grab my hand but I jerked it away.

"Do not touch me," I hissed.

"I had a PI. Her name was Ana. She worked in a strip club by the docks—"

Shame made him pause as he pulled against his neck.

"They killed her."

"So you thought you would get me killed as well? So she could have company?"

His eyes opened wide in shock.

"Of course not! I wanted to avenge Ana. I was so

279

consumed by my guilt that I didn't realize I was putting you in danger too. You were just supposed to spy on him! Things got out of hand—"

"So it's my fault?"

Well, maybe it was a little bit my fault. Ethan never asked me to follow Hector on the docks and, with hindsight, he might have tried to warn me about Gabriel... Shame warred with guilt inside me. Pushing both these feelings aside, I decided to hold onto my initial fury instead.

"Sloane, stop putting words in my mouth. I never said that," he said, bending toward me. "I'd have never forgiven myself if something had happened to you. You're the most obstinate, infuriating woman I've ever met. But thanks to your stubbornness, Varela is finally caught and on his way to jail."

He dove for a kiss, eyes closed. Mine were open, and so was my hand that slapped him right across the cheek. I smiled as I registered the shock on his face.

"You're a liar. You've manipulated me from the start—"

It was absolutely incredible. Every time a man disappointed me, there was always another one trying to outdo him, like they were participating in a *let Sloane down* contest. I wanted to strangle Ethan just as my lips itched to kiss him again.

"I never want to see you again!" I screamed. "Do you hear me?"

Afraid I would fall into his arms, just as I said the opposite, I decided now was a good time for a dramatic exit. I slammed Ethan's chest away from me as hard as I could and jumped down from the bed. A searing pain shot from my ankle, blurring my vision.

Ethan was by my side in a matter of instant.

"Sloane..." he said.

I never got to hear the end of his sentence because the world suddenly turned black as the night and I fainted.

The light filtering through the window was bright. I

blinked and shook my head from side to side, a feeble attempt to dissipate the fog in my skull. I felt like I had been run over by a horde of elephants. Every inch of my face was sore.

I stretched under the sheets and a sharp pain radiated across my chest. *Nope. Not elephants. Mammoths.* They had bounced on my ribcage apparently. I stuck to shallow breathing onward to minimize the ache.

Think. I propped myself in a half sitting position, reclining on my elbows. Yesterday had been Saturday. Saturday had been – Tom's moving day. I'd turned him down. My chest swelled with pride. I had stood up for myself.

Bizzy had noticed. She had apologized. Bizzy with the girls. She had agreed to babysit. I had needed her to babysit because –

Memories hit me like a whiplash. The drive to the docks, machine guns and tulips, Tom, Gabriel's house, and Hector's vicious blows. Heat rushed to my aching cheeks as I recalled Ethan in the bedroom, our kiss, the fight that had followed.

And then nothing. For the second time since meeting Ethan, my way back home was lost to me. I checked the alarm clock on the nightstand to my left. 3 p.m. Last I remembered the sun was beginning to rise. Maybe 5 a.m. What had happened in between?

My first intelligent thought was for my daughters. A longing to see them, to hold them close overpowered me. I swung my legs on the floor to my right then allotted myself thirty seconds for the shaking to recede. If I stood up too abruptly, I feared I might faint again.

I was relieved to find out I was wearing clean sweatpants and a tank top, although it meant that either Ethan, or Bizzy, had changed me into those. I couldn't have handled waking up in my blood stained, grime- and plaster-covered outfit from yesterday.

I spotted my super spy clothes stacked in a heap next to the bathroom door. The way they were huddled together, it looked like some corpse in a murder scene. The only thing missing was the chalk outline on the floor around it. Once again, it reminded me how lucky I was to be alive and well.

I forced my stare away from the morbid vision and looked for my cellphone. It was nowhere in sight. Instead, I found two pink folded cards erected on the nightstand. One was from Rose, with a sparkly princess glued to the front. Inside she had written with her neat penmanship.

I love you, Mummy. Hope you feel better soon. Big kisses. Rose.

The other card was from Poppy. She had drawn something that could have been a dog, or a bush, but most probably was a pony on the cover. Inside, she'd scrawled her name on one page. On the other, Rose had written.

"Poppy says you look like a blue sleeping beauty. She has tried to kiss you but it doesn't work."

I smiled despite the pain of curling of my lips brought. Thank god for children's resilience. My daughters would be fine. A huge chunk of the dread that weighted me down lifted suddenly, allowing me to stand up at last.

I pulled on a robe to hide the bruises on my arms then checked the girls' room. It was total havoc in there but no little girl in sight. I went downstairs.

The sound of Bizzy and Claudia's laughter welcomed me as I neared the ground floor landing. I followed the unexpected sound to the kitchen. Both women were sitting side by side at the kitchen counter, tall glasses of ice tea half empty before them. *Probably spiked.*

Bizzy's blonde hair was down over her shoulders, the tips bright pink.

"I thought you had dyed your hair back to normal," I said as I stepped inside the room.

Bizzy chuckled warm-heartedly.

"I thought I would surprise your father. The pink is growing on me."

She turned around to face me.

"Honey. You look—"

Awful. Her mouth contorted into a disapproving pout before she reined it in.

"A little out of sorts," she said instead.

"Finally! She's awake." Claudia raised her hands into the air like a preacher in a gospel church.

"It's good. You needed the rest." Bizzy nodded.

"I only slept for a few hours. How are you still standing up?" I asked Claudia.

Her eyebrows shot up to her blue hairline.

"Mom, where are the girls?"

"In school."

"What? On a Sunday?" My voice sounded shrill.

I pictured them roaming the streets, their backpacks too heavy for them, all alone; a modern version of *Hansel and Gretel* with Hector in the witch lead.

"We need to call the cops! We need to go look for them. They could be harmed! They could—"

Both women exchanged incredulous stares.

"Sloane, today is Monday," Bizzy spoke carefully.

"We must... Wait. What?"

"As in Monday, beginning of the week, school is in," Claudia spelled it out for me. "Rose and Poppy are fine."

"You slept all Sunday, Sloane," Bizzy told me.

So I hadn't just lost my way back home. I had lost all of Sunday as well. *Damn Ethan Cunning!*

"How did I get home?" I asked wearily.

"Ethan drove us."

"Us?"

"Yes. You, Sven, and me. You just missed him."

Bizzy winked at Claudia, who blushed like a teenage girl in love. Apparently, my friend slash housekeeper had chosen herself a new confidant. I swallowed back the jealousy quickly. They got along at last. It was a good thing.

"You spent the weekend here? Where did you sleep?"

"The couch. Well, couches. Separate ones. I'm not an expositionist."

283

Exhibitionist.

"Good to hear."

The house must have been a joyous mess.

"What else happened while I slept?"

"The usual," Claudia replied. "Gabriel was arrested. They found your phone with him."

"Some MI5 agent called this morning," Bizzy said. "Thanks to the pictures, they arrested some Russian mobster as well." *Yuri.* "The agent said he would call back later so you can testify against him."

Her eyes grew stern, in full scolding mom mode.

"Seriously, Sloane. What on earth have you been up to? Spying on mobsters? Meddling in weapon smuggling?"

"I think it's badass," Claudia commented.

The doorbell rung, startling me. I cowered behind the counter, half expecting Hector to barge in.

"Saved by the bell." Claudia smiled.

"I'll get it," Bizzy said, exiting the room.

I used the time alone with Claudia to express my gratitude.

"Thank you. For everything. I don't what would have happened if you hadn't shown up when you did."

She nodded, her serious expression bringing me back to that night, lying half-conscious on the rug.

"You would have done the same for me."

Bizzy came back in the kitchen, holding a bottle of gin in her manicured hands.

"Your friend Katherine is in the living room," she said, putting the bottle down on the counter.

I looked at Claudia before realizing Bizzy was talking to me. *My friend Katherine? Katherine as in Kate?* I swallowed painfully.

"Did she say what she wanted?"

Bizzy shook her head while she uncorked the bottle and poured two large tumblers of gin with ice cubes. She dropped a little gin in hers and Claudia's ice teas as well before putting the bottle down.

"Here," she said as she handed the two tumblers to me.

"Where did you hide her?" Bizzy eyed the bottle lovingly. "Such a thoughtful friend."

Such an alcoholic.

"I won't ask if you want to fix yourself up before you go?"

"I don't care."

She sighed.

"Go. Kate's waiting," Bizzy said as she shooed me out of the kitchen.

I dragged my feet across the hallway. What could Kate want from me? *Tom.* I had forgotten about Tom. I ran back to the kitchen, spilling half the drinks on my sweatpants as I did.

"How's Tom?" I whispered from the doorway.

"He's fine. He was discharged yesterday already," Bizzy answered. "Why the sudden concern?"

"Kate is waiting for me. As in Tom's Kate," I hissed before leaving both women with their questions.

I beamed. I quite liked my big exit.

Kate sat in Bizzy's armchair, concentrated on removing some invisible lint from her pencil skirt. The room was utter chaos, Claudia's clothes scattered across varied pieces of furniture, and pillows and sheets stacked under the chimney. If Santa Claus chose to visit in July, his arrival would be cushioned nicely.

I walked just close enough to hand Kate her drink without risking touching her then recoiled to the sofa nearby. I took my time settling into a comfortable enough position, folding my legs under me on the couch.

"You look dreadful," she said.

"Thank you." I rolled my eyes.

"I don't usually drink in the middle of the day," Kate said, eyeing her glass. "I didn't know what the appropriate gift in this circumstance was."

"What circumstance would that be?"

"I'm glad you didn't get killed?" she offered tentatively.

Good. She didn't come to kill me over Tom then.

"I'll drink to that," I said.

She raised her glass. "Cheers."

The transparent liquid burnt my throat but I pretended to enjoy it to avoid talking. I suspected Kate was doing the same. She broke the silence first.

"Tom told me what happened. Apparently, I'm one employer lighter."

"Sorry?"

Was that why she had come? She expected me to apologize?

"Oh, don't worry. I don't need Gabriel."

So it was about Tom then?

"I'm sorry Tom broke up with you."

She chortled.

"Tom didn't break up with me. I dumped him after the gala."

"So you came to rub it in? To tell me Tom tried to come back because you dumped him?"

"No. Of course not. Gosh! You truly think the worst of me." She shook her head. "I was quite impressed when he told me you'd turned him down."

"He did?"

"No. He pretended he'd dumped you. But I know men the likes of Tom. They can't stand to be alone. It didn't take a genius to figure it out."

She drank again.

"I came to apologize. All along, it was easier to despise you. And you did behave madly sometimes."

I would have loved to argue with Kate but considering our history, she did have a point. Mad didn't begin to cover the way I'd stalked her.

"The truth is, I did steal your husband. Not on purpose, believe me! I never wanted this to happen. Being in a relationship," she said with a shudder, "is definitely not for me."

"Then why?"

"Things got out of hand. First it was fun. The usual thrill of a married man. Then he asked for a divorce, and you began stalking me, and I guess I felt like I had to give him a shot. So I could justify breaking up your marriage. Very, very unfortunate idea."

"Tom's fine, by the way."

"I heard. I don't really care. The guy is a jerk, isn't he?"

Amen, sister.

"So you'll quit seeing married men?"

"I could say it, but neither you nor I would believe it." She grinned. "I'm just sorry it was you."

Kate stood up.

"Anyway, I've apologized, and now I'll be on my way."

Seriously? That was the most surreal conversation I'd ever had. I followed Kate to the hallway and held the door open for her. The sooner I could get rid of her, the better by me. She stopped on the doorstep.

"I'm glad."

"About what?"

"To see that you're all right. People usually bore me but you've turned out to be a worthy opponent. Turning down your ex-husband, and the thing with Gabriel – it was brave."

Or foolish. I chose to see it as a compliment. For some crazy reason, I enjoyed holding Kate's admiration.

"Take care, okay?" she said with a ghost of a smile before she walked down the steps, her perfect hourglass figure sashaying away.

I closed the door and dragged my poor, aching body back to the kitchen. Everywhere I looked on the way, the surrounding mess struck me. I shook my head as I muttered to myself. I couldn't expect my daughters to live this way.

I was relieved to find Claudia looking unoccupied, still sitting at the kitchen counter.

"Everything okay with the bitch?" she asked as she spotted me.

I shrugged. "I guess."

I searched for the right words but then decided that bluntness was the best course of action. After all, Claudia was supposed to work on Mondays.

"Do you think you could tidy up a bit?"

She nearly choked, she laughed so hard.

"No way! I almost took a bullet for you. That deserves at least two weeks off work."

She flipped open a magazine.

"Don't be ungrateful, Sloane." Bizzy frowned. "The girl saved your life. Give her a break."

Bizzy Harper: from tyrannical boss to union worker representative.

I raised my arms in defeat. They didn't care that my rib was splintered and that I needed to rest. Neither would my daughters when they came home from school. The life of a mother continued no matter what. No break, no holiday.

I addressed words of gratitude to whoever sat up there in the clouds. I wouldn't trade this life for the world. I had lived to be a mother one more day and hopefully many more to come.

I was lucky. They might not help me do the cleanup, but the women in my life were there when it really mattered. I was single but very far from being alone.

"See you later," I told Claudia and my mother before heading upstairs.

First, I needed to get rid of the stinky, disgusting clothes in my bedroom. This was one reminder I didn't need of my close brush with death. I brought a garbage bag with me to the room.

First, I stuffed my tank top in it. Good riddance. I pretended it was Tom I was disposing of. I felt lighter.

Then I threw my socks. *Gabriel. Goodbye.*

The sweatpants were last. The tattered piece of clothing emitted a rustling noise as I crumpled it into a tight ball. I checked the pockets. The right one was empty. In the left one, I found a folded piece of paper. My fingers shook as I smoothed it open. It simply said,

I'll find you.

Oh, Ethan! I couldn't wait...

THE END

Fantastic Books
Great Authors

CROOKED
CAT

Meet our authors and discover our exciting range:

- Gripping Thrillers
- Cosy Mysteries
- Romantic Chick-Lit
- Fascinating Historicals
- Exciting Fantasy
- Young Adult and Children's Adventures

Printed in Great Britain
by Amazon